SENTINALS BANISHED

SENTINALS BANISHED

BOOK FIVE OF THE SENTINAL SERIES

HELEN GARRAWAY

Published by Jerven Publishing

Cover by Jeff Brown Graphics

Content warning

This is an adult epic fantasy with mature adult themes. There are scenes of violence, substance abuse, abduction, consensual sex, and non-consensual sex.

eBook ISBN: 978-1-915854-00-1

Paperback ISBN: 978-1-915854-01-8

Hardcover ISBN: 978-1-915854-02-5

Sign up to my mailing list to join my magical world and for further information about forthcoming books and latest news at: www.helengar-raway.com

First Edition

For Michael Strick
Alpha Reader Extraordinaire
Thank you!

ALSO BY HELEN GARRAWAY

Sentinal Series

Sentinals Awaken

Sentinals Rising

Sentinals Justice

Sentinals Recovery

Sentinals Across Time

Sentinals Banished

SoulMist series

SoulBreather

DragonBound (2023)

Anthologies

Creatures of Magic and Myth

(Free, Sentinals Discovery)

VESPIRI
NEW VESPERS
ELOTHIA
OLD VESPERS
WATCH TOWERS
DEEPWATER
VELMOUTH
GREENSWATCH
KING'S PORT
THE GROVE
DALEHURST
TWO BRIDGES
EAST ROAD
STONEFORD
LINTEL
LOWALSTALL
TEROLIA
EAST FORD
APPLETREE
MARCHWOOD
MORTELIN
EAST WATCH
WOODBRIDGE
MARSHFORD
BIRTOLI

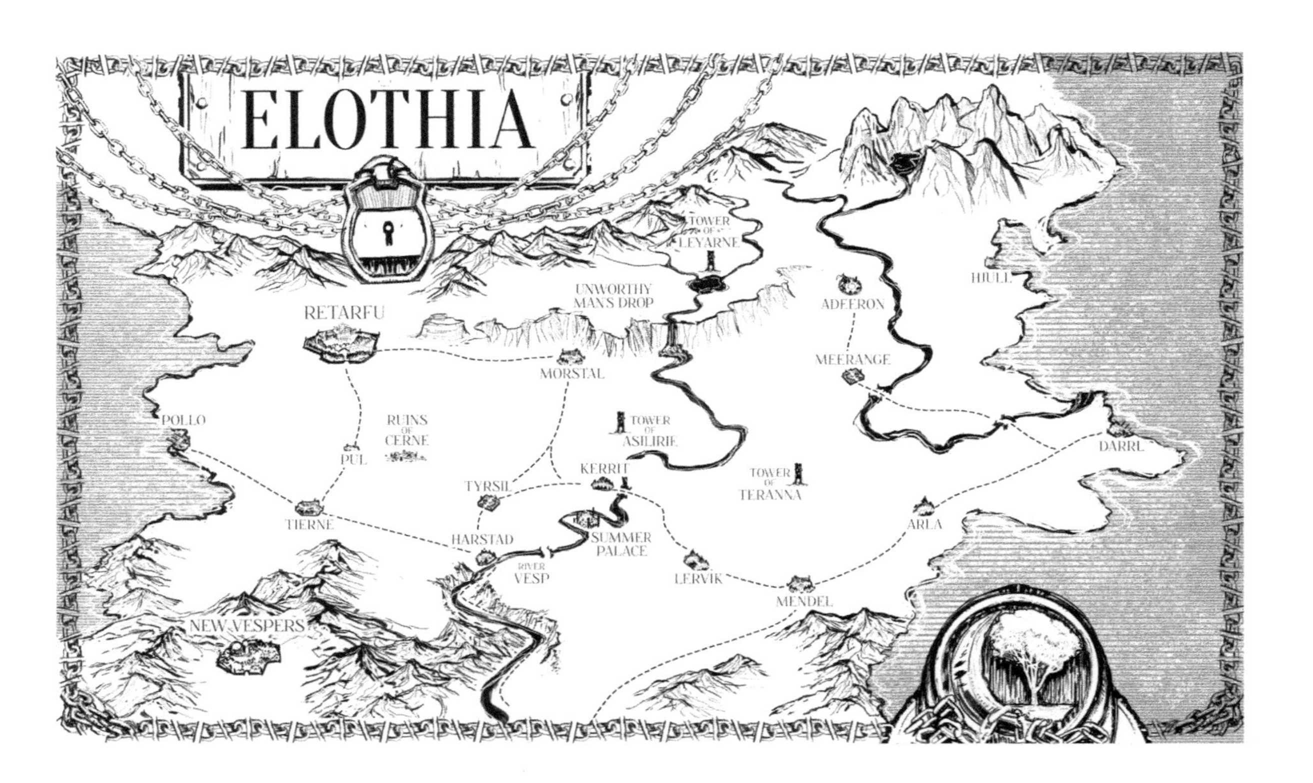

ELOTHIA
TOWER OF LEYARNE
UNWORTHY MAN'S DROP
RETARFU
ADEERON
HIULL
MEERANGE
MORSTAL
POLLO
RUINS OF CERNE
PUL
TOWER OF ASILIRIE
DARRL
KERRIT
TYRSIL
TOWER OF TERANNA
TIERNE
ARLA
HARSTAD
SUMMER PALACE
RIVER VESP
LERVIK
MENDEL
NEW VESPERS

BIRTOLI
POST-FLOOD
MORTELIN
WOODBRIDGE
VESPIRI
AGUINTI
NIKRI
MARSHFORD
HARBOUR
LAKRI
MOLINTI
PORLI
SENTI
POINT
DONA
STORM WALLS
AMRILTI
AMRI
CHERNI
EYTI
ASTILLE
PAUUL
DUYLI
SERROL

1

STONEFORD KEEP, VESPIRI

Birlerion laughed as he face-planted Leyarille in the dust. "You've got to move faster than that! Your feet are like clay."

Leyarille took a deep breath and spat out dirt. Glaring at Birlerion, she rose to her feet. The Stoneford Keep sparring ring was thankfully free of spectators. At least there wouldn't be any taunts at dinner of her eating dirt, yet again. Not that she cared. The apprentices were jealous of the fact that she got to spar with Birlerion and they didn't. Holding her sword out in front of her, she gritted her teeth, determined not to rise to the bait. Her father had told her over and over that keeping your temper was one of the most important rules in combat. She wouldn't let Birlerion rile her.

Sunlight caught the gleams of silver threading Birlerion's black hair, but his body was lean and strong. His hair was long enough for her to run her hands through if he would ever let her close enough to do so and just reached his collar. She observed the tall Sentinal closely, watching for his tells. She knew every curve of his face, every guarded expression that he allowed to escape. His silver eyes glinted at her with a challenge. He was a Sentinal; he was what she wanted to be.

Patience was another important trait, her father said; wait for your opponent to move first, watch his body language; there are always tell-tale signs just before they commit. She watched Birlerion circling slowly.

"Afraid?" he taunted, watching her in return. Leyarille stiffened, but she continued circling. She cringed as she remembered all the times he had made her fly into a temper, losing all control. She didn't know why, but Birlerion always managed to pierce her guard. This last year though, she *had* improved. She had made him work harder to keep ahead of her, though she knew he would never admit that to her. Shifting her weight, she observed his instant response, and then he stilled, a predator waiting to pounce. At least she had grown, and now her head reached his chin. She was taller than both her parents and her brother and sister.

Birlerion's silver eyes, the same as hers and her fathers, watched her closely, observing her minute adjustments. She had come prepared for battle today. The last session he had managed to flummox her by snicking the tie that held her hair back and blinding her with her cloudy hair. She had twisted it up out of the way today; she had learnt that lesson.

Another cringe at the memory of the time she had stormed up to her mother, demanding she cut her hair short, but her father, the Lord Warden of Stoneford Watch, had put an end to that. He told her to learn to fight with what she had. Her hair was too beautiful to cut, just like her mothers. She had flounced about the keep for days after that, only her father's amused gaze preventing her from chopping it off herself.

Suddenly shifting her balance, she struck low and hard. Birlerion only just managed to deflect the blow and parry the follow-up strike to his head. He took a step back and whipped his sword in front of her, making her skip back, but she was back into his space, immediately pressing him back, using her speed to counteract his strength. She hooked her leg around his and, using her momentum, took him down into the dust. He landed with a woof of breath, grinning up at her jubilant face. He scythed his legs and brought her down on top of him, winding himself in the process. He wrapped his arms around her and rolled her over.

"Never stop to celebrate in the middle of a fight," he wheezed down at her, trying to catch his breath.

"Not wanting to interrupt or anything," a sarcastic voice spoke above them, and Birlerion released her. Leyarille flipped neatly to her feet, glaring at the boy leering at her.

"What do you want?" she asked, anger flushing through her.

The boy grinned up at her. "You're late. You're supposed to be in the stables."

"Ascendants balls," she cursed, throwing her sword at Birlerion. "You made me late again."

Birlerion laughed as he caught it.

"I know, I know. I'm old enough to read the time," she huffed as, brushing herself down, she turned towards the stables. Her father had insisted all his children learn to ride and practice regularly, but even after years of lessons, she was still uncomfortable around horses and dreaded every session. She swore the horse knew and deliberately tried to unseat her. And having to brush them down afterwards, well, all that muscle trying to step on her feet just unnerved her. The fact that her brother could ride blindfold practically from birth galled her, but then he did have a Darian stallion. The mind link between the two of them must help. Why couldn't she have one too?

She stomped around the edge of the keep and into the stable block wiping her face clear of resentment as she entered the inner courtyard. The stable master stood waiting impatiently, and she silently groaned. "My apologies, master, I was engaged in a sparring session and lost track of time."

"If you paid as much attention to me as you do your sparring master, you might actually make progress," the horsemaster snapped.

Leyarille flicked a startled glance at the man, but his expression was without guile. It was only the lads who taunted her. She heard a soft snicker from the boxes and her heart sank. They had heard him. They would take it at face value. She didn't care for herself, but to accuse Birlerion of impropriety incensed her. They wouldn't say it to his face.

"Yes, sir," she replied.

"Come on, saddle up Winter. Let's see if you can do it in under ten minutes for a change."

Leyarille seethed, another unintended barb hitting her vanity. She was too slow, too clumsy; the list went on. She sighed and tried to shake the anger off; it wouldn't help. She peered over the stable door at the white mare called Winter. The mare nickered softly as she unlatched the door. Leyarille steeled herself and entered the box. She fumbled for the head rope in the gloom and stiffened her knees as she pushed the horse's rump away from her as she turned the mare around and led her out. Winter obliged by docilely following her. Leyarille tied her to the ring in the inner courtyard and collected her bridle and saddle from the tack room. She had spent the evening before polishing them all, punishment for another fight she had found herself in. It wasn't fair. Just because she was the daughter of the Lord Warden of Stoneford, she was supposed to keep her temper and ignore petty insults.

She heaved the saddle over the wooden stand and sorted out the bridle straps, and taking a deep breath, she approached the mare. Winter shook her head up and down

er flinch back. "She's only
" Leyarille muttered to
stroke her neck. She
outh, Winter taking it
traps. Leyarille leaned
ed the reins. She stared
en so simple.

y. You need a saddle as
m behind her.

ter flinch, and all her new-
e turned back for the saddle.
e had heard her father do to soothe
mare. Everyone had a Darian except
ht angrily, conveniently forgetting that her
n't have one.

e slapped the saddle onto Winter's back, and Winter
ifted away from her, making the saddle slip. Leyarille lunged and spooked the mare. She bent to pick the saddle up from the floor and breathed in a deep, calming breath. It's not the horse's fault, she said to herself. Concentrate.

She began to croon again, stroking the mare's neck; it was so soft. "I'm sorry, I didn't mean to scare you," she whispered. The horse's ear flicked back towards her. She smoothed the mare's back and carefully placed the saddle over her. Reaching under her belly, she inhaled the musky smell of her skin as she pulled the girth strap around and buckled them up. She cinched the girth strap a second time, hoping the mare wasn't holding her breath, and stood back to admire her work.

"Better," the horse master said. "Make sure it's tight. She's a bugger for breathing out; she doesn't like the strap too tight. The saddle will just slide round when you try and mount otherwise."

Leyarille gritted her teeth, and kneed the mare, and

cinched the girth in two notches. She gr
back to the master.

"Well done, now you can get on her."

Leyarille's grin faded.

"You're perfectly capable; you just need
enjoy it. The tenser you are, the more difficult you

Leyarille looked at the white mare and sighe
was supposedly the most docile horse in the stable
couldn't ride her, she had no hope of riding any
others. She reached up for the pommel and slotted he
foot in the stirrup. She launched herself smoothly into the
and swung her leg over, feeling for the other stirrup. Wint
sidled as she found her balance, but she was up. She gathered
in the reins and smoothed the mare's neck. "There that
wasn't so bad, was it?" she murmured, more to herself than
the horse.

Kino, Birlerion's honey gold stallion, poked his nose out of his stall and nickered encouragingly at her. Even Birlerion had a Darian, though she didn't resent him his one bit. He was gorgeous and had the most delightful personality to go with it. Birlerion needed someone who just loved him.

"Take her around the perimeter. A good trot will do her good, and when you reach the far end, break into a canter and then drop back to a trot as you approach the keep. Off you go." The master nodded and walked away, coiling the lead rope he had removed.

Leyarille walked the mare out of the stable block and under the arch, her shod hooves clopping loudly on the stone under her feet. She squeezed her knees, and the mare extended her legs into a trot. As they bounced around the edge of the keep, Leyarille held her face up to the weak sun that broke through the clouds and smiled with pleasure. They found a rhythm and more comfortably trotted around the fields. Leyarille wondered why she fought this so much. She signalled a canter, and the mare's stride smoothed out.

Her mind drifted, thinking about Sentinals, and one in particular. What did she have to do to get the man to pay attention to her? He may be older than her, but so what? His age meant nothing. Her father had awoken him after the Lady had placed him in a preserving sleep for over three thousand years. Tall, elegant sentinal trees had been scattered across Remargaren, each protecting one of the Lady Leyandrii's personal guards. Birlerion had been asleep in the sentinal tree in Old Vespers and had been the first Sentinal her father had woken. That had been nearly twenty years ago.

Lifting her eyes, she scanned her surroundings and eased back into a trot and then a walk. Smiling as Winter tugged on the reins, eager to canter again, Leyarille held her to a walk. Her father had been the Lady's Captain; in fact, he still was as far as she knew; no matter what the king said. The Lady's Captain who preserved the Lady's guardians. He had swept through the four kingdoms of Remargaren and awoken all the Sentinals he could find. They had formed the Lady's Guard under his command and battled to remove the threat posed by the ascendants, a group of men who believed magic was the answer to everything and who had set about destroying the Lady and all that held Remargaren together.

Unconsciously, she urged Winter on, and the mare extended her stride. Her father and his Sentinals had succeeded in defeating the ascendants after many confrontations. Many had been lost, many hurt; her father and Birlerion included. Her lips pursed at the thought, especially of her father. After all he had been through to preserve the Lady and their world, he was slowly being side-lined.

She had been born after the final confrontation when, legend had it, her father had absorbed the bloodstone, had become one with the Lady and the Land to heal the stone and the Veil that protected their world.

She wasn't sure how much of that she believed as her father never spoke of it. Oh, she knew all the stories, but how many were true? All she knew was that only Sentinals had silver eyes. She had been born with silver eyes like her father, but she wasn't a Sentinal, even if everyone assumed she was. She didn't know what she was, except a problem for everyone.

Leaning forward to pat the mare's neck, Winter shied at a loud crack right beside them. The mare veered to the left, but Leyarille kept going right. She landed in an inelegant sprawl, her hand automatically gripping the reins; another adage of her fathers: never let go of the rein. The mare jerked away from her, wrenching her shoulder, though she hung on to the leather straps, her palm stinging as the leather slid through it. She tightened her grip and Winter stopped tugging.

She lay gasping on the ground before gingerly sitting up and scanning the undergrowth. A glimpse of tousled hair meant it had been the lads from the stables, but they were long gone now. They should know better! Winter could have been injured. A spike of pain flashed through her shoulder, and she hissed as she stood. She had strained her shoulder. Served her right for not paying attention.

Checking Winter over for injury, she gathered the reins and led her a few steps to make sure she hadn't hurt herself. The mare quivered beside her, and Leyarille soothed her. "It was just those horrible boys. It's all fine now. They are just silly children. It's alright; they've gone."

She gathered the reins and awkwardly heaved herself into the saddle, leaning over the pommel as sparkly stars blurred her vision. She gasped at the pain in her shoulder and once she settled, she asked Winter to walk on. They slowly walked around the rest of the perimeter and approached the arch to the stables.

The stable master came out frowning. "I thought I told you to give her a good canter?" he said, reaching for the bridle.

"I fell off," Leyarille said. There would be no hiding it.

"Off Winter? How?" the master asked, giving her a keen inspection.

"There was a loud noise; it startled her."

"Are you alright?"

"I'm fine. I'll just go brush her down." Leyarille leaned forward and rubbed Winter's neck. "Silly old lady," she crooned.

The master eyed her but let her walk on into the stables. Leyarille tensed as she eased down to the ground and then led Winter to her box and unstrapped her saddle, wincing as she reached to pull it off.

"You're not alright, are you?" the Master said from behind her, and tears sprang into her eyes as she heard the sympathy in his voice. Why was he being so nice to her? She blinked them away furiously.

"I hurt my arm," she admitted.

"Then get yourself to the infirmary now. I'll see to Winter. You'll only make it worse lugging her tack around; go on with you." The horse master guided her out of the box and made sure she was headed to the infirmary before he turned back.

"So what really happened then, missus? You don't shy at anything," he murmured to the white mare as he removed the saddle and settled it over the box wall. He ran his hands down her legs, checking for heat, but she seemed fine. He would keep an eye on her overnight. Removing her bridle, he took it to the tack room for cleaning.

Jerrol Haven, the Lord Warden of Stoneford, watched his daughter slowly climb the hill above Stoneford Keep. His back was warmed by the trunks of two tall trees that twisted as one up into the night sky, sheltering him with the large pointy leaves that formed its canopy. His sentinal tree curved protectively over him, his presence part of a gentle hum in Jerrol's mind, along with the occasional snippet of complaint from his Darian mare, Zin'talia.

The other part of the hum was the bloodstone that ran through his veins. He had indeed absorbed the stone and joined with the Lady to seal the Veil. Most of the stories had an element of truth.

While he waited for his daughter to crest the hill, he reached for the Veil, checking the weave, making sure it was still sealed. He had seen signs of damage recently; nothing significant, maybe it was just wear and tear over time. After reworking the bindings and sealing the ends, he remained vigilant. He intended visiting the Watchers in the towers above Velmouth just to check if they had observed anything.

He followed his daughter's progress. He knew she'd had a difficult week; reports from various masters and his own observations told him she was ready to fly and that Stoneford had become a loving cage that she needed to break free from.

Was he about to do the right thing? He wasn't sure. The timing was ominous, but then, she wasn't his daughter for nothing. He sighed gently as she crested the hill. At least she was on time. He had asked her to meet him away from the keep. What he wanted to discuss with her was important but not something to be discussed in front of other people. First, though, he needed to deal with the frustration currently consuming his daughter.

"What's the matter?" Jerrol asked as she paused by his feet and turned to look back down over the moonlit keep. Shadowy buildings sprawled below them. The yellow glow of a lamp, gilding a door or window frame, evidence of those working inside.

Leyarille turned back to him, her silver eyes a soft gleam in the dark. She opened her mouth as if to say 'nothing' and sighed the breath out. Jerrol's lips twitched. She knew he wouldn't believe her, and he wouldn't let her go until she told him. Her mother she could sometimes deflect; him never.

"I'm seventeen," she said as if that answered everything.

"That you are," he replied, watching her closely.

"I'm not a child anymore."

"No. You are not."

"Then why do I feel that I am still treated like one?" she complained.

Jerrol's eyebrows rose. "I can assure you that I do not treat you as a child," he began.

"Not you," Leyarille interrupted him, flinging her arm out.

"Ah." Jerrol smiled, though he wiped his face clean at the sight of her tense face. "I see," he said, and he did. He had done his best to protect his family, yet here, he was out of his depth. He couldn't prevent her from leaving him, as he knew she was about to do. She had grown up, and it was time for her to spread her wings and experience the world for herself.

At the keep she would always be a child; a daughter of the warden. His long-time retainers looked at her in no other way, though he had a feeling it was one particular retainer that was annoying her right now. "Take a seat," he offered, shuffling over. "What do you want me to do about it?" he asked.

"Nothing," she began, her voice strident, and then she stopped as the sentinal warmed her back in greeting, and she relaxed with a sigh. "I want," she said, "to be a real Sentinal."

"That is between you and the Lady."

"Not the king?"

"No, the Sentinals are the Lady's."

"And there hasn't been any new ones since she sundered the bloodstone."

"Except you."

"Except I am not a real Sentinal. She hasn't asked me, and I don't have a tree," she said mulishly as if that point sealed the argument.

"Maybe the right moment hasn't come yet," Jerrol suggested. "Have you asked her?"

Leyarille straightened and looked at him. Jerrol's heart thumped as he took in his graceful daughter. She had morphed into an elegant woman overnight; it was quite disturbing. Her silver eyes glinted at him. "I ask her every day what it is she needs of me, but she doesn't answer."

"Sometimes," Jerrol spoke slowly, "it's not what *she* needs, but what *you* see needs to be done. She is behind the Veil; it is oftentimes difficult for her to reach us. She needs us to help her protect her people when others fail."

Leyarille twisted round on her knees so she could watch her father's face, her silver eyes widening.

Jerrol sighed and made himself more comfortable. "When Benedict died, we lost more than a king. We lost a staunch supporter of the Lady. Someone who understood the deep bonds between Lady, Land, and Liege. His son hasn't the depth or experience to understand it and is consequently suffering. I know Benedict told him, I just don't think he truly believes it."

"But Anders is the king!"

"Kings are human too. They are fallible, can be swayed by other opinions. He's never truly experienced real contact with the Lady, or he would believe," Jerrol said with feeling. "But I cannot impose my will on a king. I am no longer the Oath Keeper; that died with Benedict. I no longer captain his guards. I cannot influence Anders, especially when he doesn't want to listen. He has all but banished the Sentinals, us included," he said, patting the roots beside him. "Sent us all into retirement. For some, it was time; others resent the way he has treated them.

"After all, they didn't ask to be brought three thousand years into their future; they didn't have a choice. The choice didn't matter when they were serving the king and ultimately the Lady. That was all they knew. But without the king, they are lost. Their reason for being has been taken away, and they find time hangs heavily on their hands."

"Not Birlerion or Fonorion; they are as active as you are."

"They work with me to protect the Watch and the towers, the Lady's last foothold. As do Tagerill and Denirion in Deepwater; they have a purpose. But Leyarille, the king does not want or value Sentinals. He does not see the cracks in his kingdom as a result, and he won't listen to me. He had me removed from court the last time I visited. Jennery won't even go there anymore."

Leyarille gasped, covering her mouth with her hand, and Jerrol grimaced. Alyssa and Jennery were Lord and Lady of the neighbouring Watch called Deepwater and long-time friends of theirs. Leyarille had grown up with their children. They called each other cousins; they were family.

"Uncle Jennery and Aunt Alyssa are the mainstays of court; why, they spend as much time at court as at Deepwater."

"Not any more. Tagerill visited yesterday. Jennery and Alyssa spoke out against the king's plans to divest Terolia. As a result, their holding is at risk. The king was angry."

"But Pa, why would the king want to divest Terolia? That would be giving away half his kingdom! Who is he thinking of giving it too?"

"I don't know. I think, maybe, you need to go and find out."

In a swift movement, which emphasised her lithe grace, Leyarille rose to her feet and took a step back. "Me?"

"Yes, you. We have to stop Anders before he destroys Remargaren. He won't listen to me; he's instructed me to hand Stoneford to Mikke. He no longer sees me as a trusted advisor."

Leyarille tensed as she stared down at her father. Jerrol waited for her to absorb his words. She spun away from him and faced the peaceful keep, before turning back around. He inhaled. With the moon behind her, she looked so like her mother. "Mikke won't take Stoneford from you; he knows how much you love it."

"He doesn't have a choice if we want to continue to protect it."

"But what about you and mother?"

Jerrol shrugged, feeling the ache in his shoulders. "We'll go to Senti for a while, spend more time with Margareth. She is showing signs of improvement in that warmer climate. It was the right decision to let her go, even if we do miss her. We'll let the king's anger die down, and then we'll see."

Face tightening, Jerrol thought of his youngest daughter, Margareth. Born three years after Leyarille, she had never been strong. Jerrol rubbed his face. Margareth had always been different, easily distracted. It was as if something drew her attention away, often giving her an absent expression. The healers had recommended they send her to the islands after she'd had a sudden growth spurt the previous summer and it had left her pale and listless, more distant than before. At least the dry heat of the Birtoli climate was helping.

He waited, suddenly feeling his years. Not that he was old, but he knew the abuse his body had received was beginning to show. Maybe a break would do him good. He wasn't getting any younger, and his son, Mikkeal, was more than capable of guarding the Watch.

"Pa," Leyarille said softly as she sat down and leaned against him. "I'm not you."

Jerrol smiled, wrapping an arm around her shoulders and kissing the top of her head. "I should hope not, but you are just what the Lady needs. The next generation; new life, new blood, a new view on how Remargaren should grow and develop. We can't stand still, but that doesn't mean we have to go backwards either."

"The king won't listen to me. I have even less clout than you do."

"He's not ready to listen; you have to show him. Leyarille, go. Join the rangers. Show him what honour and loyalty mean. Find out what is really going on. You'll know where I am when you need me." The moonlight reached for him, gilding his sentinal's leaves, and Jerrol lifted his face and smiled gently in acknowledgement. Leyarille smoothed her hand over his, wrapping her fingers around the stumps of the two missing fingers on his right hand.

"Take Birlerion with you," Jerrol said. She stiffened. "Please, take Birlerion. You don't know what you'll find when you get to Old Vespers."

"He might not want to go." Her voice was devoid of expression. "And anyway, he can't join the rangers; he's a Sentinal."

"He can visit Niallerion and Marianille, find out what they know. Speak to Bryce and others. He won't be with you, but you'll have a friend nearby."

Jerrol felt her glance on his face. "He'll treat me like a

kid," she complained, and he smiled, knowing that she would take him with her.

"Give him time. He's been teaching you for years. He has to adjust to the fact that he is no longer your teacher but a companion. That change won't happen overnight." Jerrol rose and offered her a hand.

"He'll never change," she muttered under her breath as she allowed him to pull her to her feet.

Jerrol grimaced. He was counting on it. Wrapping his arm around her waist, he gave her a gentle hug. "Come on, it's getting cold and your mother will be wondering where we are," he said as they walked down the hill and back into the keep. He thought back to his earlier conversation with Birlerion and smiled to himself as he considered how similar the arguments and the sudden capitulation had been.

Bidding his daughter goodnight, he made his way around the keep on his nightly round, acknowledging the sentries before heading to bed.

Taelia's face wore a frown as she folded back the bed covers, and Jerrol knew she was worrying about Leyarille travelling to Old Vespers. They had discussed it before he had spoken with Birlerion.

"You do know she's in love with him?" she said, getting in bed. Her light brown hair was loose and clouding around her heart-shaped face. Her beautiful turquoise eyes fixed on him in worry. "I thought she would grow out of it but instead she is more determined."

Jerrol smiled. "I think she can figure it out for herself."

"But what about Birlerion?"

"He's always been part of our family; this will be no different," Jerrol replied.

"But he sees her as a daughter; he practically raised her."

"Not for much longer." Jerrol chuckled as he climbed into bed beside her.

"Aren't you going to say anything?"

"Oh no, I'm staying right out of it."

"But you approve; shouldn't you tell him?"

"I'm not getting involved and nor should you. If she wants him, she'll let him know. Knowing Leyarille, it will be long and torturous, but I'm sure he's got the stamina." Jerrol began to laugh.

Taelia thumped him. "It's not funny. We're talking about our daughter's happiness."

Jerrol continued to laugh as he blew out the candle and wrapped his arms around his wife.

"Stop laughing," Taelia grumbled.

Jerrol's shoulders shook. "Just imagine Birlerion calling you mother."

Taelia gasped, then she began to chuckle too. "Oh dear, I never thought of that."

Jerrol inhaled her comforting scent and kissed her throat before snuggling closer to the woman who was his whole world. He sighed with happiness as he kissed her neck.

"Do you think Mikke is ready?" Taelia asked.

"He's been ready since he was two!" Jerrol replied with a huff. "It will do him good to have real responsibility for a change. I would have thought you'd be happy to have me all to yourself," he murmured, pulling her closer and kissing her ear.

"Of course I am, but first losing the king and then the Sentinals and now the Watch. Jerrol, you're not ready to retire; we are not old. There is still much to do."

"Well, think of it as a well-earned rest then. Bright sunshine, golden beaches, warm turquoise seas, my undivided attention. And to top it all, you'll be with Margareth. What's to complain about?"

"Nothing, it sounds like bliss. But we won't be able to come back, and this is our home." Her voice wavered, and Jerrol stopped his exploration of her neck and rested on his elbow, looking down at her.

"Of course we can come back. We can visit. We have our cottage. We'll just have to find some new excavations to keep you occupied; start a new chapter. I'm sure I'll be able to find you something." He concentrated on distracting her as he began to remove her nightclothes.

He smiled against her skin as her arms slid around his body, and he redoubled his efforts.

2

STONEFORD KEEP

Mikke strode through the courtyard with his Sentinal, Serenion, at his shoulder. He was glad his father had instated Serenion as the Watch Sentinal; it gave him a sense of continuity in a time of momentous change. Not to mention the fact that Serenion was one of the youngest Sentinals, if you ignored the three thousand-years he had been asleep in his sentinal tree.

Leyarille and Birlerion had already left for Old Vespers, and now it was his turn, but he would ride. He was not using the waystone, no matter how much his sister teased him. Considering he was about to be confirmed as the new Lord of Stoneford, there was no way he would arrive in Old Vespers puking up his guts. Once his appointment was acknowledged by the king, he would return to be confirmed. After that, his parents were going to Birtoli to visit the island of Senti before deciding on their next adventure, as his father put it.

Mikke didn't know how his father could stand down. His father loved Stoneford just as much as Mikke did. He had asked them to stay, but his father had been adamant; they would come back and visit, but the Watch was Mikke's, and he needed a clear delineation of the handover. As did the people.

After all his father had suffered to save Remargaren, the king was throwing him away, and he had no idea he was discarding his best protection at the same time. Mikke stifled his growing anger at King Anders that he should treat his father so.

No matter what his father said, he was taking his banishment badly. New lines creased his face, and Mikke was sure his hair was greyer. It was unacceptable. But Mikke kept his own counsel and had watched as his very close-knit family was pulled apart. First Margareth had left, off sunning herself in Birtoli, and now Leyarille.

He thought back to the night Leyarille had left home. She was already missed, as was Birlerion. You didn't realise how much younger sisters shaped your daily life until they weren't there. And although Birlerion was often silent, standing in the background, his absence was noted by everyone.

They'd had a family meeting; their last get together for what would be some time. His mother was concerned, he could tell. She had watched his father with worried eyes. No matter what he said, they all knew this wasn't going to be easy for him. In effect, his father had handed the keys of the Stoneford Watch over to him that night. Serenion had formally acknowledged him as the Lord Guardian, as had Birlerion and Fonorion. It was also the first time he heard that Leyarille was going to join the King's Rangers. He'd thought she would be a Sentinal, but it seemed that wasn't straightforward either. The king interfering again.

"Pip? Are you ready?" Mikke thought to his black Darian

stallion as he strode towards the stables. The stallion's name was really Pil'penia, but Mikke had christened him Pip on their very first meeting, and it had stuck.

"Always ready," Pip replied, filling Mikke's head with his happiness at a long journey.

Zin'talia shifted in the stall next door. She was his father's white Darian mare and Pip's dam. She was not happy at the impending changes, and Mikke paused by her stall to rub her nose. *"I know, I'm sorry. We'll be back as soon as we can."*

She snorted. *"You know how you'll be forgiven."* He grinned at her acerbic reply. He would have to see if he could find any baliweed for her. His pa had intended leaving her in Stoneford while he found a house on Senti; he was not convinced he should take her as the island was so small, but Zin'talia had other ideas and whinged at anyone who could hear her, namely Mikke and his pa. Jerrol had given in after Mikke had begged him to stop her mental bombardment.

Mikke led Pip out of his stall. The stable lad had already saddled him, his travel pack tied behind the saddle. Serenion accepted a dappled grey mare from one of the other lads and efficiently began checking the straps. The black-haired Sentinal tucked his staff under his saddle flap, adjusted his sword belt, and mounted the mare. Serenion originally hailed from Elothia, the territory to the north of Vespiri, but he had been part of the Stoneford Watch Sentinals for as long as Mikke could remember.

After a quick glance around, Mikke swung up into the saddle and led the way out of the keep and under the portcullis, his guards forming up around him. They had already said their goodbyes, though he wasn't surprised to see his father waiting for him by the grove where the Sentinals used to guard the Lady's temple, just outside the village.

His pa gripped Mikke's knee as he stared up at him, and

Mikke almost expected him to trot out the usual comment about his turquoise eyes being so like his mother's, but he didn't. "Trust your instincts," he said. "Don't believe all that you hear." He ran a gentle hand down Pip's neck. "Don't forget to honour the Ladies; both of them!"

Mikke smiled. "I won't." He dismounted and hugged his father, suddenly realising how careworn he looked. He gripped his father's shoulders. "We'll be fine," he said, his gaze holding his father's silver eyes.

Jerrol nodded and let him go. He saluted Serenion, one of the youngest Sentinals he had awoken all those years ago, now matured and competently filling the role of the Lord Warden's personal guard. Moving back to let them pass, he watched them until they rode out of sight before entering the grove.

Kneeling by the grey stone altar, Jerrol prayed to the Lady for the safety of his children. There were no sentinal trees here now; both Chryillion and Saerille had fallen before his children had been born. Their trees graced the plains of Oprimere, along with the other Sentinals who had fallen in that final battle. Jerrol often thought it would have been better if they had returned home to Stoneford; it wasn't right without the trees here. It had broken Jason, the former Lord Warden. Darllion, another Sentinal who had transferred to Stoneford after their loss, had long since retired to a quiet island in Birtoli, and the grove was empty now.

It wasn't until Jerrol had taken over the Watch three years later that the Sentinals had truly returned. Birlerion and Fonorion had accompanied him, and their trees had relocated to the keep. A permanent presence; though even now, Mikke would be down to one Sentinal. Birlerion had left with Leyarille, and Fonorion would accompany Jerrol and Taelia to Senti. He prayed to the Lady that the Watch would thrive under his son's leadership and that the king would find the Lady's path. Somehow, he knew all his children were destined to be involved; he could see the Lady's hand drawing them together. He had done what he could; it was up to them now.

3

KING'S PALACE, OLD VESPERS

The king's court at Old Vespers was a place of gaiety and excess. King Anders had commanded it. He'd had enough of his father's dour parties and constricting propriety. He wanted to have some fun before it was too late. What was the point of being in charge if you couldn't do what you wanted when you wanted?

Anders strolled down the corridors of his palace to his receiving room, pleasantly unattended. Once lean and fit, he had let himself go. The late nights, excessive alcohol and drugs had ravaged his once handsome face. His eyes were bloodshot, his face sallow. His body sagged as if it had given up the fight against depravity.

He had finally dispensed with the Sentinals, even Parsillion, who had been like a dog with a bone, refusing to let go. He didn't like them constantly watching him. He had even had to drum it into Bryce that, yes, he needed security, but he didn't need to *see* them. They should be invisible.

The Sentinals had served their time and were no longer needed in his peaceful world. The Ascendant threat was dealt with, and Anders didn't see the point of having ancient guardsmen getting in the way with their antiquated ideas. They only reminded people of the recent troubles and what they had lost.

He was fed up of being told how his father wouldn't approve of his decisions or where he was going wrong. His reign would be new and refreshing, ushering in a bright new future of fun and gaiety. And he knew just the right people to help him achieve that.

The footmen hurried to open the ornately carved double doors before him, and he entered his throne room. Patterned tiles formed a mosaic of a tall sentinal tree and the Lady's moon on the floor. Not that you could see it. People stood everywhere dressed in colourful silks and elegant suits. He smiled genially as they all dropped into deep curtseys and low bows before him. Reaching the dais, he sat in the plush velvet chair with the gilt scrolls decorating it and scanned the room. Behind him, red curtains were draped across the stone wall. He nodded at the musicians, and they struck up a dance, and the room returned to its party.

A willowy, blond-haired woman who hovered at the foot of the dais caught his eye. She wore a stunning low-cut dress. Swathes of green silk descended to the floor, accentuating her pale skin and inviting his eyes to dwell. He smiled. "Ellie, where have you been? We've missed you."

"I've been procuring a new dream for you, Your Majesty. One that will make you feel out of this world." Ellie's voice trilled over the music, light and girlish.

The king's face brightened. Here was a woman who understood him; she knew how to meet his needs. "That is excellent news. The last one didn't please; don't bring that one again."

"As you wish, Your Majesty, though maybe you should try it with something else; combined it may have the effect you desire."

"What have you brought?"

"Be patient, Your Majesty, let's not spoil the surprise."

"Later then," the king agreed, casting his eyes over the room; the night was yet young. Where was his Administrator, Gillian? Anders wanted to discuss some of his ideas for Terolia.

"Maybe we could go somewhere more private; you'll enjoy it more," Ellie suggested, fluttering her eyelashes, her silver eyes gleaming.

"Not now, my dear. I have all these guests. Let's enjoy the entertainment here."

Ellie curtsied. "As you wish, Your Majesty."

Leyarille and Birlerion stepped out of the waystone in Deepwater. It was still early, and they intended staying only for a few chimes before travelling on to Old Vespers. Waystones were a magical transport system left over from the time of the Lady, allowing one to travel large distances in seconds.

Although all magic had left the world of Remargaren when the Lady sundered the bloodstone and brought down the Veil, the waystones were linked to the Sentinals, and the Sentinals had enough residual magic to be able to use them. The Lady's Captain, Leyarille's father, had woken them much as he had woken the Sentinals. Not that anyone explained how he'd done it.

Leyarille blinked in the bright spring sunlight as they led their horses up the slope and passed the graceful sentinal trees belonging to Denirion and Tagerillion. She fairly flew into the arms of the auburn-haired woman who appeared at the top of the steps to the red-bricked manor house. Her

Aunt Alyssa, the Guardian of the Watch. Leyarille engulfed her in a hug, towering over her.

"Leyarille, Birlerion, what a surprise. We weren't expecting you," Alyssa said as she hugged her surrogate daughter. She had been proud to stand with Jerrol and Taelia in the name of the Lady and bless this child with her promise. "Come, Jared and Saranne are inside; they'll be pleased to see you both. I'll send word for Lea. He and Hugh are out checking the new plantings with Peppins."

"We are only stopping a couple of chimes, auntie. We need to get to Old Vespers before dark; Marianille is expecting us," Leyarille said as she handed the reins of her horse to the hovering manservant. Birlerion patted Kin'arol, grinning as he was led away, muttering about having to go through another waystone.

"What? You come all this way and you're not going to stay and eat with us? Didn't your mother teach you better?" Alyssa teased as she led them indoors, her deep brown eyes flashing with mock anger.

Leyarille laughed. "Of course she did, but we can't stay; not this time. We only stopped to let you know Mikkeal is on his way and intends stopping over night with you, if that's alright? He is riding from Stoneford with Serenion. I expect he'll be glad of a meal by the time he arrives."

"He still avoids waystones, then?"

Leyarille grimaced. "I don't think he's prepared to give it another try. He has Pip, and he prefers to ride." She didn't know why she could travel them fine when her brother couldn't. If you weren't a Sentinal, waystones were the most uncomfortable way to travel, causing most folks to be violently sick when they reached the other end.

They entered a small drawing room where Alyssa's children were awaiting them. Jared, Alyssa's second son, was a good foot taller than his mother. He had his father's vivid blue eyes, but black hair instead of blonde; a striking combination. Leyarille hugged her cousin with pleasure. "Jared, you've grown again," she accused as she stepped back; she had to look up to his face.

"I'm the same height as Tagerill now." He grinned as he shook Birlerion's hand. He was even taller than Birlerion.

"Is uncle Tage here?" she asked as she turned to Saranne, the only daughter of the house. Saranne was small and dainty like her mother, with the same colouring and vivacity. At sixteen, she was as striking as her brother in her own way.

Saranne's voice was soft and musical. "He'll be on his way I expect; he'll have heard the waystone." She blushed as Birlerion bent over her hand, still not quite comfortable with Sentinal courtesy.

"Come sit, tell us why you are going to Old Vespers. I'm surprised your father agreed, Leyarille. Court is not what it used to be," Alyssa said, selecting her words with care.

"It was pa's suggestion," Leyarille said as she sat. "He said it was time for me to expand my training, or words to that effect. He suggested I apply to join the King's Rangers."

Alyssa's face pinched as she flicked a glance at Jared, and then she looked at Birlerion. "Surely, you are not applying as well?"

Birlerion laughed. "No. I don't think the king allows Sentinals to join up anywhere anymore. I'm going to visit Niallerion and Marianille; they keep asking me to. I'm escorting Leyarille to Old Vespers as I was going anyway."

Alyssa nodded. "Give them our love and tell them to visit us; they haven't stopped by for years." She looked up in welcome as Tagerill entered the room. His face lit up as he saw the visitors.

He was across the room, hugging his brother immediately. "Birlerion, what brings you here? And Leyarille, my dear, it's lovely to see you." Tagerill was one of the Deepwater Watch Sentinals. Tall, silver-eyed, and still with a tousled mop of deep red hair, even if time had soothed his temper. "How's your father?" he asked.

Leyarille knew Tagerill had been one of the first Sentinals her father had awoken, and if not for a serious injury that had confined him to Deepwater for many months, he probably would still have been at his side.

"He's fine, thank you. He has Fonorion watching over him," Leyarille said.

Lady Miranda, Tagerill's wife, and Alyssa's mother arrived with the tea tray, and the room broke up into natural groups. Leyarille and Jared were accompanied by Saranne talking up a storm, whilst Tagerill and Birlerion sat with Alyssa and Miranda and reminisced over old times and recent concerns.

Jared frowned at Leyarille. "How did you manage to get your father to agree to you joining the rangers? Mine won't budge."

Leyarille shrugged. "He suggested it. He said it was our time; our generation need to help the king."

"Help the king? It sounds like he doesn't *want* anyone's help."

"Then we need to show him he's wrong. Uncle Anders wasn't always the way he is now. I think we need to remind him of his responsibilities."

"He's not going to listen to us," Jared said, his voice loud in a sudden lull of conversation. He dropped his voice as Saranne hushed him.

"Someone has to tell him," Saranne said. "I don't think he realises the risk he is taking. He has forgotten he only rules with the people's support." Saranne blushed as they stared at her. "He *has*. His people will only put up with so much."

Leyarille looked thoughtful. "You're right." She was

interrupted by the arrival of Lord Jennery and his eldest son, Hugh. They filled the room, broad-chested and loud, their presence dominating the conversation. Leyarille's ribs were at risk of cracking as Jennery gave her a big hug. "You've grown too, Leyarille. You are nearly as tall as Jared. What is it coming to when our children outgrow us?" he asked as he wrapped an arm around Alyssa's trim waist.

"It's alright for you," Alyssa complained. "What about me and Saranne? We get a crick in the neck looking up at you all. Everyone, sit down for pity's sake." They all sat, and the conversation came back round to why Leyarille was going to Old Vespers.

"That's cracked it, then," Jennery said, staring at his younger son.

Jared held his father's eyes. "If Uncle Jerrol agrees that Leyarille can go, then why can't I?"

"Old Vespers isn't safe," Alyssa began, but she stopped as she saw her husband's expression.

"When has it ever been safe?" he asked, his voice gruff. "The children have to learn how to deal with it in their own way. We have to trust in them and the Lady."

"Lea," Alyssa began, a warning in her voice.

"No, my love, it's Jared's choice; he is old enough to make his own decisions."

Jared blinked in surprise. "You mean …?" He turned to Birlerion. "Birlerion, Leyarille, would you let me travel with you?"

"We're waystoning it," Leyarille warned.

Tagerill groaned and covered his eyes. "Waystoning? What sort of word is that?"

"Healer Clennin can give me something for the sickness, I'm sure," Jared replied, ignoring Tagerill. "Father? Do you mean it?" he asked, his colour heightened.

Jennery smiled sadly at his son. "If that is your choice."

Jared dampened his elation at he saw his mother's distraught face. "Mother, I'll be careful, I promise."

"You're not leaving today? It's too quick. Maybe in a month." Her voice quavered at the thought of one of her children leaving her.

Jennery jerked his head at his eldest son, and Hugh hurried Jared out to get his things. Jennery set to reassuring Alyssa. "You knew this day was coming, love; you can't keep him here forever. He'll be safe with Birlerion keeping an eye on him. Niallerion and Marianille are there as well."

Leyarille saw Birlerion grimace, but he didn't speak. She was sure he wouldn't be able to do anything once they joined the rangers. They would be part of the system then; no longer under his protection.

"I'll keep an eye on him," Leyarille promised, hoping she would be able to keep to her word. "I didn't mean to upset you, Aunt Alyssa. I didn't realise that Jared was so keen or that we would cause such an upset."

"You haven't and you didn't," Jennery said. "This was brewing long before you arrived. She hasn't upset you, has she, Alyssa? We're very proud of her, aren't we?"

Alyssa wiped her eyes and smiled; she'd heard the warning in her husband's voice. "Of course you haven't, my dear. Lea is right. Jared has been determined to go; the timing just didn't seem right before. I think your arrival must signal the Lady's intent. I must admit, I'll feel happier knowing he is with family. I know you'll look out for each other."

A chime later, Jennery allowed Alyssa to tearfully hug her son before he hustled him out of the house and down to the waystone. He tucked some coins into his son's backpack as he parted with a stream of instructions. "I'm proud of you son, never forget it, and know we're always here if you need us. Make sure you write; your mother will be upset if you don't."

He gave Jared a big hug and stepped back as Birlerion and Leyarille approached. He hugged Leyarille. "Be safe," he murmured in her ear and turned to clasp Birlerion's arm and rub Kin'arol's soft nose in farewell.

Birlerion herded his charges through the waystone before anyone could begin another round of goodbyes and breathed a sigh of relief as they all stepped out behind the Chapterhouse in Vespers. Jared's face paled, and he steered him to the bushes.

"I'll be alright; the healer gave me a tablet."

Birlerion grinned. "Well, they don't always work."

"Now he tells me," Jared said as his stomach heaved and he threw up. He wiped his mouth and gratefully took the canteen Birlerion handed him. He glanced at Leyarille. "So why are you joining the rangers? You're a Sentinal, aren't you? You've the cast-iron stomach, the name, the eyes." His stomach roiled again, and he thrust the canteen at Birlerion as he turned away.

Leyarille grimaced. "I am not a Sentinal; I'm the daughter of one."

"What's the difference?" Jared asked. A sheen of sweat covered his pale face, and Birlerion rubbed his back, offering the water again.

Leyarille rolled her eyes in frustration.

"Jared has a valid point. You know you're going to get ribbed by the others; they'll assume you are a Sentinal, even if you're not. Until you both earn their respect, you're going to find it tough," Birlerion warned.

"That's why I'm going through the open admission. If my father got me a place, no one would believe I earned it on my own merit. If I can't get in on my own capabilities, then there's no point joining."

"Even so, your name alone will cause you problems. It is unfortunate but true."

"Jared will have as much trouble as I will. Jennery is as well-known a name as Haven. I guess we'll have to bolster each other when we're down.

Once Jared had recovered, Birlerion led them past the Lady's temple, through the temple gardens, and under the tall sentinal trees next to the front door of Marianille's home. He smiled, acknowledging their soft greetings as he tethered Kin'arol. The wooden door opened before he could knock, and they were effusively welcomed into the Sentinal's home.

4

OLD VESPERS

Birlerion's sister, Marianille, was beautiful. Her lustrous black hair curled around her face, setting off a complexion of cream and roses which was to die for. Niallerion, her husband, was thinner, dark-haired, and watchful. He worked in the Chapterhouse, translating the recovered documents they were still excavating from the lost chambers in the depths below. A highly intelligent man, he was very clever at improving mechanical designs and making things work more efficiently. He waited for Marianille to finish her effusive welcome before he added his quiet greetings.

Marianille grinned at Leyarille and Jared as she pushed them into chairs. "It's been so long since we've seen you. You've both grown so much. I can't believe it's time for you to join the rangers. Doesn't time fly?"

"It hasn't been that long. Ma and pa say you're welcome any time you want to visit," Jared said. "And Tagerill sends his love."

Huffing out her breath, Marianille glared at Birlerion. "And he thinks that is sufficient?"

Birlerion grinned at her. "You'll have to take it up with him."

"I will, don't worry."

Niallerion appeared in the kitchen door. "I hope you're hungry. Marianille prepared enough food for an army."

"That's probably a good thing," Birlerion said, his gaze resting on Leyarille and then Jared. "If Jared is anything like Leyarille, you'll think you've been hit by locusts. I know Taelia is always complaining about how much the kids eat."

"That's because we're not kids anymore," Leyarille snapped as she followed Marianille into the dining room.

Dinner, a rich meat stew with vegetables and rice, soothed Leyarille's brief flash of irritation with Birlerion. She joined in the discussion about how they would go about applying to join the rangers. First, though, Leyarille had to make her curtsey to King Anders, which meant a visit to court.

"I don't see why I have to be presented when Jared doesn't," Leyarille complained.

"That's what you get for being so close to the royal family," Jared said.

"Not me; my parents."

Jared shrugged. "Same thing."

Niallerion raised an eyebrow at Birlerion. "How do you think Anders will react to you being back in Old Vespers?"

Frowning, Leyarille glanced between the Sentinals, wondering why Birlerion returning was a problem.

"No reason for him to even notice me," Birlerion replied, gaze focussed on his glass as he twisted the stem.

Marianille choked on her drink. "Even you, Birlerion, cannot be so dense as to think Anders will ignore your presence in Old Vespers. You should not go to court."

Birlerion shrugged. "It's unavoidable. He'll just have to put up with it."

"What will the king have to put up with?" Leyarille asked.

Marianille's smile was pure evil. "Birlerion often manages to … irritate the king, shall we say?"

"Not deliberately," Birlerion said.

Niallerion chuckled. "You shouldn't be so honest. Anders likes to be pampered to. Unfortunately, our Birlerion seems to lose his sense of diplomacy when it comes to the king."

Birlerion rubbed his temple. "I don't know what it is, but seeing the king being deliberately misled riles me, and I have to put him straight."

"Even if he doesn't want to be," Niallerion added.

"He should be pleased someone is trying to keep him informed," Birlerion said with a scowl.

"No one likes to be told they're wrong," Niallerion said, trying to suppress a laugh.

Birlerion scoffed. "He's the king. He should act like it."

Leyarille stared at Birlerion in awe. "You told the king he was wrong?"

"No!" Birlerion glared at the chuckling Niallerion. "It's not funny."

"Oh, it is. I can't wait to see how long it takes you to upset Anders."

Marianille and Niallerion joined Birlerion to escort Leyarille to the palace the next afternoon. As soon as they arrived, Marianille tucked her husband's hand in her arm and dragged him off to greet an acquaintance of hers. Birlerion went to see Bryce, an old friend of his and the Commander of the King's Justice, whilst Leyarille waited for her presentation to the king.

The courtiers were all stirred up, muttering amongst

themselves like a flock of iridescent pigeons. They hovered in the outer chambers pecking at the juicy titbits of news as they fell. The king had granted a private audience to the daughter of Lord Jerrolion of Stoneford, and they were waiting with great anticipation to see what happened. Marianille and Niallerion circulated, listening to the gossip.

Leyarille was wearing her only gown. Her mother had made her pack it as she had foretold that Leyarille would have to present herself to the king. She fidgeted with her dress as she waited for King Anders to arrive. She hated being restricted in skirts and petticoats; trousers were much more comfortable. Gazing around the throne room, she was shocked to see that the wall behind his throne was covered in velvet curtains, the King's Oath engraved in the wall hidden and ignored.

Birlerion had been insistent that when she presented herself to the king, she be polite and circumspect, no matter what the king said. Which was quite amusing seeing as he was apparently unable to restrain himself. She wondered what he expected the king to say and frowned as she remembered her father's concern. She wished Birlerion had been able to attend the audience, but he would have to loiter with the courtiers in the outer chambers. A private audience meant it was *private*; just her and Anders. She suddenly wondered what the king wanted.

She sank to the floor in a curtsey as the door opened and King Anders entered. He was resplendent in a navy-blue suit with gold epaulettes and a gold cord looping from his chest to his right shoulder. His clothes were immaculate in stark contrast with his bloodshot eyes and pasty skin; the king did not look well.

"Rise." His voice was gruff, not the clear, precise tones she was expecting.

She rose at his word as he seated himself on his throne. "I was expecting your brother."

"He is on his way, Your Majesty. I expect him to arrive by the end of the week. I was fortunate to travel with Sentinal Birlerion via the waystone."

"But your brother did not?"

"No, sire, he prefers to ride as he does not travel well by waystone."

"But you do. Interesting. Are you come to tell me you are a Sentinal, then? If so, you are wasting your breath; I have no need of Sentinals."

"I am not a Sentinal, Your Majesty. I am only the daughter of one."

"Then why are you here?"

"I came to pay my respects, Your Majesty, and to offer you my oath as I am applying to become a King's Ranger."

The king watched her. "Following in your father's footsteps, I see. Applying, you said? Did your father not secure you a place? Surely, he could assist you."

"I asked him not to, Your Majesty."

"More fool you. You'll only get somewhere in the world by using every advantage you have. I wonder, are you going to ask me to speak for you?"

"No, Your Majesty, I wouldn't dare to presume. I assure you I will apply through open admission."

"As you wish." Anders leaned back on his throne, his eyes narrowing. "You said Birlerion came with you? What does he want?"

Leyarille paused at the edge in his voice. Niallerion had been right; there was a sudden tension in the king when he spoke of Birlerion. "He came to visit friends."

"And you expect me to believe that?"

"I am sorry, Your Majesty, I don't know what you mean."

"Sentinal Birlerion does not just visit friends."

Leyarille hesitated, observing the king. "He didn't tell me anything different."

"Well, you can find out for me. I want to know why he is really here. Can I trust you to do that discretely?" The king leaned forward. "After all, you came to swear your oath to me; that means you'll do what I ask, doesn't it?"

"For the good of Vespiri, Your Majesty."

"Are you suggesting my request is not for the good of Vespiri?"

"Of course not, Your Majesty."

"Then swear your oath."

Leyarille shivered as she knelt before him; this was not what she had expected. "Your Majesty, I swear to uphold your rule; to serve and protect you and your kingdom as long as there is breath in my body."

"Nice. I expect you to be an exemplary ranger. Now, do as I tell you like a good little girl. I expect a report by the end of the month." He rose and left Leyarille kneeling on the floor.

She rose, her stomach somewhere around her knees as the footmen opened the doors and began setting up the room for the king's entertainment. She couldn't believe it. Had the king just ordered her to spy on Birlerion? She couldn't do it. Swallowing the bile that rose in her throat, she realised she had no choice; the king had commanded she do so.

Birlerion entered the room, and she stiffened under his keen inspection. "Everything alright?" he asked, and she eased her shoulders, comforted by his presence.

"Yes, he was pleased I was joining the rangers, and he accepted my oath." Leyarille glanced around the room, avoiding his eyes. She fiddled with her hair and tucked it behind her ear.

"That's good, then," Birlerion said. He continued speaking, his voice calm and measured, and she relaxed a little more. "We'll be expected to be in attendance for the evening." He snagged a glass of wine off a passing tray. "Here, drink this, slowly," he said with a smile as she took a gulp. "You're not used to it; don't drink too much. You can't afford to embarrass yourself in front of the king."

As the evening progressed, Leyarille wondered why she couldn't embarrass herself when everyone else seemed to be, including the king. The throne room and receiving chambers were dimly lit and piles of colourful velvet cushions were stacked in the corners.

Birlerion warned her against accepting a drink from anyone, nor to accept any of the freely available phials of colourful liquid. Leyarille stuck close to Birlerion and watched as the king eagerly accepted a blue phial from a blonde-haired woman she knew to be Sentinal Elliarille. He flopped back on his throne, and allowed Elliarille to sit on his lap.

Elliarille, was one of the Sentinals she knew least because she and her twin brother, Ellaerion, rarely visited Stoneford. Leyarille knew they had been trapped in the strands of the Veil until her father and the Lady had saved them in the final confrontation with the ascendants.

Courtiers relaxed and began to drink more freely. They shed clothing like leaves and Leyarille blushed as their hands wandered everywhere. She was relieved when couples began to retire to the plush cushions tucked in alcoves and she didn't have to watch all that exposed flesh.

As the night wore on, Birlerion's face grew stiffer and paler. Leyarille averted her eyes from another scene of debauchery and sidled her way around the bodies. How could they blatantly maul each other? There was no indication of tenderness or love; it was pure fornication. She shuddered delicately and searched for Birlerion.

She found him talking to a tall, powerfully built Sentinal

whose blonde hair was swept back off his broad face into a short queue. She smiled in recognition. He had been the king's bodyguard before he was discarded like all the other Sentinals. "Parsillion." She gave him a swift hug and looked at Birlerion. "Can we leave yet?"

Birlerion gave her an appreciative grin, though his eyes looked strained. "Parsillion was just leaving; he will escort you back to Marianille's. He'll update them on the situation here. I'll meet you there in a bit."

"I can wait for you if you want. It's just …" She wrinkled her nose in distaste.

"I know. The king's lack of restraint and that of his lackeys is worse than we thought. Go with Parsillion. It's not going to get any better. Niallerion already took Marianille home. You don't want the king making any inappropriate suggestions. You would have to obey him, and as this is your first night let's not test your oath straight away." He grinned persuasively, his silver eyes glinting at her, and she gave in; she never could resist those glints.

Parsillion smiled at her, though he too seemed a bit strained; the smile didn't reach his silver eyes. "Let us go while we still can," he murmured, and Birlerion moved to cover their departure.

He sighed in relief as they made it out the door and worked his way around the room, drifting nearer the king.

By the time he reached the dais, the king was barely sitting on his throne. He was sprawled, an arm draped over the side, a bottle in his hand. Birlerion hesitated. This was not the time to be teasing the king.

He watched as Elliarille insinuated herself back into the king's embrace and she began whispering in his ear. The king's face firmed for a moment in interest before blurring back into sodden inebriation. Elliarille frowned and then shrugged before expertly extracting herself. This was obviously a practised manoeuvre. She was joined at the foot of the dais by a man who could only be her twin brother, Ellaerion, they were so alike. Her brother did not look happy. Birlerion drifted closer, stepping behind a trellis work that concealed him.

"You take too many risks." Ellaerion's voice was low and bitter.

"Pah, he won't remember anything. They never do."

"Ellie, please, you need to be careful." Their voices faded away, and Birlerion stepped out of the shadows, staring after them. He glanced around the throne room. Benedict must be turning in his grave. Most courtiers were sprawled over the floor on cushions; none were sober. He wondered how they had the stamina to do this every night.

Shaking his head, he left. The king was threatening to slide off his throne, and he wondered who would have the guts to tell him it was time for bed. He couldn't be bothered to wait and find out.

It was nearly two in the morning by the time he arrived at Marianille and Niallerion's home and tapped on the door. A soft light glowed in the parlour, and Parsillion was still seated, conversing with Niallerion. Leyarille and Jared had gone to bed.

Marianille pulled him in and shut the door. She placed a glass of water in his hand, and he gulped it greedily as if it could wash away the taint of the palace. He leaned back in his chair and closed his eyes. His head thumped. He never had dealt with stress particularly well; he could foresee a lot of headaches in the future.

He opened his eyes as the low toned conversation ceased.

"Well?" Marianille asked.

Birlerion sighed. "The king is completely addicted to whatever Elliarille is giving him. He has lost all sense of propriety or any idea of his duty. He has forgotten why he is on the throne."

"Are you sure Elliarille is his supplier? I mean, he could be being supplied by anyone."

"We saw her giving him a phial, and the contents had an immediate effect. But it's proving she is his procurer that's the problem. Just because he favours her won't stand up to the justice's inspection."

Leyarille froze behind the bedroom door. The knock on the front door had woken her, and upon hearing Birlerion's voice, she had slipped out of bed to listen better. Justices? Was the king right? Were the Sentinals really plotting against him? She shivered at the thought. No, she couldn't believe it, not of Birlerion of all people.

Birlerion was still speaking and she leaned against the door. "I'll have to stay and keep an eye on them. Marianille, Niallerion, I can move to an inn if it's an inconvenience. Leyarille and Jared will be at the barracks once they sign on; at least they'll be safe there."

"Don't be daft. You can stay here or you can stay with Parsillion. He had to find rooms when the king dismissed him."

"Yes, about that, you ought to avoid the palace, Parsillion. You know the king will be angry if he sees you," Birlerion said.

"I don't trust them." Parsillion's voice was low, and Leyarille wasn't sure she had heard him correctly. He didn't trust the king? The floor creaked as someone stood, and Leyarille turned and clambered back into bed, her heart thumping rapidly, obscuring the voices in the other room.

In the outer room, Birlerion stood and gripped Parsillion's shoulder. "We'll find a way to get him back; the Anders we know would be distraught if he realised what he was doing."

"He needs protecting from himself." Parsillion was almost in tears.

"We will protect him; I swear it, Parsillion," Birlerion said, his voice low and intense as he tried to comfort his friend.

The next morning when Leyarille left her room, she found Niallerion busy in the kitchen. "Where is everyone?"

Niallerion grinned. "Jared and Birlerion took Kino down to the hostelry before the neighbours started to complain. Marianille is lying in as she was overtired after yesterday, and Parsillion went home. I expect we'll see him later. Come sit, have some breakfast. I think Birlerion was planning on showing you some of Vespers before you and Jared go and complete your application this afternoon."

Leyarille sat down with a thump. "This afternoon?"

Niallerion's grin widened. "No point waiting. Get it over with. It's either today or two days hence. Jared wanted to do it today, so …" Niallerion turned back to the stove with a shrug.

Leyarille was demolishing a pile of fried potatoes and eggs when Birlerion and Jared returned. She watched amused as Jared tried to beat Birlerion to the chair. Jared was in fine spirits, excited about everything and eager to get out exploring.

"What's the plan then?" she asked as she put her fork down.

"W-ell, I thought we could start at the Lady's temple and thank her for the support she's going to give you this afternoon." Birlerion gave her a fleeting smile. "Have a quick look over the Chapterhouse, we won't have time to go into much depth today, and then swing by the markets and bring back some fresh produce for Marianille; she's promised to cook up a feast this evening. We need to get to the garrison for two this afternoon, so you can sit the entrance exam. After you pass that, the next stage is combat skills, and once you pass that, you become a cadet and move into the barracks."

Leyarille was glad he hadn't said 'if'. She glanced at Jared; he didn't seem worried at all. Ignoring the nervous flutter in her tummy, she grinned. "Let's get going then!"

Jared, grounded in the present and interested in the now, asked questions about the current city. Leyarille, steeped in history, longed to know more about why things had changed. Both of them wanted to know how Old Vespers differed from the Vespers Birlerion had known over three thousand years ago.

They were seated on a grass bank staring at the Chapter-house, munching apples, when Leyarille twisted to look up towards the palace. "Pa said there was an amazing bridge, the most beautiful structure he had ever seen, between the Chapterhouse and the Lady's Palace."

"The Lady's bridge, built by Captain Guerlaire," Birlerion said.

"Tell us about Guerlaire. How come he isn't here with you?" Leyarille asked.

"How did Uncle Jerrol see the bridge? How is that possi-ble? Why don't I know about this?" Jared's voice rose in indignation.

Birlerion laughed. "We have all week. You don't need all the stories today. Anyway, Jared, I thought your father or Tagerill would have told them to you by now."

"If only. My father isn't much of a storyteller, especially when he isn't in it. He can be quite cagey. He gives you a titbit and then won't tell you anymore. Unless it's all about him of course, then you can't shut him up."

Birlerion laughed again. "He hasn't changed much then. Marianille and Niallerion were at the Lady's court; they can tell you more about the Lady's palace and life at court. I moved about a lot, then I ended up at the palace with Tagerill and Serillion before they were reassigned to the Watches."

They were silent a moment, aware that Serillion had been a close friend of Birlerion's until his death at the hands of the ascendants. Birlerion didn't speak of him often. "Tell us about Guerlaire," Leyarille said. "Why did he never return like the rest of the Sentinals?"

Birlerion sighed, his eyes distant. "Guerlaire was an intense man; very practical but deeply emotional. He built the Chapterhouse as part of his endless quest for knowledge. He roamed the land looking for new things and bringing them home to catalogue. The Chapterhouse kept expanding, was meant to further our understanding of the world and everything in it. Today, the scholars have spent years looking to the past, excavating instead of exploring, though they have nearly uncovered all the rooms now, so who knows, maybe they'll look to the future again soon. Though there may still be another level yet to occupy them.

"Guerlaire loved the Lady Leyandrii very much, and although it's said he built the bridge just because he wanted to prove he could, I think it was for Leyandrii.

"It was the most unbelievable structure ever built; it was so fragile and gossamer-like. It was a miracle it stood, but it did. It spanned from the Chapterhouse to the northern spire of the Lady's palace. And it glistened. It sparkled in the sunlight, but it glowed at night under the light of the moon. It was amazing." Birlerion fell silent, a soft smile on his face. Leyarille and Jared exchanged glances and kept quiet, afraid to disturb his line of thought.

"He would never tell us how he did it or what it was made of. At the end, when the Lady sundered the bloodstone, he wouldn't leave her." He glanced at Leyarille. "Your father met him just before the end. Did he tell you?" As she mutely shook her head, he continued. "Guerlaire was consumed in the final wave with the Lady and drawn away with her as she banished herself and the ascendants. He cannot cross the divide. And so he is lost to us." Birlerion was silent again, brooding.

He became aware of the silence and began speaking. "And then the Lady blessed us with your father, and Guerlaire passed his sword on, and Jerrol became the Lady's Captain. As he still is, Lady be praised." He looked about him and stood up. "Come, we need to get back. You need to have some lunch, freshen up. Later, I'll tell you about the first time I met both your fathers," he said, and Leyarille and Jared teased him to tell them the story all the way back to Marianille's. It was rare for Birlerion to share any stories.

5

THEATRE, OLD VESPERS

Birlerion was waiting for them outside the Rangers Garrison when Leyarille and Jared finally walked through the gates as the sun began to set. Their applications had been accepted without comment. They had sat the entrance exam, four chimes it had taken; a paper on arithmetic and reasoning, a paper on comprehension and the written word; a paper on the history of Remargaren, one on the territories of Remargaren, and a final half-chime interview with the recruitment office as to why they wanted to join the King's Rangers.

Leyarille looked pale and wrung out, and Jared didn't look much better. He was mumbling about whether the easternmost port in Terolia was Seril or Feril, and wasn't Aguinti the third largest island in Birtoli?

"Enough!" Birlerion said firmly. "It's done now, you can't change it. Forget about it for now. Marianille has prepared a delicious meal for us, and then we are taking you to the theatre as a special treat. Everyone's coming. It will be great!" It diverted them from their worries as he had intended, and they badgered him all the way home to tell them more.

After the meal, more Sentinals arrived. Niallerion's home was heaving with Sentinals, and when Birlerion thought about it, nearly every Vesper Sentinal was here tonight. He, Niallerion, and Parsillion wore their collarless, silver-green Sentinal uniforms, as did Frenerion, a more elderly Sentinal with greying hair. Marianille had chosen another stunning gown, saying she didn't often get the chance to dress up so she was making the most of it, and she dragged Leyarille off to see what she had that could be made to fit her.

Jared was fiddling with the dress shirt his brother Hugh had the forethought to shove in his pack when he looked up and his jaw dropped. Birlerion looked round to see Leyarille emerge from Marianille's room. Leyarille wore a deep green gown tucked in at the waist with a sash accentuating her curves. The neckline was modest but flattering. Her hair was twisted into ringlets that curled around her neck, and the sleeves made her arms look long and slender. Marianille hovered eagerly behind her to see the response on the male audience, her gaze lingering on Birlerion.

Birlerion couldn't help the pride he felt at the sight of Leyarille. She was so beautiful, and he felt the need to tell her. She blushed rosily as he shyly said, "You look stunning." Suddenly aware of his sister watching him, he wiped his expression clean.

Marianille bustled around, admiring Jared; he did look handsome, his deep blue eyes and dark hair an attractive combination. Birlerion was relieved as she drew attention to herself and Jared instead of him and Leyarille.

"Is everyone ready? Then let us proceed. The Royal theatre awaits us, and I have seated tickets you'll all be glad to know." Niallerion waved his tickets in the air with pride.

"How clever of you, my darling," Marianille said as she tucked her arm through his and Jared's and led the way through the Lady's gardens towards the market square and the new building that housed the theatre. The gardens were lit by torches guiding the way, and a soft murmur of voices rose around them as they joined the people converging on the theatre.

Birlerion tucked Leyarille's arm in his and followed. "You do look lovely," he said softly as they followed Marianille. "Green suits you."

"The Lady's colour," Leyarille replied with a smile.

"True." His gaze dwelled on her, memorising the way she looked. Once she was in the Rangers, she would rarely be out of uniform.

Arriving at the theatre, Marianille handed out the tickets and organised the seating. Her thoughtful gaze rested on Leyarille and then Birlerion as she sat them together in the front row.

The theatre was a round wooden structure constructed by an artistic enthusiast. The artiste Merani had toured the kingdoms with his troupe, offering tableaus and playlets, but he had greater aspirations, and he had wanted an appropriate venue to display them in. One half of the structure was taken up by a raised platform that was overlooked by galleries where various musicians were located. Opposite, tiers of seating rose from the pit in the centre and rows of wooden seats ringed the walls. Torches were lit everywhere, positioned around the galleries and providing a warm glow that softened the stark edges.

Niallerion had procured seats in two rows almost in the centre and on the third tier; they looked over the lower levels and had a clear view towards the stage. To the left of the stage, a red velvet bedecked box was prominent, though empty. Merani was sure the king would one day realise what he was missing and deign to grace his theatre.

Niallerion finally pulled his wife down into the seat next to him. "Stop fussing and relax," he grumbled, and Marianille draped herself over his arm and fluttered her eyelashes at him until he laughed.

"Stop flirting, you two, and tell us what this show is all about," Parsillion interrupted them from his seat behind them.

Marianille laughed. "The Great Merani presents 'A comedic journey of two halves.'"

"A comedy." Frenerion's voice was tinged with doubt. "Are you sure this was a wise choice?"

"I've heard it's hilarious. We'll be rolling in the aisles, or so they say," Marianille promised. She turned back to the stage as the musicians began tuning their instruments and the light started to dim as torches were extinguished. Part of the stage was cleverly lit, leaving the rest in darkness.

Birlerion watched Leyarille's face. Her eyes shone in anticipation, and her lips parted as she waited for the show to begin. He shifted so he could watch her expression and still see the stage and smiled as her face lit up with amusement as the show began.

"Birlerion, all this laughter. I need a drink. Be a dear and see if you can find one for us," Marianille pleaded, holding her ribs when the show paused for an interval; one the patrons badly needed.

Birlerion smiled as he rose and bowed. "As madame commands," he said grandly before leaving on his errand. He eyed the heaving mass of people around the drinks stand and sighed as he joined the queue.

He was patiently waiting for his turn when he became aware of muttering behind him. Belligerent voices were beginning to build. Turning around, he was surprised when the men behind him flinched back.

"See, I told you so. He's one of them. Sucks your blood and then tosses you aside to die," a skinny man with pock-marked skin spoke in a loud whisper.

"I can assure you I do no such thing," Birlerion said, unable to keep the sharpness out of his voice.

"O' course he'd say that, wouldn't he?" The man nodded wisely. "Kills 'em he does, and tosses their body in the street as if it's rubbish."

"If I killed a man in fair combat, I certainly would not disrespect him so," Birlerion retorted, trying to relax tense muscles as he stiffened against the accusation.

"See, he admits it; he's killed men. He kills innocent young men for sport."

"I assure you I do not. Wherever did you hear such tales? Even Merani could not better them."

"Sentinals have powers. You're all mad after what you been through. You're ancient. Got to affect the brain, ain't it?"

"I am quite sane. What makes you think I'm not?"

"You were seen. A man with silver eyes accosting young Perks down at the wharves, and then he turns up dead across town. That's the second one in as many months."

Birlerion frowned with concern as the men muttered between them. "Have you reported this to the King's Justice? Surely, they would be the ones to tell."

"They laugh at us, don't believe us. We're not … what was it they said we weren't, Tom?"

"Reliable witnesses," an elderly man replied. His grey hair was neatly trimmed, as was his moustache. He was straight-backed; ex-military, Birlerion thought.

"Very well. Will you meet me tomorrow? At a place of your choosing. I would hear more. I assure you, Sentinals are not to blame, and Vespers should be safe for all. On my honour as a Lady's Sentinal, I will take it to the Justices if you tell me everything you know."

The elderly man considered him and then sighed. "What we got to lose? Some help's better than no help."

"But what if it's him? You could be next," the skinny man whispered, shocked.

"It's not him. Meet me at the Docker's Tavern on Gart Street at eleven tomorrow morning. Ask for Tom."

"Agreed, eleven at the Docker's Tavern." Birlerion turned away, drinks forgotten.

When he returned to the balcony, he had lost his seat to Jared, and he slipped in beside Frenerion.

"Where have you been? The ladies noticed their lack of refreshment," Frenerion said.

"I was detained. I'll explain later."

Birlerion was aware of Frenerion's sharp glance, though he fell silent. Birlerion missed most of the second half as his mind turned over what he had heard. He didn't laugh once, even though his companions were shrieking with laughter.

Marianille held her sides as they gathered outside the theatre. "Oh, my ribs; such agony. I haven't laughed so much in all my life."

"Wasn't the man with the exotic bird so clever? To make it behave so and when he wanted it to as well." Jared's eyes were shining with excitement. "Imagine being able to train a bird to do such things."

"I thought the parable about the poor man who was actually the richest was the cleverest," Leyarille chimed in.

Marianille turned to Birlerion. "And you, dear sir. Such utter failure. What happened to our sustenance? I had such faith in your capabilities, and now they are all dashed."

Birlerion made a tragic face. "My lady, you destroy me with your words; there were too many barriers to reach the victuals, and then I heard the laughter and could not delay further and so miss the show."

Marianille laughed at him and then groaned. "Don't make me laugh! My ribs ..."

Leyarille smiled to see the Sentinals so relaxed; the banter of old friends was comforting. She was looking forward to making such worthwhile friendships. She eyed Jared thoughtfully. Maybe he was a good place to start. She smiled as Parsillion offered her his arm, Marianille having dragged Birlerion off with her. "Thank you," she murmured as she fell into step.

"Which part did you enjoy most, Parsillion?"

"The narrator," he said quietly. "The art of keeping your attention is how you weave the story throughout the acts. Merani is truly a great man."

Leyarille frowned in thought, trying to remember the thread of the story. She had laughed her way through each sketch, not paying much attention to the man who spoke at the beginning of the act.

"And what did you perceive to be the moral of the story?" she asked, her voice soft in the night air.

"To not forget what you hold in your hand, lest you end up in need of that which you already lost."

Her brow creased in thought. "I don't understand. How is that funny?"

"It isn't, Leyarille, it isn't."

Warm light spilled out before them as they arrived home, and they wearily collapsed into chairs, kicking off shoes. Niallerion put the water on to boil, and Marianille set out glasses on the table. "A drink before you leave, Parsillion, Frenerion. It was a lovely evening. I haven't had so much fun in ages. We must do it more often."

"It was an interesting show," Frenerion said. "One has to hope that the king will condescend to attend, though whether he will appreciate it as much as we did, time will tell. Let us hope not for dear Merani's sake. I would like to attend another show one day."

Niallerion laughed. "I think Merani is safe for the foreseeable future, even if the king does attend."

Leyarille frowned at the undercurrent in their voices, and Jared was leaning forward, listening avidly. What did he hear that she didn't? She would ask him later. She cast a glance at Birlerion. He had been silent since they'd returned and his eyes were distant. He sensed her attention, and she saw him visibly shelve whatever was concerning him and attempt to join the conversation, though he was nowhere near as carefree as the beginning of the night. She wondered what had happened to affect him so.

She never had the chance to ask him as he walked Parsillion and Frenerion out at the end of the night and Marianille shooed her off to bed, saying she would be following straight after.

The next morning, Birlerion had already left when Leyarille rose, and Niallerion offered to take them down to the harbour. Jared leapt at the offer, and she had no choice but to follow.

Niallerion reminisced as they walked down the road to the harbour, and Leyarille and Jared listened in amazement. The scent of the sea grew stronger, the tang of salt heavy in the air, and as they rounded another curve in the road, the harbour spread out below them.

"I remember Tagerill telling me a story once about the time he met your father here, Leyarille. Your father had single-handedly sailed a boat no bigger than that fishing boat over there," he pointed to a small sailboat with a single mast, "from what was then Plini on the east coast of the Birtoli mainland all the way here, offering his fish for sale. He went to the Chapterhouse and paid for a trading license for the Jerven shipping company. Birlerion still has the pearls Jerrol traded him for the coin for the payment."

"Jerven shipping company? If my father started that company, we would be rich!"

Niallerion chuckled. "Roberion was fortunate to ride that wave. He got in early, had the inside track you might say. That's how he made enough money to build the *Miracle*," he said, referring to the elegant frigate that frequently sailed between Vespiri and the other territories.

"Leyarille, do you mean to say Birlerion has never told you any of these stories?" Jared asked in disbelief. "If my father had lived over three thousand years ago and came home safe and sound, I would want to know all about it."

"Well, Tagerill didn't tell you either," Leyarille retaliated.

"My father didn't travel back in time."

"Did he really? Travel back in time, I mean?" Leyarille asked Niallerion in bewilderment.

"Oh yes, I met him. As did Birlerion, Tagerill, and Serillion, amongst others. Lady's blessings, I remember the three of them. They were a year ahead of me. They were infamous in the academy. They were what every cadet aspired to be and every tutor dreaded." He laughed, remembering, then he sighed. "Those were the days, whilst they lasted, but it wasn't to be." He shrugged off the memory and turned to the harbour and began pointing out where the old harbour finished and the new harbour began.

They walked down the long hill and followed the track around to the wharves.

Leyarille stared at the small boats. "My father hates water; there is no way he would have sailed in a boat that small."

Niallerion looked at the boat sadly. "There is a reason for

that, but I am not the one to tell it. He was a great sailor; even Roberion will attest to that."

"Exactly when was it that Uncle Jerrol travelled back to Vespers?" Jared asked with interest.

"About seventeen years ago, just after Leyarille was born."

"No, I mean when in your time."

"It was the end of 1123, a few months before the Lady sundered the bloodstone."

The blood drained from Leyarille's face. "Are you telling me my father was involved with defeating the ascendants? That he was actually here when the Lady graced the lands?"

"Yes," Niallerion said.

"Unbelievable. All those history lessons, you mean he was telling it from experience?" Leyarille's voice rose.

Niallerion grinned, rubbing his chin. "Well, not knowing what stories he told, it's possible."

"You wait till I get my hands on him, and Birlerion - he used to chip in comments as if it was common knowledge, both of them." Words failed her, to Niallerion's relief, and Jared burst out laughing at her expression.

"Leyarille, you have to share. No wonder you know so much about Remargaren; you have inside knowledge. I wish I'd known before the entrance exam. It could have made so much difference."

"You'll do fine, both of you. Anyway, time is passing. Let's head back if you've seen all that you want to." Niallerion herded them back up the hill, wishing he had kept his mouth shut.

6

DOCKER'S TAVERN, OLD VESPERS

Birlerion arrived at the Docker's Tavern at eleven sharp and entered the dim taproom. He searched the room before walking up to the bar. "I'm looking for Tom," he said to the large man behind the counter.

The man inspected him, his eyes squinting in the gloom as he travelled down Birlerion's nondescript brown jacket and trousers to his booted feet and back up to his silver eyes. He held the silver eyes as he jerked his head. "He's in the backroom waiting for you. He stood you an ale if you've a mind for one."

"Thank you." Birlerion accepted the offer. He took the mug and placed some coins on the bar. "For a refill." The barman nodded and swept the coins off the bar.

Birlerion walked to the back of the room and ducked through the low doorframe. The backroom was dark, lit by a couple of candles that barely dispersed the gloom, and daylight struggled to pierce the dirty windows. The elderly man from the previous evening was seated at the single table, a clay mug before him. An empty chair was drawn up beside him, and Birlerion sat.

"Thank you for the drink, and thank you for meeting me."

Tom nodded. "As the Lady says, it's no skin off her nose."

Birlerion's lips twitched, but he disguised it by taking a sip of his ale. The musky aroma of hops filled his nose, and he placed the mug on the table. "Indeed," he agreed politely.

"Did yer mean it? You would take our concerns to the Justices fer us?"

"Of course. People going missing cannot be ignored. We need to find out what happened to them, for their family's sake if nothing else, let alone the fear it must be generating in general."

"But yer a Sentinal, aren't yer? One o'them the king says have no use?"

Birlerion dipped his head. "Well, I wouldn't put it quite like that, but yes, the king no longer requires our services."

"And what did Commander Haven have t' say about that, then?" Tom grinned evilly in anticipation.

"Well," Birlerion said with a keen glance at the man opposite him, "after some protest, he accepted the king's command and asked us to find other occupation."

"Good man, Haven. I served in Stoneford's third unit, volunteered. Saw him at Oprimere. You too, I'm thinkin'."

Birlerion stilled. "If you were at Oprimere, then yes, I was with Commander Haven at the end."

"Got yerself blasted, didn't yer. Saw yer go flyin'. Thought you'd 'ad it, 'specially when them trees started appearing. Uncanny it was." He shuddered, his eyes seeing a scene long in the past.

"I was fortunate, I recovered. Many didn't," Birlerion said.

Tom nodded. "Yeah, lost m' brother there. M' ma was never quite the same after that." He sighed, staring at his mug. "But you Sentinals, you kept us together; you stood with us. I didn't think it could be you."

"Could be us doing what?"

"Killin', snatching innocent kids off the street."

Birlerion tensed. "Tell me everything you know." He took out a notebook from his pocket and leaned forward, listening intently, not noticing when the barman thumped another mug beside each of them.

Tom nodded. "It started about six months ago. A couple o' kids went missin' one after the other. First one turned up wandering around the backstreets, claimin' he'd seen the Lady. She'd chosen 'im to show her the way, he said. The second one turned up dead down by the 'arbour."

"How did he die?"

"No one knows. Not a mark on 'im. He weren't even fifteen; just a kid."

Birlerion made a note. "What was the date? And their names?"

"It was just after Lady's day, last Octu, that Brant was found. He was mumbling about stars and the Lady. None of it made sense. He still doesn't make much sense. His mother is at her wit's end; don't know what to do with 'im."

"Where does he live?" Birlerion wrote down the address as Tom dictated it. "And the other?"

"Poor Will. He just started out, apprenticed to the carpenter up near the mill, you know; the one they built where those old warehouses used to be." He continued as Birlerion nodded. "He lived down by the new builds. All those new 'ouses that sprung up a couple of years ago. He was found down by the 'arbour, 'is body tossed in the water. Why would someone do that?" Tom took a gulp of his ale. "Not a mark on 'im, though his ma said his clothes weren't his."

Birlerion looked up. "What do you mean?"

"She said his clothes were too fine to be his." Tom shrugged as if it didn't matter. "And then a couple o' months later, another body turned up, left behind the Chapterhouse in the midden, half covered with the peelings and the waste. Again, no marks. Young lad called Perks, lived across the square with his pa. His ma died the year before. His pa was distraught losing them both, spends most of his time in 'ere now, drowning 'is sorrows."

Birlerion stiffened as he stared at his notebook. "And there is a witness says it was a Sentinal?"

"There were one, but 'e retracted his statement," Tom said carefully. "'e refused to speak to yer."

Birlerion stared at him. Tom was sitting straight-backed and watching Birlerion just as intently. "Do you think someone persuaded him not to speak?" Birlerion asked.

"That's the word on the street." Tom nodded.

"And now you say there is another?"

"Yeah, another young lad, young Jake. Snatched a week or so back, turned up a couple of days ago, apparently collapsed, drunk, behind the Galley Arms. When he was found, he claimed a glowing spirit had attacked him because she wanted his body. Most laughed at him, but if he wasn't tellin' the truth, where had he been? 'e couldn't explain, kept mumbling about needing to go back. Just keeps wandering off back around the Justice buildings, looking for something. His ma can't keep 'im at home."

"Do you think she would let me speak to him?"

"At this point, I think she'd be glad of any help."

Birlerion nodded. "So, four young men, two dead, two wandering lost and confused. All in the last six months."

Tom sighed. "I'm not sure, but there might be one more, another lad. 'is ma said he'd gone off to join the army, but I 'aven't been able to find out if he joined up or not. No one's seen 'im for about a month."

"But there hasn't been a body."

Tom shook his head.

"His name?"

"Sam Gort. He's seventeen, brown hair, brown-eyed, strapping lad; caught the girl's eyes, yer know." Tom nodded sagely. "They were all not bad looking lads."

Birlerion leaned back in his chair. "I'll see what I can find out. How do I get hold of you?"

"Leave word here; I'll find yer."

"Very well." He pushed his untouched mug of ale over to Tom and levered himself to his feet. "I'll be in touch soon."

Tom nodded and looked down at the mug. "Yer need to stop them before we lose another."

Later that day, Birlerion entered the dim halls of the Chapterhouse, searching for the duty scholar. He found him after many redirections in the depths of the storerooms. The scholar blinked at him from behind round lenses that made his eyes seem abnormally large.

"Maps? You want a copy of a street map of Vespers? Of course we have copies. Five coppers each. We have maps of everything; cities to harbours to Watches, you name it."

"Just of Vespers at this time," Birlerion replied, a little bemused as the scholar stacked pads of creamy coloured paper in his arms.

"You can help me take this back upstairs. This Elothian paper is a blessing; the novice's get through it as if it were water."

"Maybe you should teach them how it's made. Once they realise how long it takes, they might be more considerate." Birlerion helped deliver the supplies and then managed to escape with his map, a pad of paper, and a pencil and found an empty desk in the library. There he spent the morning, making notes of his conversation with Tom and mapping the homes and the locations where the lads had been found on his map. He was frowning off into the distance, a crease between his brows, when Frenerion found him.

Pulling up a chair, Frenerion sat beside him. "I've been looking everywhere for you; a message came for you. A woman called by and said her son would speak to you tomorrow morning at eleven. A lad named Jake?"

"Ah, good. Look, this is what I've found so far. There have been four, possibly five, lads go missing in the last six months. These marks are where they lived; those are where they were found."

Frenerion stared at the notations Birlerion had made on the map. "It must be particularly worrying for those who live in the new houses in the south-east," he said thoughtfully.

"Indeed. Do you think you and Niallerion could set up a watch and see if you can see why that area is more at risk? See who visits, where the youngsters go. I am sure this isn't going to stop." He indicated the map.

"Of course. Who is this lad you want to speak to?"

"Young Jake. He lives at number four, Princes Court. One of the new builds in the south-east. He was found wandering, confused, down by the Galley Arms." Birlerion scowled. "I'm wondering if there is a connection between the lads disappearing and the influx of drugs at the palace."

Frenerion pursed his lips. "I know Parsillion is concerned that someone is using drugs to influence the king. Maybe they think if they can get him addicted enough; he won't notice he is no longer ruling. But I can't see the connection with young lads going missing."

Rubbing his temples, Birlerion sighed. "Maybe there isn't a connection. So who is holding power if Anders isn't? That would be an indication of something. Can you identify a specific group being more vocal? I hadn't heard that there was an influx of new administrators. The chancellor is still Pelori, isn't it?"

Frenerion nodded. "He's been in place for years and, so far, is still in the king's favour."

"Maybe I'll stop by and have a chat with Bryce, see what he thinks. The Inquisitors must be aware that something is going on. Disbanding the Sentinals was not an insignificant step, and then to interfere without reason in the Watches, yet no one blinked." Birlerion leaned back in his chair and stretched his arms. "What have the kids been up to?"

Frenerion laughed. "Do not let them hear you call them that. They will not be happy."

"True. I need to get out of the habit. Are they still exploring Vespers?"

"I think Niallerion is regretting offering to show them around." Frenerion grinned.

"Well, I expect they are back. It must be time for dinner. Jared is sure to have dragged them home. He'll be starving by now." Birlerion stood, collected his paperwork, and followed Frenerion out of the library.

By the time Birlerion reached Marianille's house, Mikke and Serenion had arrived. Chaos reigned as his troop of guards led their horses off to the nearest hostelry, and Marianille insisted Mikke and Serenion stay with them. It made the house crowded, but they were family, so there were no complaints.

The evening meal was loud, as everyone spoke at once, demanding news and updates. Leyarille and Jared groaned over the entrance exam, though were more excited about the upcoming combat tests. Once the table was cleared, they all sat around it, nursing their mugs of coffee, or kafinee as the Sentinals called it.

Birlerion glanced at Serenion. "Good journey?" he asked.

"Fine," Serenion replied as he leaned back in his chair.

Mikke snorted. "For you, maybe. Pip complained the whole journey about not being able to canter. He wanted to stretch his legs."

"Too much traffic," Serenion supplied succinctly when Birlerion raised his eyebrow.

"Coming to Vespers or going?" Birlerion asked.

"Both," Serenion said. "The roads were really busy."

"Why is that important?" Leyarille asked, glancing between the Sentinals.

"No reason," Birlerion murmured, trying to look uninterested, but he knew Leyarille was intrigued. She always paid attention to anything he said and picked up on the smallest of points; it was uncanny. It also meant he had to guard his words, though he was used to that now. He smiled at her. "You'll have to persuade Marianille to lend you another gown. Two visits to see the king in as many days. We're being spoilt."

Leyarille blushed rosily, and Marianille huffed her breath out. "I think we've had enough of the king and his antics. The Watches seem to be a much healthier place to live." She exchanged glances with her husband, and he nodded in agreement.

"Stoneford is a lovely Watch for raising families, and Mikke has but one Sentinal remaining," Birlerion said, raising an eyebrow in Mikke's direction.

Mikke frowned at him for a moment, and then he stared at Niallerion and Marianille. "You would always be welcome," he said in a rush as he caught the hint, and a slow smile grew on Niallerion's face.

The conversation moved onto Mikke's audience with the king. Niallerion slipped out to confirm the time with the king's secretary, and by the time he'd returned, Serenion was sharing a story about Taurillion, a friend of his in the Elothian court.

"Grand Duke Randolf would have it that Taurillion should be present in the receiving chambers, but Taurillion was adamant that he should vet the people requesting the audience first. I think he thought his stern expression would frighten the supplicants to keep their requests short.

"Only he didn't realise that there was a book running to see who could get Taurillion to crack a smile first. Even the duke was in on it." Serenion chuckled. "The administrators persuaded people to present the most ridiculous issues. And do you know the one that finally made Taurillion crack?" He smiled at his audience. "A request to build a duck bridge. So the ducks could walk across the river instead of paddling."

Everyone burst into laughter, and Birlerion was relieved to see the pensive expression on Mikke's face ease. It wasn't surprising the boy was nervous about his audience with Anders. None of them knew what to expect, really. Birlerion suddenly wished Mikke was being presented to Randolf in the Elothian court. He was sure it would go more smoothly.

7

OLD VESPERS

Birlerion rode through the streets of Vespers the next morning, winding his way to the outskirts and the houses built on the surrounding fields. Vespers was growing fast. *Old* Vespers he corrected himself. Even after nearly twenty years, he still thought of the city as Vespers, as Leyandrii had first named it.

It didn't take him long to find the house where Jake lived. A terraced house in the midst of rows and rows of housing. Birlerion stared at the profusion of dwellings in surprise and suddenly wondered where all the people had come from and how they could afford them.

Dismounting, his smoothed Kin'arol's golden neck. *"I'll not be long."*

"You'll be as long as you need to be," Kin'arol replied, his voice a soothing caress in Birlerion's mind.

After knocking on the door, Birlerion stepped back and inspected the house. It was sturdily built, with glass windows set in the stone both upstairs and downstairs. *"I wonder who built all these houses and how much they charge for the rent?"*

"Easy enough to find out." Kin'arol shook his head, his golden mane rippling down his neck.

The door swung open to reveal a plump woman with blonde curly hair. She hesitated a moment and then opened the door further. "You'd best come in," she said in a low voice, her gaze flitting up the road and back. Birlerion entered and paused in what looked like the parlour as the woman closed the door.

"My name is Birlerion, and I'm here to speak with Jake," Birlerion said, noting the dark shadows under the woman's eyes.

"Jake's upstairs in his room." The woman paused and clasped her hands tight. "I don't know how much you were told, but he's not right. He doesn't know where he is and keeps trying to leave, but when you ask where he's going, he stares at you all confused." Her face crumpled. "My son is lost, and I don't know how to bring him home. The Lady doesn't answer my prayers."

"Maybe she has," Birlerion said, as he squeezed her hand gently.

The woman's eyes widened as she stared at him, and then she nodded. "Come up then," she said, leading the way. She pulled a key out of her apron pocket. "I have to lock the door, otherwise as soon as I turn my back, he's gone, and the night guard have to bring him home. They've been very good about it, but they are starting to say they'll have to charge me. Only joking, I know, but still." Having unlocked one of the two doors on the landing at the top of the stairs, the woman stepped back and gestured Birlerion forward.

A single bed was pushed against one wall and a table stood in the corner, a pile of books sitting on top. At first, Birlerion didn't see its occupant, and then he realised the boy was crouched under the table.

"Jake? There's a Sentinal here to see you," the woman said from the doorway.

Birlerion stepped into the room and smiled at the woman. "Don't worry. We'll just have a chat. Why don't you go and have a hot drink? I'll make sure he doesn't leave."

The woman nodded and then closed the door, but she didn't lock it. Birlerion watched Jake as his head twitched and then stilled. The boy had a mop of curly brown hair, but that was all Birlerion could see. He shuffled back and leaned against the door, crossing his ankles. "You know, Jake, the Lady listens to everyone's prayers, but not everyone hears her answers."

Silence.

Birlerion continued speaking. "She watches over us all, removed as she is. The moon casts her gaze over the land and gilds us all in her regard."

"Stars watch," the boy's muffled voice came from under the table.

"And the stars watch," Birlerion agreed. "There are many stars in the sky above. The expanse spreads out forever, night black pierced by pinpoints of light and swirling strands."

"Yes! You've seen it," the boy said, crawling out from his shelter and staring up at Birlerion.

"Yes," Birlerion agreed. "How did you see it?"

"Silver eyes see all," he said and then tucked his head in his knees as he began rocking. "She cast me out. She showed me all and cast me out."

"The Lady would never cast you out," Birlerion said gently. "Who showed you the stars, Jake?"

"The Lady, all shining silver, took me."

"Where did you meet this lady?"

"She said I was chosen and she would show me the way." Jake's eyes grew vacant. "Shiny stars," he mumbled and lurched to his feet, darting for the door. Birlerion was quicker and grabbed his arm.

"Jake? Where are you going?"

"Need more stars." His expression changed from desperation to yearning. "Stars and eyes. She promised."

"What did she promise?"

Jake began swaying. His face turned to the ceiling as he wrapped his arms around himself. An incoherent mumble spilled from his lips. His eyes were vacant as his gaze dropped to the floor.

"What can you see?" Birlerion asked.

Jake stilled and then charged for the door again. Birlerion caught him around the waist and hauled him back. "What is it you see?" he asked again as the boy struggled in his arms.

"Stars and eyes, eyes and stars. Stars and eyes ..." Jake mumbled.

Birlerion held him close until the mumble died away. "The Lady blesses you, Jake. She grants you peace," Birlerion murmured as the boy relaxed in his grip. He lay him on the bed and knelt beside him, placing his hand on the boy's forehead. His skin was flushed but he was cool to the touch. "Lady bless you, child," he murmured, unsure how to help him. He would ask Healer Francis if he could help. The boy had seen past the Veil, and yet how was that possible?

When he was sure the boy slept, he rose and left the room.

It was mid-afternoon by the time Birlerion arrived at the palace and hurried through the corridors to the king's throne room. His chat with Jake had taken longer than expected, and his inability to help him, rankled.

Working his way through the courtiers, Birlerion paused

as he saw Mikkeal standing before the king with Elliarille circling him like a predatory butterfly.

"You're Jerrolion's boy, aren't you?" Ellie asked, running her finger across Mikke's chin as her light blue gown swished around her legs as she circled him again. "You look just like him. All except the eyes and the hand, of course."

"Yes, my lady." Mikke's voice barely quivered.

"Ah, he has lovely manners. Stoneford is turning out good stock I see, Your Majesty." She threw a quick glance at the king as if gauging his mood. She smiled secretively, although she wiped the expression from her face as Birlerion approached. "And he has such pretty eyes."

"And what does Stoneford's whelp want from Vespers?" the king asked, lounging on his throne as his courtiers tittered.

Mikke's shoulders stiffened, though his voice remained calm. "Your Majesty. I am here as requested, to be confirmed as the next Lord of Stoneford."

"And why would I do that?" the king asked

"Because you commanded it so, Your Majesty, and the Lady signals agreement."

"And does the current lord command you so?"

"My father abides by your word, Your Majesty, as do I."

"Ah yes, your father. He wasn't so yielding the last time I saw him. I suggest you make up for it," Anders said, staring at the boy. Birlerion noted the tension running through Mikke and was relieved as he knelt swiftly enough, dark lashes hiding his eyes, head bowed.

"So your father agrees that he is no longer competent enough to retain the Watch?"

"No, Your Majesty, my father is quite capable of holding the Watch."

"He can't be. Your father must be weak to concede his power so easily, don't you agree?"

"No, Your Majesty. You mistake honour for weakness."

The courtiers stirred.

"Well, the Lady obviously thinks he's weak, as you say she agrees with me. Everyone heard him say it, didn't they?" The king looked around his audience, and they all murmured agreement. "She agrees that your father no longer holds our favour. His time has passed. It's time for him to bow out and remove his contentious voice."

"Yes, Your Majesty." There was a slight tremor in Mikke's voice, and the king smiled coldly.

Birlerion grabbed Leyarille's arm as she went to step forward, her face pale with anger. She stilled in Birlerion's grasp, though she didn't acknowledge him.

The king's attention was caught by her movement, and he smiled at her obvious discomfort, noting Birlerion's restraining hand, though his smile faded when his gaze rested on the Sentinal. "Ah, I see your sister is not so obedient. Do you need your sister's protection? Not man enough to fight your own battles? If that is so, how could you possibly defend a Watch?"

Leyarille flushed with chagrin.

"No, Your Majesty. I am here at your command, obeying your orders. My father stands ready to step down. I await your acknowledgement of Stoneford's obedience to your word." Mikke's voice was steady and back in control.

"But here you kneel before your king, begging me to confirm you. You are begging, aren't you?"

"I am paying you the respect you are due as the King of all Vespiri and Terolia, Your Majesty, but if it is your command, then I will beg."

The throne room held its collective breath at the boy's bold reply, their respect for him growing as he continued to respond to such blatant provocation with calm and respectful responses. He said nothing that was disrespectful, though the same could not be said of the king.

Birlerion gritted his teeth as the king continued to bate Mikke. Anders ought to be ashamed of himself, but Birlerion could tell he was enjoying it.

"Do you see who stands before you, Anders?" Birlerion asked, deliberately drawing the king's attention to him as he stepped forward next to Mikkeal.

"Stands? I only see a beggar on his knees," Anders hissed angrily, not noticing Birlerion's use of his personal name, though the awe-struck audience did.

"I wonder, Your Majesty. You seem so preoccupied these days. Maybe the Lady Elliarille could shed some light on the reason why? I fear your eyesight has been affected along with your other senses. I thought maybe you had missed that Mikkeal Haven pays you the fealty you requested."

The room was silent, stunned at the unfolding drama. The king frowned, picking through Birlerion's cold words. "How dare you, Birlerion? Do not think that you have license to …"

"Do you see Mikkeal Haven?" Birlerion's voice cracked across the throne room, interrupting the king. Even the king flinched. Leyarille and Serenion watched the normally reserved Sentinal in amazement.

"Of course I see him," Anders snapped, instinctively responding to the command in Birlerion's voice.

"Good. Serenion, escort your lord out. He has performed his duty. Niallerion awaits you outside." Birlerion moved to stand in front of Mikke as the boy stood. Mikke's body was rigid as he bowed towards the throne, his face carefully blank. The king stared at Birlerion, perplexed, as if not quite sure what had happened.

"Pip is waiting for you." Birlerion's calm voice steadied the boy, and taking a deep breath, Mikke turned on his heel and walked out of the throne room with Serenion by his shoulder.

They were met by a livid Niallerion, who escorted them out of the palace, leaving his wife, Marianille, who was elegantly attired in a deep rose-coloured gown, to enter the throne room. Her lustrous black hair and creamy complexion caught many admiring glances as she calmly crossed the throne room to the small group by the king. Leyarille simmered with fury, her face flushed, and Marianille gently gripped her arm in warning as she passed.

Elliarille broke the stunned silence. "No, no, call him back. Make him stay. Let us get to know him more."

"Surely not, Elliarille?" Birlerion smiled through gritted teeth. "I would think you eat lads such as young Mikkeal for starters. Surely you need more challenging meat for your entertainment?"

"But the king was enjoying himself, and we are here for his entertainment," she replied, flicking a coy smile at Anders.

"Maybe not all of us want to be entertainment," a soft voice drawled from behind her, and Elliarille stiffened as she glared at the man who stopped by her side. He raised a monocle to his eye and inspected Birlerion and then Elliarille. "I thought Sentinals had better things to do these days."

"Ah Gillian, you've just missed all the fun," Anders said with a laugh.

"Lord Gillian," Birlerion murmured as he gave the elegant man who was one of Anders senior administrators a slight bow. "Elliarille is bored. I'm sure you are just the man to liven up her evening."

Gillian's lip curled. "Only you, Birlerion, would dare to suggest the king's company was boring."

"I said no such thing. The king knows Ellie's love for parties and is well aware of her short attention span."

hsst! Gillian wouldn't know what fun is even if it hit [illegible] in the face. Go back to your stuffy office if you don't want to be entertained." Elliarille flounced towards the king, twisting her pale blonde hair in her fingers. "Anders, darling, what do *you* want to do? Shall we dance? Set up some competitions? Your courtiers would love to win your favour."

Anders arched a brow. "You mean *your* favours, don't you, m'dear?"

Marianille linked her arm through Birlerion's, squeezing his arm in gentle support. "I see Ellie hasn't improved much," she said. "Still chasing after any pretty face that passes by."

Ellie flushed. "You are not welcome here, Marianille. I thought you had been given your marching orders."

"No more than you have," Marianille replied, her face serene. "Your Majesty," she said, sinking into a deep curtsey, "you look ravishing tonight."

The king smiled in response. "And you look gorgeous, Marianille. Retirement suits you."

"Why thank you, Your Majesty. I find having time to wash my hair makes all the difference."

"Well, my dear, it was time well spent," he said, leering at her in appreciation.

"Thank you, Your Majesty, you are kind to say so."

Ellie flounced impatiently at the pleasantries. "Come, Your Majesty, tell them to go."

"I thought you said the king wanted entertainment. Do you speak for the king now, Elliarille?" Birlerion asked, trying to keep his voice light and teasing, attempting to ease some of the ratcheting tension in the room.

"Of course not, but why didn't you let the boy blood his claws, Birlerion?"

"I thought he did. Is your skin so tough and your wits so addled that you didn't feel them?"

Ellie scowled as the king gave a bark of laughter and Gillian chuckled as he hovered, watching the Sentinals closely.

"He got you there, Ellie," Gillian said, his voice dripping with condescension.

Anders leaned back on his throne. "Where's your riposte, Ellie? Birlerion stay. Ellie needs the practice."

"Are you sure, Your Majesty? We wouldn't want to bore you." Birlerion smiled even though the idea of staying nauseated him. Adrenaline rushed through his veins making him feel light-headed; he should never have confronted Anders, not in front of all his court. And baiting Ellie was never a good idea, she would take her revenge at the first opportunity. She didn't seem happy to see Lord Gillian either, which wasn't surprising, he supposed, seeing as how Gillian drew the attention of all the courtiers away from her as he tilted his head to hear the king's response. Gillian stood with one gleaming boot on the first step, his muscular legs set off to perfection by his tight-fitting trousers, obviously revelling in the attention.

"Oh yes." Anders dismissed Gillian with a negligent wave of his hand, and after a quick glance around the room, Gillian bowed himself away. Anders clapped his hands and music filled the silence. The courtiers relaxed and began to mingle.

Birlerion dipped his head as Marianille murmured in his ear, and he nodded. Marianille linked arms with Leyarille and almost pulled her out of the throne room.

"Tell us what she said," Ellie demanded, frowning after Marianille.

Birlerion smiled. "But what if it is a secret? You like secrets, don't you, Ellie? Would you tell me yours?"

Ellie stared at him, suspiciously. "It wouldn't be a secret if I told you," she replied, her lips tightening.

irlerion smiled as if she had said something

l, sure she was missing something, but the
as her brother caught her attention, and she
aerion led her out of the throne room, and
Birlerion sighed with relief.

He looked around the room, nodding at Parsillion hovering discretely out of the king's sight. Anders would have been furious if he'd seen him. He shouldn't have taken the risk, though word of the situation with Mikke had obviously gotten around as he also caught sight of Frenerion slipping out of the room.

Birlerion took a flute of champagne from a passing tray and knocked it back. He took a steadying breath and tried to hide the tremble in his hand. Continuing to circulate, he ignored the king's frequent glances in his direction. Remaining calm and relaxed, he conversed pleasantly with various courtiers, lords, and ladies as his guts roiled at the release of the tension and terror he had felt for Mikke.

He paused as a gruff voice detained him. "Well, you've got balls of iron, that's for sure."

Birlerion turned, smiling in pleasure at the stocky, grey-haired man before him. He wore the uniform of the Commander of the King's Justice. "Bryce, what are you doing in the king's throne room at this time of night?"

"I heard Jerrol's lad was in difficulty," he said, his brown eyes flashing with anger.

"Nonsense, he managed just fine."

"So I saw. Enough to make an old man proud. I promised Jerrol I would look out for the boy. I was here to keep that promise."

"And I'll tell Jerrol when next I see him," Birlerion replied.

"He didn't need me; he had you."

"This time. I don't think this is over."

"No," Bryce grunted. "Come find me tomorrow. Be... Anders doesn't see me here. I don't come often, wouldn't want him to think he can drag me here every night." Bryce held his eyes before he gave a brief nod and left.

Birlerion let his breath out. The king seemed occupied. Ellie had long departed with her brother, so he took the opportunity to slip away after Bryce. He found Kin'arol in the palace stables and thankfully made his way through the streets of Vespers towards the home of Marianille and Niallerion behind the gardens of the Lady's temple.

"The King forgets his responsibilities," Kin'arol said, his voice a velvet caress in his mind.

Birlerion huffed under his breath. His Darian often surprised him with his comments. *"Indeed he has."*

"I thought Mikke did well, though Pil'penia was furious. They stay, though Mikke wanted to go home."

Birlerion wasn't surprised. The Darian would reflect Mikke's true feelings no matter how much he tried to conceal them. After stabling Kin'arol at the hostelry, Birlerion walked through the temple gardens to his sister's house.

Niallerion was waiting for him. "I've managed to keep him here, but only just. He was ready to leave as soon as he left the palace grounds. The boy is justifiably angry, but Birlerion, he cannot be seen to be."

"I know," Birlerion murmured as he ducked through the low doorway and straightened up in the crowded parlour of Niallerion's home. He stifled a sigh as he met Mikke's scorching glare. Leyarille was just as bad, and he could tell she was angry at him. He wasn't sure he could cope with all the swirling emotion in the room.

"Mikke, come walk with me. We should give our thanks to the Lady for her support tonight," Birlerion said.

Mikke's pent up anger released with a whoosh of breath as he stared at Birlerion. Niallerion hid his smile as he ducked his head. Why hadn't he thought of that? He had been at his wit's end trying to keep the boy calm, and Birlerion did it with one sentence. He watched Birlerion wrap a comforting arm around the boy's shoulders as they left.

The tension in the room dropped significantly after the door closed behind them. Serenion let his breath out and finally sat down. He rested his head back against the chair and closed his eyes. "Politics is exhausting. Give me a good old fight any day," he murmured.

Marianille rubbed his shoulder as she passed.

Niallerion eyed Leyarille. "Birlerion will calm him down," he said, thinking to reassure her.

Leyarille glared at him. "Why did he allow it to go on for so long? To allow the king to humiliate Mikke, in front of the whole court, and to denigrate my father after everything he's done and still does! None of you said anything."

"It wasn't our place to say anything," Serenion said, his eyes still closed. "Your brother petitioned the king. He was the one who had to respond."

"Why?"

"Because Mikke had to prove he could be the Lord Guardian. That he could hold his own against the king. You saw how the king reacted when you made to protest. You just gave him fuel to bait your brother with."

"But why attack our father? Why try to reduce him to nothing?"

"To provoke a response. But Mikke didn't give him one, so the king failed to make his point, don't you think?" Niallerion said, massaging his temples. "And Mikke can't be seen to be reacting after the event either, and neither can you. You both have to forget it ever happened. The king granted

Mikke his guardianship. He got it, and that is all that matters."

"No, he didn't," Leyarille frowned. "The king didn't grant anything."

"Birlerion made the king acknowledge Mikkeal," Serenion said. "By doing so, by saying he saw him, the king granted Mikkeal's petition and the Guardianship of Stoneford."

"And Birlerion did so at great risk," Marianille said, entering the room with a tray, which Niallerion took from her and placed on the table. "You do not force the king to do anything and live these days."

Leyarille swallowed and collapsed in the chair opposite Serenion. "I had no idea."

"You did well to hold your tongue; you would have made it so much worse if you had spoken out." Marianille smiled at her.

"Not by choice," Leyarille admitted rubbing her arm. "Birlerion nearly broke my arm; he has a strong grip," she said with a weak smile.

"Let me see that." Marianille nudged Serenion to sit up and take his drink and then knelt beside Leyarille, her silks swishing across the floor. She tutted at the sight of the livid bruising; Birlerion's grip had left dark marks. He must have been desperate to have been so rough with Leyarille. "We need to treat that," she said, rising. She returned with a salve and smoothed it over Leyarille's skin. Leyarille hurriedly rolled down her sleeve as the door latch rose and Mikke entered. Leyarille looked over his shoulder and relaxed as Birlerion ducked his head and entered behind Mikke.

She sipped her drink. Marianille had laced it with brandy, and she almost choked. She managed to swallow and took a breath before smiling anxiously at her brother as he squatted on the floor beside her. He leaned against her legs.

"That's no way for a Lord Warden to sit," she teased, stroking his dark hair. She offered him her mug, and he took a sip, choking like she had. Though he took another deeper swallow before handing it back. She sighed. "I'm so sorry, Mikke. I never meant to make it worse for you."

Mikke turned startled eyes on her. "Don't be, you didn't. I would have been disappointed if you hadn't tried to defend Pa."

"It's a good job Birlerion was there."

"It's a good job they were all there," Mikke replied.

"All?"

"Knowing that the Sentinals believed in me, that the Lady believes in me. That was what helped me stay calm. What I was doing was right, and the king acknowledged that in the end. That's an end of it, Leyarille. You don't mention it to anyone ever again unless it's me or Birlerion."

Leyarille nodded, her gaze following Birlerion as he made an effort to smile as Marianille pulled him into a tight hug before pushing him into a chair. She had a mug in his hand as soon as he was seated. He returned Leyarille's smile and relaxed as his sister fussed over him.

Birlerion raised his mug. "Lord Mikkeal," he said with pride. "May Stoneford flourish under your guardianship with the Lady's blessing."

"Lord Mikkeal," the others repeated, raising their mugs.

Mikke blushed, but he raised his mug in acknowledgement. "To my friends, my family; I wouldn't be here without you."

Birlerion looked at Niallerion as he relaxed into his chair and sipped his drink. "You asked him, then?"

Leyarille frowned. "Asked him what?"

Birlerion tutted. "You really must pay more attention, Leyarille," he said in his teaching voice, and Leyarille threw a cushion at him as Mikke laughed.

"Niallerion and Marianille are going to relocate to Stoneford," Mikke said with pleasure.

A smile lit up Leyarille's face. "That's wonderful. You'll love it there; though we will miss you dreadfully."

"That's why you'll have to come home regularly; that's what waystones are for," Mikke said with a grin. "To Stoneford," he said, raising his mug.

Jerrol walked down the dusty road towards the empty sentinal grove. It seemed diminished without the Lady's guardians gracing her temple. Maybe he would suggest his sentinal move here, though he felt resistance to the idea in the gentle connection he had with his tree; he was obviously staying put. Jerrol frowned. Why would he not want to relocate to the Lady's temple?

He knelt in the springy grass by the stone table, which was the Lady's altar, and prayed to the Lady to protect his family. Mikke and Leyarille taking their first step in their new lives; his gentle Margareth still seeking her purpose; Taelia, who was fretting at the loss of their home and, he knew, concerned about him; Birlerion, who was precious as a brother and missed as much; Jason, frail and lost in his memories. Jerrol sighed. Jason would be making his final journey soon, travelling to join Jerrol's foster mother, Hannah, who had been gone these five long years. He wished she was still here to help guide his son's steps as she had his.

Creakily, he rose, his joints stiffening in the damp grass. He flexed his legs. Surely the bloodstone should make him more flexible, but maybe the years were just catching up with him after all. The thought of the warm sun and blue skies of the Island archipelago of Birtoli suddenly sounded attractive, and he smiled. He could use a break; he couldn't remember the last time he and Taelia had had time just for themselves.

His smile faded, and he folded as a shaft of pain struck through his chest. He collapsed beside the altar, gasping for breath as tears blurred his vision; he couldn't breathe.

The Lady's presence surrounded him. *"Relax, Jerrolion, you only make it more difficult. You of all people should know better."*

His vision cleared as he took in the delicate face framed by long blonde tresses and the deep emerald eyes of the Lady Leyandrii, the Lady of Remargaren. The eyes, he realised suddenly, of his youngest daughter.

"My Lady," he gasped as she wavered in his vision, and he reached a shaking hand. The Lady folded the remaining fingers of his hand over and rested it on his chest.

"You know what to do, my Captain," she said, and she faded away. A soft chime shimmered through the grove, and Jerrol opened his eyes.

He took a shaky breath and slowly sat up, leaning against the stone table for support. He wished she would give him some warning that she was going to visit. He opened his hand, which was clamped against his chest, and looked at the three emerald seedpods nestled in his palm. He drew in his breath in wonder; three new Sentinals.

He sat for a moment in the peaceful grove, catching his breath and waiting for his heart rate to slow. He closed his eyes and drifted until the strident call of a blackbird made him open his eyes and grin. The Lady was impatient, was she?

He climbed to his feet and was confronted by the happy meeping of a small furry creature, a cross between a small, mackerel-striped cat and a lizard with wings. Ari, the Lady's Arifel, had responded to her presence and popped into the Grove. He perched on the altar and flipped his scaly wings neatly onto his back as he mewed in disappointment that the Lady had gone.

"Where have you been?" Jerrol asked as he smoothed a finger down Ari's soft white chest. Ari butted his hand with his head, forcing his fingers to his ears. He hadn't seen the little Arifel in months. He flitted about the Kingdoms with his mate, Lin, and his kits at his leisure these days. Jerrol dutifully scratched his ears. "Are you coming with me to Marchwood?" He opened his hand and showed Ari the seeds. Ari nosed them and then meeped happily. He stretched his wings and popped out of sight.

"Alright then," Jerrol breathed as he left the Grove, heading for the waystone. His Darian mare, Zin'talia, crooned a query in his head. *"I'll be back soon,"* he answered.

"Shouldn't you tell Taelia and Fonorion?"

"I won't be long."

"Famous last words," Zin'talia sighed as she shifted in her stall.

Jerrol stepped out amongst the fragrant blooms of the famous Marchwood rhododendrons. They bloomed almost all year round, scenting the air with their sweet perfume, the red and pink blooms vibrant against the dark green waxy leaves that were their backdrop. The leaves rustled as he pushed his way out and onto the road leading up to the Marchwood manor house. He wasn't surprised when Laerille and Anterion, the Watch Sentinals, appeared at the top of the road waiting for him.

Laerille glanced over his shoulder and frowned. "Are you alone, Captain? Where's Birlerion or Fonorion?"

Jerrol hugged them both before answering. "Birlerion is in Old Vespers, and Fonorion is back at the keep with Taelia. I couldn't leave it unattended."

"But you shouldn't travel alone, Captain. In these troubled times, you don't know who is afoot," Anterion's deep voice rumbled in concern.

Jerrol smiled at the blond-haired man who towered over him. "I came straight from the Stoneford waystone to here; there was little opportunity for anyone to intercept me."

"Does Fonorion know you came here?" Laerille asked, her silver eyes glinting anxiously.

"He won't even know I've gone. Seeing as I'm here, let's find Lord William." Jerrol started walking. Their questions and concern were worse than the catechism his sparring master used to give him when he turned up late when he was a kid.

Lord William descended the steps as he heard their voices. "Jerrol, what are you doing here?" His eyes drifted over Jerrol's shoulder, and he too frowned, though he held his tongue. Jerrol opened his hand, and Lord William's eyes widened. "I see," he said, his face brightening at the sight of the seeds. "Laerille, be a dear and go call Garner for me." He looked at Jerrol. "When did you get these?"

"This morning. I came straight here. Keep them close, William; the king will not approve. Sentinals are not currently in favour."

"Of course, he won't find out from Marchwood. They'll just be more trees in the nursery until they are needed. Whilst they are saplings they won't even be noticed."

"Thank you, William."

"Our pleasure. We've missed the youngsters; it will be nice to have them around again."

Jerrol laughed. "I thought you were pleased when I reallocated them all."

"That was Anterion. I think the twins were the last straw."

"Yes, Elliarille was always a handful. They both seemed to have settled alright in Vespers though. They seem to be thriving at court. Maybe it's reminiscent of the Lady's court."

Anterion frowned. "If what we hear is true, King Ander's court is nothing like the Lady's." They were interrupted by the arrival of Garner, Lord William's head nurseryman. Jerrol handed over the precious seeds. His breath hissed through his lips at the physical wrench of letting them go. He breathed shallow breaths for a moment, letting his body readjust to the emptiness.

"I'll escort you back to Stoneford; you should rest, Captain." Laerille watched him in concern.

"Go with the Lady, Jerrol. Be safe." Lord William was more interested in the seeds, and he turned away with the nurseryman.

Jerrol grinned at William's preoccupation and allowed Laerille to escort him back through the blooming rhododendrons to the waystone.

8

OLD VESPERS

Jared smoothly stepped into his opponent and twisted. Ignoring the catcalls and whistles, he rotated his body, so his momentum took most of the pressure off his back as he threw him over his shoulder. He stepped back as the boy regained his feet, glaring at him as he brushed himself down.

The examiner made a note on his pad. "Next," he said, turning his attention to the next pairing. Jared moved out of the ring and accepted Leyarille's thump on his shoulder in congratulation. She had dealt with her opponent easily, even though he had been much heavier than her.

Leyarille was a noticeable minority in this intake; one of only three female applicants. The boys were suspicious of her and her silver eyes, and once they knew her name, they were even more antagonistic. Jared had kept close, though from her display in the ring, she clearly didn't need any help. But he watched all the same just in case some idiot thought ganging up on her would be a good idea.

They rotated to the next discipline; archery. Here, Leyarille excelled again; she hit everything that was presented to her. Jared didn't fare so well, maybe hitting half the targets. He preferred a sword or an axe. Leyarille grinned at him with excitement, her face flushed. "This is so much fun. Imagine doing this all day!"

"I don't think that's how it works. I am sure there will be other things to do apart from combat skills," Jared replied with a laugh. "Anyway, you don't need any more practice; you are terrific."

"Birlerion is an excellent teacher. I couldn't let him down now. You should ask him for some tips."

Jared whistled. He should have known. Birlerion was renowned for his archery skills. There was a story that he had once taken out two assassins in the middle of a ball at the palace without hitting anyone but his targets. You couldn't get any better than that. And in front of King Benedict as well.

Leyarille faltered at the next rotation. She was capable with a sword, but the heavier the broadsword or axe the more she struggled to control the unwieldy weight. Jared proved his strength as he demolished his opponents and happily proceeded to the next weapons station.

They stood on the sidelines and watched a young lad with dusky brown skin and blue-black hair give a demonstration of how to throw a dagger. He hit the bullseye with every blade. Jared frowned as he watched. "He's not even looking," he complained.

"It's all in the body position. Look how loose he holds himself, and he ends up facing the target every time." Leyarille squinted more closely. "He looks vaguely familiar," she muttered as Jared was called forward. From the off, Jared was too stiff and the waiting lads laughed at him as his daggers landed well off the mark. "Relax," Leyarille called.

Jared shook out his arms, but he stiffened as the catcalls continued. He heard Leyarille shouting to ignore them, but

our tense, and the boys only jeered more at her
reciated her support, but some support was
my. He was glad to get rid of his last dagger
s he went to collect them.

t standing upright when a dagger thunked into the target right next to him. Jerking back, he glared up the range at the thickset boy smirking at him, flipping another dagger lazily in his hand. Jared pulled out the blade as the examiner's sharp voice reprimanded the boy who had thrown the knife.

"Fenton, stand down or I'll reject you now."

The boy scowled and stepped back as the examiner docked his turn as punishment.

"You missed," Jared said, handing him the blade. "Try again."

Stiffening, Fenton took the blade. Jared held his pale blue eyes before walking over to where the dark-skinned boy was watching with interest. The boy grinned at Jared before holding out his hand. "Kayen Landis," he said, his voice deep and smooth.

"Jared Jennery," he replied, shaking his hand. "You were amazing. I wish I could throw a dagger like you."

Kayen shrugged. "Practice. My mother's favourite weapon, along with the scimitar."

"My father prefers the broadsword or an axe," Jared admitted.

"Which are fine in their place," Kayen agreed, "but tend to be a bit heavy-handed."

Jared laughed. "True, they lack a bit of finesse, much like my father at times." They watched Leyarille take Fenton's place. She wasn't as smooth as Kayen, but her blades hit the target, and she collected them before walking over to Jared and his new friend.

Jared introduced them, and Leyarille smiled. "I thought I

recognised you. You used to visit Stoneford with y parents."

Kayen grinned. "My mother and father both thought I should meet the Captain; they wanted me to appreciate him as much as they did."

"I'm so glad I'm not the only one here with a Sentinal for a parent. Kayen's mother is Sentinal Kayerille of Mistra, and his father is Oscar Landis, the Commander of the Terolian King's Rangers. Kayen, you're so lucky you don't have the silver eyes."

Kayen grinned. "Shhh, no one knows about my parents except you two."

Leyarille rolled her eyes as they walked over to the last test, an obstacle course. They joined the queue, waiting their turn. The examiner repeated his instruction as each applicant crouched at the starting line.

"You have one chime to complete the course. Each task must be completed in order along the route. Collect the tokens from the steward at each station once you're done. Hand the tokens in when you finish." His voice was bored as he repeated the instruction over and over, releasing each runner in thirty-second intervals.

Leyarille waited her turn as Jared and then Kayen started, and then she was off, following the track around the field, relaxing into a comfortable rhythm as her long legs ate up the ground.

She caught up with Kayen as he scrambled up and over a net slung across a beam, landing nimbly beside him. Kayen flashed her grin as they set off together and gestured her ahead; she was obviously quicker than him, and she pulled away and entered the dim tunnel ahead of him. Wrinkling her nose, Leyarille scrambled through the tunnel on her hands and knees, sloshing through the thick mud without hesitation. She rose out of the tunnel and approached the first task station as she wiped her hands on her filthy clothes.

A steward stood beside a makeshift table, a plank of wood resting on two barrels. A stone weighed down a pile of paper, and a wooden box held pencils. The steward pointed at them as Leyarille arrived. "Take a paper and pencil. Complete the puzzle and return it to me."

A couple of boys were standing to the side, frowning over the paper, though it looked like Jared had already left. Leyarille scrubbed her hands on her trousers again before taking the paper and pencil, and she scanned it. It was a code. You had to replace symbols with the correct letters to complete a sentence. She annotated the paper with her changes and handed it to the steward who glanced at it and gave her a token, and she was off as Kayen arrived.

Running down the path through the trees, she followed the track and began to climb towards the palace. She pulled off her jersey as she started to warm up and stuffed the token in her pocket. The hill kept going, and she was glad when it finally levelled out. Sides heaving, she approached the next task station. A line of horses waited patiently, their tack in a confused heap beside them. She took the horse assigned to her and began untangling the bridle from the saddle; it was all wrapped around the stirrups. She smiled at Kayen as he joined her, quietly swearing as he began untangling.

"Don't waste your breath," she gasped, glad to have a chance to recover hers. She couldn't believe Jared was so far ahead of them. Kayen's nimble fingers were faster than hers, and he was soon positioning the bridle over the horse's head.

Leyarille followed shortly after. Smoothing her hand down the horse's neck, she deftly looped the bridle on before turning to the saddle. She was so glad her father had insisted she persevere with her riding lessons. She kneed the horse to tighten the girth as the steward inspected Kayen's efforts and gave him a token. She stood back as Kayen ran off and waited for the steward to pass her efforts. She left him removing the tack, her token in her pocket as she ran after Kayen.

The track led back down the steep hill, and she leant back as the track steepened and shortened her step as she almost shuffled down the incline. Crossing the creek at the bottom, she was off through the trees, heading back towards the garrison.

Leyarille almost tripped over Kayen. He was kneeling over Jared, who was lying flat out on the track, a muddy line across his chest. She dropped to her knees beside him, scanning the undergrowth intently. "What happened?"

"Don't know. He was like this when I arrived." Kayen gently slapped Jared's face, but there was no response. Leyarille ran back to the creek and scooped up some water in her hands. She rushed back, dribbling what remained over Jared's face. He moaned and then stirred and began coughing.

Kayen helped him sit up as a boy ran past, looking down at them in interest but not stopping.

"Jared? Are you alright?" Leyarille asked as she supported him with an arm around his shoulders.

Jared gave a weird groaning sound and gulped in air. "I think he was stunned," Kayen said.

They helped him stand. "Jared? What happened."

Jared wheezed. "Ran into a rope; nearly took m'head off," he gasped.

Kayen looked around, but there was no sign of anyone or a rope. "Long gone."

"Do you still have your tokens?" Leyarille asked urgently.

Jared patted his pocket and scowled. "No." They looked around, scuffing the ground as another boy passed them and then another; the tokens were long gone too.

"Why would someone target you? It makes no sense."

Jared shrugged. "Who knows. Come on, we'd better finish the course." He started walking. "Go on ahead. You two might as well finish in time. No point all of us failing."

Leyarille gave him a hug. "Don't be silly. We both finish or neither of us do. You can have one of my tokens."

"Absolutely," Kayen agreed. "We'll split what tokens we have between the three of us when we get to the finish. Come on. We haven't got much time left."

They began running, Leyarille and Kayen keeping the still shaky Jared on course. He rubbed his chest gingerly, and there was an angry red graze under his chin that was oozing blood. They approached the next task station together. The steward observed them but refrained from comment. They were given a map each and told to plot the most efficient course from King's Port to Daarl.

Leyarille spread her map out on the ground. "Look, Daarl is on the east coast of Elothia, Kings Port is Vespers."

Three dark heads bent over the map. "Quickest is up the Vesp through Deepwater and up to the Summer palace before cutting East at Kerrit," Jared suggested.

"The river valley is quite steep. Look at how close the lines are. They're ravines. Wouldn't it be quicker to go via Tierne? Shortest is not always quickest," Kayen pointed out.

Leyarille frowned. "Good point." She looked at the steward. "May we ask a clarifying question?"

The steward nodded, watching them with interest. "Ask."

"By 'efficient', do they mean the shortest route or the one that gets you there faster?" she asked.

The steward smiled. "Good question. They mean the one that gets you there faster."

Leyarille grinned at the boys. "Right then, we go with Kayen's suggestion; do you agree, Jared?"

"Yep, good call, Kayen," Jared agreed. Leyarille plotted

the course on all their maps and handed them to the steward. He gave them a token each and then he gave Leyarille two extra tokens.

Leyarille looked at him in surprise. The steward nodded. "One for using your initiative, one for showing leadership, and one each for teamwork."

Leyarille grinned and handed two of the tokens to Jared. "There, that replaces your missing ones; we've all got the same. Come on, we must be nearly out of time." They ran down the path, out of the trees, and back on to the track that ran around the edge of the training fields, arriving at the finish line last but all together. They crossed the line with minutes to spare and handed in their tokens.

Jared collapsed to the ground, his sides heaving as Leyarille went to get him some water. Kayen hovered over him with concern as Leyarille dampened her hankie and pressed it under his chin.

"Ouch," Jared complained, flinching away.

"You're bleeding," she said as she folded the cloth over and dampened it again.

"What a bunch of losers," Fenton said as he loomed over them. "Last place. Who'd want you on their team?"

"It wasn't about winning," Kayen said calmly, inserting his body between Fenton and Jared, and Leyarille still crouched on the ground. "It was about completing the tasks in the allotted time."

Before the boy could reply, an even deeper voice interrupted. "Correct, Mr Landis."

They all turned in surprise and stiffened as the Commander of the King's Rangers approached them. Commander Stafford took in the scene in one glance. His gaze halted on Fenton. The boy swallowed nervously under the direct stare. "Mr Fenton, it seems you were under a misapprehension; nothing was said about being first." His gaze moved on to Jared now shakily standing beside Leyarille. He noted the marks on his chest and chin. "Are you alright, Mr Jennery?"

"Yes, sir, I'm fine. Ran into a low branch, sir."

The commander raised a sceptical eyebrow but nodded. "I see." His eyes dwelled on Leyarille and then he nodded before he turned away.

Kayen let out his breath. "Well, I didn't expect to see him here today."

Leyarille smiled at Jared. "Come on, let's go home. Marianille will sort you out." She looked at Kayen. "Where are you staying? Do you want to come back with us for dinner? We are at Niallerion and Marianille's house. Birlerion will be there too, I expect."

Kayen smiled with pleasure. "I'm at an inn in town, but that would be great, if you're sure they won't mind?" He looked down at himself. "I'd better get changed first."

Leyarille laughed. "You're no worse than the rest of us. Grab a change of clothes. We can use the bath at Marianille's. They'll be so pleased to know you're here."

Birlerion was waiting for them outside the garrison, and his face lit up at the sight of the three of them. "Kayen, why didn't your parents tell us you were coming?"

Kayen smiled shyly. "I didn't want them to make a fuss," he admitted.

"Idiot," Leyarille poked his shoulder.

Birlerion grinned. "Come on, you all look like you need a bath. How did it go?"

He was overwhelmed by the enthusiastic response, each of them talking over the other. "Alright, alright. One at a time." He held up his hands.

"We need to stop and get Kayen a change of clothes. Which inn are you staying at?" Leyarille asked as they walked down the street.

"I've got a room at the Crown," Kayen replied.

Birlerion immediately veered down a side street. "This way, then. We'll cut behind the market," he said as he led the way. They soon arrived at the inn, and Kayen dashed inside the dim interior. Birlerion grasped Jared's chin. "What happened to you?" he asked as they waited.

"I ran into a low hanging branch," Jared replied, rubbing his chest.

"One that almost took your head off. Let me see," Leyarille said, tugging his shirt.

"Get off." Jared pulled his shirt out of her grasp. "I'm not stripping in the street."

"You've been rubbing your chest ever since we found you; it obviously hurts. And anyway, you said it was a rope, not a branch."

Jared glared at her. "Stop fussing."

"Enough, you two. We'll take a look when we get home. And here's Kayen, so let's get going. Marianille will have dinner cooking by the time we get there."

"Thank goodness, I'm starving," Jared replied.

Marianille shrieked in horror at the sight of them, and she hustled Leyarille into the bathing room first. But not before hugging Kayen in delight. Jared collapsed in a chair and closed his eyes. Birlerion squatted beside him. "Show me," he said, his voice gentle.

Jared sighed and eased upright. He winced as he struggled to take his shirt off, and Birlerion hissed at the sight of the vivid welt across his chest.

Marianille appeared beside him. "How did that happen?"

"Someone pulled a rope up in front of him," Birlerion replied as he steadied Jared, who suddenly paled.

"He was unconscious when we found him flat out on the ground," Kayen said, hovering behind them.

Birlerion gently prodded his chest and Jared paled further, drawing his breath in. "I think it's just badly bruised." He smiled as Marianille anticipated him and passed him a pot of salve. "This will help ease the ache. We'll put some more on after your bath, but the sooner it's applied," he said as he scooped a good handful out, "the sooner it starts working. Kayen you go next. Give this time to work and then Jared can have a bath." He gently smoothed the salve over Jared's chest. "And then we can eat!" He grinned at the boy, and Jared gave him a weak grin back. "You'll do. Leave your shirt off for now. It needs washing anyway." He gently wrapped a blanket around Jared's shoulders and left him dosing in the chair.

Leyarille entered the room, rubbing her hair with a towel, and Kayen gratefully went for a bath. She squatted on the floor by Jared. "You alright?" she asked in concern.

"Fine, thanks, just aches," Jared mumbled, his eyes closed.

Leyarille looked up at Birlerion. "But who would try to hurt Jared? Why?"

Birlerion looked at Jared thoughtfully. "It's difficult to tell."

"I bet it was that Fenton boy. He threw a dagger at you too," Leyarille said.

"Fenton?" Birlerion repeated.

"A lad twice the size of Jared. He was behind Jared on the range. When Jared went to pick up his daggers, Fenton threw one at him; it only just missed him. I don't think he intended hitting him, but he wasn't that good of a shot. He was lucky it didn't hit Jared."

Jared opened his eyes and looked at Birlerion. "You know the name?"

"There was a Commander of the King's Rangers called Fenton. I'll look into it. Maybe he's related."

Kayen came out at that moment, and Jared levered himself out of the chair and drew in a breath. Marianille gave him a careful hug. "Dinner will be ready when you're finished; it's your favourite. I roasted a chicken in celebration of you finishing your tests."

Jared's eyes brightened, and he hastened into the bathing room.

He was back out shortly after, his hair slicked back and his face flushed but clean. Marianille pounced on him and reapplied the salve before he could protest and then she sat him before a plate piled high with food. He sighed in bliss, and after a brief prayer to thank the Lady, they all tucked in.

The evening was a boisterous one. Even Jared regained some of his usual vitality. Kayen kept them laughing all night with his stories about his parents, such opposites yet so well matched. Leyarille was enamoured by the fact that a beautiful Sentinal, whom she was sure could have chosen anyone, and an obscure captain of the King's Justice had managed to cross paths in Terolia and ended up getting joined.

Birlerion laughed at Leyarille. "Oscar was never obscure. He was one of the most reliable and resourceful men I have never known."

Leyarille flushed. "I meant no disrespect." She smiled disarmingly at Kayen. "It just seems odd that your mother didn't choose a Sentinal. I mean, Sentinals always seem to gravitate to each other. Look at Marianille and Niallerion or Tianerille and Venterion."

"You forget," Birlerion said, "you don't know them all. You can't make such sweeping assumptions. Roberion joined with Lilith; she is a Birtolian. Tagerill joined with Miranda. It is not so unusual. Sentinals are not so different. We may be closer to the Lady, from a different time, but that doesn't mean we don't feel or hurt the same."

Leyarille was silent.

Jared's chuckle broke the awkward silence. "Well, I can safely say that there is no Sentinal in my bloodline, just a Jennery, and I am assured he is more than a match for one!"

Birlerion began to laugh.

"What's so funny?"

"Your father is a Sentinal."

"What?" Jared sat up in shock and gasped as his chest throbbed.

"The Lady made him a Sentinal when she made Jerrol her Captain, only he became a Lord of the Watch instead. I don't know why he never fully became a Sentinal, with a tree and all. Maybe the Lady was preoccupied and never got around to it?" Birlerion nodded. "But he is a Sentinal alright."

Jared frowned. "How can he only be a part Sentinal?"

Birlerion shrugged. "He was a member of the Lady's guard when I first met him. I must admit, things were a bit hectic when we were first awoken, so I never thought much of it, and then, well, he and your mother got Joined and took on Deepwater. I don't think he had much time to assimilate what being a Sentinal meant before he became a full guardian of Deepwater with your mother."

Jared smiled in delight at the fact he was part Sentinal. Birlerion grinned at the expression on his face.

The following day, word arrived at first light. Leyarille and Jared had been accepted into the cadets, and they were to report to the garrison at nine the next morning. Kayen arrived soon after, excitedly waving his acceptance letter to join in with the celebrations.

9

OLD VESPERS

The next morning, Birlerion escorted them to the garrison to be inducted into the cadets, and after hugging all of them, he strolled off into the city, leaving them to walk through the gates. Staring after him, Leyarille felt a sense of loss as he disappeared into the throng of people, until Jared tugged her through the gates and into the garrison.

Leyarille listened avidly as the commander welcomed them into the cadets. They would each be allocated into a unit, of which there would be five this year, undergo provisional training for a period of two years, and then on passing the final exams, they would be promoted to full ranger status.

Leyarille was thrilled that she and Jared were allocated to the same unit under Lieutenant Parnent. Kayen was allocated to unit four under a Lieutenant called Kopka. Each lieutenant stepped forward as they were named; they all looked lean and fit.

Congregating into their units, the lieutenants marched them off to their barracks to settle in. Rules were relaxed on day one, but thereafter: break the rules, take the punishment, and Lieutenant Parnent was very clear about the punishments, as if he relished handing them out. Once he left, the room was filled with babble as the cadets introduced themselves and grabbed beds.

"You're one of them Sentinals, aren't you? Whatcha doing here? The king don't need your sort now." It was the stocky lad, Fenton.

Leyarille frowned at him. "My father is a Sentinal; I am not."

"But you've got the silver eyes. Makes you a Sentinal."

"It's a sign of the Lady's regard. Maybe you don't follow the Lady?" Jared suggested.

Fenton stepped into Jared, but he found he was shorter and his intended jibe fell flat. "And you," he sneered. "A Jennery elevated above his position."

Jared laughed. "Is that what this is about? Position? I'm sure you'd have one if you'd earned it." Jared turned away, and Fenton grabbed him. Jared moved fast, twisting out of his grip and grabbing Fenton's arm, wrenching it up behind his back until the boy hissed, and then he released him. "Don't start," Jared said, staring him straight in the eyes, "what you're not prepared to finish."

Fenton stepped back, scowling. "This isn't over," he said as he moved away; the other boys following him and muttering.

Leyarille pulled Jared back to his bed. "You didn't need to step in; I could handle him."

"I know you could, but his beef is with me. If he wants to fight, then he should deal with me, not threaten my friends."

Leyarille sighed. "You heard what Parnent said. We can't fight. That's what Fenton wants. He'll get you kicked out."

"Then he'll get kicked out too," Jared replied rebelliously.

It wasn't an auspicious start, and things deteriorated

quickly over the next week. Their belongings would go missing, messages weren't passed on, and finally things came to a head in the sparring ring. Their opponents began fighting dirty when the master wasn't looking.

Leyarille was sparring with Lucas, one of Fenton's sidekicks, when a flailing arm came out of no-where and caught her in the face. She turned into the body of the boy crowding her and retaliated. The boy dropped back, howling, blood rushing from his nose as Leyarille engaged the second boy, twisting him around and planting his face in the dirt.

"Release!" the master called, and she immediately stepped back and stood at attention, her face still smarting from the unexpected blow.

The master stood in front of her. "Explain."

"Lucas and I were sparring, sir, when two other boys attacked us. We defended ourselves, sir."

"I see." His lips twitched at the sight of the two boys. "Creel, stop wailing and go to the infirmary. Thirrel, stop your whining and get back to your partner. I will deal with you in a moment." He looked back at the silver-eyed cadet. "The use of force should be tempered in practice. I understand they took you by surprise, but control is key, cadet. If this happens again, you will fight with one hand strapped behind your back, understood?"

"Yes, sir!"

"Good. Go get your eye checked out and report back immediately."

"Yes, sir." Leyarille headed off to the infirmary. Jared's grinning face lifted her spirits as she left. She submitted to Healer Hollin's rough and ready treatment, hissing as the ice touched her cheek.

"You are going to have a lovely shiner. Not as bad as his."

He jerked his head at the boy lying groaning on the other bed. "You broke his nose."

"I didn't mean to. He came at me from behind."

"Well, he won't do that again," Hollin chuckled. "Come back after your practice is finished. I'll give you another compress to reduce the bruising."

Three days after Leyarille and Jared had joined the academy, Birlerion ducked under the low door frame into the dim interior of the Docker's Tavern and caught the barman's eye. "He's out back," the barman said before Birlerion could speak. He smiled his thanks as he entered the small back room. Straightening, he saw three men seated around the table.

"I received your message," he said, taking the empty seat.

Tom introduced his companions. "These are Porter and Timmin. Porter works on the docks. Timmin is a brakeman on a goods wagon that travels to and from Retafu every month."

Birlerion nodded at the men. "Pleased to meet you."

Porter was a brawny man; his bare arms were thick, attesting to his work on the docks hauling goods and produce, whilst Timmin was whip thin, with dirty brown hair, a straggly beard, and sharp eyes. He watched Birlerion closely and was the first to speak.

"I hear you're looking for Euphoria." He shook his head. "Bad stuff."

"Is that what it's called? Then, yes, we need to get it off our streets before anyone else dies," Birlerion replied.

Timmin nodded. "Wish we could, but once it's here, it's here. Difficult to get rid of."

"We have to try, or at least educate people of the risks."

"It's expensive, and supply is difficult; you gotta have the brass, yer know." He rubbed his fingers together in emphasis. "Not much on the streets yet."

"Yet there are bodies appearing in the city," Birlerion said.

"And the docks," Porter said. "Right unnerving it was, seeing that body floating in the water."

Birlerion grimaced in sympathy. "There seems to be a supply of Euphoria entering the palace. Do you know where it is coming from?"

"Elothia," Timmin replied promptly.

"Elothia? Do you know how? Who is bringing it in?"

"I wouldn't like to say, them being pretty private yer know, but wagons go back and forth all the time. Easy to slip a package among the goods, if yer know what I mean."

Birlerion stared at the man. "I don't suppose I could persuade you to look a little more closely next time, could I? A name, a description, anything to help us track them down would be useful."

"That's what Tom said." Timmin stared at Birlerion as if making a decision, and then he sighed. "I'm scheduled for a run next week, goods train to Retarfu. It'll take two weeks to travel to Retarfu, unload and reload, then another two weeks for the return trip."

"That may be too late," Birlerion frowned in concern. He would have to go to Elothia himself. He looked up. "Whereabouts in Retarfu do you unload? I will try and meet you there."

Timmin looked at him doubtfully. "Yer a bit, yer know …" He gestured at him. "People notice yer, if yer know what I mean."

Birlerion smiled. "I'll try not to be."

Tom elbowed him, and Timmin glared at him. "Alright, I

..s gonna tell him, gimme me a chance. We offload at the Valley warehouse, back of Jarlsgard street, west side."

"Very well, I'll meet you there in two weeks."

Timmin sighed and supped his ale.

Birlerion turned his attention to Porter. "You said you saw the body in the harbour? A lad called Will, wasn't it?"

Porter shuddered. "Yeah, pulled 'im out."

"When was this?"

Porter looked at Tom. "About four months ago."

Porter nodded. "'e were nobut a lad. Who would want to hurt him?"

"You said there were no marks on him? No injuries?"

"Not that we saw. Drowned, they said, but he weren't; he looked nothing like a drowner."

"You think he was dead before he went in the water?"

Porter shrugged. "Dunno. He didn't look right for drowning."

"We took him to the Justice's. They said he must have fallen in; they weren't interested," Tom said bitterly. "Even when we told them later about the clothes, they still weren't interested. And by then, he was with the Lady."

"His mother said the clothes weren't his?"

Tom nodded. "Too fine. They were linen, she said, draw string trousers and shirt; he'd never owned the like."

Birlerion sighed. None of it made sense. "Do you think I could speak to Will's mother? And the first victim who survived, Brand?"

"I expect I can arrange it. What did Jake say?" Tom asked with interest.

Birlerion tapped his fingers on the table as he thought. "Not much. As you say, he is confused. Talked mainly about stars and a yearning to go back, though he didn't know where. And wanting more, of this Euphoria, I suppose.

Nothing that would tell us about what happened. I doubt he is even sure who he is now," Birlerion said.

Tom sighed. "We'll help where we can, but there's only so much we can do."

"I've asked a healer I know to look at him, see what he can make of it."

"'Tis good of yer; his ma will appreciate it."

Birlerion rose. "Keep in touch. Let me know if you hear anything further."

"And you." Tom held out his hand, and Birlerion shook it. "Let us know if you need us. For anything!" he said, staring at Birlerion.

Birlerion nodded slowly and left.

10

RANGERS ACADEMY, OLD VESPERS

Commander Bryce of the King's Justice frowned as he watched a silver-eyed cadet haul a stinking bucket across his path and empty it in a cordoned-off area behind the sparring ring. He watched her return. "What are you doing, cadet?"

Leyarille stiffened to attention, the stink from the bucket drifting before her. "Moving the midden, sir."

"And who told you to do that?"

"Lieutenant Parnent, sir."

"And are you doing this by yourself?"

"No sir, Cadet Jennery is helping, sir."

"I see." And he did. "And who gave you the shiner, Cadet Haven?"

"It happened in practice, sir, in the sparring ring."

"I hope your opponent came off worse?"

"Oh yes, sir."

Bryce's lips twitched at her enthusiastic response. "Excellent. Carry on, cadet."

"Yes, sir." Leyarille escaped, and Bryce continued on his way. Once he returned to his office at the king's palace, he called his assistant, Captain Deron, into his office. The captain stumped in and waited for his commander's instructions. Bryce was frowning into the distance. "Remind me, Deron. Which unit of the academy is Parnent in?"

"Second, sir."

"And who do we know in the academy?"

Deron wrinkled his brow in turn, leaning on his crutch. He had lost a leg in a battle protecting the king, and subsequently Commander Haven had enlisted him as his aide. He had never left. "Well, the Academy commander is Reece. He's a good bloke, plays by the book; his adjutant is a good friend of mine, Captain Calver."

"Good, good. Could you have a word? Unofficially of course. Ask him to keep an eye on two new recruits, Haven and Jennery. Not to interfere, but to let you know if things get out of hand, you know what I mean. We wouldn't want our brightest hopes demoralised from the start, now, would we?"

"Certainly, sir, I understand." Deron stumped back out. Bryce watched him go, a good man. He had inherited him from Jerrol. Deron knew everyone, and Bryce found him indispensable.

Leyarille sighed despondently and eased her aching back. She dropped the bucket at her feet and stared at the stinking pile of rotting leftovers and slimy vegetation still before her. Rubbing her blistered hands, she gritted her teeth as Jared paused beside her. "It'll take us weeks to move this," she hissed through her teeth.

Jared dropped his bucket next to hers and slumped on the floor with a groan. "Well, what do you suggest?" He stared at his hands; he had blisters on top of blisters. They had been shovelling muck for two days.

"I am fed up of us being continually punished for stuff that isn't our fault. I bet Parnent doesn't even check the facts, he just assumes we are at fault. Why is everyone so jealous of us? It's not as if we stopping them from progressing." She kicked her bucket. "We went through the admissions process; we work just as hard as they do. All of this goes on our record and it's not fair."

"Who said the cadets would be fair?"

"I thought we would be learning something new, not wasting our time shifting stinking shit!" she said, pacing back and forth.

"Getting angry about it is a waste of energy," Jared replied, slowly stretching his stiff back, and he sucked in his breath as his muscles pulled. "We need to either get our orders changed or put up with it."

Leyarille came to a halt and stared at him. "What did you say?"

"We either ..."

"No, no I heard you the first time. Get our orders changed; you are a genius. I could kiss you."

"Ugh, please don't." Jared scowled at the thought.

Leyarille chuckled. "Don't worry, I won't." She frowned, thinking furiously. "What are the rest of our unit doing? Do you know?"

"Of course I do. Fenton had great delight telling me they were moving onto observation and intelligence gathering." Jared smiled, impressed at the curses that fell out of her mouth. "You're improving," he said calmly. "Your mother will flip out when she hears you."

"Put your excellent mind onto how we get our orders changed. We should be there as well."

Jared frowned. "I would suggest that the sparring master

will not be impressed by the new location of the midden. When he finds out he'll have to put up with this stench right beside his sparring rings every day, he's going to have a fit. Why don't we make him aware of who ordered it to be moved? Once we explain what we've been ordered to do and why, maybe the sparring master can get the order rescinded. It's not as if we've done anything to earn it."

"But what if he just orders us to move it elsewhere?"

Jared thought a bit more. "Then we challenge the orders validity. I don't know why Parnent has got it in for us, but I bet he didn't have the authority to have the midden moved. It's been where it is for years; you can tell by the stink. Let's walk back past the Adjutant's office. He'll be bound to smell us and investigate. If he knows, then maybe he'll challenge Parnent's decision and get the order rescinded."

Leyarille stared at her cousin; he was brilliant. "Let's make sure he'll smell us," she said with a vicious grin, staring at the stinking mound.

Captain Calver stopped them as they crossed the quadrant. They had loitered outside his office for a good ten minutes before moving on. "Cadet Haven, Cadet Jennery, halt. Why are you so filthy? You are a disgrace to the uniform of a King's Ranger."

Leyarille and Jared stiffened to attention. "Yes, sir," they chanted in unison.

"What have you been doing?" Calver stared at them, his gaze suspicious. They looked like they had been rolling in muck.

"Lieutenant Parnent ordered us to move the midden, sir. We have been transporting the midden to the location marked out by the lieutenant, sir."

"I see." Calver stared at Leyarille. "And where is the new location?" he asked.

"Behind the sparring ground, sir."

Calver choked. "Is it, now? Show me."

Leyarille and Jared led Calver to the sparring ground and proudly showed him their work. "It's taken us two days just to move that much, sir." They held out their filthy hands as proof.

Calver drew in his breath at the sight of their blistered hands. "I see," he said again. "Go to your barracks and wait for me there."

"Yes, sir." They saluted and made their escape.

It was a good half chime before Captain Calver arrived with no lesser person than Commander Reece himself. Leyarille swallowed nervously. The barracks stank, as did they.

Reece's nose twitched as he entered, and he stared at them long and hard. "Cadet Jennery, report."

Jared stiffened. "Sir, we are two days in to moving the midden, as ordered. I'm sorry, sir, it's taking longer than anticipated. I think there is a lot more of it than Lieutenant Parnent said, sir."

Reece raised a brow at Calver, and Calver shrugged, trying to keep a straight face. "Show me your hands."

They both displayed their filthy, blistered hands, proof of their dedication to their duty.

"Go to the baths and remove this stink, then you will report to the infirmary and get your hands treated and await further orders. Understood?"

"Yes, sir," they chanted in unison, and Reece dismissed them.

Reece considered his options. "Separate them, move them into units under Kopka and Scott. Accelerated path.

No point wasting such dedication. And tell Parnent to report to me immediately."

"Yes, sir," Calver replied, following his commander out of the barracks with alacrity.

Leyarille sighed in bliss as she ducked under the hot water again. Her hands stung, but she finally felt clean. She relaxed against the side of the bath and grinned as she heard Jared sloshing about in the neighbouring bath. He had been complaining the whole time; his hands were worse than hers, and she winced in sympathy. Though he hadn't complained once while they shuttled the buckets to and from the midden. Her respect for her cousin was growing. Not only was he smart, but he was also a reliable partner. She was beginning to get an inkling of the camaraderie her father had with Jared's father and his Sentinals.

They got out of the baths when their skin began to wrinkle. Leyarille had washed her hair four times, hoping she had finally got the smell out. They dressed in clean uniforms; their dirty ones were probably being burnt, or so they hoped.

"Do you think we can detour by the dining hall on the way to the healerie? I'm starving."

"You are always starving," Leyarille replied. "And no, we are following Commanders Stafford's order to the letter. Straight to the infirmary. Your hands don't look so good."

She marched him to the infirmary, and, after one look at his hands, Healer Hollin whipped Jared into a side room. His assistant smiled at Leyarille reassuringly. "Come, let's sort you out, and then you can rejoin your unit. Congratulations, I hear you've been reassigned. Kopka is a good lieutenant. You'll learn a lot from him."

"We've been reassigned?" Leyarille repeated in surprise.

"Let's deal with your hands, and then you can read Commander Reece's orders," the healer said comfortably. She hissed as he swabbed her hands in a dark brown liquid.

Leyarille was finally released as dusk was descending, hands bandaged, orders read. She reluctantly left Jared in the healerie. He was feverish, and Hollin was taking no chances. They had fed him, so he was happy. She wasn't so pleased about being sent to different units, but she was sure they would find some time to exchange notes.

She arrived at her new barracks and hesitantly knocked on the unit leader's door. Lieutenant Kopka was a tough-looking soldier, broad-shouldered and square-faced. He looked up, and she met his gaze. She knew he knew who she was. Who didn't? Though he didn't make reference to her background. Leyarille straightened her back, hoping he wouldn't comment on her fading bruises or her bandaged hands.

As he stood, Leyarille realised he was shorter than her. "Haven, welcome to unit four. You're in bed seven. Get settled, meet your team, get a good night's sleep. Be on the training field for sixth chime."

"Yes, sir."

"Your belongings have already been moved. See you in the morning." He nodded dismissal, and Leyarille saluted and went to find her bed. She perched on the edge and wondered where the rest of her team were.

She soon found out as they trooped in. Nine other cadets who would soon be her whole world. She tensed as they stood around her in a loose semi-circle. A stocky lad with a shock of blond hair grinned. "Welcome to the best unit in the rangers. I'm Sid." He held out his hand, then he laughed and held up his hands as he saw her bandaged hands. "Don't worry, we can shake later."

They went around introducing themselves, until Kayen said, "Don't worry, you won't remember us all."

Leyarille nodded, smiling at Kayen in relief as she stood; she had forgotten he was in this unit. "I'm Leyarille; it's good to meet you all."

Sid grinned. "Tell us how you did it."

"Did what?"

"Got Parnent and the rest of 'em on midden duty," Sid laughed.

Leyarille sat back down on her bed in surprise. "For real?"

Sid grinned at the others. "Told you so. A Haven wouldn't stitch up her unit on purpose." He turned back to Leyarille. "They've got to move the midden back. The Sparring master was furious."

A smile spread over Leyarille's face. "Well, it wasn't really my idea; it was Jared's. He said we had to find a way to get our orders changed, otherwise we would still be there. It would take years to move that pile of shit."

Kayen laughed. "We heard Calver was accusing his runners of all sorts of things as he tried to find where the smell was coming from."

Leyarille grinned. "We did stink."

"I'll bet," Kayen paused as a bell rang. "Lights out in ten minutes. Get a good night's sleep. We're on an accelerated path; it's tough but worth it. See you in the morning." They all melted away to their own beds and left her in peace. She smiled as she lay in the darkness. What a difference a team made, and an accelerated path; she couldn't wait to tell Birlerion. She fell asleep thinking how pleased he would be.

11

RANGERS ACADEMY

Between classes, fitness training, and combat training, Leyarille didn't have time to worry about anything except making sure she was in the right place at the right time. She was slowly realising that what she had thought was 'fit' was a far distant condition to what the sparring master expected. Even though she had always thought Birlerion a hard taskmaster, he obviously hadn't been tough enough. She was lucky to have the disciplines. Her father had taught her those from an early age, and her hand-to-hand combat skill was far above the others. No one could better her unless they ganged up on her, and even then it took four to bring her down, and as Sid said later, it would have taken more except she was trying not to incapacitate them, thank the Lady.

She began to understand why they had a variety of activities. Her aching muscles had a chance to recover while they did book work. They also progressed onto different weapons. When they were presented with the heavier broadswords, she could barely lift one, though Jared seemed to excel at it. "My father used to carry a long-handled axe; he used to teach us at home," was Jared's explanation. The sparring master took one look at Leyarille and took the broadsword away. "That will never be your weapon. You need to learn how to fight *against* one. Use this." He tossed her a much lighter sword.

As the weeks passed, Leyarille and Jared had few opportunities in their spare time to catch up and exchange notes, but they did whenever they could. Kayen joining them more often than not. The powers that be watched the beginnings of a strong friendship develop and kept them too busy to find trouble.

They were fortunate enough to be in the same lectures on observation and fact-finding, the lecturer only allowing them to sit together because they were his most attentive pupils. They spent two weeks studying the practice and methods and were then put on assignment. They were each given a mission and a target, and they had two days to find an example of the target and track and observe their behaviour. Leyarille's heart sank as she read hers. Her objective was to track a Sentinal without them noticing her. Fat chance!

Leyarille tussled with her conscience. The king was expecting a report from her on Birlerion's activities, and this was the ideal opportunity to track Birlerion without her feeling guilty about it. She didn't have to struggle too hard; she was interested in what Birlerion was up to as well, and her curiosity had been peaked by the king's request. Why was the king worried about what Birlerion was doing?

Early the next morning, Leyarille was in position behind the shrubbery in the Lady's garden. Birlerion emerged from Niallerion's old house, dressed as usual in his silvery-green uniform. Leyarille hadn't really noticed before, but his uniform shimmered in the early morning sunlight. His black hair just touched the collar of his jacket. A white linen shirt peeped out at the neck, and he hadn't done his top button up. For Birlerion that was relaxed.

Her eyes dwelled on his face. She had missed him these passed weeks, no matter how busy she had been. She smiled as he ran his fingers through his hair before striding off through the Lady's gardens. He stopped at the entrance of the temple and entered through the open door. Did he visit every day? There was a lot she didn't know about this man whom she thought she knew so well.

She took the opportunity to reposition herself on the other side of the gardens while he was in the temple. It was about half a chime before he re-emerged, his face calm and relaxed. She was surprised when he turned back into the gardens, and she carefully followed him as he walked up to the front door of the foundling home.

The Lady's supporters funded the home for orphaned and abandoned children; she hadn't realised Birlerion was one of them. He opened the door and let himself in, disappearing into the dim interior. She drifted around the building to the back gardens, a grassy area which was fenced with wooden boards, to provide privacy and safety, she assumed. She managed to find a loose board and pushed it aside, so she could see in.

Two blond-haired children, a girl and a boy, were playing in a sandpit. Another child with dark brown curly hair tipped water from one bucket into another, methodically filing his blue cup with water and pouring it into the other bucket. The cup leaked, losing half the water in the transfer, doubling his work.

The two children in the sandpit squealed in delight when Birlerion entered the garden with an elderly woman wearing a long grey robe. He had two more tiny children hanging onto his hands. "Philip, come play wiv' us," the children called.

The little boy with the bucket of water ignored them and continued his pouring.

Birlerion knelt by the sandpit and lifted a tiny girl into his lap. He began helping her to fill a cup with sand. They turned it over together, chanting a tune Leyarille couldn't quite hear. They tapped the base and Birlerion helped the little girl lift the cup. She clapped her hands at the resulting mound of sand before demolishing it. "More," she laughed.

Leyarille heard Birlerion's low laugh and watched in amazement as he teased and joked with the children. They were climbing all over him, wanting him to help them too, and he didn't seem to care when he ended up with sand all over him; Birlerion, who was always so immaculately dressed.

Birlerion spent about half a chime with the children in the sandpit before he rose, and, removing his jacket, he shook out the sand. He folded it over his arm and went to sit by the solitary little boy with his water bucket. The linen shirt moulded to his back and rippled with his muscles as he sat.

"Hi, Philip." Birlerion's voice was soft and gentle. The little boy ignored him. "I visited the Lady today and she asked me how you were getting on."

Philip continued filling up his cup and transferring the water.

"I said you were much better, thank you very much, and that if Mother Mabel allowed it, I would take you with me next time I visited her. Would you like that?"

Leyarille couldn't see any change in the boy, but Birlerion seemed to take it as an assent because he continued speaking. "That's good, then. She will be pleased to see you." He paused as he watched Philip work. "Oh, I almost forgot, she gave me a gift for you. Here." Birlerion placed a bright red cup next to Philip.

The little boy didn't acknowledge him, but he smoothly

put down the blue cup and picked up the red one and began scooping water. His shoulders relaxed as the red cup held the water. Birlerion rested a soft hand on his curly head before rising, and taking the blue cup with him, headed back to the house. Leyarille gasped as the little boy stopped scooping water and watched him leave with a look of such naked longing that it brought tears to Leyarille's eyes before his face became an expressionless mask and he returned to the water.

After the Foundling home, Leyarille followed Birlerion to the Chapterhouse, where he spent the rest of the morning in the library, frowning over some scrolls. Leyarille had managed to borrow a scholar's robe and strolled through the courtyard and down the corridor beside the library. She had spotted Birlerion at one of the larger tables, with maps laid out before him, jotting notes on a pad. She wished she could go in and ask him what he was studying. She had almost been caught when two scholars came past and asked her why she was loitering outside the library. Shouldn't she be inside learning? She had managed to talk her way out of that, but then she spotted Parsillion crossing the courtyard, and she made good her escape.

She waited outside the Chapterhouse gates, having returned the robe to the office she had found it in. She almost missed Birlerion leaving as he used the back entrance and not the front as she had expected. Parsillion had come out of the front entrance on his own. She followed Birlerion and was worried when he and Parsillion met outside the Black Dog inn, entered together, and both seemed happy to see each other. She suddenly wondered if she should have made sure that Parsillion had actually met Birlerion inside the Chapterhouse. She couldn't assume just because they were in the same building that they had met. Maybe they hadn't. Perhaps she ought not to record it as she couldn't prove it.

Her tummy grumbled at the thought of food. She hadn't thought to request some sandwiches to take with her, though she was sure Jared had. He was always so prepared. Maybe she wasn't as cut out to be a ranger as she had thought.

Observation was a lot harder than she had expected. In practice, it all sounded so straight forward, but in reality, there wasn't that much cover in the streets. She was sure that trying to follow someone in the countryside would be worse. She couldn't get close enough to hear what was said most of the time. If she had time, in future, she would get to know a person's general habits first so it would be easier to see what was out of the ordinary, and if she knew where she was expecting someone to go, she could prepare better observation posts. Ducking into doorways felt a bit conspicuous, and she was surprised Birlerion hadn't seen her yet. She had thought his powers of observation were far superior to hers.

Leyarille was also concerned at how little she really knew him. She had spent almost every day of her life in his company, yet now she thought about it, he never said much about himself. She had no idea what his favourite part of the day was or what he was really doing in Old Vespers. She flushed as she realised she didn't even know where he was born. He was always there, but in the shadows, watching and silent. And she thought she loved him. There, she admitted it. She did love him, and she hated not being with him. Was that love? Or Lady forbid, did she just have a crush on him as her mother had said all those years ago? How embarrassing that would be.

She also learnt that observation could be boring and very tiring. She found it difficult to concentrate when nothing was happening, and her attention kept wandering. She considered sliding into a booth in the inn and getting a meal, but it didn't look that busy and she would stand out being a lone female. There was much to be said in having a partner.

Maybe she and Jared should have worked together on this assignment. She sighed. It was too late to be thinking of that now. She shifted her position behind the pillar again. Her feet and her back ached.

She eased away from the wall as she saw the two Sentinals leave the inn and cross the street, heading towards the market square. Following, she wondered what they had been talking about all afternoon. She should have tried to enter the inn; she was kicking herself at another missed opportunity as she paused at the end of the street. The market was full of people; leaving work, meeting friends at the cafés and inns, doing some last-minute shopping. She spotted Parsillion and darted off after him. She was across the square by the time she realised he was alone. Scanning the crowd, she frowned in annoyance; she had lost Birlerion.

She searched each of the streets that led out of the square, but he was nowhere to be seen; he had vanished. She cursed under her breath before collapsing into a seat in a café and finally ordering some food.

She started jotting down all the things she had done wrong. If nothing else, she could learn from her mistakes. She would wait for him in the temple gardens. Birlerion always went home through the Lady's gardens, and she had a feeling he visited the temple morning and night. She would find him there.

She was so relieved when Birlerion walked into the Lady's temple later that night that she almost rushed up to hug him. She had been right. He spent half a chime in the temple and then wandered home through the gardens, and he didn't leave again until the next morning.

Leyarille slept in the Lady's temple, tucked uncomfortably behind the bookshelves. She had dreamt of the Lady, unsurprisingly, she supposed. In her dream, the Lady had been calling her Sentinals forth. She watched as Birlerion fell to his knees before the Lady, accepting her blessing. His black and grey uniform of a ranger shimmered into the silvery green uniform he still wore today. She could even see that he'd had blue eyes; a beautiful deep blue, which turned opaque as a film of silver covered them, and then the familiar silver eyes framed by the dark lashes that she knew and loved stared directly at her.

Leyarille awoke abruptly, aware of footsteps in the temple. She carefully peered around the bookcase to find Birlerion kneeling before the Lady's altar, laying some freshly picked flowers on the step.

He chanted the Lady's prayer and then began talking to the Lady as if she was there beside him. Leyarille eased back, concerned she was eavesdropping on a very private conversation. She screwed her eyes shut and plugged her ears, determined not to listen. She opened her eyes as she heard a soft chuckle. She looked around, horrified to be caught, but there was no one standing over her, and she realised that Birlerion had stood and was leaving the temple.

Leyarille crept out and hesitated by the altar, then knelt and touched the flowers. *"I am sorry. I've never thought to bring you anything but myself."*

"You will do just fine, young Leyarille." Leyarille turned in shock, but the temple was empty. The sun was slowly working its way down the wall, illuminating the dust motes swirling in the air. Leyarille hurried out of the temple, concerned she would have lost Birlerion, but he was strolling across the gardens towards the central square.

She followed, pausing at the edge of the gardens as Birlerion seated himself outside one of the cafés. He ordered his breakfast and started to read a newssheet. Her stomach growled as she watched him eat an omelette and enjoy his coffee. She had never seen him take so long to eat. He finally paid his bill and headed off through the Justice quarter.

Leyarille had an inkling she knew where he was going, and she turned out to be right. Birlerion led his Darian out of the hostelry, mounted up, and took the road that began the long climb up to the switchback. There was absolutely nowhere she could hide. She sighed and hovered by the last concealing stone wall. She would have to wait for him to get to the top before she started, and that would mean she would have no idea who he was meeting.

Birlerion paused at the end of the road, his stallion gleaming in the golden sun, and twisting in his saddle, he looked down the road and stared straight at her before smoothly moving his gaze on and turning back towards the palace.

Leyarille cursed under her breath; how long had he known she had been following him? She reviewed her notes and cursed again. He must have known since the start. Whatever she had observed, he had allowed her to observe. It was all innocuous, someone innocently going about their business, except for the three chimes between five and eight last night when she had lost him in the crowds in the market square and picked him up again heading home through the Temple gardens.

Her respect for him deepened. He hadn't given any sign that he knew he was being followed. His behaviour hadn't changed at all, and yet when he had wanted to, he had managed to lose her easily and without raising her suspicions. She wondered uneasily what he had been doing the previous night.

And then he had let her know in the end that he knew she was there. Why? She thought about that for a long time, sure there was a lesson she needed to learn. Remembering his leisurely breakfast, she hissed her breath out; he had been taunting her, and she hadn't realised. The more Leyarille thought about it, the more she realised Birlerion had let her observe him, giving her an insight into his life. Heat flushed through her as she held her head in her hands. She hated spying on him, and yet, at the same time she loved the little insights. Reluctantly, she began to chuckle as the funny side hit her before she thankfully headed back to her barracks. She needed a shower and some breakfast before she could begin writing up her notes and her honest opinion of her success or lack thereof.

12

STONEFORD KEEP

The next morning, after handing in her assignment, she was advised that she and Jared had been given a day's leave for her brother's confirmation. They would be met at dawn the next day and were to be back by eight the following morning. Not too much celebrating then, she thought ruefully, though she was pleased she was able to go; she had thought she would have to miss it.

Somehow, she wasn't surprised when it was Birlerion who was waiting for them outside the garrison gates before dawn the following morning, and she flushed under his amused gaze. Jared was too busy trying to tell Birlerion about everything to notice her discomfort, and she was able to recover as they walked towards the Chapterhouse.

The streets were eerily quiet in the grey pre-dawn before the day truly arrived. Once they stepped through the waystone to Stoneford, Jared peeled off to throw up in privacy. Leyarille grimaced in sympathy at the sight of his pale face gleaming with sweat. Birlerion jerked his head at Leyarille to continue while he stayed with Jared to make sure he was alright. Leyarille hurried up to the keep, excitement bubbling in her stomach at the thought of seeing her family.

It was sometime later when she saw Birlerion and Jared enter the keep. Jared was talking fast, waving his hands in the air, and Birlerion was frowning. He asked a sharp question, and Jared answered. It looked like Jared was trying to convince Birlerion of something. Birlerion looked up and across the courtyard and caught Leyarille's eye. She dropped her gaze and flushed. He'd caught her watching him *again*. She couldn't help it though. She missed him. Her eyes were always searching him out, just because she wanted to see his face.

"What's the matter, Leyarille?" Birlerion asked from beside her.

She started; she hadn't even seen him cross the courtyard. His concern made her feel worse. "Nothing," Leyarille replied, forcing the words out. Her guilt was eating her up. She couldn't stand to be near him, knowing he would be disgusted in her, and yet the thought of not being with him made her stomach curdle.

"It is not nothing. You're struggling with something. You've been asked to do something you are not comfortable with. I can see it, Leyarille," he said as she opened her mouth to dispute his words. "Oaths are funny things. You should only swear them for the right reasons. If you swear one, you have to mean it. They are non-negotiable.

"If the person you've sworn the oath to strains the parameters of your oath, you need to consider why they did it. Maybe if you understood why they want you to do what they've asked, you could more easily give them what they need." Birlerion smiled. "Sometimes they don't realise what it is they are really asking for. Don't worry so, believe in the Lady and she will keep you straight. You know right from wrong, Leyarille. Your heart is good, and I hear you are shaping up to be an excellent ranger. Embrace it, enjoy it. This is your life. Worrying about something that may not happen is a waste of time and energy."

Leyarille exhaled. "Birlerion …"

"No, don't tell me. Keep safe, my dear." He kissed the top of her head and walked away.

Leyarille stared across the courtyard, feeling inordinately relieved. She had a feeling Birlerion had some inkling of what the king had asked her to do, and he hadn't vilified her for it. He had told her to understand why.

She mulled over his words. He was right. Why would the king be concerned about what Birlerion was doing? Birlerion had been out of Vespers for years. He was here on a visit. Why would the king think otherwise? She put her concerns aside as her sister dragged her off into the kitchens to help the cook prepare the food for the expected hoards that would be celebrating with them.

Jared, now fully recovered, lugged tables past her as she covered yet another plate of delicious looking cakes. Jared lent the table against a stack and headed back into the keep. He was soon back, hauling more tables out into the courtyard. It appeared everyone had been tapped to help.

She delayed long enough to hug her Uncle Jennery and Aunt Alyssa as they arrived with her cousins, Hugh and Saranne, and she was pleased to see Tagerill and Miranda. They were loaded with what looked like more food and a cart stacked with wooden barrels; the ale had arrived. Leyarille linked arms with Saranne and, laughing, dragged her off to help in the kitchens, leaving her parents to sort out where everything should go.

The sun rose, bathing the morning of Mikke's confirmation as Lord of the Watch in brilliant golden light. The keep had been decorated with streams of bunting and jugs of fragrant flowers. The air was filled with the scent of Summer and the renewal of life. Even the birds seemed in great voice, trilling in the day with gusto.

Jerrol stopped by his son's room early before the chaos of the day took over. The keep was packed to the rafters with friends, lords, and family. It was the largest gathering of people in a single Watch in years.

Serenion stepped out with a nod as Jerrol entered. "Ready?" Jerrol asked.

Mikke stared at him. "I don't think I'll ever be ready. Pa, are you sure this is the right thing to do? You have years left here. I'm too young to be a lord."

"You're old enough; you're older than Simeon was when he was confirmed. Age has nothing to do with it."

"The king will get over his spat. What will you do then? Ask me to stand down?"

"Of course not. Once you are lord, you are lord for life."

"But that should apply to you as well, then. I don't understand why you have to stand down."

"Because it is the only way we can protect the Watch. The Watch is what is important, not me or my feelings."

"I'm not ready."

Jerrol smiled at his son's last-minute nerves. He gripped his arms, staring into his turquoise eyes, so like Taelia's. "Of course you are ready. You've been running the Watch for months. Everyone defers to you already as the young lord. This is a natural progression. It was expected; it's just a little sooner than we had planned."

"But what about you, Pa?"

Jerrol realised his son was worrying more about what was to become of his father than of becoming the new lord. "I will be fine. Everyone dreams of early retirement, and I've certainly done my bit. Your mother deserves some of my undivided attention; I've been promising it to her for years. We will relax in Senti and enjoy the sunshine."

Mikke's smile lacked conviction.

Jerrol shook his son gently. "It will be well, truly. The Lady approves, so she must have other plans for me. I am so proud of you, Mikkeal. You will be good for the Watch. Enjoy your day; it will be very special." He kissed him on both cheeks before hugging him close. "Embrace it, be proud. Stoneford will be watching."

Mikke nodded, though his eyes were shadowed as he watched his father leave. He sighed and concentrated on fixing his cuffs. He looked up when Serenion returned. "Ready?" he asked, keeping his voice light.

Serenion laughed. "About as ready as you are, but we'll cope together."

Mikke relaxed; he was right. They would meet whatever they needed to deal with together.

The Sentinals carried Jason down to the grove in his wicker chair. He was frail now and rarely left his room, but he had insisted; he wanted to see his grandson confirmed, and Jerrol couldn't refuse him.

His eyes lit up as he saw the graceful trees curving over the Lady's temple. "Chryllion, Saerille," he said joyfully. His eyes clouded over in confusion as Niallerion crouched beside him, holding his hand. "I am so sorry, Jason, they are mine and Marianille's."

Jason's face cleared. "Of course they are, and welcome they are too. The Lady is pleased."

Marianille leaned over him to tuck a rug around his legs and another around his shoulders. She gently kissed his papery cheek, creased with the history of his life. Jason touched her smooth face with his gnarled fingers in thanks and settled in his chair, eager to see his grandson. He peered around the Sentinals, pleased to see the villagers lining the grove, happy to be involved.

The air in the grove shimmered as Jerrol led Taelia and his daughters into the clearing, Fonorion at his shoulder, with Birlerion behind them. Jason sighed in pleasure. So many Sentinals and all in his grove. His eyes dwelled on his granddaughters. He was so blessed to have such a loving family. He smiled gently as Margareth came over and hugged him. Such a lovely child. He drifted in pleasant memories, remembering when she had been born.

Taelia and Leyarille joined them, their faces bright and cheerful, and the sense of expectation rose in the grove.

Jerrol waited by the stone table, the Lady's altar, and tried to control his emotions. He was so proud of his son, and he knew the Watch would be in safe hands. He hadn't expected it to be so difficult to let it go. His life had been entwined with this Watch. It was where he had been born; he had grown up in the corridors of the keep, always under Jason's feet. It had always been his bolt hole, his home, where he came back to lick his wounds and recover. He was glad he'd had the opportunity to give something back to the Watch.

Now it was time to pass it on. His stomach churned at the thought, and Zin'talia crooned softly in his head offering comfort. He sighed. The Watch wasn't his; he was but its caretaker, and younger heads were needed now. Maybe the Lady had other duties for him; she just hadn't told him yet. His heart eased at the thought. He may no longer be the Commander of the King's Justice, nor the King's Oath Keeper, and now no longer Lord of Stoneford, but he was still and always would be the Lady's Captain.

He felt a tug and raised his eyes to the sentinal trees, his eyes seeing far beyond. The comforting hum of his sentinal in his bones increased as he reached. The gentle yearning of the Veil grew stronger as it acknowledged his presence. His blood warmed as the crystal of the bloodstone within him stirred, resonating with the Veil.

A gentle voice in his mind drew him back from the Veil. *"Pa, it's time."* He dropped his eyes in shock as he sought his youngest daughter's eyes. She smiled at him, her normally green eyes luminous, no colour at all.

He smiled back at her, acknowledging her intervention. *"I'm here."*

He glanced around the grove as the murmur grew. Jennery and his family stood with Tagerill and Miranda. He sought Birlerion standing with Taelia and his daughters, the other Sentinals, and the Lords of the Watches. They all faded as his son, Mikkeal, entered the grove, Serenion at his shoulder. His heart burst with pride. His son was calm and poised, ready for the next step.

Jerrol forgot all the petty machinations of the king and as he embraced his son, the sentinals' pointy leaves rustled above them in greeting. Jerrol released his son and looked deep into his turquoise eyes. "Ready?" he asked.

Mikke grinned. "Always ready, Pa."

Jerrol smiled, and he turned to the congregation. Opening his hands, he began speaking, his quiet voice reaching the far edges of his audience. Everyone watched in anticipation. "Welcome to Stoneford Watch on this glorious day. We stand here today, in the eyes of the Lady, under the protection of the Land and oversight of our Liege to pass the keeping of Stoneford Watch on to the next generation. Our son." Jerrol's eyes settled on his wife's emotional face. "Our son, Mikkeal takes his first step on the Lady's path, embracing this Watch as his responsibility for him to keep."

He turned back to Mikkeal and rested his hand on his shoulder. "Mikkeal, in sight of the Lady, do you swear to honour the Watch, to protect and nurture its lands and people?"

"I so swear," Mikke's voice was steady. The sentinals' silvery trunks began to glow, and the audience stirred.

"In sight of the Land, do you swear to honour the Lady and our Liege; to guide your people safely and securely?"

"I so swear." The sense of anticipation in the grove rose.

"In the sight of our Liege, and at his behest, do you swear to uphold the rules of the land and to join in the protection of Vespiri and Terolia should he so desire?"

Mikke didn't falter. "I so swear."

"And so, in the presence of your people and under the blessing of our Lady Leyandrii and the embrace of our Lady Marguerite, I declare that Mikkeal, son of Jerrolion and Taelia, be known as Lord Mikkeal of Stoneford. His to keep and honour for so long as he shall live."

Jerrol stood away as he felt the guardianship pass. He flexed his shoulders as if a weight had lifted, and he smiled in sympathy as Mikke braced as the guardianship settled across his shoulders and sank through his body. Mikke's face lit up with amazement as people began cheering. The whole grove visibly glowed with the Lady's blessing.

Jerrol relaxed as Taelia wormed her way under his arm, watching proudly as their friends crowded round to congratulate the new Lord Warden of Stoneford. She looked up at her husband and squeezed him gently. "The Lady approves," she whispered. "You should be very proud."

"We should be and are very proud," he whispered back, hugging her into his side.

He watched amused as his son fought his way through the crowd of well-wishers. "Pa." Mikke engulfed his father in a huge hug, and then he looked at him in concern as he released him. "Are you alright?"

Jerrol grinned. "Of course. I told you. The Watch is yours, enjoy your day. I think everyone is ready to party; you ought to lead the way."

And so the party began. As the music struck up, Mikke twirled his mother onto the dance floor. Jerrol dragged a protesting Leyarille with him, and the dance floor slowly filled.

"Why so pensive?" Jerrol murmured to his daughter, frowning as he had to look up to meet her eyes. "And will you stop growing; this is insufferable," he complained.

Leyarille laughed. "Sorry, Pa, out of my control." She let him spin her out and back in and sighed. "Nothing is as easy as I thought it would be," she admitted.

Jerrol laughed. "It never is, my dear, it never is."

"But how do you learn it quick enough? In theory, it is all so straight forward, yet when you go to do it, there are all sorts of problems."

"That's because people are never predictable. Some skills you can learn, others you have to live. You can't beat experience."

"But that means I'll never be ..." she faltered.

"What?"

"Nothing."

Jerrol gave her a sharp glance. "Sometimes you just need to be yourself. Stop forcing yourself to be what you think someone else wants you to be and all else will follow."

Leyarille frowned at her father, and he grinned. "This is a day of happiness." He swung her into the path of another couple. " Come, Birlerion, swap, I need a lady more suited to my height." He handed Leyarille off to the willing Sentinal and smiled down at Saranne. He twirled her away, leaving Leyarille staring at Birlerion's chin.

"Relax," Birlerion murmured. "This is supposed to be fun."

Leyarille finally looked up and met his eyes. "When did you know?"

Birlerion had the grace to blush. "Almost immediately."

"But how? Was I that obvious?"

Birlerion smiled into her eyes. How could he tell her he had a preternatural awareness of her? He always knew when she was in the vicinity, especially when her eyes were on him. "I have a sixth sense," he murmured finally. "It's a feeling you get when you are being watched."

"So, no matter how good I was, you would have known?"

"Probably."

"That morning, in the café, that was deliberate, wasn't it?"

"I'm sorry," Birlerion said with some contrition. "I was hoping you'd come and join me."

"And blow my cover?"

Birlerion smiled, and Leyarille grinned as her cheeks flushed pink. "Oh, alright, I had no cover, but still, you can't say I didn't persevere."

Birlerion laughed.

"Where did you go that night? I lost you in the square. Was that deliberate as well?"

Birlerion's smile faded. "This is a party. Enough shop. Look, do you think your father is matchmaking?" Birlerion nodded at Mikke and Saranne twirling around the floor.

"I expect so," she laughed. "He would be delighted I'm sure to have a direct relationship with Deepwater."

Birlerion knew he had distracted her for now, but she was tenacious, she would remember later. He made the most of having her in his arms, taking the opportunity to draw her close as the music soothed into a slow waltz, and they melded into each other's arms and twirled around the dance floor with ease.

Taelia watched as she swayed in her husband's arms. "They do look good together," she said, a hopeful expression in her eyes.

"Have patience, my love. You know Leyarille never does anything the easy way."

"Poor Birlerion," she sighed, and then her face brightened. "But Mikke seems quite interested in Saranne. It's been a while since they last saw each other."

Jerrol burst out laughing. "Give them a chance, this is only their first dance."

"I knew from the first time you touched me," she complained as she allowed Jerrol to spin her off the dance floor.

He squeezed her tight and gave her a kiss. "Time for a drink?"

Taelia sighed. "I'll be with Marianille and Alyssa. Bring it over there."

"As you command, my love." Her tinkling laugh followed him to the table where the refreshments were laid out. He selected two glasses of wine and caught sight of Parsillion and Tagerill in deep discussion. He drifted in their direction. "Everything alright?"

Tagerill grinned. "Of course. This is an excellent party, Jerrol. It has been far too long since we had a get together like this."

"I think it's the first time we've ever had a get together like this. We haven't had so many Sentinals in one place in history, I think. The ladies are spoilt for choice."

Parsillion laughed. "I thought Roberion and Lilith were coming?"

"They were, but young Idril was poorly and they had to delay. Roberion might arrive later. If not, I'll see him in Senti."

"So you still intend on leaving for Senti?" Tagerill said.

Jerrol nodded. "We'll stop at the Watch Towers and then leave for Senti straight after."

Tagerill stared at him. "The Watch Towers? Why the Watch Towers?"

Jerrol shrugged. "Just a feeling."

Tagerill scrunched his face up in concern. "Let me know if you need help. It's time you let Fonorion retire; he is beginning to struggle. With Birlerion in Vespers, I hate to say it, but you need a younger Sentinal looking out for you, especially in light of the king's attitude. You never know what he is going to do next."

"I'll be fine, and anyway, Fonorion will let me know when he is ready to retire. Until then, he is my guard."

Birlerion paused beside them, two glasses in his hands. "Fonorion will be fine; the sun will do him good. At least it will be warmer than Elothia."

Jerrol raised an eyebrow. "You are off to Elothia?"

Birlerion nodded. "I thought I'd drop in on Randolf, seeing as Leyarille and Jared are settled. I'll waystone to the Summer Palace and ride from there."

Parsillion interrupted them with a chuckle. "Jerrol, I think your wife is getting desperate for her drink."

Jerrol looked across and saw Taelia frowning at him and holding her throat. He laughed. "I guess so. Speak to you later." He joined Taelia, passed her a glass and, as he sat down, swept a glance around the courtyard. Birlerion and Leyarille were chatting, glasses in hand. Mikke was escorting a laughing Saranne to a chair. All was well, and he relaxed; it was no longer his responsibility.

Marianille smiled at him, recognising his momentary sadness. "It will take time to let go," she murmured. "But I have some news that will set your mind in a new direction." She smiled as Niallerion came up behind her and rested a hand on her shoulder; she reached up and clasped his hand. "*We* have some news. Niallerion and I have not only relocated here to Stoneford, but we are also expecting a baby."

"Marianille," Jerrol gasped in delight and rose to embrace her. "Niallerion, congratulations." He shook Niallerion's hand before pulling him into a hug.

Taelia squealed. "I knew it! I was sure you were, especially when you refused the wine. Sentinals never refuse wine!" She jumped up to hug Marianille and then Niallerion, Alyssa close behind. The noise they were making soon attracted attention, and the happy news spread around the courtyard.

Mikke arrived with glasses. Saranne beside him with more. "A toast," he proclaimed. "To Marianille and Niallerion, and our newest Stonefordian."

They raised their glasses in salute.

Jerrol laughed. "I see our new lord is on the spot." He stood back as the Sentinals crowded round, eager to congratulate Marianille and Niallerion. Mikke came and stood beside him. "The Lady blesses you, Mikke. The Watch will take this as a sign; the first Sentinal baby in years."

"Why now, Pa? Why has it taken so long?"

Jerrol chuckled. "You'd have to ask a healer that. Maybe it just took time for them to recover from being asleep for so long. Or maybe the Lady thought it was time. Whatever the reason, it is welcome news, though you will need to take extra care of them."

Mikke frowned. "They intended taking a house in the village. Maybe they ought to stay here in the keep."

"I'll leave you to discuss it with them." Jerrol smiled and made to move away.

"Pa," Mikke said, and Jerrol paused. "Thank you."

Jerrol looked at him in surprise. "For what?"

"Everything! For being you; for making sure I would be ready. I know how much this means to you, and I've watched you these last few months. Saying goodbye. It doesn't have to be goodbye, you know, there is room for both of us in this Watch."

Jerrol smiled. "Thank you, Mikkeal. You will make a wonderful lord. We'll see how it goes. I am sure we will be back, even if it's just to visit." He moved off, eventually stopping beside Lord William and his wife Imelda, before Mikke lost sight of him in the crowd of people.

Serenion drifted up beside him. "It's been a wonderful day but people are beginning to leave, my lord. You ought to see them off."

Mikke raised startled eyes to him, and Serenion smiled. "Did you not think we would call you 'my lord'? You are the Lord of the Watch now. It is an appropriate address in public, in private, however." He shrugged. "I'll probably forget."

Mikke grinned. "That's a relief then. Serenion you are my friend and trusted confidante; please don't ever let my new position prevent you from speaking plainly. I trust your counsel."

"As you command, my lord. Your guests?" Serenion answered with a slight bow. Mikke laughed and took the hint.

13

STONEFORD KEEP

The next morning, the keep slowly set itself to rights. Leyarille, Jared, and Birlerion were up, breakfasted and gone before most of the stay over guests thought about rising. Jerrol and Taelia were among some of the earlier risers intending to travel to Velmouth with Margareth before heading south. They hoped to find a vessel large enough to take them and their horses at the port of Mortelin off the coast of Marchwood.

They set off with Fonorion and an escort of guards that Mikke insisted they took, and Jerrol, with an eye to his wife and daughter, didn't argue. Zin'talia happily burbled in his head, eager to get on the road, keeping him entertained with her snippy comments on the confirmation and the people she knew.

They arrived in Velmouth as evening descended, the journey leisurely for once. Jerrol found it strange not having to be somewhere by a certain date. There were no agendas, no emergencies, nothing for him to manage or worry about. He had nothing to do except escort his wife and daughter from one place to another.

He dismounted and helped Taelia and then Margareth dismount. The lieutenant took their horses to the stables and, a lady on each arm, he led the way into the inn. Their rooms were soon allocated as Jerrol had booked them just in case. They spent the evening relaxing in the small sitting room, only venturing out to eat dinner before retiring for the night. Jerrol was trying to keep a low profile, hoping to travel onwards without the town officials tracking him down. His luck ran out the next morning as they prepared to leave. Councillor Sellins appeared beside him as he checked Zin'talia's saddle.

"Lord Jerrol, you should have told us you were visiting," the elderly man complained.

Jerrol laughed. "I'm not here in any official capacity, councillor, just passing through. Lord Mikkeal is the person you need now."

"You should have come to dinner. I would have been delighted to spend time with your family."

"Another time, maybe," Jerrol murmured.

The councillor held out his hand as he grinned. "Stop by on your way back; we should talk."

Jerrol stared at him and nodded slowly before shaking his hand. "Very well, though we have a long journey ahead of us. I don't want to delay too long."

"Stop for lunch. The ladies will need a rest before you journey onwards," the councillor said persuasively.

Jerrol sighed and mounted Zin'talia. "Don't forget," the councillor said as they rode off.

Taelia rode beside him. "What was that all about?"

"No idea, but it looks like we'll be stopping for lunch in Velmouth on the way back. I was hoping we would get to East Ford before we needed to stop."

"Never mind, we don't have to stop long." She looked around at the rising pines and snow-capped peaks that filled the horizon, mesmerised by the view. "To think I missed all this for years. It is so beautiful up here."

"That it is. Even the air smells different," Jerrol replied as they began the climb to the Watch Towers. Taelia may have been blind when they first met and instilled in him an appreciation of his other senses as a result, but since the Lady had blessed her with sight, she absorbed her surroundings and colour as if it was the only chance she would see it.

The conical roofs of the grey stone towers peeped through the dark foliage of the ranks of pine trees. A narrow track led up through the trees, and they followed it, the sound of the horse's hooves muffled by the pine needles.

Margareth gasped in delight as the plateau opened before them. The clear waters of the lake filled most of the plateau, and the reflection of the clear sky made it look very blue. The small village of tower Hamlets nestled along the shoreline over the far side. The trail wound around the edge of the lake and kept climbing until they reached the tall, imposing gates of the Watch Towers, now open and guarded by a single sentry.

He waved them in, and they clattered into the courtyard, the noise drawing other soldiers out to greet them. The bull-necked Sentinal, Venterion, strode across the cobbles and reached to lift Taelia out of the saddle before she had a chance to dismount. He engulfed her in a hug. "Taelia, it's good to see you."

Taelia laughed, trying to catch her breath. "As it is you, Venterion. You are looking well."

"Good food, good company, what more can you ask for?" he said as he more gently helped Margareth dismount.

Jerrol grinned as he joined them. "I'm glad you are happy in your work."

"What brings you here, Captain? We weren't expecting you," Venterion asked as he led the way out of the courtyard.

They passed under a stone arch and into a garden full of flowers. There were lounge chairs located in little alcoves, some on their own, others grouped together.

Taelia gasped and clapped her hands together. "You finally finished it, and it looks lovely. Tianerille must be so pleased."

"So are the Watchers. They've begun to come down to relax out here. A bit of sunshine does them good and gives them some colour," he said, looking around the gardens proudly.

A fierce-looking woman exited one of the towers, a frail-looking man in her arms. She gently deposited him on a chair and wrapped a rug around him. The man spoke, and she laughed. A huge smile spread over her face as she saw Jerrol and Taelia, and she made her way through the troughs of flowers. "Captain, Taelia, what a lovely surprise." Her deep voice filled the garden as she hugged Jerrol.

"We were just admiring your flowers. What a difference it makes," Jerrol said as he looked around the courtyard. Flowers of all colours were planted around the base of the towers, softening the grey stone and brightening the courtyard. Tianerille had obviously found joy in gardening, and the towers were draped in her artistic efforts, the plants responding enthusiastically to her care. "You have been very busy."

"We all have. It's taken us a few years, but it's worth it. We wanted to get the Watchers out of their towers, but there wasn't much point when they would only be looking at more stone. Now, they get to relax in this clear air and inhale this wonderful perfume; they are responding so well."

"Not much conversation yet, but we'll get there," Venterion said. "I'm trying to persuade Germaine over there to have a game of chess. But he's not taken the challenge yet. He is the one most eager to come outside though, so I have hope. Let me introduce you." He led the way over to the elderly man lying in the lounge chair. He knelt beside him. "Germaine," he said softly, "we have visitors. Look, here is the Captain come to say hello."

Germaine opened his eyes and stared at Jerrol. His eyes were a very pale blue. His skin was almost transparent, the blue of his veins very clear.

Jerrol smiled as he leaned over him. "Germaine, how are you?"

Germaine raised a shaky hand and Jerrol clasped it. "Where have you been, boy?"

"Looking after Stoneford," Jerrol replied with a grin.

"Ah, yes of course, I forgot." His watery eyes moved. "And is that Taelia I see and young Margareth?"

"Yes, we came to say hello."

"Good, good, nice place this is." His eyes focussed more intently. "Margareth, come talk to me."

Venterion moved out the way to allow Margareth to perch on the edge of the seat. Germaine took her hand. "You're late," he said.

Jerrol froze as Margareth laughed. "I know, I wasn't sure."

The old man huffed. "Of course you know; she was very clear."

"To you, maybe, but you know how all this works. I don't."

"Then you'll learn, girl; the chair's been waiting."

Jerrol swiftly wrapped an arm around Taelia's shoulders as the meaning of the old man's words became clear to him. Margareth was going to be a Watcher? Why hadn't the Lady warned him? Or come to that, why hadn't Margareth said anything? Taelia's shoulders stiffened under his arm as she realised what they meant too.

"What?" Taelia gasped.

Margareth smiled up at them, her eyes luminous and far seeing. "I've always liked it here," she murmured distantly.

"Are you sure?" Jerrol asked.

"Of course she's sure, don't be daft," Germaine snapped.

Margareth laughed and patted his hand. "We've known about this for ages, but this is the first they've heard about it. Be nice."

"How long have you known?" Jerrol asked, inspecting his daughter. She seemed a lot more confident, more comfortable in her body; it was if she had finally found her calling.

"Since our last visit. I could have stayed then, only I knew you weren't ready."

"*We* weren't ready?" Taelia repeated, her voice sharp.

Margareth smiled at her mother as she rose and gave her hug. "I am sorry, Ma, but this is where I belong."

Taelia let her breath out in a huff and set her daughter away from her. "We always knew you had a calling, we just didn't know what it was. We want you to be happy."

"I know, and I will be."

Jerrol looked across at Venterion and Tianerille watching them in concern. "It looks like you've got another Watcher to look out for," he said. "I think you'll find she might be a bit more of handful than your other tenants."

Tianerille laughed. "She'll be like a gust of fresh air through this place, if I'm hearing what you're saying right. Margareth is going to take up the vacant seat in the tower and join us as a Watcher?"

"Looks like it," Taelia said with a sad smile. "She'll keep the place lively."

Margareth gave Germaine a gentle hug. "You'll play chess with me won't you, Germaine?"

"Of course, my dear," he said with a gentle smile before he dosed off.

Margareth chuckled as she watched him. "I didn't mean

for it all to come out so quick; I'm sorry if it's been a bit of shock."

Jerrol laughed. "I had a feeling we came here for a reason. I just wasn't expecting to be leaving you here."

Margareth turned towards him and wrapped her arms around his neck. She kissed his cheek. "You knew, it's been building for a while; you've caught me reaching a few times."

"True, but if you're going to do this, you need to learn it properly. No gallivanting off into the Veil on your own. You know how dangerous it is."

"I know, Pa, I won't. You've warned me enough times. There are enough experts here to guide me."

"If you can keep them awake," Venterion interjected with a grunt.

They all laughed, the tension broken, and Tianerille invited them inside to have some lunch and discuss logistics.

"We rotate the towers. Each day we bring the watchers down from one of the towers, sometimes by tower, other times by floor. We're trying to get them reacquainted with life in general, as well as each other. They seem very isolated otherwise," Tianerille was explaining as she poured the wine. "Our resident healer, Saffron, has been doing some gentle physio to get their limbs moving again. Having slept like us Sentinals for so many years, they have petrified in those chairs. As they didn't have a sentinal tree to watch over them, it's a slow process, but we're not going anywhere. It's been interesting talking them." Tianerille flicked a glance at Taelia. "You should come and visit some time. They have much to say about the stars and the burden the Lady placed on them. They have been watching over Remargaren for centuries and no one really understands what they have been doing."

Pursing her lips, Taelia nodded. "It is a part of our history that we have overlooked."

"You're doing great work, Tianerille; it is already making such a difference to their quality of life," Jerrol said.

"The Watchers are still important. They watched the stars long before Leyandrii created the Veil to protect us. While we have the Veil, we are safe and hidden from anyone beyond the stars, but we should not ignore the fact that there is life out there. We are not the only world in existence, Leyandrii was always clear about that."

"Not something that is widely accepted though," Taelia said deep in thought. "We should start a chapter here; the scholars would learn so much from the Watchers now they are back with us. Even after all these years, we haven't really studied these Towers or understood the full extent of their purpose." She glanced at Margareth. "A few younger people around here might help your long-term plan of rehabilitating the Watchers."

Tianerille brightened. "Do you think so? I suggested it a while back, but Liliian didn't seem to be interested, and I didn't push it. After all they had just found another floor and were busy excavating."

Taelia frowned. "We need to be looking forward, not back all the time. I'll speak to her when we get back from Senti."

"You're off to Senti then. We wondered where you would go," Venterion said, taking a sip of his wine.

"Just for a break," Jerrol said. "I'm sure the Lady has much for us to do. I'm not ready to retire yet, though a rest won't go amiss."

"He's been promising me his undivided attention for years." Taelia laughed. "It's about time he lived up to the promise."

"Well, looks like you're gonna get it if Margareth is deserting us." Jerrol smiled at her with a glint in his eye.

"Aww, Pa, don't." Margareth rolled her eyes.

Jerrol mock frowned at her. "Just you wait until it's your turn, young lady. You'll be singing a different tune then."

She shuddered as Venterion rose, chuckling. "I'll be back soon. I need to go check on Germaine."

"Do you want to put your gear in your rooms? You are staying tonight, aren't you?" Tianerille rose as well. "Margareth, although you'll have your tower, you should sleep here with us. I suggest you move straight into the annexe, then your parents will know where you are."

Taelia and Margareth followed, arms wrapped around each other's waists, and Jerrol smiled at the sight as he rose to follow them.

14

WATCH TOWERS, STONEFORD KEEP

Jerrol got as far as the door and felt a tug; he drifted back out into the courtyard, his senses questing, and found himself next to Germaine.

"You'd better sit down," a gruff voice sounded beside him, and Jerrol was surprised to see Germaine standing.

"What?" he said, his eyes distant as he reached for the Veil. He was vaguely aware of hands guiding him down, and he broke through the clouds and reached further. The expanse of the Veil stretched out before him, the glittering stars a brilliant back cloth. He frowned in concern as he felt the sharp edges. The Veil was damaged, strands were torn and stretched thin, the ends questing for him, caressing his skin. Jerrol pulled the edges together and sealed them. The Veil roiled angrily beneath his touch, charged and virulent. Something wasn't right. He quested further, checking the weave. There were other areas of damage, slight to be sure, but they weakened the overall integrity of the Veil. He sealed the edges and moved on to the next.

Margareth's touch bumped him. *"Pa?"*

"What are you doing here?" he thought as he scanned the Veil.

"You've been gone for ages. Ma is getting worried."

"I have?"

"Yes, you need to come back."

"Look, look at how the weave is worn here; there are many areas of damage like this. You'll need to keep an eye out for them and let me know if it needs repairing."

Margareth chuckled in his ear. *"I am your daughter; you can show me how it's done. I have the Bloodstone and the Oath in my blood too, you know."*

Jerrol faltered. *"I suppose you have,"* he said in wonder. *"We'll come back tomorrow and I'll show you how. If I've been up here that long, you'll understand how easy it is for the Veil to beguile you."*

"I know, Pa, come back." Her voice faded as Jerrol followed her back to his body. He opened his eyes to a dimly lit courtyard. Torches had been lit, and he was laying in the lounge chair covered in blankets. Taelia was lying in a chair next to him, watching his face and holding his hand.

"Hi," she said softly as he turned his gleaming eyes towards her, lit by an inner glow that made them even more luminous.

"Hi." Weariness dragged at him. He had forgotten how draining the Veil was.

"You missed dinner."

"I'm sorry. I didn't mean to stay so long."

"What was wrong? You're normally in and out."

"There were patches of damage, like the weave had frayed. In many different places."

"Does the Veil normally suffer from wear and tear?" Taelia asked in surprise.

"Not on this scale. I've never seen so many patches at once."

"Do you think someone is deliberately causing it?"

"I'm not sure. The Veil was overexcited, but it wasn't feeling threatened. We'll just have to keep an eye on it."

"We?"

Jerrol grinned. "It seems Margareth has the knack. She came and got me."

"Our daughter, a Veil Watcher; who would have guessed," she murmured.

"I don't know why we are surprised. As she said, she has both the Bloodstone and the Oath in her blood. If we'd thought it through, it would have been obvious."

Taelia chuckled as she sat up. "And here we thought we were the intelligent ones. Come on, Tianerille saved you some supper."

"Good, I'm starving." He allowed her to pull him up out of the blankets. She wormed her way under his arm, and he snugged her in tight as they walked into the main building, intent on finding food.

Jerrol slept deeply that night, the exhaustion catching up. Taelia left him sleeping in the morning; it was rare he slept in, and she made the decision that they would stay one more day. She advised the lieutenant, who returned his men to the barracks. The Veil had obviously taken more out of Jerrol than he realised.

She joined Margareth and Tianerille for breakfast. "Where's pa?"

"Still asleep. I left him in bed; he obviously needs it."

Margareth looked at her mother in concern. Her father never slept in. "Is he alright?"

"Of course, he's just tired. It's been a stressful few weeks, you know. He really does need this break. He's not just teasing."

"You would tell me if something was wrong, wouldn't you?"

"Sweetheart, he's fine, just a little tired. A few weeks

relaxing in the sunshine will do him as much good as it did you."

Tianerille looked at her across the table. "Do you think you'll get that long?" she asked cynically, looking over her coffee cup.

"At least," Taelia said tartly. "The king certainly isn't going to come looking for us in a hurry."

"More fool him," Tianerille muttered under her breath.

Taelia took a sip of her coffee to hide her grin. "True. Hopefully he'll come to his senses soon, but not till Jerrol's had a rest. Who knows what will be expected of him next? We've been in Stoneford for over seventeen years; it's quite an adjustment for him."

"And for you," Tianerille said astutely. "What about you?"

Taelia shrugged. "As long as I'm with him, I don't care where we are. Yes, I'll miss Stoneford, but Jerrol is my home. And now all our fledglings have flown the nest." She smiled at her daughter. "I guess it's time for the next chapter of our lives."

Taelia finally went up to wake Jerrol at her daughter's urging. Margareth couldn't get over her father sleeping in so late. Taelia quietly shut the door and, easing off her shoes, climbed onto the bed. Lying down beside her still sleeping husband, she ran her hands up his chest and kissed his bare shoulder. She breathed in the scent of his skin and desire tingled through her body.

Jerrol stirred and pulled her closer, his lips finding hers even with his eyes closed. His forehead creased as his hands explored her body. "You have too many clothes on," he murmured sleepily.

Taelia's low chuckle made him smile. "That's because I'm up and dressed, and it's time for you to get up too."

"You'll need to get rid of some of those clothes, then," he

said, his voice strengthening as he woke up and kissed her more firmly.

Taelia gurgled. "Jerrol, love, it's nearly lunchtime. We need to go downstairs."

"We're on holiday," Jerrol replied, concentrating on undoing her buttons. He kissed her bare shoulder as he worked her shirt down her arm. His lips fluttered across her chest and worked his way up her neck to her ear. She shivered under his touch and capitulated. Helping him shed the rest of her clothes, she burrowed under the sheets to get as close to him as she could.

He was hot, his skin slightly damp from his extended sleep, his legs tangled in the sheets. He stretched and his hot skin slid the length of her cool body, and Taelia shuddered against him. Kissing his chest, her fingers lightly traced his rib cage and the many tiny scars that covered his body. He shivered as he folded himself around her, and Taelia smiled as the man she loved showed her how much he loved her.

It was much later when a lazily replete Jerrol finally came downstairs and sat at the table to eat a late lunch with his wife. Fortunately, Tianerille had taken Margareth off to inspect her tower room, and by the time they returned, Jerrol and Taelia had relaxed into an easy banter and were drinking coffee, looking as if they were just waiting for whoever would show up first.

Tianerille cast a knowing look at them, noting the way they leaned into each other, always touching no matter how they moved. "Margareth is happy with her room; she'll show you later. I believe Venterion is out with your lieutenant checking the walls or something equally interesting. It's nice having a few extra men here; gives our lads a bit of a breather. It does tend to be an intense three-month tour when they are here."

"Do you think the tour needs to be shorter?" Jerrol asked, his fingers absently caressing Taelia's knuckles.

"Or more men. It is a long shift, and although it's usually quiet here, it's the one time something happens that we could be caught short."

"You ought to send Lord Mikkeal a request; he can't deal with it if he doesn't know," Jerrol replied.

Tianerille nodded. "Good point, I will."

Jerrol looked at Margareth. "I'd better show you how to seal the Veil and the locations where it seems damaged."

Margareth sat up, eager. "I'll be glad to help. It's about time I did my bit."

Jerrol smiled. "You'll soon be wishing you were back in Molinti, sunning yourself on the beach."

Margareth laughed. "No. I always burnt; it's much better here."

"So be it," Jerrol said, rising from his chair. He leaned over and kissed Taelia lightly on the lips before leading the way out of the dining room. "Let's go to your tower. I somehow doubt you'll need it, but the grid helps the focus. You do need to find an assistant though. As you could tell from last night, it is easy to lose track of time, and to be honest, if the Veil had its way, it would never let you come back. It is voracious; no matter how much it tries to persuade you otherwise, don't forget it can kill you."

"Yes, Pa."

Jerrol flicked a glance at her, but she was serious. He hoped she was for her own sake.

Her room was on the second floor. A brown leather reclining chair, recently polished by the scent of beeswax in the air, stood in the centre of an otherwise empty room. Jerrol gestured for her to take a seat.

"Rule number one: the Veil is insatiable; always be on your guard. Rule number two: never ever let it touch you. If it gets its thread into you, you won't be able to return home. Rule number three: always seal from the inside out. The integrity of the Veil depends on all layers being repaired, not just the outer layer. And finally, Rule number four: don't be afraid to ask for help. You don't have to do this alone."

Margareth stared at her father wide-eyed. She repeated the rules back to him.

"Don't ever forget the four rules. I'll be your anchor today. So off you go; I'll meet you up there." He sat on the floor, leaning against the wall, and grinned at her.

Margareth squirmed in the chair to get more comfortable and stared at the grid in the ceiling.

Jerrol wasn't surprised when she broke through straight away, the tumbling expanse of the Veil before her. *"The weave is normally clean and smooth, but there are patches like this where the surface is abraded. You can see the threads are weakened as if something has repeatedly brushed against it. You need to reseal the threads and check the weave."* He demonstrated, his movements quick and efficient, and then led her to the next patch. *"You try."*

She tried to copy his movements, but the Veil writhed under her touch. It was not as easy as he made it look.

"It's not just about sealing it; it's about control. You have to command the Veil to be still and then seal it. The Veil will not allow you to repair it otherwise. Remember, the veil wants you, therefore it will try to draw you in. You have to be the one in control."

Margareth glared at the Veil. *"Be still,"* she said, and the Veil stilled under her gaze. She sealed the threads and stood back to inspect her work.

"Well done. Return to your room now." Jerrol waited until she had returned to her body. She gasped as sensation returned.

As she sat up, Jerrol observed her eyes as they shimmered briefly before solidifying back into her usual emerald green.

"You may think it's simple, but using your mind is exhausting, and until you get used to it, you need to return after each repair. If you get too exhausted, the Veil will trick you, and you'll get stuck there forever. This is very serious Margareth, you must pay attention at all times."

Margareth nodded. "I understand."

Jerrol stood. "Alright, let's get some food. You'll find it uses up a lot of energy, and you will eat a lot more than you used to," he said with a brief grin. "We'll go back and do another repair afterwards."

Venterion entered the dining room and veered towards Jerrol and Margareth seated at the table. Immediately, the kitchen staff brought out another pot of coffee for him. It looked like Jerrol and Margareth had worked their way through two plates of sandwiches by the nearly empty plates on the table and were deep in discussion of the merits of various knots and weave patterns when Venterion collapsed into the chair next to them. Shaking his head at their preoccupation, he stole their remaining sandwiches and smiled his thanks as a kitchen boy brought out another plate.

He watched bemused, as they both helped themselves and continued their discussion. He looked up as Tianerille entered the hall, and Venterion gestured at the pair beside him. "Like father, like daughter," he said, scowling at them.

Tianerille laughed and dropped a kiss on his head. "She's only got him for today; she needs to wring him dry before he leaves."

"They could stay another day or two," he complained.

"Don't bet on it. He only intended staying the one night, remember?"

15

OLD VESPERS

Birlerion, Jared, and Leyarille stepped out of the waystone behind the Chapterhouse in Old Vespers the morning after Mikke's confirmation. Jared groaned as his stomach roiled, and he turned away as he began to retch. "Doesn't it ever get any better?" he complained as he wiped his mouth.

"Doesn't seem to," Birlerion said as he handed him a canteen of water. They waited patiently as Jared emptied his stomach.

The rising sun glowed on the yellow stone of the Chapterhouse and slowly brought the town of Old Vespers to life as they travelled through the empty streets. Shutters clattered open as housewives opened up the houses and store fronts were put out, carefully displaying their wares.

They soon arrived at the barracks, Jared grumbling under his breath at the lack of a horse. Leyarille tutted at him. "The exercise, cadet, think of the exercise. Think how much we've missed in just a day. I'm sure we'll be expected to catch up." Leyarille noticed that Birlerion wasn't even out of breath, and she idly wondered when he trained. He hadn't made any mention of it. Life in the cadets was very restricting.

Birlerion gave them a flip salute as he continued passed the barracks towards the hostelry, leaving them to make their way around to the office where they checked back in and joined their class on the training field. As Leyarille had said, the fitness master was eager for them to catch up under his critical gaze.

Arriving at the hostelry, Birlerion found a restless Kin'arol, peeved that he'd been left behind. *"Since we used the waystones, there was no point dragging you to Stoneford,"* Birlerion said as he stroked Kin'arol's glossy neck in apology and began to tack him up.

"I don't care; I want to be with you."

"Well, you're with me now," Birlerion replied as they left the hostelry and walked past the Justice buildings and on up the switchback to the palace. He soothed his stallion by telling him all about the confirmation.

Arriving at the palace, Birlerion made his way round to Commander Bryce's office. Deron was just setting out his desk, preparing for another busy day. "Is Commander Bryce in?" Birlerion asked as he hovered by the open door.

"Yes, go right in, he's just arrived. Shall I order you a coffee as well?"

"That would be great, thanks." Birlerion smiled and entered the Bryce's office. It was little changed from when Jerrol had possessed it. A plain desk with a chair and shelves behind it took up most of the space, maps of the various territories were pasted on the walls, and notes were pinned against a range of different locations.

"What time did you leave to arrive so early?" Birlerion grinned.

"I left last night. I need time for my stomach to recover; those waystones are really nasty. Convenient but very nasty."

Birlerion grinned in sympathy. "Who did you find who was sober enough to take you through?"

"Serenion did the honours. He's a good lad, and he'll be good for Mikke. What a day. Not one I expected to see for years. Olivia refused to come home with me. She's travelling back with Jennery and Simeon, and Simeon will bring her home."

"Sensible woman." Birlerion smiled, thinking of the lovely woman who kept Bryce in order. He had been lucky. Birlerion diverted his mind from that line of thought and returned to the king. "The king has much to answer for. I am at a loss to understand his rationale."

"You and me both," Bryce sighed. "I'm beginning to think your suspicions are correct. His mind must be compromised for him to think his recent decisions are good for Vespiri. Sit down, Deron will get us coffee. I followed up on that lad you said was missing. The report arrived yesterday, and I've dispatched some men to follow up. There is no record of a Samuel Gort applying to the King's Justice, or the rangers. We're seeing if we can trace his whereabouts from his last known position. We got a reasonable likeness down on paper from his mother, who is understandably worried. I've also put the Inquisitors on the case, and they are pulling all reports of missing lads in the last two years." Bryce frowned. "The concern is that if little was done to investigate at the time, then the trail will probably be cold by now, but they may find something. It's worth a try." He paused as Deron placed two mugs on his desk.

"We may need to tighten up the process for handling reports of this nature, even if some turn out to be reported in error. We can't afford for to miss those that aren't," Birlerion said as he reached for the coffee.

"Already done. I had the Inquisitors pull the procedures; they are looking at them now to see how we can improve them."

"I've been cultivating a couple of men who first approached me about this. They want to help. I'm afraid they don't have much faith in the Justices."

Bryce sighed. "I'm not surprised, for us to have missed this for so long."

"Do you think there could be anyone in the Justice department concealing the information? It does seem unusual that your people would have missed it."

"An interesting thought. I'll add it to the list of things to cross check."

"I asked my contacts to see if they could find anything out about the drug Euphoria. It must be in the city as well as up here at the palace; if they can find where it is coming from, we might be able to trace it back to the source."

"Where do you think it's coming from?"

"I'm not sure. I don't think it's Birtoli; the islanders would be aware and they wouldn't put up with it. Jerrol was going to ask around just in case, but I don't think it will be the islands. It's more likely Terolia or Elothia, and the only noise I'm hearing is from Elothia."

"Not the Watches?"

Birlerion scowled at the map of Vespiri on the wall. "It's possible. We ought to warn the Watches to be on the look-out for any new ventures. Though, I'm not sure we've the right climate for it. Too damp. Most spices and exotics grow in the dry air of Elothia or the heat of the desert. And both those kingdoms have a lot of empty space that could hide such an enterprise. I think I'll probably try Elothia first."

Bryce nodded. "Keep me informed. I'll let you know if we find anything."

"I'm staying at Marianille's house. Parsillion will know

where I am if you can't find me, though he's asked me to keep an eye on the king seeing as Anders banned him from the palace. I'm not sure Anders will be any more pleased to see me than he would Parsillion. For some reason, Elliarille and Ellaerion seem to be the only Sentinals in his good graces. Elliarille was always good at finding the right connections. It's a shame she never makes the effort to influence them to help others. We were never close, and now, I know them even less. To be honest, they aren't my first choice of Sentinals to trust with the king."

"No? I would have thought you could use their close proximity to the king to your advantage."

"Even though they've mellowed over the years, I don't think anyone really understands what they went through while they were trapped in the Veil, nor do we know how much they remember. It must have affected them. I just hope their trees helped soothe the worst memories."

"I'm sure they have. It always amazes me how all of you have adjusted to life here." Bryce waited patiently as Birlerion stared off into the distance. "Birlerion?" he said finally.

Birlerion refocussed on the grey-haired man across the desk from him. "Just a thought." He grinned. "It needs work."

Bryce grimaced. "Well, don't take too long. I have a feeling that time is important; the incidents seem to be happening more frequently, and I don't want another body turning up."

"Let's hope you find Sam."

"We'll give it a week. If we have nothing new by then, I suggest you go visit Randolf anyway. It can't hurt to get him checking, and he's more likely to do it for you. The king would not approve such a request from me. But you, he has no control over anymore, does he?" Bryce grinned evilly as he relaxed back in his chair, and Birlerion laughed as he rose to leave.

"I'm not leaving it a week. I'm going to go tomorrow."

"Birlerion." Bryce leaned forward, suddenly serious. "Be careful. I have a bad feeling about this. Don't take any unnecessary risks, please?"

Birlerion stared at him before slowly nodding.

That evening, Birlerion showed his face at court and made sure King Anders saw him. Elliarille shot him a filthy look, which he serenely ignored, and he stayed longer just to curb some of the courtier's excesses and prevent her from coaxing the king away, though Birlerion was sure Anders was completely infatuated. Birlerion found that just his presence, with his perfected icy stare, seemed to deflate the most buoyant courtier.

He had already planned his trip to Elothia. The only waystone near Retarfu was at the Summer Palace. He would have to ride from the Summer Palace up to Grand Duke Randolf's principle seat in Retarfu. That meant at least a day's ride, possibly two, through some tough terrain. He visited the scholar at the Chapterhouse, bought a copy of the latest map of Elothia, and spent the last of the evening studying it, reminding himself of the roads; it had been a few years since he had last visited.

Birlerion briefed Frenerion and Parsillion. Frenerion agreed to haunt the palace whilst he was gone; Parsillion would stay at the house. He hoped Parsillion would be an acceptable alternative contact should any of Birlerion's liaisons show up.

Birlerion felt his lack of companions keenly, but there

were just not enough Sentinals in Vespers anymore. He knew Bryce would have offered his men if he'd asked, but coupled to the fact they didn't travel via waystone so well was that Bryce had need of them himself. Since very few people knew where he was going, he hoped that would be enough.

Early the next morning, just as the sun rose and turned the sky a delicate peach, Birlerion led Kin'arol out of the waystone at the Duke's Summer Palace and checked with the guard on the gate to make sure that Randolf had relocated to Retarfu. He waited outside the crenellated grey stone walls as Allarion, one of Randolf's four remaining Sentinals, came to check who had used the waystone. Each grey wall ended at a tall tower, one in each corner. Three sides of the palace were protected by the deep curving river that flowed on down through Elothia and became the River Vesp as it entered Vespiri and wended its way through Deepwater.

Allarion was blond, bearded and broad chested; his thick neck made it seem like his head sprouted straight out of his body. Birlerion winced as Allarion gave him a bone-crunching hug. "Enough, you big oaf, put me down."

"But it's been years since you were last here. You are staying for a drink, aren't you? Come on, just one. We can catch up. It gets boring round here with them all gone."

"Just one," Birlerion agreed with a sigh as he led Kin'arol through the small gate cut out of the larger portcullis gate. A stable boy came running to take Kin'arol and he reluctantly let him go as he followed Allarion into the familiar palace. He scanned the inner courtyard as they crossed, but it all looked unchanged from Birlerion's last visit. They entered the South tower and climbed the stairs to the captain's office on the first floor.

"Come in, the place is ours. There's just a basic staff to keep the place running just in case the Duke or Duchess decide to visit. I think the Duchess much prefers this palace to Retafu. More relaxed." He grinned as he sat beside the desk.

Birlerion sat in the chair opposite and accepted the ale that Allarion pushed into his hand. "I can't stay; I need to get to Retarfu."

"You've got all day; what's the rush?"

Birlerion laughed. "It's not exactly a direct road you know."

"It is if you go via Tierne. The Duke had a whole road building project going on for years. There's a nice broad road now from here to Tierne and then up through the ruins to Retarfu."

"Isn't it quicker to cut through the pass to Morstal and then up?"

"Well, not always, depends on the weather. As you say, it's more challenging."

"I'm travelling alone; I'd rather do the unexpected."

"You shouldn't be travelling alone," Allarion said, concern colouring his voice. "I'd go with you, but I can't leave this palace unattended."

"I didn't expect you to," Birlerion reassured him.

"But why are you here? What's happened? And what's this we hear about the Captain stepping down in Stoneford? That's not correct, surely?"

"Unfortunately, it is. Vespers seems tainted with a new favourite pastime, and it's affecting those who make the decisions."

"You mean the king."

"Alright, I mean the king. He is taking his enjoyment for some entertainments to the extreme. He is experimenting with some new recreational drugs that have entered the palace. We need to find out where they are coming from. These drugs are mind blowing; they can damage your mind and even kill." Birlerion leaned forward. "Have you heard of a drug called Euphoria?"

"Euphoria, of course, it's a great relaxant. It's never been a cause of death that I am aware of. You must have the wrong drug."

"You mean it's a common drug in Elothia?"

"Yes, many people use it. It relaxes your body, sensitises your skin, good for … you know, when the ladies visit," he said with a leer.

Birlerion frowned at him. "Do you know who supplies it?"

Allarion shrugged. "Who knows, but it's easily accessible from any village. It's not even classed as a drug; it is a recreational stimulant, I think the term is. People are quite protective of it; it's an everyday thing, so be careful you don't make them think you're trying to take it away."

"The drug called Euphoria being supplied in Vespiri is not a stimulant," Birlerion said slowly. "It is a potent drug. It must be a more concentrated version, because the damage it is causing is permanent. We have young lads who are confused, don't know who they are or what they are supposed to be doing. They are lost. The healer describes it as if they suffered a mind trauma."

Allarion shook his head. "That doesn't sound like Euphoria. Euphoria is a powder; you mix it with water."

Birlerion leaned back with a sigh and sipped his ale. "Well, someone has created a different drug with the same name, and it is causing great damage in Vespiri. I need Randolf to help find out who is doing this and stop it."

They both looked up as the waystone chimed. "Are you

expecting any other visitors?" Birlerion asked as he frowned in concern.

Allarion cast him an astute glance. "No. I wasn't even expecting you." He levered himself out of his chair and led the way back down the stairs. "All this excitement in one day means nothing else will happen for months."

When Birlerion stepped out of the gate behind Allarion, he wasn't altogether surprised to see Leyarille standing beside the gate house. She was shifting from one foot to another as she gripped the reins of her horse, unsure how he would take her following him a second time in as many weeks.

"I'm sorry, Birlerion, Commander Bryce sent me after you," she blurted before he had a chance to say anything.

Allarion looked at Birlerion quizzically. "You know this Sentinal?" he asked.

Birlerion smiled. "This is Leyarille, Captain Jerrolion's daughter. Leyarille, this is Sentinal Allarion of Elothia."

Leyarille did a funny sort of bob, which made Birlerion's smile deepen; she was completely out of her depth.

Allarion grinned. "Well in that case, come in, join us. We were just having a drink. It's very rare one Sentinal comes to visit, let alone two!"

Leyarille smiled uncertainly but followed the Sentinals through the gate, allowing the young stable lad to take her horse. She glanced around the inner courtyard, her eyes rounding in amazement as she drank in the ancient stone and metal work. "How long have you been stationed here, Sentinal Allarion?"

"It's just Allarion among friends," he laughed. "I'm on a yearly rotation. One year here, one year at Retarfu. Been doing it for years."

Leyarille nodded as if she knew what he was talking about. Birlerion knew she was dying to ask more questions, but she hesitated, overawed by the palace and, he thought, the huge Sentinal.

"We'll sit in the library. More room," Allarion said as they came out on the first floor. He waved them on, and Birlerion led the way, leaving Allarion to collect their drinks.

"What did Commander Bryce tell you?" Birlerion asked as they sat in the more comfortable chairs in the library.

"He said I was on assignment with a mentor; you." Leyarille shrugged. "All I know is that I was to follow you to Retarfu and connect as soon as I found you. He gave me a letter for you."

"Give it to me later," he murmured as Allarion entered the library.

"We can have a party now," Allarion said happily.

"I've already told you, Allarion. I can't stay."

"Well, Leyarille and I will have a party, then," he laughed.

"Leyarille is travelling with me."

"Don't be such a spoil sport." Allarion frowned. "You're such a killjoy, Birlerion. Relax for a change."

"You know why I can't stay."

Allarion scowled. "So you say, but still, you will have two drinks with me. That's the least you can do."

Birlerion sighed and gave in.

The Sentinals relaxed and reminisced across time as Leyarille sat and listened. Surrounded by a library of ancient books and two Sentinals over three thousand years old, who remembered the world as a much different place even after being awake for twenty years, Birlerion thought it must be very disorientating listening to them, when he caught her wide-eyed stare.

"What was the Lady really like?" Leyarille asked as they came to a halt.

Birlerion's face softened. "She was the most wonderful

person you could ever meet. I believe everyone's experience was personal to them, but she truly had the best interests of all at heart."

"I still can't believe she shattered that stone and banished them all behind the Veil. Why would she do such a thing? She could do so much more if she was here, with us," Allarion complained, his eyes darkening.

"She *is* here with us," Birlerion replied, his voice soft.

"You know what I mean, Birlerion, it's not the same. And Guerlaire. Where is he?"

"With the Lady."

"He should be here. He's the Captain; his place is here with us."

"His place is with the Lady. We have a captain, Captain Jerrolion."

"Who is currently banished from Vespiri," Allarion said, his face taut.

"He won't always be," Birlerion said very carefully.

"But he is now. What use is he?"

"My father is watching," Leyarille said sturdily. "Wherever he may be, he will always be watching."

Allarion flushed. "Of course, of course, ignore me, young lady. I mean no harm."

Birlerion put his mug down. "I think it's time we made a move; we have a long way to go."

Allarion didn't try to stop them, and he gave Birlerion a ferocious hug on parting. "I'm sorry, I didn't mean it, it gets lonely out here."

"I know, I'll try to visit more often," Birlerion promised as he waited for the stable lad to bring round their horses. "Hold the course, the Lady is with you, and the Captain, as Leyarille said, will be watching. You are never alone, Allarion."

Allarion ducked his head and after giving his arm a final

squeeze, Birlerion mounted Kin'arol. Leyarille smiled as she shook Allarion's hand. "It was good to meet you, Allarion. I hope we meet again soon."

"It was my pleasure, Leyarille. I will no doubt see you on your return, when you both will stop for longer. It will give me something to look forward to." He gave her a grin and tossed her into her saddle.

Birlerion was aware of Leyarille watching him as they rode down to the river crossing. Deep in thought, he ignored her, worrying about Allarion and other Sentinals who might also be struggling on their own. Kin'arol drew to a halt at the river bank, and Leyarille joined him as they waited for the river ferry to make its way back across the water.

"Why was Allarion so bitter? I thought all Sentinals were glad to be awoken."

Birlerion glanced across at her. "Not all, and Allarion's Sentinal was petrified, so he didn't have his tree to sustain him like most of us did. He really shouldn't be alone. We always used to be assigned in pairs, so we always had a back-up, but there are so few of us now …" Birlerion's voice trailed off and he sat on his horse, frowning off into the distance.

Leyarille dragged her gaze from him and watched the ferry pull its way across the river. The creaking ropes dipped and rose over the water as the ferry man worked.

"Here, Commander Bryce said to give you this." Leyarille handed him the letter.

Birlerion cracked the wax sealing the paper and unfolded Bryce's message. Leyarille watched his face as he briefly read the contents, but his expression didn't change. He looked up and met her eyes. "Looks like you get to be my partner. Bryce thinks you need the experience and I need the back up." He grinned wryly.

Leyarille exhaled in relief. "You don't mind?"

Birlerion shrugged. It was concerning that Commander Bryce was worried about him, and he briefly wondered why Leyarille had been sent and not some more experienced ranger, then he shelved the thought. “Not at all, I could use the help. Let’s get across this river and I’ll tell you what I know so far and why we’re going to Retarfu.”

16

MORTELIN, MARCHWOOD WATCH

Jerrol and Taelia rode into Mortelin two days later, having stopped overnight in East Ford, his troop of guards still faithfully following along with their bags. They went straight to the harbour, hoping to find a vessel large enough to take them to Senti. Jerrol halted abruptly on the wharf and stared at the tall three-masted frigate moored in the middle of the harbour. It dwarfed all the other vessels.

Zin'talia complained in his head. *"Give me some warning that you want to stop, why don't you? And I'm not getting back on that boat."*

"Ship," Jerrol corrected. *"And you're the one who wanted to come with us."* She snorted as she shook her head, her mane flapping. "What is Roberion doing here?" he asked out loud.

Taelia chuckled. "Someone is meddling."

"You don't say," he breathed, taking in the graceful lines of the *Lady's Miracle*. As they watched, a small boat cast off and rowed its way across the harbour. "I guess we're about to find out," he said as Roberion stood up in the boat and waved his cap, his brown hair ruffled by the breeze.

Jerrol ran a soothing hand down Zin'talia's neck as he dismounted. *"Sorry,"* he thought as she rubbed her cheek against his, and she crooned gently in his head in return. Jerrol helped Taelia dismount and, wrapping an arm around her waist, they waited for the rowboat to tie up at the jetty.

They were soon engulfed in a warm hugs as Roberion laughed in sheer delight, his laugh a deep rumble. "I'm sorry I didn't make the confirmation but when I heard you needed a ship, I thought the *Miracle* was exactly what you needed!"

"Well, she'll certainly be more comfortable than one of the smaller vessels," Jerrol agreed, grinning at the broad-chested Sentinal.

"I'll just arrange to berth at the quay and we'll get you onboard, and then we'll be off." Roberion cast a glance over at the soldiers behind them. "Are they all coming too?"

"No, they were our escort; they'll return to Stoneford now." He looked up at the lieutenant. "Seems we have our ride, lieutenant. We'll just offload our bags and you can be off. I thank you for your care."

The lieutenant grinned. "Yes, sir." A couple of quick commands and their baggage was offloaded and piled on the ground beside them. Roberion returned from the harbour office and waved his cap. A flag ran up the mast in acknowledgement, and the sound of the clanking anchor being raised floated across the harbour. A short time later, the *Miracle* was berthed neatly at the quay, and boards were run out from the deck.

Jerrol led Zin'talia up the gang plank. *"Come on, you've done this before. It's a solid plank of wood; you'll be just fine."*

She rolled her eyes. *"It's a bit narrow,"* she snapped as she hesitantly placed a hoof on the board.

"It's quite safe. I'm with you, come on." She skittered across the plank and down the ramp into the hold. *"There,"* Jerrol soothed. *"That wasn't so bad, and look what I have for you."* He

emptied a cloth bag into a hay net that Roberion had already supplied.

Her head went straight into the net. *"Hmmm, hmm, my favourite, baliweed,"* she murmured happily, ignoring the sailors slotting the planks of her temporary stall around her. He chuckled as he climbed out through the slats.

Jerrol found Taelia up on deck with Roberion as he prepared his ship for sea. He stood behind his wife and wrapped his arms around her waist, kissing her neck in greeting. She smiled up at him and leaned back into his embrace.

"Brings back memories, doesn't it?" she murmured.

"It does indeed," he agreed. "Doubt we'll get becalmed this time though." He laughed quietly as they both thought of their Joining ceremony on the *Lady's Miracle* over twenty years ago. Roberion had performed the ceremony whilst his ship was becalmed in the middle of the sea under the brilliant Lady's moon.

The next moment they were moving. The *Miracle* was eager to be back to sea. They eased out of the harbour, and at Roberion's signal, the sails were run up; they billowed in the breeze and caught the wind, and the *Miracle's* prow lifted as she cut through the waves.

"Straight to Senti? Yes?" Roberion asked.

"Yes, Senti please," Jerrol agreed.

Roberion called up to the helmsman, and he acknowledged the command spinning the wheel. The sailors on the *Miracle* knew the Birtolian waters well, having sailed here with Roberion ever since he had first commissioned her.

Jerrol breathed in the clear salt air and smiled into Taelia's neck. The breeze off the sea was moist and warm, the first sign that they were in the southern waters of Birtoli. The sky was a brilliant blue, and fluffy white clouds with flat bottoms scudded across the horizon as far as the eye could see.

The island of Aguinti was a hazy grey mound on the horizon as the sheer cliffs of the western edge of the island of Molinti loomed up on their starboard bow as the *Miracle* headed south.

Once into the open sea, the sails billowed, and the Miracle cut her way through the waves until they slowed to skirt the shoals of Lisilti, a low-lying mass of rocks that caught many a sailor unaware, and then they scooted through the gap between the tail of the Island of Senti and the island archipelago of Eyti before turning sharply north-east to reach the unusual harbour of Senti.

Glittering harbour walls curved east and west, sheltering the entrance to the harbour as the *Miracle* approached. The walls were an amazing feat of workmanship, and many stories had been told of their construction, none of which, Jerrol mused, were true. The truth no one would believe, and it was safer so. He relaxed as the thrum of his Senti sentinal perched on the headland and the Oath buried deep below the harbour walls welcomed him home, filling his mind with images and stories of what he had missed whilst he had been away.

Taelia glanced at his face; his silver eyes were far way. There was a slight smile on his lips as he raised his face to his sentinal tree, and she knew he wouldn't hear anything she said. She stood next to him and watched the sentinal as it shivered in delight as they entered the harbour.

Vespiri

It had been two days since Birlerion had left for Elothia when Parsillion answered the knock on the door. A young boy hovered on the step. "Tom says meet him at the usual place at 11 tomorrow morning," he parroted glibly before turning tail and legging it through the dark gardens.

Parsillion chuckled under his breath. It was a good job Birlerion had told him where the usual meeting place was, else he would have been stymied. He was about to close the door when he spotted Frenerion making his way through the gardens. He smiled in welcome as the Sentinal came into the light, but his smile faded as he saw the expression on Frenerion's face. He pulled him inside.

"What is it?"

"You've got to speak to Bryce." Frenerion was shaking with anger.

"Frenerion, sit down, take a deep breath. What has happened?" Parsillion crouched beside him in concern; the grey haired Sentinal looked like he was going to have heart failure.

"Th-The king. He is a disgrace. You have to stop him before he destroys all we worked to protect." Frenerion stared at him desperately. "You need to get Birlerion back here; he seemed to keep the king and his court within the bounds of decency, but this … he's out of control, Parsillion."

"I'll speak to Bryce tomorrow, but there is little he can do if the king denies him."

"He can be present. The king needs to see that his behaviour is not acceptable." Frenerion paused as if to gather breath. "Gillian is spreading rumours that he is the king's representative. He is handing out orders as if he is the head of the Administration, instead of Pelori, and the king does nothing to stop him. When I pointed this out to the king, he told me to leave and not return; it seems my scowling face is not welcome. And Elliarille, she is encouraging him."

"Maybe we should investigate Elliarille a bit more. I know it goes against the grain to distrust a Sentinal, but she is leading the king away from the Lady's path. Why?" Parsillion wrinkled his brow. "It doesn't make sense. Why would she break her vow to Leyandrii?"

"We have to get her away from him."

Parsillion smiled wryly. "More easily said than done, though you are right, we need Birlerion. He has a way about him that cuts right to the point. I never would have thought it, but it seems he can influence where we cannot, and he has been a lot more forthright about it than usual," he finished, frowning in thought. "I'll speak with Bryce. I've been watching the housing estates as Birlerion asked, but all is quiet. I was going to suggest we begin to patrol the docks and the warehouses; that's where the bodies turn up. I know it would be too late, but it would help if we could get a line on who is involved; just something we could track." He sighed. "Let's hope Birlerion finds something. There is nothing here."

Frenerion nodded. "Bryce will have to go to court; we can't leave the king compromised like this. If he is not careful, he will betray his oath and lose his throne, and then the future of all Vespiri will be at risk."

"I'll speak to Bryce tomorrow. This is getting ridiculous; we have no Sentinals we can rely on. Maybe I'll speak with Ellaerion. He seems to be popular with the king."

"Don't. It's his sister we're trying to protect the king against. We can't trust him to do right by Anders. If we could, he would already have done it."

"True," Parsillion rubbed his face. "Alright, maybe Bryce has some officers we can borrow."

The next morning, Parsillion hesitantly entered the Docker's Tavern. Jim stared at him suspiciously from behind the bar. "You lost?" he asked.

Parsillion smiled, trying to look innocuous. "No, I am here to meet a man named Tom."

Jim peered passed him. "Where's t'other one?"

"Birlerion asked me to come today; he couldn't make it."

"Doubt Tom will like that," he said, jerking his head behind him. "He's through there."

Parsillion ventured further in and ducked under the low door frame. The room was dark, and Parsillion peered through the gloom.

A firestick flared, lighting the sole occupant, and sharp eyes raked over him. "Where's Birler?" a gruff voice asked.

Parsillion twitched at the use of Birlerion's former name. "He had to travel out of Vespers for a while. I'm his friend, Parsill."

"Parsill, Parsillion? You the king's protector?"

"I was," Parsillion agreed.

"I see." Tom considered him, obviously deciding whether to trust him. "I wanted Birler to know that I got word of where the stuff is going."

"You did?" Parsillion said carefully, sitting opposite him.

"Yeah," he ruminated for a moment. "You said he went out of town?"

"Yes, he travelled to Elothia. He wanted to track down the supply chain."

"Shame I didn't catch him before he left. I wanted to warn him; he needs to be careful. It seems one of the king's administrators, Gillian, is involved."

"Lord Gillian?" Parsillion asked, his eyes widening.

"He owns half the warehouses out back. I'm thinking he's decided to start a new type of import," Tom said with a sour grin.

Parsillion leaned forward. "That is not good. Are you sure?"

"Yeah, he's been seen collecting packages in person; packages he is keen to keep out of sight."

"That doesn't prove he is involved," Parsillion said.

"It does when it becomes a regular delivery and people who see too much go missing. There is quite a turnover of men at his warehouses; he keeps moving people around. It makes it difficult to tell when folks disappear."

"Who is missing?"

"We've made a list; there's more than you think," Tom said, handing over a grubby piece of paper. "We believe all these are missing. They are not in Vespers, nor we believe at Gillian's estate in Marchwood."

Parsillion glanced down at the paper and then stood and held out his hand. "I appreciate you taking the time to keep us informed. I will get this list checked out. You can find me at Birler's house until he comes back if you need to contact me."

Tom shook his hand and watched him leave, and then sighing deeply, he struck another firestick and lit his pipe.

17

RAVINE, ELOTHIA

"What's the matter?" Leyarille whispered as she glanced around the small clearing that Birlerion had stopped in. Sheer stone cliffs rose above and descended below them. Shadowed clefts were filled with trailing greenery and wiry bushes. The narrow trail wound onwards following the deep ravine carved by the river far below. Boulders strewn at the base of the cliff had splintered and were covered by deep green velvety moss.

"We're being followed," Birlerion replied as he dismounted, slid out his bow, and unhooked his quiver. *"Kin'arol, wait in the shadows,"* he thought as he crossed to the edge of the ravine and peered down at the craggy outcrops and sparse bushes to the river far below.

They had been following the river for at least three chimes, hoping to reach the crossing and the road to the ruins of Cerne before dark. He didn't want to camp on the trail overnight. But if they were going to have to fight, it would be better to have a little space than risk it on the narrow trail.

Exhaling, he turned away from the sheer drop. "You take

the left," he began to say, but Leyarille took him by complete surprise when she threw herself across the clearing and her weight took them both over the edge of the ravine. He released his weapons and grabbed at her as they bounced off the rock face and came to a sudden abrupt halt as Birlerion snagged a bush; it slid through his hand, skinning his palm, and they dropped again, scraping skin against rock before he managed to grab another bush. He hissed as he tightened his grip, holding onto her arm in a vice-like grip, and she dangled below him as they slowly rotated, the sudden silence oppressive.

"Are you mad?" Birlerion growled through gritted teeth. His grip on the wiry bush slid, and they jerked as he hung on, the bush the only thing between them and certain injury, if not death, in the turbulent river below them. His shoulder burned as he hung on, sweat beading on his face.

"They were going to shoot you," Leyarille replied, calmly looking up at him. "And me no doubt."

"And this is better, how?"

"Well, at least you're not skewered with lots of arrows." She grinned as she reached for a sturdier looking bush sprouting out the side of the steep ravine. She pulled them towards the rock face, hauling herself up so he could hold her more firmly. He released her arm and his grip convulsed around her waist.

They hugged each other tight, and she tucked her face in his neck as a barrage of arrows skimmed past them. "You were saying?" Birlerion said.

"They are just making sure. They can't see us, otherwise they would have hit us." She squirmed and Birlerion's grip tightened.

"Stop wriggling. You'll slip out of my grasp."

"I've got a rope. I just need to unwrap it from round my waist."

"You mean you planned this?"

She chuckled at the resigned tone in his voice. "Not really. My father said there were a lot of long drops in Elothia. He always said if I ever went to Elothia to make sure I had a rope. You'll be glad to know I listened to him," she said with a quick grin. "It was unfortunate that it all came to a head here."

"Unfortunate," Birlerion repeated, trying to find purchase with his feet against the rock.

"Birlerion? Are you alright? There are men everywhere. They surround us." Kin'arol's panicked voice filled his mind.

"We're in a bit of a predicament."

"So am I. They look for you, though they didn't expect to come across us here."

"Let's hope they assume we fell in the river. Stay calm, Kin'arol. They don't know who you are."

"Calm?"

Birlerion grimaced at the panic in Kin'arol's voice. "Kino says he is surrounded by many men. So keep still for a moment, while I calm him down."

They hung in silence, and he was aware of Leyarille watching his face.

"The Leader is angry. He wanted to speak to you. He knows your name."

"How does everyone know I was coming to Elothia?" Birlerion demanded.

"I don't know, but I can't escape yet. There are too many of them. They say we are heading for Harstad."

"Do as they say for now. We'll follow when we can." Birlerion exhaled.

"They've taken Kin'arol and your horse. Kin'arol says they are heading south."

"Well we need to get out of this ravine. Have you got me? I need my hands."

Birlerion swallowed and hugged her tight against him. "I've got you." His voice was gruff, and he cleared his throat.

Leyarille let go and leaned away from him so she could loop the rope, and then she squinted up the rock face. "There's an overhang just above us. If I can loop the rope over that; it will give us some leverage."

"Let me make sure they've all gone first."

"Can't see anyone, but we can't stay here."

Birlerion silently agreed. His left arm felt like he had dislocated it; his shoulder was numb and yet it seemed to burn at the same time. *"Kin'arol, did they leave anyone behind?"*

"Not that I can tell. They think you drowned, otherwise they would have stayed longer."

"Get on with it then," he muttered out loud as sweat trickled down his face.

Leyarille glanced up at him before she flicked her rope up and snagged it over the rock. Birlerion hissed as his grip slid, his boots scraping the rock as she jerked against him.

"Sorry," she murmured, contrite.

"Did you get it?"

"Yes, let go of me. I'll climb up if you could hold the rope? I'll be as quick as I can."

"Be careful, they might have left someone up there." He reluctantly let go of her and grabbed the rope, keeping it as still as possible as she scampered upwards. Releasing the bush, he grabbed a protruding rock instead and flexed his shoulder. Pain exploded through his tortured muscles, and he rested his forehead against the rock. He wrapped the rope around his right arm and carefully looked up. The rattle of stone and grit eased as Leyarille's boots disappeared over the top.

Her tousled head soon returned. "All clear. Can you make it up on your own? I don't think I can pull you up."

Birlerion gritted his teeth and began to climb. Taking

most of his weight on his right arm, he slowly worked his way up the cliff face. The rope made all the difference, and he finally belly flopped over the edge with a drawn-out hiss; he couldn't have defended himself if his life depended on it. He lay on his back breathing heavily with his eyes closed, exhausted. He reached for Kin'arol, as his Darian's fear permeated his thoughts. *"Kin'arol, are you alright?"*

"Are you alright? They say they shot you." Kin'arol's voice was high and jittery.

"I'm fine. We'll follow. We'll find you. Where are you now?"

"We go south."

"Let me know if that changes."

Birlerion broke off his silent conversation with Kin'arol as Leyarille took his skinned hand and gently begin wrapping it. He rolled his head and opened his eyes. He frowned at the tender expression on her face. Suddenly realising he was watching her, Leyarille looked up. "I'm sorry," she said, tying off the strip of cloth. "I guess it wasn't such a good idea."

"Beats being killed," Birlerion murmured with a slight smile. Trying to stifle a groan, he sat up. "Are you alright?" He looked her over. Apart from a few grazes, he couldn't see any obvious injury.

"I'm fine." She pushed her hair out of her eyes in a gesture reminiscent of her father, and Birlerion felt a tension ease within him. "I think you took the brunt of the fall. I am sorry. You've hurt your arm, haven't you?"

Birlerion started to shrug and stopped as his abused shoulder protested violently. "It's just a pulled muscle. I'll be fine," he said as he carefully rolled to his feet. "Come on, we should get out of here before someone thinks to come back and check."

"Why do you think they tried to attack us? Is it related to what you are investigating?"

"I don't know. I suppose it's possible, but there are only a few people who know what I'm digging into, or even that I was going to Elothia. I don't understand how anyone knew I would be here. We'll have to tell Owen, Randolf's commander, that he needs to pay more attention to the safety of his visitors."

Leyarille was silent for a moment and then she said, "Are you still in contact with Kino? Is he alright?"

"Yes, he's unhurt. The bandits are headed south towards Harstad. Guess we'll have to follow."

"What makes you think Elothia is involved in the missing boys?" she asked as they started walking down the narrow track that would eventually lead out of the ravines and into the rolling hills of the Elothian plains.

Birlerion sighed and eased his shoulder. "There is a connection between the supply of a new drug called Euphoria, which has started to appear in the palace, and the recent disappearance of far too many young lads from Vespers."

"What does that have to do with the king?"

Birlerion shrugged and hissed as his shoulder jabbed. "Don't know," he said through gritted teeth.

"Take your belt off. I'll buckle it to mine and we can support your arm. So it doesn't drag so." Leyarille watched him struggle for a moment before pushing his hands away and unbuckling his belt herself. Her nimble fingers pulled his belt off him and buckled the two belts together. She leaned around him, breathing in deep as she slung the belt across his chest and buckled it behind his rigid back. She carefully tucked his arm through the loop, but he still swayed as the pain rippled through him. "We can stop for a bit if you want," she suggested, a little breathlessly.

"Not yet, let's get as far as Harstad. Who knows, Kino may be there, and if not, we should be able to get horses and we can rest."

"So you're trying to find out why these boys are going missing?" she asked.

Birlerion tried to concentrate. "Yes, two have turned up dead, two were found wandering confused, their minds affected by a drug, possibly Euphoria, but there is also one called Distant Stars according to Brant, the other boy who survived. He gave Leyarille a wry grin, "That's who I went to meet that evening you lost me. Healer Francis believes they suffered some sort of trauma whilst under the influence of the drug, which has damaged their minds. So you could say they've been deprived of life as well; in effect, their lives will never be the same again."

"But that's terrible. What is the king doing about it?"

"I haven't told him yet, and even if I did, I don't believe he's currently in the mood to listen. I don't have the proof yet. I don't understand how this is all linked together nor who is involved. The king can't do anything until we know who to go after."

"You can't do this on your own, Birlerion."

Birlerion smiled at the concern in her voice. "Don't worry, I'm not."

"What is in Elothia?"

"I think this is where the drugs originate. I want to ask Randolf to look into it, see if he can find the source and turn it off."

"Grand Duke Randolf?"

"Of course, he is a good friend."

Leyarille gaped at him. "And just when did you make friends with Grand Duke Randolf the fourteenth?"

Birlerion chuckled. "Many years ago, before you were born. Your mother was held hostage at Retarfu for quite a few months whilst your father and I joined the Elothian army. We got to know him then."

"Why did you never talk about this?"

"It was a time of loss," Birlerion said gently. "It reminds us of those who died at Oprimere. Your father doesn't like to be reminded of his Sentinals' death. He blames himself."

Leyarille raised stark eyes. "I'm sorry, I didn't know."

"How could you? We don't talk about it. Don't worry, we have a long way to walk. Plenty of time for me to tell you all about it, it'll help pass the time." And so Birlerion hitched his trousers up and started to tell her about the time her father had gone to Elothia as a diplomatic emissary and Taelia, Marianille and Niallerion had been held hostage in Retarfu, not long after her parents had first been joined. Once they left the ravine behind, he led her across country, following tracks and trails, though he never referred to a map. He was still talking as dusk began to descend and the town of Harstad came into view.

"How did you know how to get here? You haven't used a map once."

Birlerion tapped his head. "It's in here. Maps get lost, as you now know from experience. Lose your horse, you lose all your equipment too. Best to know the country you intend to cross beforehand and keep your essentials on you and not in your saddle bags," he said as he hitched his trousers yet again.

They cautiously approached a tavern on the outskirts of the town, and Leyarille, insisting Birlerion wait, went to make sure the bandits weren't in residence. She was soon back, saying all was quiet. He dug out some coins from an inside pocket as they entered the dimly lit inn.

His coins purchased them a room and a meal. Trying to reassure Leyarille, he agreed to rest on the large bed, and he let her help him out of his makeshift sling. He did protest at her unlacing his boots, but he gave in, knowing he wouldn't have been able to do it himself anyway. Between his hand stinging and his shoulder burning, he knew he wouldn't sleep, but he felt her eyes on him as she sat on the chair, so he dutifully closed his eyes and lay still.

Leyarille was wrestling with something; he could feel it. There was a tension about her, as if she was resisting whatever she had been ordered to do. When she rested her head in her hands and whimpered, the slightest of sounds, but he heard it, he was up, lifting her out of her chair and hugging her close.

"What's the matter?" he asked. At first, he didn't think she was going to tell him, but then she suddenly relaxed into his embrace.

"This is all my fault," she mumbled to his chest.

"What makes you say that?"

"I told the king you were coming to Elothia."

Birlerion huffed. You couldn't say she wasn't tenacious. "How did you find out I was coming to Elothia?"

"I overheard you telling Parsillion at Mikke's confirmation."

"That doesn't mean he sent someone out after me."

Leyarille raised her eyes to Birlerion's; her eyes teared up as she met his. "He sent me."

"Why do you think he sent you?" he asked gently.

"He seems suspicious about what you are doing."

"Do you think he is suspicious or is someone else making him suspicious."

Leyarille stilled and frowned in thought. "I thought it was him. He seemed very sure, and I felt it was like a test; he was waiting to see if I would do what he asked."

Birlerion nodded. "You are probably right, which means he probably has other people watching both of us. So don't worry about the fact you told the king. He probably knew already."

Leyarille shuddered. "I didn't know what to do. I couldn't tell you, yet it felt wrong to spy on you."

Birlerion hugged her. "Silly. I told you, life in the rangers would be interesting, just keep the reason why you are doing it clear. Maybe we should tell the king more, then he would be able to make clearer decisions. Assuming he won't listen is my failing, not yours."

"You lost your bow and quiver." Leyarille's tearful voice was muffled against his chest, and Birlerion laughed.

"They are just weapons. They can be replaced."

"And Kino. What if they hurt him?"

"Kino is fine. They have no reason to harm him. We'll get him back." He rubbed her back and then realised his arms were full of her lithe body and tried to ignore his own reaction to her close proximity. Now was not the time. He couldn't abuse her trust, especially as he was supposed to be her mentor. "Maybe we ought to go and see what is for dinner," he said gruffly, letting her go. The scent of her hair and the feel of her body under his hands had brought him to his senses. He stubbornly ignored the fact that there was only one bed in the room. He would deal with it later. Maybe he could sleep in the barn?

18

HARSTAD, ELOTHIA

Leyarille and Birlerion sat together in the small taproom and discussed in low tones how to rescue Kin'arol. Birlerion was in constant contact with him as he reported the bandits' progress. The bandits had skirted Harstad and headed for Tyrsil, choosing to set up their camp near a wooded area to the north.

Leyarille watched Birlerion's expression closely as she chewed her lip. This was all her fault. Birlerion's injury, Kino being captured. She blamed herself for the lines of strain on his face.

How her report to the king had resulted in them being attacked Leyarille had no idea. All she had reported was that Birlerion was going to the Summer Palace and riding to Retarfu. Nothing else. Was it sheer chance they were attacked? Or was the king involved in something more serious?

The bar was empty but for them, though they were still careful about what they said. They leaned back as the food was placed on the table, surprisingly fresh bread and a bowl of stew. The gravy was almost black, but the aroma that rose from the steaming bowl was delicious. They stopped talking and concentrated on the food. Birlerion ordered wine, and the meal became quite convivial, Leyarille teasing him about his having to hitch his trousers up all the time, and Birlerion accusing her of getting lost.

"Thank goodness dinner wasn't fish. Your father hated fish stew, and I must admit, I'm not a fan."

Leyarille wrinkled her nose. "It doesn't sound very appetising."

"It's not, especially when they leave the bones in." Birlerion grinned at her expression. His face stilled, the liveliness disappearing as his eyes narrowed and went distant again. Leyarille waited as he conversed with Kino, wishing she had a Darian.

"It seems we have gained some company," he said softly. "Kino says some of the bandits have come into town. They have just arrived."

"Do you think they'll give us our horses back?"

"No idea. You had a better look at them than I did. I only saw one of them before a flying tackle took me into a ravine. They just came into the bar."

Leyarille grimaced and slowly rotated. She glanced at the door before slowly easing back. "He's definitely one of them; he had a silver scar on his cheek; it was quite clear."

"One wonders how they know we're here and what they want. They didn't have a chance to demand anything last time."

"It's a little worrying that they have travelled so deep into Elothia. Do you think they are locals?"

"Good question, though I'm unsure. He's coming over, so I suppose we'll find out."

Leyarille looked at her empty bowl. "At least we got to eat first," she said with a wry twist of her lips.

Birlerion relaxed against the back of the bench, though

Leyarille saw his hand didn't stray far from the hilt of his sword. She watched, waiting to see how he played out the situation.

The man was typically Elothian. He had blond hair and beard, and it wasn't clear where one finished and the other started. His light blue eyes flicked over her and went back to Birlerion. He had the widest shoulders, and Leyarille wondered how he had got through the door. A flick of his fingers had his companion with the scarred cheek waiting by the bar. "You made good time. We didn't think you would make it this far." The man's voice was accented, though Leyarille couldn't tell from where.

Birlerion held his gaze. "If you knew we were alive, why didn't you help us back up the ravine?"

The man shrugged. "I figured, if it was meant to be, you'd find your own way, and here you are."

"Why are you so interested in us? There is freedom of travel in Elothia these days."

The innkeeper watched them nervously, some sixth sense warning him there could be trouble.

The man laughed. "You left so quickly I didn't get a chance to introduce myself. I am the Bandolier di Kvalla and I rule those places others do not wish to bother with."

"Oh?"

"Yes, I understand that you are looking for me."

"I am?"

"Yes."

"What makes you think that?"

"You look to eradicate my business. I thought we could talk. Maybe you would change your mind."

"You didn't want to talk earlier. You sent arrows down after us."

"Maybe I was a bit hasty."

"What makes you want to talk now?"

Kvalla smiled slowly. "A careful man. I like careful men." He made a show of making himself comfortable and ordering a bottle of wine. "Join me," he ordered, pouring out three glasses when the innkeeper had scuttled back behind the bar. Leyarille waited, watching for Birlerion's response. He calmly watched the other man.

Kvalla smiled and raised the glass to his lips and drank. "Nice, this is a wine from the borders, made from a hardy grape and fermented. This year is not too bad. It can be a bit hit and miss." His beady blue eyes stared at Birlerion in challenge.

Birlerion reached for his glass and took a small sip. "Bold," he said.

"Ah yes, much as us Elothians are. It's too cold up here to prevaricate; we are direct people."

Leyarille filed away the information he was freely providing.

"So what do you want?"

"Ah, another direct man. We will get on well, I think." Kvalla took another sip of his wine and ruminated thoughtfully. "I want you to stop interfering in my business."

"I wasn't aware I was," Birlerion replied, raising his eyebrows.

"And I won't kill you."

Birlerion smiled. "I think you'll find I'm not so easy to kill."

"You have such a lively distraction. I expect she would help us." Kvalla leered at Leyarille.

Leyarille remained silent, her expression cold.

Kvalla chuckled. "But I digress, my business, yes, you are hampering my exports."

"I am?"

"Yes, yes. People asking questions, more guards on the borders. You are stirring interest in things you don't understand. The Grand Duke will be most upset to lose the taxes I pay. It is a large part of his income. I pay tax, the Grand Duke leaves me be."

"But your exports are causing harm. If you kill your buyers then you will run out of market."

"No, no my exports have never killed anyone. They are, shall we say, recreational, harmless."

"Even used as a distillate or in combination with other drugs?"

"No one uses it distilled. For one, it is too expensive and two, it would taste too bitter. It has to be cut and diluted, presented like a dessert to be enjoyed whilst relaxing." Kvalla kissed his fingers and splayed them out.

"I think someone is ignoring your recommendations and cutting you out of the sale. Distillates have been found in Vespers. I imagine if someone is selling the distillate, then you are losing out on your cut of the market share. Who is your buyer in Vespers?"

Kvalla frowned. "I am not telling you that. No one is selling distillates. That would be ridiculous."

"I can assure you it is happening and there have been deaths as result. That is why the King's Inquisitors are investigating, not because of me."

"Nonsense, Gi …" he came to an abrupt halt as Birlerion's eyes widened. "Bah, I don't believe you, but I will check myself. This is my business; I control it. I am Kvalla the Wise and Beneficent. Keep your nose out of my business and I will leave you alone; interfere and you will regret it." Kvalla rose and tossed some coins on the table. "I will be watching you."

Birlerion smiled. "Make sure you leave our horses in the barn when you leave. I wouldn't want to start our new acquaintance by accusing you of theft, especially as I know who you are."

Kvalla laughed and touched his finger to his head in salute as he left the bar.

Birlerion watched him go.

Leyarille studied Birlerion. "Who do you think he was going to name?"

"Possibly Lord Gillian, one of the old families. He has an estate in Marchwood and another north of Stoneford on the borders. Works for the chancellor as one of his administrators, but has ideas above his station. I wonder why he would be involved in drug smuggling? He certainly doesn't need the money as far as I know."

"Maybe he's fallen on hard times."

Birlerion nodded. "Indeed. Maybe it's time to look a little closer and see what Lord Gillian has been up to."

Leyarille watched as his face grew distant and his mind grappled with the new information. He suddenly smiled and focussed on her, and she warmed under the expression in his eyes. "Time for bed. I'll check the horses are in the stable. Kino is unhappy and not sure whether they've all gone. Why don't you go and get some sleep? I'll bed down in the barn."

"Don't be daft, Birlerion, your arm is still paining you. I can see it in your face. You need to sleep in a proper bed. We'll both go and check the horses, and we'll both sleep in the bed. Don't be so old-fashioned." Leyarille chuckled. "You can put a barrier of pillows between us if it helps, but you are sleeping in a bed tonight, so don't think otherwise."

Birlerion surrendered though Leyarille laughed when he did put a pillow between them. She was acutely aware of him lying beside her, resolutely staring up at the ceiling. She relaxed when he finally closed his eyes and his breathing slowed.

. . .

Birlerion froze as he woke the next morning with Leyarille in his arms. Her arms were wrapped loosely around his waist and he stiffened as they tightened as he tried to pull away. She snuggled into him, and he silently groaned. He was in so much trouble. Kin'arol chuckled in his head at his discomfort. He opened his eyes and breathed a sigh of relief. She was still asleep, her face relaxed, even though her grip had instinctively tightened as he moved.

He briefly entertained the thought of kissing her; she looked so peaceful, so beautiful. But his common sense returned just in time. She was his partner, and he was here to teach her how to be a ranger, a Sentinal even, Lady willing. Not to take advantage of her when her defences were down. He eased himself out of her grip, hesitating as she murmured a protest. He gently kissed her cheek as he covered her with the blanket and went to find breakfast and to make sure Kin'arol had recovered from his fright.

Leyarille opened her eyes and stretched as she heard the door close, and she smiled; he had kissed her. A warm feeling spread through her body; he had held her in his arms and he had kissed her, yes it was a chaste kiss on her cheek, but still, it was a start. She slowly sat up, reluctant to let the moment go.

By the time she had washed and descended the stairs, Birlerion had led their horses out of the stable. They were both saddled and still had their saddle bags attached.

"So Kvalla has some honour; I wonder why he gave them back?" Leyarille said.

"It's possible he hadn't intended killing us; he may have just wanted to give his warning. I expect the next time he won't be so forgiving."

"You mean I threw us over the edge of a ravine for no reason?" Leyarille asked dryly.

Birlerion laughed as he flexed his shoulder. She noted he

was wearing his belt back around his waist, though he had a clean handkerchief around his skinned hand. "I said it was possible. Only he knows what he intended. Your quick thinking got us out of a possible scrape. We're still here to talk about it; that's what matters. Just make sure you keep hold of your rope," he said with a disarming grin, which made her laugh in return.

They rode off, munching crisp bacon sandwiches, which the innkeeper's wife had insisted they take with them. Birlerion was eager to make up lost time. They took the road to Tierne, choosing to avoid Tyrsil, and then turned north on to the road leading to Retarfu. Riding past the ruins of Cerne, Birlerion reminisced on the temple that used to be there, bringing the past to life so clearly that Leyarille swore she could see Marguerite running through the fields, flowers springing up around her.

The day was drawing to a close as the outskirts of the city of Retarfu finally came into view, the air cooling as the sun descended. Leyarille's breath plumed in the air and she shivered.

Birlerion led her through a warren of small streets, always seeming to know where he was going. The streets gradually widened and then opened into the main approach to the palace.

Leyarille drank in the sights. She knew her father had brought her here when she was small, but she didn't remember it. Birlerion smiled as her head swivelled from one sight to another. Retarfu was an impressive city. The palace walls glowed a golden yellow in the setting sun, and tall columns graced the entrance and curved away on either side. Vaulted arches led into the depths of the palace.

Birlerion halted by the guard house and saluted the guard on duty. "Sentinal Birlerion and Cadet Ranger Haven of Vespiri requesting an audience with Commander Owen."

The guard ran his eyes down a list and visibly swallowed as he reached the bottom. He looked up and recognised the silver eyes. "Of course sir, please follow Symms. He will take you to Commander Owen's office."

"Thank you." Birlerion dismounted. Leading his horse, he followed Symms through the vaulted archway, Leyarille close behind him. Their horse's hooves echoed as they passed under the arch and into the inner courtyard. Symms sent a runner off as stable lads arrived to take their horses. Birlerion pulled his saddle bag off Kin'arol and smoothed his hand down his neck as the stable boy led him away. Leyarille copied him, nervously hovering behind him.

By the time Symms had led them up the steps and into the palace, a large bluff man with blond hair and startling blue eyes had arrived. He had a closely clipped blond beard, which he smoothed with his fingertips as he watched them approach.

"It really is you," the man said, a broad grin spreading over his face as Birlerion mounted the steps. Birlerion dropped his bag as he was engulfed in a huge hug. Owen set him back and shook his shoulders. "What took you so long?"

Birlerion laughed. "We can't always be on leave, you know. Some of us have to work."

"Rubbish, you're a national hero. You know perfectly well you never have to work again."

Leyarille and Symms watched in awe as the Commander of the Elothian army hugged Birlerion again. He finally ordered a footman to take their bags and virtually dragged Birlerion into the palace, talking furiously. "Where are Jerrol and Taelia, why aren't they with you? Wait till Randolf and Guin'yyfer hear you've arrived. Promise me you'll come have a drink with me. Once they get hold of you, I'll never see you again." Owen suddenly swung around. "And who's this? I don't recognise your companion."

Birlerion chuckled. "This is Leyarille, Jerrol's daughter."

Owen gasped. "Never!"

"Leyarille is a cadet in the King's Rangers."

"Welcome to Elothia, Cadet Haven. Last time I saw you, you were just a small child. Birlerion, I can't believe you left it so long to return."

"You can't talk. What stopped you from visiting Stoneford?"

Owen chuckled. "True," he said and led them deeper into the palace.

19

RETARFU, ELOTHIA

Leyarille looked around her in amazement as they were led through the palace, past the large oil paintings that lined the walls, interspersed by colourful frescoes of temples and beautiful young women. Leyarille stopped abruptly before one of them. The woman had long blond hair and green eyes. She had her arm clasped around the waist of a younger girl with brunette hair and vivid blue eyes; they were both barefoot and carefree and seemed to leap off the wall.

"Ah, a woman of taste, I see." A deep voice spoke behind her, and Leyarille spun in surprise. A slender man stood before her. He was elegantly dressed in a dark blue uniform with gold braid and had blond hair and blue eyes like the majority of Elothians. The man's eyes widened as he took in her silver eyes.

"Your Grace, Birlerion has just arrived," Owen said jovially, and Leyarille realised it was the Grand Duke himself standing before her. "And this is Jerrol's daughter, Leyarille."

The Duke's face lit up in welcome as he caught sight of the Sentinal. "Birlerion." He smiled gently at Leyarille. "And

Leyarille, daughter of Jerrolion. Welcome to our home." He frowned at Owen. "Owen, where are you taking them? Bring them to our rooms."

"I was going to let them freshen up first, Your Grace," Owen replied. "I'm sure you and the Duchess can wait half a chime for them to get rid of their road dirt."

The Duke laughed. "Only a half chime, mind you." He stepped forward, and Leyarille was amazed when he too embraced Birlerion, even if he was covered in grime.

Owen hurried them off to a pair of stately rooms situated next to each other, pointing out the bathing room as they passed. "I'll be back in half a chime," he said with a grin. "Be ready, once the Duchess knows you're here, she'll come and find you herself if you take too long."

Birlerion had begun stripping off his uniform before the door was closed behind him, and Leyarille followed suit, rummaging in her saddle bags for clean clothes and a cloth to wipe down her boots. She heard Birlerion's door open and close and assumed he'd made a dash for the bathroom. She brushed her hair out and left it loose to cloud around her face. She heard his door close and hurriedly made for the bathroom. She sluiced her face and neck and washed her hands. There wasn't much time for more.

Returning to her room, she undressed and changed. She was polishing her boots when there was a light tap on her door. "Come in," she called as she scowled at her boots.

She looked up as Birlerion entered. His hair was still damp and slicked back; it made him look younger, and he was dressed like her, attired in a white linen shirt and dark trousers. He looked very handsome. His silver eyes gleamed in appreciation as he in turn inspected her.

"You'll have to leave those outside your door later. They'll polish them for you for tomorrow, but they'll do for tonight."

"I didn't realise you were so well known in Elothia; more stories you and pa never shared?" she asked tartly as she pulled on her boots.

"I suppose there is quite a lot we didn't tell you about," he admitted. "It never seemed relevant or appropriate; they were difficult times."

She cast a glance about her room as she stood. "Do I need my jacket? It needs a good brushing really."

"No, tonight will be informal; you look fine."

Leyarille grinned. "As do you, kind sir."

Birlerion laughed. He seemed quite carefree, as if he had shed his worries with his uniform. She couldn't quite put her finger on it, but it was as if an edge had softened, as if he was no longer on duty. She shelved the thought. "Well, I suppose we ought to go before they come looking for us."

Birlerion smiled and offered her his arm, and she took it gladly. "Do you know where we are going?" she whispered, overawed by the tall ceilings and ornate decorations.

Birlerion looked affronted. "Of course. I know this palace inside out."

"Good," Leyarille grinned, "because I don't have a clue."

"I won't ever let you get lost," he murmured, and she felt comforted by his promise.

They were approaching some rather ornate wooden doors when Owen arrived. "I'm glad to see you remembered your way."

"As if I could forget," Birlerion replied as Owen preceded them into an even grander room. Leyarille swallowed as her eyes flitted around the exotically papered walls and ceiling-to floor-length oil paintings of far too many grand people.

"I thought you said it was informal," she whispered, eyes wide.

"Relax, you're in the Grand Duke's personal apartments. What else would you expect?"

"Birlerion," a light voice interrupted them and Birlerion let go of Leyarille's arm to approach an elegant middle-aged woman with long blond hair and light blue eyes.

"Guin'yyfer," he said with pleasure, and he formally bowed over her hand, before she laughed and pulled him into an embrace.

"It is so lovely to see you, and you've brought Leyarille with you?" Guin'yyfer turned to Leyarille who curtsied awkwardly. It didn't seem to work so well when not wearing a dress. "My, haven't you grown since you were last here. Welcome to Retarfu. We'll be joined for dinner by my children. You probably won't remember them, but we wanted Birlerion to ourselves for a bit before they took over." She rolled her eyes, and Leyarille smiled uncertainly.

Guin'yyfer led them into the inner room, and Leyarille relaxed in the more comfortable furnishing. The upholstery of the chairs and sofas were a soft pastel blue, and tall vases of flowers stood on dark wood furniture.

"Come sit, you must be weary after your journey. Randolf will be here shortly, he just had to deal with something. Please, sit, a glass of wine while we wait." She turned her attention to Birlerion. "So, Birler, where have you been all these years. Why haven't you visited."

Leyarille choked on her wine and Guin'yyfer laughed. "It's his name. Does no one use it anymore?"

"No, they don't, and you won't either if you know what's good for you," Birlerion said. "I prefer Birlerion."

"You're not threatening my wife already, Birlerion? It's a record." The Grand Duke paused in the doorway and smiled at his wife, a tall, bronze-eyed Sentinal at his shoulder.

Birlerion rose as Guin'yyfer gave her husband a radiant smile, and Leyarille smiled with her. She was infectious. "Taurillion!" Birlerion strode across the room and embraced the Sentinal.

"Birlerion. It's wonderful to see you. Marguerite never said you were coming!"

"Is she here with you?" Birlerion asked.

Leyarille watched them, her stomach fluttering at the thought of meeting Lady Marguerite. Were they casually discussing a goddess? Marguerite was Lady Leyandrii's sister. She had bonded with the Land, and Leyarille thought the stories of her appearing in Remargaren were just that, stories.

Taurillion's face fell. "No, she rarely manifests these days. She says it is too exhausting. Though you being here might count as a special occasion."

Birlerion squeezed his arm before returning to his seat.

Leyarille rose as the Grand Duke entered the room. "Please sit, we are informal tonight. By the Lady, Birlerion, it is good to see you," he said.

"It's good to see you too, Randolf," Birlerion smiled as he sat back down.

Randolf chuckled. "What have you been up to? How is everyone?"

Leyarille sat and listened as Birlerion ran through a surprisingly long list of people that the duke and duchess obviously knew. He glossed over the passing of the Watch to Mikke, and the duke's eyes gleamed with questions, though he didn't press the point. "And Landis is still commanding the Terrolian Guards. He's based out of Mistra with Kayerille; their son, Kayen, is a cadet in the King's Rangers like Leyarille here."

"When you next see Oscar and Kayerille, make sure you tell them to visit. We miss them." Guin'yyfer turned to Leyarille. "Did you know that Captain Landis, well, he was a captain then, was seconded to the third Chevron with your father? For a while it was only the Vespirian guards keeping us safe. I must admit I thought they all had funny accents," she said with a peal of laughter. "It wasn't until Owen arrived with the rest of the Chevron that we found out they were escaped Vespirian prisoners rescued by Captain Finn."

"I'm afraid Leyarille, doesn't know all of her father's adventures," Birlerion said carefully.

Guin'yyfer turned contrite eyes on Leyarille. "Oh, of course, I'm sorry, I never thought."

Leyarille turned confused eyes on Birlerion. "What don't I know? Is there more you haven't told me? I know my father was Captain Finn, that he joined the Elothian army for a while before the battle of Oprimere."

"Ah, yes," Guin'yyfer said pensively. "So many lost, so many good people." She visibly shook her sadness off and smiled. "But you know Oscar's son. What is he like? Do you know his parents?"

"I know Commander Landis and his wife Kayerille, they visited my father often. I didn't really know his son until I joined the rangers; my brother knew him better. He reminds me of his father, though. He is very calm under pressure and always has an answer; the masters haven't caught him out yet," she said with a grin.

Randolf laughed. "And what does the betting book say?"

Leyarille chuckled. "I think it's split, but the astute amongst us expect him to outlast the masters."

"Glad to hear it." The duke looked up as the door opened and two young men entered the room, followed by a much younger girl. "Ah, the family are here; Gerhard, Wilhem, Rosie, look who has come to visit."

Birlerion rose as the duke's children crossed the room. Wilhem reached him first. "Birlerion, you promised you would return before now. Where have you been?" Leyarille realised he was younger than he looked, maybe fourteen, fifteen? Gerhard was the eldest. He was the Crown Prince and the spitting image of his father. Wilhem was thinner like his mother. Birlerion enthusiastically returned their hugs and bent to pick up Rosie up as she tugged on his shirt to get his attention. Rosie squealed in delight as he twirled her around and sat her on his lap as he returned to his chair.

Guin'yyfer looked resigned. "Well, that's the last we get of Birlerion. Rosie will vie for his attention with the boys. Leyarille, you'll have to entertain us instead. Tell us about the rangers; how long have you been enrolled?"

Leyarille laughed and began talking about life in the rangers, the good and the bad. She noticed that Gerhard was listening closely despite what his mother said.

"You sound like you love it already," Guin'yyfer said thoughtfully.

"Oh, I do. I've made some good friends, learnt loads, though I still have a lot more to learn. I'm having trouble putting the theory into practice. That's why I'm with Birlerion, to get some experience out in the field."

Randolf looked at Birlerion. "So you are not just here on a social visit then?"

Birlerion grimaced. "Afraid not, but it can wait until tomorrow."

Randolf nodded and smiled indulgently as his daughter patted Birlerion's face to draw his attention back to her. Gerhard sat beside Leyarille and started asking her questions about the rangers and what she had to do to join.

Rosie eventually gave Birlerion up to Wilhelm and climbed in her father's lap instead. Guin'yyfer watched her son and Leyarille with a keen eye but left them to chat. They all moved to the dining room for dinner, and Leyarille found herself spending an unexpectedly pleasant evening with the ruling family of Elothia.

Birlerion had surprised her again. He was relaxed and comfortable with the royal family. He knew the children well, and Leyarille wasn't very surprised to find that he stood as sponsor to Wilhem. He must be a close friend for the Duke and Duchess to choose him to watch over and guide one of their children. She wondered when he had visited; she didn't remember him being away for long periods of time. She also wondered what part he had played in her father's life all those years ago to be so well respected by such important people.

The next morning, Leyarille walked through the palace corridors with Birlerion to the Grand Duke's study. Randolf had been insistent they meet first thing. When they entered his study, Taurillion and Gerhard were already present.

Once seated, Randolf gestured to Birlerion to begin. Randolf was just as shocked as Leyarille had been when Birlerion explained the recent events in Vespers. "I'm trying to find the link. There has been an influx of drugs into Vespers, drugs referred to as Euphoria and Stardust. We've have had a spate of deaths, all young men, their bodies scattered throughout Vespers. Two have survived, but their minds are confused, lost; they no longer know who they are or where they are. The healer says it's a result of a trauma whilst under the influence of a drug. We have to find the source and stop it before someone else is killed. I'm sorry, Your Grace, but as far as I'm aware, Euphoria originates from Elothia."

Randolf shook his head. "It can't be Euphoria. It is recreational and widely used across Elothia. There have been no reports of any adverse effects."

"I'm concerned someone is doctoring it. I don't think it is the same strength or dosage as used here."

"Now that is possible," Randolf said thoughtfully. "Once it is out of our control, I suppose it could be used for other purposes." He looked at his son. "Maybe your suggestion of tighter controls was not such a bad one."

Gerhard frowned. "If one person has found a way of doctoring it, it won't take long for others to do the same. Especially if the business is as lucrative as Birlerion is saying."

"We also encountered a man named Kvalla on the way here; he seemed quite upset with me. Went out of his way to tell me not to investigate any further."

Taurillion growled. "Kvalla? You mean he came out of his hole for once? We have been searching for him for years; he is elusive."

"What did he say?" Randolf asked, leaning forward.

"He said I was interrupting his supply and that you would be most upset at the lost taxes. He pays you taxes; you leave him alone."

Randolf spluttered. "The gall of the man; who does he think he is?"

"More powerful than he truly is," Gerhard responded with a wry smile. "I told you if we left him unchecked, he would cause more trouble. He is actively expanding across Elothia. Do we really want everyone dependent on him?"

"He said he controlled the areas no one else wanted to, Your Grace," Leyarille spoke hesitantly. "Wouldn't that suggest he is holed up in the more remote areas?"

Taurillion laughed. "Maybe it's time for your army to earn some of its pay? A few sorties out towards Adeeron and Hjull wouldn't hurt."

"He was also talking about wine; that is fermented on the borders. He seemed quite knowledgeable. It's possible he is also hiding in plain sight; I imagine vineyards are quite big and remote too?" Leyarille asked.

Randolf looked at her thoughtfully. "An interesting point. There are some vineyards out towards Arla." His eyes dwelled on his son. "Maybe your next visit should be in that direction."

Gerhard nodded. "I'll inform Commander Owen."

Birlerion grinned. "Kvalla will be upset if you disrupt his supply lines. Be warned, he will retaliate."

"He will learn to be more circumspect or go out of business," Randolf growled. "He is a citizen of Elothia, and he will abide by my laws."

"To be fair, he had no knowledge of the distillates, Your Grace. He was as annoyed that someone else might be cutting into his business. So he may deal with it himself."

"I don't think we'll wait for him. Birlerion, how long do you remain here?"

"Well, I thought I'd give Leyarille a quick tour of the city, seeing as she's unlikely to remember it from her last visit, and then I am meeting an acquaintance down in the warehouse district. A possible lead into how the drugs are entering Vespiri."

"Oh?"

"Yes, it seems the goods wagons may be the way it's being transported. I thought I'd hitch a ride on the way back."

Randolf studied Birlerion. "And where's your back up? You are not travelling alone, are you?" Randolf smiled at Leyarille. "No offence m'dear, but the likes of Birlerion, and your father of course, always seem to find trouble."

Birlerion shrugged. "There aren't enough of us. The king disbanded the Sentinals as you know; we are now undesirable in Vespers. Niallerion and Marianille relocated to Stoneford; Jerrol and Fonorion left for Senti. I left Parsillion and Frenerion in Vespers, but their hands are tied. They try to keep an eye on the king, but he makes it difficult."

"So, no back up," Randolf said bluntly. "You're no good to us dead, Birlerion. You are poking into murky waters, and you've already said they are prepared to kill. Take Taurillion with you. He can go on the wagons with you. Leyarille can take your horses back and warn Bryce; they can be waiting for you when you arrive in Vespers."

"I can't take Taurillion, Your Grace," Birlerion protested. "You need him."

"Allarion will stay here with me, and I have Owen and his whole army. Your need is greater. Taurillion will blend in better." He frowned at Birlerion. "For that matter, how do you propose to blend in? You are rather distinctive you know."

Birlerion grinned. "Without the uniform or weapons, you'd be surprised how nondescript I can look."

Randolf gave a bark of laughter. "Believe that when I see it." He shook his head. "I think you are deceiving yourself." He said more seriously, "You will never be nondescript, my friend."

"We'll see," Birlerion replied, unconcerned.

Leyarille watched the interplay with interest. Birlerion responded with a blend of subservience and authority; mostly authority, she noted. He had made the issue in Vespers their issue too, and he had achieved his goal. No one was trying to stop him; they were figuring out how they could help him the most. She was a little peeved about being the one taking the horses back to Vespers, though she didn't complain; it made the most sense. She just wished he'd mentioned it beforehand.

Birlerion was as good as his word and acted as her tour guide as he showed her the city of Retarfu, a city it was clear he loved. "This is Marguerite's temple. The people of Elothia are very close to the Land and Lady Marguerite. Her guardians are closely linked to both the Dukedom and the land itself." He paused at the end of the road to give her a ıe architecture, an elegant grey stone lome and a spire.

"

ıld be most upset if we didn't."

hat?" Leyarille asked with a laugh.

ıd Leyandrii aways liked visitors."

tension as he walked up to the ornate altar the centre of the temple and knelt on the step and bent his head.

Leyarille glanced around her in concern and tensed as Birlerion froze, and then he chuckled and Leyarille cast a glance at him. He was looking contrite and amused at the same time.

She concentrated on her own prayers and felt a soft caress on her face before the feeling faded. She stood and drifted off around the central altar, walking all the way around; it was an intricately carved image of a young woman holding a large bunch of lilies and orchids. If you concentrated, you could smell the scent of lilies and hear her light laugher on the still air. Three marble steps led up to the effigy from all directions.

Leyarille reached her starting point. Birlerion was still kneeling where she had left him. She went to look at the engravings on the walls. It was a beautiful temple.

She was staring at an image of a sentinal tree and a young woman when she sensed Birlerion standing beside her. The name 'Yaserille' was engraved under the image; next to her was another tree curving over a young man who was reaching up to the stars. The name 'Lorillion' was engraved beneath.

Birlerion ran his fingers over Yaserille's name. "We miss you," he said softly, as his fingers moved on to trace Lorillion's. "We miss you both."

Leyarille was concerned to see a tear trace down his

cheek, and she gripped his arm in sympathy. Birleri
his cheek and cleared his throat. "Come on, there's
more to see," he said solemnly as he led her out of
temple. He seemed to shake off his sadness as the sun brok
through the cloud cover.

"Let's get some lunch. If I remember correctly, there is a really nice café down this street. We can sit down for a bit and decide whether you want to see the governments buildings, which are rather fine, or the food market, which is one of the largest markets in Remargaren."

Leyarille laughed as she sat in the chair that the waiter held out for her. "Birlerion, honest you don't have to show me everything."

"You should make the most of it. Who knows when you will be able to come back and visit?"

"But we're not here to do as we please. Where do the delivery wagons enter the city? We need to assess the best way to get you onboard."

Birlerion smiled. "After lunch. What will you have?" He handed her a menu.

20

RETARFU, ELOTHIA

For the third day, Birlerion and Leyarille watched the comings and goings of the warehouse district in the west side of Retarfu. Every few chimes, Birlerion had changed their position so they could get a different view. They had tracked the timings of deliveries, the procedures for onloading and offloading, the types of wagons and their approaches, the different mechanisms to offload, dependent on the size and weight of the goods.

There was an army of men that came and went like the tide with the arrival and departure of the wagons. One minute they were buzzing about the wagons like a swarm of worker bees as they were offloaded, and then they were gone as the wagons pulled away empty to the loading station.

Each day, Birlerion had adjusted his clothes, matching as closely to the typical work clothes of the men. Today, he had pulled a cap down low over his eyes and mingled with the last influx of workers as more wagons pulled in. Leyarille lost sight of him in the mass of people; he did blend in.

She tried to spot him, but she didn't see him until there was some sort of altercation near a newly loaded wagon, where horses squealed and reared up. There was a sudden cry as someone was caught by a flying hoof. She saw a man leap up onto the wagon and grab the reins before the horses bolted. She realised it was Birlerion as she heard him shout commands at the men around him. She recognised his voice, even though he tried to temper it.

With the horses under control, he leapt back down and ducked under the traces. She assumed he was checking the horses weren't injured. A thickset man with a clipboard hurried out and began shouting at the men, and they dispersed. The man ran a hand through his dirty blond hair and scowled at the wagon and then the man lying on the ground.

Birlerion ran his hands down the nearside horse's leg, and the horse stamped his foot. He was fine, fortunately. The same couldn't be said for the driver, who was laid out on the cobbles, his forehead split open where the horse's hoof had caught him. Serves him right, Birlerion thought savagely, the way he had treated the horses, he deserved it. The driver was dragged away and the oversee demanded a reserve driver step forward.

"Come on, we haven't got all day. This wagon needs moving. You," he pointed at the brakeman, "move it."

"I'm a brakeman. Ain't my job to drive the 'orses," the man replied stubbornly, running his fingers over his straggly beard.

"I'll drive them, if you pay me the wages for it," Birlerion said, ducking out from under the traces when the oversee was showing signs of desperation. He kept his cap down low over his eyes.

"Name?" the overseer rapped, barely looking at him.

"Bernie, sir."

"Alright, pull the wagon over behind that one. You're number eight in that train to Vespers." He handed him a board with the number 8 on it. "You'll be met in Vespers and directed to your drop off point. You get paid on your return, one tesla for the trip. Place your mark here, if you accept." The man thrust his clipboard under Birlerion's nose, and Birlerion pressed his thumb against it. His finger left a grubby mark.

Birlerion climbed up on the back of the wagon and began checking the load, testing the ropes and slats that held the boxes in place.

"What are you doing? Move that wagon now. We are behind."

"I'm making sure it's loaded right. Wouldn't want to lose the whole lot on the first hill now, would we, sir?" Birlerion said with a touch of sarcasm as he threw a tarpaulin over the top and began efficiently tying it down, wrapping the rope in a figure of eight around the hook, and passing it through the rings on the side of the wagon, and flinging the rope to the other side to repeat the actions.

The overseer watched and then grunted before moving to the next wagon, leaving the man to his job; he obviously knew what he was doing.

Birlerion moved the wagon to end of the train and turned to the brakeman. He was a squat man, broad across the chest but with thin arms and legs. "How long have we got before we move out? I need to get my stuff."

"You got no time, we'll be leaving once those two wagons are loaded, 'alf chime, maybe?"

Birlerion nodded and held out his hand, "Bernie," he said.

"George." The man grinned showing stained teeth, "I 'ope you handle them 'orses as well as it looked. The road to

Old Vespers ain't for the weak. We have some long old pulls."

"We'll be fine, these horses will get us there. Make sure you load up the grain, they need feeding too." He checked the water barrel and thumped the lid down hard to seal it.

He slipped away as George did as he'd asked and found Leyarille tucked away where he had left her. "I'm on the next train out. We leave in about half a chime, wagon number eight of ten. I have nothing on me except my daggers. Take my sword and pack with you back to Vespers. Could you get me a new bow from Taurillion or Owen? Bring them with you when you meet us at the warehousing district. We get directed to the final loading bays when we arrive. Taurillion will have to travel with you." He shrugged. "Which may be for the best." He scowled into the distance. "Tom's friend, Timmin, is the brakeman in wagon number three, so I have one contact I know if things go wrong. He says he has the package on board his wagon." He looked at Leyarille and grinned, his eyes alight. "I'll find out who the package is for when I get to Vespers. If it's Gillian, I'll know it and we'll have a connection. I'll send you an Arifel to warn you when I arrive. See if you can bring my weapons and meet me at the warehouses. Take care." He kissed her cheek and was gone. She hadn't had a chance to say a word.

He climbed back up onto the wagon. "George," he said, frowning at the horses. "Do we get an escort? Are we likely to see any trouble on the way to Vespers?"

George snorted. "You ask now? Bit late, ain't it?"

"Just wondered," Birlerion said.

"We're on our own, mate. There's a couple of swords in the box, and there's a bow, but the string broke, and some arrows, but they ain't much good without the bow, I s'ppose. We sleep under the wagon. Yer might want to get some bread. Not much food on the road."

"Good point." Birlerion looked around and dropped to the ground. He crossed out of the busy loading bays and stopped by a street seller. Buying four rolls, some dried strips of meat, and some apples, he dropped them in a sack he also purchased. He moved on and picked up a blanket and a roll of gut string. That would have to do. He'd slept rough before. He hoped it wouldn't rain; now that would be truly miserable. He would stink by the time he reached Vespers, but never mind. He returned just in time and stowed his purchases in the sword box behind the driver's seat. Finding an empty canteen, a wooden bucket, and another rug in the box, he rushed to the well and filled the canteen before climbing back aboard. He took a deep breath and sedately shook up the reins, then followed the wagon in front of him.

As Leyarille watched the wagons rumble down the road, she kept her eyes on Birlerion. He was accompanied by a rough-looking man who was chatting away, though Birlerion concentrated on his horses. He deftly controlled the horses through the streets, and his wagon rumbled out of sight. She waited for the two wagons following him to pass from view, and then she ran through streets back to the palace.

Fortunately, the sentry on duty recognised her and waved her through. She rushed up the stairs to the first floor and burst into the commander's office. "Commander Owen, where's Sentinal Taurillion?"

Owen looked up from the papers on his desk. "In the library," he replied absently. Leyarille swirled in the doorway and rushed down the gallery to the library.

"Sentinal Taurillion," she gasped as she skidded into the library. "Birlerion's left with a wagon train, headed for Vespers. He's driving one of the wagons."

Taurillion looked at her in surprise. "How did he manage that?"

"There was an accident and one of the drivers was injured, so Birlerion took his place, I think. He said the goods were onboard and we were to meet him in the warehouse district in Vespers."

"I suppose we need to go to Vespers then," he said with a grin.

"Will he be alright, though? He doesn't have a sword or his bow."

Taurillion laughed. "I should worry more about anyone stupid enough to attack them; he'll be fine."

Old Vespers

King Anders declared that there would be a week of state events. The Lords of the Watches were invited as were his commanders and state officials, to welcome and help entertain his young nephew, Prince Pierien, the heir to the throne of Birtoli.

The palace was in uproar as the staff tried to cater for so many guests and Anders was kept busy ensuring the arrangements met his approval. He was secretly relieved to have time to recover from all his recent excesses; he had maybe overdone it, just a bit. A week of more stately entertainment might give his stomach time to recover as it was starting to rebel against some of the more potent gifts Elliarille had begun to bring.

He was looking forward to his nephew arriving, though he did frown at the news that he was travelling on Roberion's frigate. He had been unable to find a valid reason to confiscate the ship. His councillors had advised that the ship was owned outright by Roberion and therefore the crown had no claim on it. His advisors were working on it. Elliarille was right; if anyone should have a ship it was the king.

Anders beckoned as he spotted her. "Join me later when this is over." He waved a hand over the room.

"With pleasure, Your Majesty." Ellie laughed gaily and curtseyed before turning away and melting into the crush, and the king turned his attention to the next supplicant.

It was much later when Anders retired to his room. He had passed a pleasant evening with good company and plenty of wine. He had revelled in the attention, forgetting that they only pampered his wishes because he was the king, not necessarily because they liked him.

He paused on the threshold when he saw Ellie sprawled across his bed; she was kicking her bare feet in the air and a petulant frown adorned her face. He had forgotten he had suggested she join him. He was a little worse for drink and not in the mood to placate a temperamental lady.

"Ah, my dear, apologies, the party went on longer than expected. Maybe we should do this another night?"

He missed the scowl that crossed her face as he crossed the room to lay his jacket on the chair.

"I've been waiting for ages, Anders. I can't wait another day. If you want to try it, it has to be now." Her childish voice took on a wheedling tone. "Come, join me. It won't take long and you can see if you like it."

Anders sighed, kicked off his shoes, and loosened the frills around his throat. "Very well, but I really don't see the point if I'm not going to feel the full experience."

Ellie smiled. "Oh, I'm sure you'll feel everything. Come, my dear, lay down and get comfortable."

"Tell me what it is first."

She pouted. "You want to know all my secrets, but I'll tell you this one time. This is called 'Euphoria'."

"Euphoria? Sounds promising." He lay down beside her and groaned as the room spun; he tried to sit up again, but she pushed him down.

"Come, Your Majesty, it's now or never," she purred, rubbing his chest. "Here, drink this." She held a vial against his lips and he dutifully drank it. She continued to rub his chest, undoing the buttons of his shirt as his pupils dilated. "Yes, that's right, relax into it." She watched as the drug took effect. Her hands moved over his skin and slowly moved down his body; she undid his trousers, her eyes intense, her lips parting as his body began to shudder at her touch and the drugs took over. "That's right," she crooned. "Doesn't that feel nice? See, I told you, getting rid of all those others, means more for you, and you only need me. I'm the only Sentinal you need, don't you agree, Anders?"

Anders mumbled in agreement. He'd agree to whatever she said as he long as she kept making him feel this good. He groaned as his body responded to her touch. His skin felt like it was on fire, his breathing quickening as his body tensed.

The inner door to the king's chamber opened abruptly, and she looked up furious, at the interruption. Her brother crossed the room, taking in the scene in horror. "Ellie, you can't. He's the king, for Lady's sake. Remember what I said. He is protected by the Lady, as are all of us. He will remember."

Ellie scowled at him. "He's so far gone he won't know," she whispered, trying to hold on to the fading sense of desire as Anders moaned beneath her.

"No, leave him. I found another for you; he'll work just as well."

"But he's almost there, it'll take but a moment."

"No, Ellie, it's too risky; do you want to lose all for this one moment?"

You've spoilt it," she hissed as she resisted her brother's grip.

"But there is another eagerly waiting for you," Ellaerion persuaded gently, careful not to startle her. "You'll have much more fun; he's ready for you, come, don't waste your chance. I'll tidy up here, you go on home."

Ellie allowed herself to be persuaded. She had missed her opportunity with the king. She would make her brother pay for that; her eyes brightened at the thought. Her brother was becoming such a bore, worrying about silly old men who had no right to tell them what to do. He was frowning over stupid books in his study instead of escorting her; she hated being alone. Then she remembered he had said there was one waiting for her at home. She picked up her shoes and flitted out of the chamber without another thought.

Ellaerion breathed a sigh of relief and turned back to the bed. He wrinkled his nose in distaste at the sickly smell of drugs and alcohol. Straightening the king's clothes, he left him sprawled on the bed. When the king's man arrived in the morning, he would think the king had just had too much to drink. He cleared away the vials and left the room, shutting the door behind him.

21

ELOTHIA

Birlerion stretched his back as he pulled his wagon up, glad the long day was done. He unharnessed the two horses. They were large chestnuts, one with a white flash down his nose, the other with white socks, and called Bip and Bop for some unknown reason. He found a nice thick verge of grass and drove a stake in the ground to tie them to and stood whilst they drank from the bucket before running a hand down their backs.

Searching a bit further, he found a quiet place out of sight of the others, where he went through some gentle disciplines and stretched out tired muscles unused to controlling a pair of heavy horses for such a long period. Shaking out his arms, he returned to the horses and began brushing them down, removing the layer of road dust that coated them. He wished he'd thought to have taken at least one spare shirt with him; he had never travelled anywhere so light. The rest of the evening was spent restringing the bow and repairing the arrows as best he could.

George joined him. "Yer know how to use it then?" he

asked as he watched Birlerion's nimble fingers tie off the gut and test the draw.

"Some," Birlerion admitted.

"Good ter know," George muttered, and he wandered off to find his blanket. Birlerion laid under the wagon and closed his eyes. He was soon asleep.

Someone shaking his shoulder woke Birlerion. Jerking upright, Birlerion relaxed as saw Timmin hovering over him, holding a shielded lantern. Timmin placed his finger over his lips and then beckoned him to follow. Birlerion grabbed his knives, silently rose and followed.

Timmin drew to a halt beside his wagon. "I thought you should see this," he whispered and drew back the canvas on his wagon. He sat the lantern on a box and tugged a paper wrapped package towards him. "This is was we're carrying."

"You opened it?" Birlerion asked.

"You made me curious. I don't like being taken for a fool. If someone stops me, I'm the one blamed."

"Is it just this one pack?"

"Always one."

Birlerion peeled back the paper. A dark brown wooden box, maybe two hands lengths and one wide, was partitioned into two rows of nine small compartments, eighteen in all, each one holding a small blue, glass bottle.

"What are they?" Timmin asked.

Birlerion lifted a bottle out, and wiggled the cork out of the top. Sniffing it, he jerked back as his eyes watered. "It's strong, whatever it is."

"You think this is what is causing those boys to suffer?"

"I don't know. It's potent. It could be." Birlerion sealed the bottle and replaced it in the box. He stared into the distance for a moment. "We have someone abducting young boys off the street and using them to test something that affects their minds. It is likely this has something to do with it, especially as it's being smuggled into Vespers. You're sure this is going to one of Gillian's warehouses?"

"Every time. Whichever wagon is number three, gets an extra package, a few moments before we leave."

"Do you have any idea how long this has been going on?"

"I don't know. The first time I carried one was about a year ago,"

"A year?" Birlerion gasped.

"Shh. I don't want anyone knowing I opened it."

"You'd better tie it back up then." Birlerion checked around them, but no one stirred. Only soft snores drifted across the camp. "At least we know it is coming from Elothia. Now we just have to prove Gillian is receiving it."

Timmin dragged the canvas back over the wagon. "I can't believe I didn't question this before."

"Why would you? There was no indication there was anything wrong with one package out of many."

"I knew there was something shady in the last minute delivery."

"Well, we're doing something about it now." He patted Timmin on the shoulder. "Thanks for showing me, but get some sleep. We've got a tough day tomorrow."

The next day started early, and they were on the road by sunup. Birlerion stared down the road, following the wagons. George spoke from beside him, "This stretch is not too bad. Pretty flat, a few climbs, but nothing like down by the river. Some tricky places there."

"How long you been on the wagons, George?" Birlerion asked with a grin, looking at the stocky man.

"About twenty years. Not a bad life yer know, out on the roads. It's nice seeing the country."

"Where do your family live? They must miss you being away so much."

"Jus' outside Vespers. The missus don't mind; she likes the money," George grinned, "and the peace, I expect." Birlerion laughed. "What about you? Where's your family from?" George looked at him in interest.

"Vespers. We used to live down by the old wharves before they were all knocked down and rebuilt. Rough area that was," Birlerion mused.

"I thought yer was one of them, yer got the silver eyes even though yer tries ter hide them. Those wharves were rebuilt centuries ago."

"Thank goodness, they were terrible. You wouldn't make anyone live in those conditions today."

"Wotcha doing on the wagons fer?"

"Even Sentinals need money. We need the work these days."

"That's right, the king don't use yer no more, does he." George watched him deftly manage the horses round a bend. "I'll bet yer know how to use a sword, then."

Birlerion nodded.

"Well, in that case, I know how to drive 'orses. I jus' don't like doing it. So's if we gets into some trouble, just fling me them reins and you do the fighting."

Birlerion chuckled. "Deal," he said softly. George nodded pleased.

The next day, they descended into the rolling plains that led to Tierne and the wagons rumbled down the empty roads unimpeded. They passed isolated stray boulders and curved masonry that were mostly hidden by the swaying grasses; signs that the ruins were near. The air was heavy as the ruins rose around them, tall shattered columns and leaning grey plinths, a desolate scene. A soft mist began to swirl around them. "George, would you walk ahead, make sure we don't lose the road?" Birlerion suggested.

George nodded, "Jus' don't run me over," he said with a grunt as he climbed down from the slow-moving wagon. Birlerion slowed the horses even more, hoping the wagon behind him was alert. George walked in between the horses, looking nervously around him. The voices ahead of them were muffled, dampened by the swirling mist, deadening the sound. Shadows loomed up beside them and then faded away. The horse's hooves were loud in the moist air, which left beads of water on everything it touched. Visibility dropped to a few feet in front of them, and Birlerion kept his eyes on George.

And then suddenly they were out into bright sunlight and there was quite a gap between them and the wagon in front. He waited for George to climb back aboard, and he shook up the horses to catch up. The ruins receded behind them.

Two days later, they began to climb the first of the steep hills. The road kept turning back on itself as it worked its way upwards. The horses strained as they turned around the sharp bend, the harness jinking as they struggled. Birlerion urged them on, and the wagon jerked as they took the strain and pulled them around. He eased off as they pulled up to the next corner. Swinging wide, he tried to help the horses pull it round the bend, and they straightened up and continued.

As they crested the rise, Birlerion could see the next hill before them and then the river winding its way down through flatter plains towards the valley that led into Deepwater. Having given Bip and Bop a breather on the run down, George frantically manning the brake, they began the last tricky rise. Birlerion rotated his shoulders as they began the pull up. The sheer rock face rising beside them crowded them towards the edge of the road, where a steep drop down a ravine to the river was gradually deepening as they rose. There wasn't a lot of room to manoeuvre.

George peered over the edge and hung on tight to the side of the wagon. "Once we're up here, it's much better," he said, his knuckles whitening as he tightened his grip. "This is the worst bit."

Birlerion urged the horses on, and they took the strain. They would have to stop after this rise; the horses wouldn't be able to take much more. He hoped the other wagons would make the same decision.

The sound of falling rock had him looking up urgently. Pebbles and grit clattered down around them, and he shook the reins to quicken the horses. Larger rocks began to fall, bouncing off the cliff face and sailing over their heads.

Bip shied as a larger boulder clattered under his feet, and Birlerion struggled to keep the horses straight. More rocks clattered around them, ricocheting off the wagon and he heard George grunt heavily beside him and yelled to get the horses moving. Birlerion flinched as his cheek stung, a ricochet had caught his face, but he concentrated on the horses. Birlerion could hear the men on the wagons behind him shouting, and he risked a glance over his shoulder. They had halted. One of the horses had reared and got tangled in its traces. The driver was desperately trying to unbuckle it whilst ducking more falling debris.

This was no place to be stopping. The horses would struggle to move a dead weight on the hill. Movement above caught his eye, and he narrowed his eyes as scanned the side of the ravine. Shadows flickered, and he saw the point of an arrow jutting down at the wagon train. He threw the reins at George. He had the bow and arrows out of the box and nocked before George had even gathered the reins. Birlerion watched the cliff face, arrow ready. He released and reached for the next arrow, climbing onto the back of the wagon. He was aware George had pulled the horses to halt as a large boulder sailed over the head of the horses and carried on down the ravine. Someone was deliberately dropping rocks on them.

"Shelter behind the wagon. There are bandits above us," he called, dropping down to the ground as more boulders rained down on them. They glanced off the wagon and he heard one of the horses squeal. The sliding clatter of stone eased, and he peered around the wagon. A shower of arrows thudded into the wood and tarpaulin. He jerked back, and then rose, releasing his arrow at target after target, and moved down to the next wagon. "Is anyone hurt?"

The men stared at him wildly and shook their heads.

"Get the horse untangled, we need to move," he said sharply as he climbed up onto the wagon, searching the cliff face. He returned to his own wagon. "You alright?" he asked George, who was holding his right arm.

"I think I broke it," he said, sounding bewildered.

"Can you hold on long enough for us to get out of here? We'll look at it at the top. Do you think you can release the brake on my word?" Birlerion boosted him up and followed. Grabbing the reins, he shook up the horses. They pulled forward and took the strain. "Release," Birlerion barked, and George struggled to release the brake. The horses pulled, and for a moment, Birlerion thought they were going to roll backwards, but the wagon moved, and they began to climb the hill again. Once they were moving, he glanced at George, who was looking quite pale, but game.

"Giv' us the reins, those bandits could be still up there," George said grimly, holding out his left hand. Birlerion handed them over without comment and took up his bow again, scanning the rising rock above them. He heard the thrum and flicked his bow out, deflecting the arrow away. He sighted an arrow towards the direction the arrow had come from, and as George urged the horses on, the curving rock face revealed an upper path, and he began shooting until he ran out of arrows.

They reached the top of the climb, and Birlerion stood on the back of the wagon watching the other wagons follow, the odd arrow stuck out of the wood, but it seemed that everyone had come out whole, or at least only slightly damaged. Birlerion touched his cheek and came away with blood.

He sat back down and took the reins off George, and they rolled down into a village north of the Deepwater border. Birlerion pulled up near the waterhole and jumped down. He helped George down, guiding him over to a nearby tree. He was looking quite grey in the face. Easing off George's shirt, he could see the massive bruise on his forearm. Birlerion gently felt his arm; the break was quite clear. "We need a healer," he said, glancing up as the other men crowded round. "Can one of you go see if there is a healer in the village?" he asked as he rested George's arm in his lap. "Don't move," he said. He came back with the rough makings of a splint and a canteen of water. Immobilising George's forearm as best he could, he cut one of the blankets down and made a makeshift sling. He offered George the canteen. "Sorry it's not something stronger," he said with a grin.

George chuckled. "You're wasted on the wagons, yer know, but I'm glad yer here."

"Rest, I need to check the horses." Birlerion covered him with the remains of the blanket and returned to the horses. He knew one of them had been hurt. Releasing them from the wagon, he took them to the water. Bip was nodding slightly and running his hand down his shoulder. Birlerion felt the heat and the swelling. Scooping the water up, he rinsed Bip's shoulder down. He remembered seeing a bale of cloth on the wagon, and he went to look, easing some of the material out when he found it.

He soaked it in the water and tied it in place on Bip's shoulder. He led the horses back to the wagon and tethered them next to it, leaving them a long enough rein to graze. Returning to George, he replaced the make-shift sling with a more supportive one made out of the cloth. And then he sat down next to him with a grunt.

George eased his shoulder. "That feels better, thank 'ee." He closed his eyes. "Do yer think they'll follow us here then?" He had seen the sword on Birlerion's belt.

"Best to be prepared, though to be honest, I'm not sure there's much we can do if the bandits turn up," Birlerion said, closing his eyes. He eased his aching back.

"Depends who they are and how many are left, I suppose," George said with a chuckle. "Shame you can't collect yer arrows."

"True," Birlerion replied, opening his eyes at the sound of approaching feet. He stood as he saw the wagoneer return, accompanied by a competent looking Captain of the Elothian Chevron.

The captain saw Birlerion, and his eyes widened. "Sentinal, what are you doing here?" he asked in surprise.

Birlerion laughed. "Just earning a crust, captain, just earning a crust."

The captain looked horrified. "Surely not. The Grand Duke would not treat you so."

"The world changes, captain. It seems you have a bandit problem in Elothia. We were attacked on the last rise coming here."

He nodded. "So your man said. I've sent a unit out to check. I'm Skellan, Second Chevron. We don't have a healer, but we have a basic field kit if that is of use?" He looked at George and crouched down to inspect his arm. "I doubt we have anything that will improve on what you've already done though," he said as he stood again. "But we can sort your face."

"Thank you, captain, I'm Bernie," Birlerion said briefly. "Some pain killers would help. I have none on me, and if there is any bran for the horses, they could do with a good meal after today, as could all of us I think."

The captain nodded. "That I can help with. I'll send some men down to look after your horses. You can come back to my camp. A good meal will set you up for tomorrow. Where are you going?"

"Back to Vespers," Birlerion said as he helped George rise, and they slowly walked up the road towards the camp, the other wagoneers following them hesitantly. "Did you see any other wagons come through here earlier?"

"Yes, six or seven came through a couple of chimes ago. They didn't stop; they went straight to the crossing. They probably camped the other side of the river."

"We'll have to try and catch up with them tomorrow." He looked back at the weary men stumbling behind them. "We're all beat."

"I can send a messenger, ask them to wait for you if you like," the captain offered.

"We'd appreciate it, Captain Skellan. I'm sure we'd all prefer to travel back together."

The captain's hospitality even extended to a bedroll in a tent and a shaving kit, and after steaming hot bowls of the iniquitous fish soup always found in Elothia, the weary men bedded down without complaint. Birlerion made sure George was dosed up, and he accepted a couple of extra packets of the pain relief powder for the following day as he was sure George would need it. He submitted to having his face cleaned, though he refused the offered bandage. There was no way he was travelling to vespers with a bandage round his head. He carefully scraped off his growing stubble, wincing at the bruise on his cheek. But after sluicing his face clean, he felt much better. It was worth it.

He awoke at dawn and peered out of the tent. George was still gently snoring, so he left him a bit longer and strolled down to the wagons. Bip and Bop looked content. They had been given a good brushing by the looks of it, and the tack had been cleaned. He wondered why the captain was being so considerate.

He found out when he got back to camp. "Sentinal Birlerion," Captain Skellan greeted him, and Birlerion scanned the tents, hoping none of the men had heard. How had the captain found out who he was? "It's an honour to meet you."

"Just Bernie will do. I'd prefer it if few knew I was on the wagons."

"As you wish. My men collected a few of your arrows." The captain handed him them. "Your skill is legendary. There weren't any bandits left to catch. You couldn't be anyone else."

Birlerion looked at him in surprise. "But I didn't really see them. I couldn't have killed them all."

The captain's lips twitched. "Well, each arrow hit true. At least this road should be safe for a while."

Birlerion smiled. "I suppose so, till the next time. If I could ask a favour? Would you pass a message to Sentinal Allarion at the Summer Palace to pass on to Taurillion for me? Could he tell Taurillion where we are? Taurillion is supposed to be meeting me in Vespers, but he has no idea when I'm arriving. We're at least six or seven days out, assuming we don't meet any other obstacles."

Skellan grinned and gave him a quick salute. "Be my pleasure, sir."

Birlerion rolled his eyes at the captain's persistence. It wasn't worth arguing about seeing his name was pretty famous in Elothia. With a sigh, he went to rouse the others. They needed to get back on the road.

22

KING'S PALACE, OLD VESPERS

Ellaerion circulated the throne room, listening for any gossip, keeping a pulse on the news. He blended into the colourful throng and listened. The king was in a bad mood, hungover they said. As long as that was all it was. Ellaerion drifted closer to the throne to make sure. The king certainly looked like he was in a foul mood. His face was pasty, and his eyes were heavy.

Anders caught sight of the blond haired Sentinal. "Ellaerion, where is your sister?"

"She is in town, Your Majesty," he said. "She went for a dress fitting or something because you said you liked her in blue, and she was determined to find a gown you would adore."

Anders frowned. "Was I supposed to meet her last night? I misremember."

"Yes, Your Majesty, but I understand you told her it would have to be another night. She was a little peeved. You know what women are like." He smiled. "I believe she had brought you something, especially for you."

"Ah yes, she wanted me to try Euphoria, didn't she?"

Ellaerion's breath caught. Did he remember after all? "I'm not sure what it was called, Your Majesty. You'll have to ask her when next you see her."

Anders nodded. "Please offer her my apologies if I mistook the day."

"Of course, Your Majesty." Ellaerion bowed himself away in relief and went to find his sister. He found her still asleep in her rooms. He had carried her there after she had finished with the young man he had brought her. It was getting more and more difficult to satisfy her. She preferred to drug them herself. Seeing them succumb to the influence of the drugs was part of the trip for her, which meant he had to restrain them without the convenience of putting them to sleep. It also meant that they'd seen him, and he couldn't afford for them to talk afterwards.

She had progressed from seducing maybe one man every few months to one every few weeks. She was becoming insatiable, and Ellaerion was afraid her increasing demands would give them away. Vespers wasn't all that big of a city. Too many unexplained deaths would be noticed.

He looked down at her. She would sleep for a few more chimes at least. She looked so sweet and innocent, like a child, but it was a woman's appetite that drove her, and him. Unfortunately, the man had survived her attentions this time. Ellaerion had dumped his well inebriated body outside a dive down by the wharves. No one would believe his stories of being attacked for his body. It would be passed off as wishful thinking.

Ellaerion sat as his desk and rifled through his correspondence. He hated it here in Vespers; it was nothing like he remembered. The people were more direct and demanding, and there were a lot more of them. He rested his face in his hands. He supposed it was a good thing for nights like last night, but he wanted to get away from the smell, find some peace away from everyone. Be himself for a while, relax.

Instead, he had to cater to his sister's whims and procure men on demand. It at least kept her hands off him. He shuddered as unwanted memories surfaced. She seemed to think any male body belonged to her to do with as she wished. The more you resisted, the more she wanted you. He had learnt that one the hard way.

If only they had something to do, it might occupy her overactive desires, but the king had disbanded the Sentinals, sent them into retirement, denied them entry into any of the other services. Those in the other territories reported that their roles were unchanged. Even in the Watches it seemed Sentinals were appreciated; it was only King Anders who didn't want them.

Ellie wouldn't relocate, no matter how persuasive he was. They could go to another Watch, another country even. He had always fancied living in the islands, amongst the warm seas. A few Sentinals had moved down there. But she had her sights set on the king, and she wasn't going to give up.

Ellaerion had a sense of impending doom, which only deepened the following day when he arrived at court and found the king actually behaving like a king, remote and austere. His throne room was elegantly bedecked in flowers, the mosaic on the floor gleaming in the lamp light. Someone had been busy cleaning. The smell of soap and polish was in the air as if all the previous decadence could be washed away.

He found Elliarille moping in the outer chambers. "He says he's too busy to see me," she complained, scuffing the toe of her slipper on the floor. "Me! He wants to see me soon enough when he wants something."

"Hush, Ellie, keep your voice down. He's the king, what did you expect?"

"I am so close. He's almost there, a few more days."

"I told you, you can't use the king, he is too protected."

Ellie laughed under her breath. "His protections are down, his guard dog is away. He's mine."

Ellaerion frowned at her, "Away? What do you mean?"

"All the other Sentinals are banned, and Birlerion left Vespers. He won't be glaring at us, spoiling our fun." Her face took on a calculating expression. "After the king, maybe it's time for me to get to know Birlerion a little better. He would do wonderfully well."

"Where did Birlerion go?"

Ellie shrugged. "I neither know or care. At least he's gone."

"Ellie," Ellaerion exhaled in exasperation, "you know he's been asking questions. *Where did he go?*"

"I don't know," Ellie snapped, losing her patience. "Ask Benarte or Gillian or one of the others. One of them said he had gone. They were just as interested in where he went as you are. I overheard them. I'm sure they'll be happy to discuss him with you."

"Ellie, please, Lord Benarte or Lord Gillian, you have to be careful with these people. They are very conscious of their position. That's what makes them useful to us, but pay them some respect."

Ellie glared at him, her eyes flashing. "You go lick their boots if you want to. They should be paying *us* respect. We are the Sentinals. We knew the Lady. Where were they?" Ellaerion watched her flounce out of the chambers; she was becoming uncontrollable.

The next day, Ellie was walking through the palace's formal gardens when the arrival of many horses interrupted her concentration. She strolled along the terrace and caught sight of Mikke arriving. She watched him intently, tapping her lip. Jerrolion's son. Now wouldn't he be a coup. He looked very handsome astride a gleaming black stallion. He blithely jumped down and ran a hand down the neck of his horse. Looking up, he laughed at something the dark-haired Sentinal who had arrived with him said. He dismissed his guards with a quick word. She frowned at the sight of Serenion at his shoulder. She would have to detach him. What was an Elothian doing here in Vespiri anyway? She would have words with the king. He should banish him back to where he came from.

That evening, the formal presentation began, and Anders welcomed Prince Pierien of Birtoli to Vespiri. The evening was one of glittering opulence and elegant dining. Ellie yawned delicately behind her fan; this was so boring. She idly looked down the table, frowning as she caught sight of Lord Jennery and his wife, Lady Alyssa, and another Sentinal, Tagerillion, who stood behind them. What was he doing here? Lord Mikkeal was seated not far from them. He was entertaining a young girl, who was watching the room wide-eyed. Obviously her first presentation at court then. Ellie dismissed her and moved on.

Commander Bryce and his wife, Lady Olivia, were seated at the head table, and she seemed to be occupying the young prince. There was little entertainment for a boy of his age at this court, she thought drearily. She sighed as another plate was placed before her. How many more courses were they going to have to sit through?

Saranne leaned towards Mikke. "Do we have to eat all of this?" she asked, staring at the plate. "I'm not sure I've got room."

"Just take a taste of every plate. No one will notice if you don't eat it," Mikke reassured her. "How are you enjoying Vespers?"

"Very well, there is so much to see. But I'm afraid we go home tomorrow."

"Are you not staying for the ball?" Mikke asked, feeling slightly disappointed.

"I don't think so. My father said the king didn't want him to stay away from his Watch for too long."

Mikke frowned at that but let it pass. "Won't you have time to see Jared?"

"We saw him this morning. He is loving the rangers. He had permission to see us for a chime as we were here. My father arranged it, I believe. Have you seen Leyarille?"

"I hope to see her later in the week," Mikke said, making a mental note to arrange it. He hadn't thought.

"I'm sure she'll like that. I wasn't sure if you would have time."

He would speak to Commander Stafford later and make sure he did.

Saranne sighed. "I know you'll think me unaccountably stupid, but which lord is seated by the king? I keep muddling them up."

"I would never think such a thing." Mikke smiled into her deep blue eyes, and she smiled back, mesmerised by his vivid aquamarine eyes.

Mikke broke eye contact and began a little breathlessly to describe who was who. "Lord Pelori is the elderly gentleman next to the king. He is the Lord Chancellor, the head of the Administration, which runs the country for the king. Next to him is his wife, Lady Amabel. Then you have Lord Benarte who is the Administrator for Trade. He is responsible for the movement of goods in and out of Vespiri and Terolia. His wife, Lady Susan, then Lord Gillian, who is the Administrator for Transport. He's the one you can blame for the state of our roads," he said with a smile, and Saranne laughed. Mikke wracked his brain for something else that would make her laugh. Her face lit up when she laughed, and her eyes sparkled when she looked at him.

Their plates were removed and small wine glasses replaced the larger ones. Mikke smiled. "We've reached desert," he said. "You'll be happy to know we'll stop eating soon."

Saranne frowned at him. "How do you know?"

"These are dessert wine glasses. The wine is much sweeter, so you get less of it." Though he had noticed she hadn't touched any of the wine. "Would you like some more water?" he offered.

"Oh," she smiled at him and his heart flipped. "May I?"

"Of course." He signalled a footman and made the request. Two tumblers were brought and filled.

"Thank you," she said in relief as she took a gulp.

The meal progressed, and Mikke rose with regret when the king signalled the meal was at an end and escorted Prince Pierien away. It was quite late, and there would be no further entertainment. The guests began to make their way to their rooms, or their carriages if they lived in the city.

The next morning, the king and some of his lords took Pierien out hunting, though what they would find on such a hot day Mikke had no idea. Mikke had not been invited and so found his way to the king's library, where he perused the book shelves and spent a quiet afternoon reading. Mikke was disappointed to find Saranne had been correct the following evening. She was not present at the ball, nor was Lord Jennery or Lady Alyssa.

He drifted up to the trim Lord of East Watch. "Lord Marcus," he greeted him. "How was your journey?"

"Long, much like yours," the Lord said with a grin. He'd had to travel the length of the country like Mikke.

"Yes, the roads don't improve much, do they? We'll have to mention it to Gillian. I hear Randolf has been improving his roads extensively."

"The Grand Duke," Lord Marcus said repressively, "has more roads to improve."

Mikke laughed. "Then you would have thought ours would be in excellent condition."

"Makes you wonder what they do, doesn't it?"

"Indeed. Did you see Jennery and Alyssa? Unfortunately, they couldn't stay for tonight."

"So I heard." Lord Marcus looked at Mikke, a warning in his eyes. "You might want to slip away earlier yourself. The court is not too healthy this time of year. Things get overheated. Those who can, are wise to remove to the country where it's cooler."

Mikke nodded. "I'll bear it in mind Lord Marcus." He turned with a smile as someone tapped his arm. His smile slipped when he saw who it was. He bowed. "My lady."

Ellie smiled coquettishly at him. "My Lord Mikkeal, I have noticed you have yet to dance. I lack a partner."

Mikkeal turned back to Marcus, rolling his eyes as he bowed. "Excuse me," he said as he held out his hand and led her onto the floor. She was a good dancer, and Mikke found himself twirling around the floor. A delicate floral scent drifted under his nose, light and sweet. He wrinkled his nose as they danced.

"You dance well, my lord," she said, moving closer. The scent grew stronger.

"As do you, my lady. It is a pleasure to dance with you."

"That is good," she breathed, smiling down at him. She was taller than him, but then she would be, she was a Sentinal. He had forgotten for a moment. "I look forward to another dance later then," she said as the music drew to an end. He bowed as she curtsied, and he watched her sashay away, a slight frown on his face. He was claimed for another dance and the evening passed by.

Mikke was taking the opportunity to grab a drink when he realised he was standing next to Prince Pierien. "Your highness," he said carefully, with a bow towards the slender young man. "Were you looking for something in particular?"

"A glass of water would be most welcome," the prince replied, "but I cannot see any."

Mikke signalled a footman and procured the water for him. He should just carry a jug around with him, he thought with smile.

"Thank you," the prince said as he drank deeply. "I'm supposed to be used to heat, but this room is stifling."

"The terrace is just out here if you would like to take some air," Mikke said, indicating a door. "The doors should be open really, but the light attracts the bugs; they are a nuisance this time of year." He led the way out onto the terrace. A few other people had had the same idea, and their voices carried on the still air. The terrace was lit by torches, the flames tall in the cooler evening air.

Pierien sighed as he joined Mikke. "What a relief. How are you, Lord Mikkeal? It's a while since you were last in Birtoli."

"Yes, it seems the older we get, the less opportunity there is for travel. And I have a Watch to keep now," Mikke replied.

"Yes, congratulations by the way. I saw your father recently. He was in Molinti."

"How was he?" Mikke asked, his face brightening.

Prince Pierien laughed. "Very relaxed, enjoying retirement, he said. Your mother was extremely happy to be back in Molinti too. My mother was pleased to see her."

"Moliniti? I thought they went to Senti."

"They did," the prince said dryly. "But once m'father

heard they were there, he had Roberion bring them to the palace."

Mikke laughed, relieved. "I was worried about him," he admitted.

Prince Pierien smiled. "Don't be, they seem quite happy. Though I will say, I believe it was your father who persuaded my father to send me here."

"Why do you think that?"

Pierien shrugged. "Just a feeling I had. I expected Sentinal Birlerion to be here," he said, changing the topic.

"I did too, but I haven't seen him. The king is not a fan of Sentinals at the moment."

"I noted the lack. Birtoli would welcome any Sentinal that wished to relocate. We have but Roberion. I have long thought we were underrepresented."

Mikke laughed. "Serenion, did you hear that?"

Serenion chuckled from the shadows. "I thank you for the offer, your highness, but I'm used to cooler climates. Stoneford will do for me."

"Shame," the prince said. He took a deep breath. "I suppose I ought to return. It was a pleasure speaking with you, Lord Mikkeal." He bowed and returned to the ballroom, his own guard at his shoulder.

Mikkeal looked along the terrace and sighed. "I suppose we ought to return as well," he said, following the prince back in doors.

23

OLD VESPERS

Leyarille stepped out of the waystone behind the Chapterhouse with Taurillion close behind her. She fussed Kino as Taurillion gazed around him with wide eyes.

"I'd forgotten how much it's changed," Taurillion said, gripping the reins of his horse.

"We'll leave Kino at the hostelry. You'll probably need to use it too if you're staying at Birlerion's place while he's away. I'm afraid the king is not very welcoming of Sentinals at the palace."

"Lead on. Birlerion wanted me to keep an eye on the city anyway." He kept glancing back at the Chapterhouse as Leyarille led him through the streets.

"He'll be back soon," she murmured to Kin'arol as she stabled him. He looked forlorn without Birlerion. "I'll come and see you every day, I promise," she said as she sprinkled some Baliweed in his haynet, and he nudged her before dipping his head. Leyarille and Taurillion rode through the city streets, up the switchback and into the palace courtyard, where lads ran out to take their horses.

Bryce rose in surprise as Leyarille led Taurillion into his office. "Taurillion, what are you doing here?"

Taurillion grinned. "Birlerion asked nicely," he replied.

Bryce laughed. "Good, so where is he?"

"He's tracking the supply route for the drugs. He believes he's found the wagon that's transporting the drugs here to Vespers." Leyarille said. "He's driving one of the wagon's back as part of a wagon train."

"Alone?" Bryce asked. "I told him to be careful!"

"It's been four days since Birlerion left Retarfu. He's probably just south of Tierne now." Taurillion pointed at the map on the wall. "He'll be at least another seven or eight days. I thought I'd take the time to familiarise myself with Vespers. It's nothing like I remember." He smiled at Bryce. "I can't believe I've not been here in the last ten years. I'd forgotten how different it is now. I was expecting the old Vespers; it is very disorientating."

Bryce nodded thoughtfully. "I suppose we'll have to arrange a welcome for them. We don't want those drugs spreading through the city. Do you know where they are going in Old Vespers?"

"Birlerion was hoping to track the package to it owner." Leyarille screwed up her face. "Wouldn't we scare them off if too many soldiers appear in the warehousing district?" She didn't think Birlerion would be amused if he lost this opportunity to prove who was involved.

"Stafford will handle it. The rangers know how to be discreet." Bryce said. "Parsillion will be glad to see you. He has been watching the docks and the warehouses. I am sure he'll be glad of your help. He can give you a tour." Bryce looked at Leyarille. "Could you see if you can find Parsillion and bring him here? Taurillion, please sit. How is Owen?"

"Much the same. He seems to have finally settled into life

as a commander. He did resist for quite a while, but Guin'yyfer wore him down in the end. Randolf is pleased."

Bryce chuckled. "Jerrol always said he was one of the most reluctant officers he had ever met."

"Where is Jerrol? Birlerion mentioned the situation here, but he didn't really go into much detail. Randolf was trying to recruit him, unsuccessfully I may add. I can assure you, Randolf would welcome more Sentinals as he has so few."

Bryce scowled. "Jerrol went to Senti. We haven't heard from him since." He grinned. "Except for an unscheduled state visit from Prince Pierien. I can see his hand in that."

"Maybe the prince will remind the king of his obligations," Taurillion murmured.

"We can always hope," Bryce agreed. He looked up as Parsillion entered his office. "Parsillion, look who's arrived." He left the two Sentinals to greet each other and nodded at Leyarille. "Thank you, Cadet Haven, that will be all. You ought to get back to your unit."

Leyarille wanted to protest, but she caught herself and saluted, leaving his office. She still had Birlerion's belongings, so she took them with her back to her barracks. Stacking his sword and the new bow beside her bed, she slid his pack underneath it out of sight. It was comforting having his things around her. She wondered how he was getting on. A stubborn look came over her face. He had told her to meet him with his sword and bow, and meet him she would. She went off to find her unit.

Birlerion was relieved when they finally passed into Deepwater. Even though the countryside looked the same, he felt like he was home. The guards at the border gave the wagons a cursory checking, and Birlerion frowned as he watched them. They were waved on, and he obediently followed the wagon in front of him. He would have words with Jennery if he thought that was an appropriate border control, especially with the directive Bryce was supposed to have sent out. It took them another two days to travel down through Deepwater to Greenswatch. Birlerion watched the Grove pass with longing eyes, but he resisted the temptation to stop and visit.

He became quite friendly with the men on the wagons behind him after the bandit incident. They shared their fire and coffee and fussed over George as much as he'd let them. He hadn't seen much of Timmin, but that was probably for the best, and he didn't try to find him.

They picked up the East Road and began the final leg. Birlerion couldn't wait to get home and have a bath. There was sleeping rough and *sleeping rough*. These wagoneers didn't know what the word comfort meant. Few hot meals and fewer stops where there were any amenities. The spectacular rainbow-coloured bruising on his cheek was hidden by a stubbly beard. He had lost weight too. He had hardly eaten for the last two weeks. He could kill for a proper cup of kafinee too. The stuff they brewed on the road was disgusting. He didn't know how they did it day after day, but they didn't complain or gripe. The wagon trail was their home.

Twelve days after leaving Retarfu, they rumbled into Vespers just as the sky was streaked in virulent reds and oranges as the sun descended behind the king's palace. The palace walls glowed as if a fire truly burned within them.

Following the King's Road up from the docks, they swung onto the new road, and passed the Chapterhouse leading to the warehouse district. Birlerion eased his back and straightened. He called Ari and when the little creature appeared beside him, he discreetly handed him a note. "For Leyarille," he whispered as Ari hovered for a moment before blinking out again. Birlerion had deliberated about involving Leyarille, but he was sure she still had his sword and bow, and even if he didn't tell her when he arrived, she would be waiting for him.

"Nearly home, George. You'll be glad to get off this wagon, won't you?" He grinned at the weary man next to him. George had ridden beside him most of the way without complaint, obstinately refusing help, even though Birlerion knew he had struggled the first few days. He was a good man, and Birlerion didn't want him caught up in whatever was going to unfold next. "Can I drop you anywhere on the way? I can deal with the unloading," he suggested.

"Nah, got to get my money anyway. I know I won't be much help, but I can hold the 'orses for yer."

Birlerion nodded. He knew he wouldn't be able to change his mind. The wagons before him started peeling off as men waved numbered boards at them. He kept going. Timmin drew his wagon into the gaping doorway of a warehouse. A man waved a board with the number 8 on it, so Birlerion pulled in behind him. Timmin twisted in his seat and watched Birlerion with worried eyes.

Birlerion steered his horses into the dim, echoey warehouse beside Timmin's wagon, and George engaged the brake. The doors screeched closed behind them, shutting out the light. "What's the usual procedure here?" he murmured, preparing to dismount.

George shot him a sharp glance. "They unload us and then we pull on out t'other side and go get paid."

Birlerion stuck out his hand. "It's been a pleasure, George. Don't stick around once you're unloaded, alright?"

George nodded slowly. "If you ses so."

"I do, this is not your fight."

"I thought there was more t'yer than just wanting a bit 'o

brass," George replied, watching him closely. Birlerion laughed and jumped down.

A foreman yelled instructions and half of the men swarming around Timmin's wagon peeled off to Birlerion's wagon, and Birlerion began to unwind the rope and flung it over the other side. A swarthy, dark-haired man with a grubby blue scarf round his throat arrived and unwound the rope and flung it back to Birlerion, and they worked their way down the wagon.

Once uncovered, more men arrived and the wagon was unloaded. Birlerion watched as the men work in efficient silence. The horses stirred, their hooves loud on the stone floor as a man suddenly appeared out of the depths of the warehouse, escorted by three guards.

"Are these the wagons from Retarfu?" The man's sharp voice cut through the thick silence, and Birlerion slowly tugged his cap down as he recognised the voice. He hadn't expected Lord Gillian to come himself. The foreman hurried across the warehouse and Gillian waited for him in the shadows, an indistinct form draped in a black cape. No one would know he was there if he hadn't spoken. There was a brief conversation between Gillian and the foreman, and then they disappeared into deeper shadows. There must be offices out back or something because they didn't return.

Birlerion tipped his cap at George. "I wouldn't hang about, if I were you," he said as he slapped Bop's rump. George grinned at him and shook up the horses, and the wagon rumbled out. Birlerion headed for the dim passageway that led under the wooden stairs as Timmin's wagon followed George's out of the warehouse. At least they were clear of any trouble that might be brewing.

Hand against the rough wood slats, and the aroma of timber filling his nose, Birlerion ventured down the passage and halted at sound of low voices. He peered around the corner and jerked back. A dull yellow gleam seeped under the door, illuminating the rough features of two of Gillian's guards. Listening intently, he recognised Gillian's strident tones, he was upset about something, and the foreman was whining. "We had nowhere else to take him. She didn't want him."

"Why not? What was wrong with him?"

Birlerion could imagine the foreman shrugging. "We attempted delivery. It was refused. You still owe us."

"Not if you didn't deliver the goods."

"The lads won't take it kindly if you don't pay them."

"Is that threat? Because if it is, those will be the last words you ever say." Birlerion shivered at the vicious edge to Gillian's voice. "Get rid of the boy. We can't afford for him to talk. And what's this about there being an ambush on the road?"

"Bandits in Elothia. Lucky one of the drivers knew how to use a bow."

"Who?"

"Dunno. Who cares? At least the wagons got through safely. I told you we need guards on the wagons."

"We don't want to draw attention to them. Find out who the driver is. Maybe you can use *him* as a guard next time."

"Maybe. You will be paying us to dispose of the lad, now, won't you?"

"Just do it," Gillian hissed. He wrenched the door open, and his guards stiffened to attention. He spoke to the brute of a man, a third guard who had been in the office with him. "Lerat! We have a problem. Make sure he deals with it." Gillian stalked off down the corridor with two of his guards leaving Lerat to wait for the foreman.

The foreman cursed under his breath. "This way," he snapped and stomped after Gillian. Birlerion followed silently behind them. The men entered an adjoining warehouse, and

Birlerion wrestled briefly with the need to follow Gillian, but a boy's life hung in the balance, and it wasn't really a decision after all. He entered the warehouse.

The two men strode across the echoey space, their footsteps loud. "He's in the back office," the foreman said, his voice resigned.

Birlerion took the longer route around the perimeter of the building. He couldn't afford one of them glancing behind them and catching him in the middle of an empty warehouse. Wishing he had his bow, and not just George's sword and his dagger, he briefly wondered where Taurillion was. Had Leyarille received his message? No matter, he would deal with it himself.

Reaching the other side of the warehouse, he peered around the partition and saw another corridor of offices much the same as the other warehouse. Silently he worked his way down the passage, passed darkened offices until he reached the door with a glow around the frame. Taking a deep breath and gripping his sword, he barged in, not waiting to adjust to the sudden glare of lamplight. He threw his dagger at the largest person he saw hoping it would slow them down. He had a brief glimpse of a young lad, bound hand and foot, wide frightened eyes, three men standing over him, and then he concentrated on the guard rushing towards him. The clash of steel was loud in the confined space. Birlerion didn't waste time with fighting nice, he was outnumbered and tired. He blocked the strike and drove his fist into the man's face, dropping him with one punch. As he turned to the next man rushing him, he hissed at the sting of metal slicing across his ribs, and he instinctively blocked, forcing the man's arm away, and followed it up with a jab of his own. The screech of the main doors opening distracted the foreman who scowled as he lunged at Birlerion.

Birlerion deflected his strike as the huge man, Lerat,

pulled the dagger out of his shoulder and threw it at Birlerion who danced back, allowing the blade to harmlessly thunk into the wall.

With a roar of frustration, Lerat lunged for Birlerion, his huge hands closing around his neck. Birlerion twisted, driving his sword into the man's stomach, but the vice around his neck squeezed tighter and sparkly pinpoints of light clouded his vision. He struggled for breath as he clawed at the man's hands but he couldn't loosen them.

Birlerion heard a dull thud, followed by a second and the vice released him. Birlerion collapsed to the floor, gasping for breath.

"Birlerion? Are you alright?" Jared leaned over him.

Birlerion squinted at him. "What are you doing here?" he croaked. His throat was raw; his voice gravelly.

"I came with Leyarille. We've been watching the warehouses for the last two nights. We saw you arrive."

Squinting across the room, Birlerion saw Leyarille standing in the doorway, bow drawn, arrow knocked. The foreman had backed away from her and was standing against the wall, his hands in the air. Gillian's guard was skewered by two arrows, Leyarille's work no doubt.

"You arrived just in time. Check the boy," Birlerion said, his voice harsh.

Jared patted his shoulder and then knelt by the shuddering boy and pulled down the gag. Coughing, the boy drew in a noisy breath, and Jared gripped his shoulder. "You're safe now, no one else is going to hurt you." He used his dagger to saw through the ropes binding him, and the boy gingerly rubbed his raw wrists.

Jared smiled encouragingly. "It's all over, they won't hurt you now," he repeated. Close up the boy's body was a mass of bruising, many already deepening to a purple. His shirt had been ripped off him and hung in tatters around his arms.

Leyarille hovered over them and stayed alert. "Taurillion is around somewhere," she said. "He was checking the other warehouses." The sound of running feet had her backing out the door. A quick glance and she was back.

Birlerion rose to his feet. "Don't even think it," he said to the foreman as Taurillion skidded through the door.

"Birlerion! Are you alright?"

Birlerion frowned at Taurillion. "You took your time." He shrugged out of his jacket and offered it to the boy

"You weren't where you said we were supposed to meet," Taurillion replied. "I had to check all the warehouses. You were lucky I ran into Timmin, and he told me you were down here."

"Well, there are two men here who were attempting to kill this boy. You can take them to the Justicers. We need to get the boy to a healer and then we'll report to Bryce."

"What about you? You're bleeding too," Leyarille said.

"None of it is mine, I'm fine," Birlerion replied, turning away from her concerned stare. "Jared, go check if there is anything in the office. Paperwork, invoices, lists, anything, especially if it references Elothia, Euphoria, or dust."

Jared nodded and went off to search.

Birlerion tugged at his arrows, but they were embedded deep. Leyarille's aim had been deadly. Exhaling, he crouched over the body. He was sure she would be horrified later. He could see it in her eyes, the shock of what she had done just hadn't hit her yet. His side twinged as he rose, and he looked down in surprise. Leyarille had been right he had taken a wound. His shirt was slowly turning red, and he sat down, suddenly queasy.

Soft hands held him upright. "Are you alright?"

Birlerion smiled at Leyarille in surprise. "You were right, I did take a hit. I didn't feel it."

She huffed and lifted his shirt and then slowly raised her eyes to his. "I can't believe you don't feel that."

Birlerion groaned. "I said I *didn't* feel it. I can now," he said as his side began to burn. Leyarille helped him out of his shirt and pressed it against the deep cut on his ribs.

"Taurillion, see if you can find something to tie this in place. He can't hold it. We should always have a supply of bandages with us."

Birlerion chuckled. "Your mother always used to say that." He winced as she pressed hard. He looked up at the boy they had rescued staring down him. "Looks like we're all in the wars," he said with a grin.

"Wh-who are you?"

"We're from the King's Guards. You're lucky we found you." Birlerion replied. "What did they want with you?"

"I'm not sure. I was locked up for a while, and then they said they didn't need me." The boy's voice quavered. "Were they really going to kill me?"

"Whatever they intended, they didn't succeed, so don't think about it. It didn't happen," Birlerion said firmly. "What's your name?"

"Charlie Banks."

Birlerion hadn't thought that he could be the missing lad that Tom had told him about, Sam Gort. It didn't sound like he had been restrained for long enough. "Were there any other boys locked up with you?"

"No."

"You don't sound too sure."

"I slept a lot. I think they put something in the food, so I can't be sure."

"Did you hear any names? Or anything that would help us identify who did this to you?"

Charlie shook his head. "I'm sorry, I don't even know where I am."

Leyarille helped lever Birlerion to his feet, and he grimaced at Charlie. "Well, let's get out of here before anyone else turns up."

Leyarille picked up his bow and quiver and helped him sheath his sword, and they left the warehouse. They started to walk back through Vespers. "Let's go to the tavern. The help can come to us. Charlie can't walk all the way up to the palace," Birlerion said and reversed his direction. Leyarille looked at him with suspicion but held her tongue.

"Taurillion, can you go and find help for us? We'll be at the Docker's Tavern, and ask Bryce to send a squad down to the warehouse to clean up."

"Won't it be shut?" Leyarille asked, her voice subdued as Taurillion headed off.

Birlerion laughed. "It's not that late. It'll be open." He flicked a glance at her and wrapped his arm around her shoulder. "Just remember, it was you or them. If you hadn't killed those men, you wouldn't be standing here."

Leyarille nodded, her expression uncertain.

As they approached the Docker's Tavern, the sound of raucous voices floated out the door. Birlerion made them wait in the shadows whilst he went in first. He soon returned, beckoning, and they slipped through the bar into the back room without anyone noticing. "What happened?" Tom appeared by his side.

"We rescued Charlie and got into some bother. We've sent for the healers. Charlie here needs seeing to." He carefully removed his jacket from Charlie's shoulders, and Tom hissed his breath out at the sight of his back.

"So do you," Leyarille's voice was sharp.

"And me," Birlerion agreed. "Any chance of a coffee? And could you add a bit of brandy or something? I think we all need a boost." The barman nodded and left the room. Birlerion flipped a chair around and made Charlie sit astride it. Charlie rested his head on his hands and closed his eyes.

Birlerion sat at the table with a weary sigh, and Jared emptied his pockets of everything he'd found at the warehouse. Tom sat next to him watching with interest as Birlerion began to rifle through the documents.

"Where did you find Charlie?" Tom asked.

"In the warehouse down the back of the Galley Arms."

Tom scowled. "Gillian's place."

Birlerion looked at him in surprise. "Yes, do you know him?"

"Know of him. Keeps himself to himself. But you don't cross him. You'll regret it if you do."

"Do you know where his estates are? Apparently, he has more than one."

Tom shook his head. "'fraid not."

Birlerion took a deep swallow of his coffee when it arrived and sighed out the resulting burn as the liquor warmed his throat. The barman stood watching him and handed him another glass. "Here, do you good. You look a bit pale."

Birlerion smiled and knocked it back under the man's beady eye. The barman nodded and turned away as Bryce strode into the tavern. Bryce looked around and zeroed in on the Sentinal. "I thought I told you to be careful," he said, glaring at Birlerion.

"We were. We're all here," Birlerion said soothingly, feeling a bit hazy from blood loss and brandy. Bryce stared at his glittering eyes and moved onto Jared and Leyarille.

"What happened?" he asked more moderately, moving aside as Healer Mathew arrived.

"Gillian came for for his package."

"Lord Gillian?" Bryce asked in concern.

"The one and only." Birlerion grinned. "He is the contact we've been looking for in Vespers. Not sure how he is involved with the missing boys, but we found Charlie locked up in the warehouse. As you can see, they weren't being very kind. They were intending on killing him." Birlerion frowned as he turned over what Gillian had said in his mind. "It seems there was agreement to deliver Charlie somewhere, only whoever it was wouldn't take delivery. It doesn't make much sense."

"The king is not going to like this. He's not going to let us go after one of his administrators."

"Maybe he will if we tell him everything. Once he has all the facts, he will act."

Bryce grimaced. "Don't be so sure of that." His voice sounded as sour as the look on his face.

After a low-voiced conversation, Charlie was loaded on a stretcher and carried off. Mathew moved on to Birlerion. He removed the makeshift bandage and began cleaning his side. "You'll need stitches," he said, and Birlerion rested his head on his arms and tried not to wince too much.

Bryce watched him. "Get some sleep, Birlerion, and report in the morning. Leyarille and Jared can fill me in on the way back to the barracks. They are out without permission. Let's not get them into any further trouble." He glared them into submission and rose, watching Jared collect the papers on the table.

"These were from the warehouse. Birlerion said we should bring them," Jared said.

"Good, I'll take them." Bryce glanced at Birlerion and then Tom. "Is there a bed here he can use? He's not going to make it home," he said.

"Oh aye, Jim will take him up. We'll keep an eye on him."

"Good, thank you." Bryce shooed the cadets out in front

of him, leaving Mathew to finish off with Birlerion. "Taurillion, walk with us, you have some explaining to do."

"Me?" Taurillion protested. "It's Birlerion you need to speak to."

"Oh, don't worry, I will tomorrow," Bryce said, loud enough for Birlerion to hear him. "I thought I said we were going to let the rangers be the welcoming committee?"

Birlerion slowly sat up as Mathew finished his sewing. Mathew patted his side dry and wrapped a bandage around him. "No strenuous activity or I'll be stitching it again. Hear me?"

"I'm just going to go to sleep," Birlerion promised.

"Make sure you do. That wound is deep, Birlerion. I'm not kidding. And what happened to your face?"

"It's just a scratch. It's nothing."

"I'll be the judge of that," Mathew said as he cleaned the wound.

"We'll make sure he goes straight to bed," Tom said gruffly.

"Take this, it'll keep the swelling down and ease the pain. I'll leave you some for the morning. You're going to need it. And a new shirt by the looks of it."

Birlerion smiled his thanks, and Tom and Jim steered him up the stairs. He fell into his borrowed bed and slept through till late the next morning. When he finally woke to the smell of bacon cooking, he found he had company. "I brought you some clean clothes, seeing as your others have pretty much had it," Bryce said from a chair in the corner. Birlerion winced as he tried to sit up. He had stiffened up overnight. "Mathew said to take the powder here." Bryce handed him a glass.

"Aren't you a bit busy to be playing nursemaid?" Birlerion asked as he drank the vile tasting liquid.

Bryce snorted. "Someone's got to. You need to take better care. Now tell me what happened."

Birlerion sighed and leaned back on his pillows and began to recap the journey and the altercation in the warehouse. "You need to keep an eye on Leyarille, she made his first kill. Her first blood. They held up well." He closed his eyes.

"You can't protect them forever," Bryce said gently.

"I know, but they were on my watch."

Bryce sighed. "I spoke to Stafford. He knows how to deal with it. He'll talk to her, keep her busy."

Birlerion nodded. "The young lad we rescued may remember something once he's recovered enough."

"Francis said he'd let me know when I can speak to him," Bryce replied. "We need to inform the king, but first, take some time for yourself Birlerion; a couple of days at least. I know I can't order you to, but you look washed out."

"Thanks," Birlerion said with a tired grin.

"Go home, rest."

Birlerion stilled. "Home," he repeated, his voice soft, and Bryce winced. The man lying in front of him no longer had a home. The king had ripped that away, along with his purpose.

24

OLD VESPERS

Birlerion, after thanking Jim for the loan of a bed, returned to Niallerion's house. Entering the quiet building, he peered in the bathing room. He would have loved to have soaked away the grime and dust of the journey in a long bath, but Mathew's warnings about keeping his wound dry rang in his head, so he made do with a thorough wash and finally a shave. He had never been one for a beard.

Washing his hair had been a mistake. His side ached after he had awkwardly bent over the side of the bath. He should have waited and let someone else do it for him. Sighing, he towelled his hair dry and eyed the empty chairs. He missed his friends. He wondered where Taurillion had got to. The house had an unlived feeling about it. Taurillion had barely made an impression, if that is, he had even slept here. Birlerion gave up worrying about it and went to bed.

The next day, feeling much better, he had a leisurely breakfast in the local café before visiting the hostelry, and after reassuring Kin'arol he was fine, rode up to the palace. Bryce had said he wanted to inform the king of what they had found out. Birlerion wished him good luck with that, but he had promised to back him up if necessary.

Bryce was not in his office when he arrived, and Deron suggested he wait, but Birlerion was feeling restless. "I'll walk around the stables for a while," he said. "You can find me there when he returns."

Deron nodded and watched the Sentinal go. He missed having them around. They were so useful, and knowledgeable, he mused. The king was wasting his resources, and who knew what they were getting up to without anything to do. Sentinals were never the restful kind. Just look at Birlerion, he couldn't even sit still.

Birlerion wandered aimlessly around the stables, stopping to rub the noses of those inquisitive enough to poke their heads over the stable door. He entered Kin'arol's stall and rested his head against his golden neck.

"We should go back to Stoneford," Kin'arol murmured.

Birlerion grimaced. *"We can't, not yet. We need to discover what is happening to these boys. It can't be allowed to continue."*

"Pil'penia is here."

"What?" Birlerion jerked his head up in surprise and peered into the next stall. He was confronted by the black liquid eye of an equally black stallion. "Pip?" He ran a hand down his silky neck as he entered his stall. "What are you doing here? Where's Mikke?"

Pip shook his head and snorted in frustration.

"He has been neglecting you, has he?" Birlerion murmured. "Now why would he do that? What could possibly draw his attention away from you? And his Watch for that matter."

Pip exhaled through his nostrils. "Indeed, a woman." Birlerion closed his eyes as he rested his head against Pip's neck and inhaled his musty scent. "And I suppose we know who, don't we?" he muttered.

Pip nodded.

Birlerion sighed deep and long. "I suppose I had better go and see what's what." He gave Pip a last pat and left his stall, latching the gate behind him.

"Be careful, Birlerion. I don't like that woman. She may be a Sentinal, but she's forgotten her purpose," Kin'arol said.

"Always," Birlerion replied. Forgetting his message for Bryce, he stopped at the well to wash his hands before walking back up to the palace and through the side entrance.

He made his way through the corridors to the throne room, acknowledging the salutes from the palace guard. Even though he no longer had any authority, the guards still treated him as if he did. He paused on the threshold of the throne room and wrinkled his nose at the pervasive smell of dank air and too many people.

Serenion almost pounced on him, he was so relieved to see him. "Birlerion, where have you been?"

Birlerion gripped his shoulders. "Why, what has happened? Why are you here? Where's Mikke?"

"Mikke and I came for the state dinner last week in honour of Prince Pierien. He arrived over a week ago. The king has been entertaining him. We were commanded to attend, as were Lord William and Lord Marcus."

"What about Jennery and Alyssa?"

"They came for the state dinner but left straight after. It was alright to begin with. Pierien and Mikke hit it off. Mikke stayed because he wanted the opportunity to get to know Pierien better. I thought it was sensible. Who knew when they would get the chance to meet again? But the king kept them apart. He always had something he wanted Pierien to see or do, and then *she* got her claws in him." Serenion scowled and jerked his head.

Birlerion scanned the room more closely and saw Mikke. He was lying half-naked on the cushions, and Ellie was draped all over him. She was running her hands over his bare chest and down towards his waist.

"How long has this been going on for?"

"About four days. I managed to keep her away to start, but she is tenacious, and with the king occupied elsewhere, she has gradually gotten worse."

"Where's her brother?"

"Haven't seen him."

Birlerion nodded, checking the room. "Where's Pierien?"

"The king suggested a private audience. He took him off about two chimes ago. I think they went to the Green Room."

"Right, come with me," Birlerion said, shrugging out of his jacket. "Once we extract them, you escort both Pierien and Mikke back to Stoneford. I suggest you get them as far as Deepwater tonight and stay there. Pip is ready to go. Once I get Pierien out, you get him and his men organised, alright? I'm sure Pierien will be just as eager to leave. Then come back for Mikke." Birlerion strode on ahead. "Don't wait for me, just get them away."

"Of course. But how do we get them out?"

Birlerion paused outside the door of the Green Room and handed Serenion his jacket. "Leave that to me."

"Sir, Sentinal, the king said he was not to be disturbed." A footman came running up.

Birlerion glared at him, and the footman gulped, taking a step back.

Birlerion opened the door and slid in, shutting it behind him. He took in the room instantly and walked forward. A young dark-haired man sat opposite the king. He had an expression of distaste on his face. "Ah, Your Highness, I've been looking for you."

Prince Pierien shot out of his chair like an arrow from his

bow. "You have?" he said, his expressive face lighting up immediately.

Birlerion tried not to smile. "Yes, Lord Mikkeal wanted to extend an invitation to you to visit his Watch. I understand you haven't visited one before."

"He does?" Pierien recovered from his surprise well. "I would be most pleased to accept his kind invitation."

"Serenion awaits to escort you to your rooms to prepare for your journey," Birlerion said, bowing the prince to the door. He saw him safely into Serenion's surprised arms and shut the door and turned back to the king.

"Your Majesty, what goes on here?" he asked as he approached the king. He took in the packets and powders scattered over the table.

Anders was slumped in his chair, staring at the fire. "Kids today," he slurred, "got no gumption."

"Gumption for what, Your Majesty?"

"Trying new things. Boring." His head fell forward and he emitted a low snore.

Birlerion stood watching him for a moment before sweeping everything off the table and into the fire. He poured a glass of water and placed it on the table near the king. Checking the room once more for anything that shouldn't be there, he left. The footman was nowhere to be seen. Birlerion caught the eye of a palace guard. "Stay here. The king is asleep. Don't let anyone disturb him."

Birlerion didn't wait for an answer but strode off to the throne room. He didn't think getting Mikke away from Ellie would be as simple. He shuddered at the thought of allowing Ellie's hands to touch him, but he gritted his teeth and entered the throne room.

He circulated, smiling blandly as he closed on Mikke and Ellie. Taking a flute of champagne, he sipped it as he drifted nearer, wincing at the dryness. Mikke was looking a bit worried as Ellie's hands strayed further down his body. Maybe it wouldn't be so difficult after all.

Birlerion undid his shirt buttons ad began rolling up his sleeves. "Why, Ellie," Birlerion drawled, "I thought you were interested in more mature company these days."

Ellie flashed an annoyed glance at him. Birlerion's smile was sharp as he glared at Mikke. "Forgotten something, haven't you, boy? Pip has been calling you. Maybe you ought to check in."

Mikke's glazed eyes focussed as he reached for Pip, and he stiffened as he made contact. Birlerion saw the horrifying realisation of his situation dawn on his face as Pip obviously told him what he thought in no uncertain terms.

Birlerion smiled at Ellie and stepped closer, distracting her from Mikke's aghast expression. He trailed a hand down her back and dropped a soft kiss on her bare shoulder. "I thought you wanted more challenging meat?" he said suggestively as he bent over her.

Ellie laughed and cupped his face in her hand. "Why, Birlerion, I thought you'd never offer. You've come to realise what you've been missing, have you?" She lifted her face to his, and he went to kiss her on the cheek. Ellie pulled him down on top of her and kissed him full on the lips, her hands running up around his ribs and up his back. Birlerion flinched before relaxing into her embrace.

Mikke watched, repelled, as Ellie forgot all about him and switched her attention to Birlerion. He was shocked at Birlerion's behaviour, that he would act so, and then flushed at the realisation that he had been behaving no better. He shivered as he became aware of his half-naked state and searched for his shirt.

Awareness of the general debauchery going on around

him seeped into his befuddled brain, and he shuddered. What was he doing? He struggled to his feet, and Birlerion broke away from Ellie to look Mikke in the eyes. Birlerion gestured to the door. "I believe Serenion is awaiting to escort you back to your Watch," he said as Ellie began undoing his shirt.

Ellie laughed. "Yes, run away home, little boy, you leave much to be desired compared to this." She ran her hands over Birlerion's bare chest smoothing his shirt open.

Mikke flushed and began to turn away.

Ellie frowned as she found the bandage on Birlerion's ribs. "What have you done to yourself?" she asked, suddenly sitting up.

"Nothing, 'twas an accident. I know how you can make me feel better though," Birlerion replied with a smile as he pulled her back down towards him, ignoring Mikke.

Serenion hovered on the threshold, a look of concern on his face as Mikke hurried towards him. "Thank goodness. Come on, Pierien is waiting." Serenion peered into the throne room, saw Birlerion and Ellie, and escorted Mikke away, his concern deepening.

"Pierien?" Mikke asked in confusion.

"Yes, he is coming to the Watch for a visit. We need to escort him home. Let's get you changed, and we can go. Pierien is already packed and eager to leave."

Mikke blew his cheeks out. "I don't blame him," he said. "Serenion, I owe you an apology."

"It's not me you owe one too. It will be Birlerion for having to put up with that harpy's hands all over him," Serenion said as he escorted his lord back to his room.

Serenion gave him enough time to wash and change, helped him ransack his room and throw his clothes in a saddle bag before escorting him down to the courtyard. Pip was waiting for him, along with Prince Pierien, who was giving the Darian a lot of attention. "I'm jealous, Lord Mikkeal," Pierien grinned at Mikke, "to have such an amazing stallion."

Mikke rolled his eyes. "It's not so amazing, Your Highness, when he's telling you what an idiot you've been!"

Pierien laughed. "You and me both, Lord Mikkeal. You and me both."

Serenion rushed back out of the palace, followed more slowly by Bryce, buttoning up his jacket. Bryce approached Pierien. "Your Highness. I understand you are off for a visit to Stoneford?"

"Yes, Lord Mikkeal was kind enough to extend the invitation," Prince Pierien replied.

"Good, good, then I won't hold you up. It will be dark by the time you reach Deepwater." Bryce nodded at Mikke. "Lord Mikkeal," he murmured before he hurried off into the palace.

Serenion breathed a sigh of relief as Mikke and Pierien's guards closed around them, and they started down the switchback leading them down to the city and thence on to the East Road which would lead them to Deepwater. He cast a worried glance back up to the palace as they rode. He had done his best. Hopefully it would be enough and Bryce would be as successful at extractions as Birlerion had been.

Bryce paused in the doorway of the throne room and scowled. He was glad to see the king was absent. That was one blessing at least. He supposed he ought to be anxious as to his whereabouts, but he would deal with him after he had found Birlerion.

He strode into the throne room and planted his feet beside the prone figures laying on the cushions. Birlerion was trying to stop Ellie from removing his shirt by nuzzling her neck and wrapping his arms around her.

"Sentinal Birlerion," Bryce said, an edge to his voice, and Birlerion immediately released Ellie and stood up, pulling his shirt around him.

"Commander Bryce."

"I was expecting to see you today."

"Yes, sir, I did come by, but you weren't there."

"Well, I'm here now," Bryce said, his eyes glinting.

"Yes, sir. Ellie, apologies, duty calls," Birlerion said, tucking in his shirt.

"You can't leave now, Birlerion. We were only just getting started," Ellie complained.

Birlerion shrugged his apologies and followed Bryce out to the throne room. "Thank the Lady," Birlerion breathed. "I'm not sure I could have put up with much more of that. Did they get away alright?"

Bryce scowled at him as he led him back to his office. "Yes, they did. Serenion said he was taking them to Deepwater for tonight."

"Good, that's one less thing to worry about."

Bryce threw him his jacket. "Serenion left this for you. Don't you think lovemaking was a bit energetic? You'll rip your stitches."

"It was the only thing I could think of in the spur of the moment to distract her. I didn't realise Mikke was here, let alone Pierien. I had to distract her from Mikke somehow so he could escape."

"Well, it worked, and where is the king? Should I be worried?"

"Probably more worried than you are," Birlerion replied. "We would have a constitutional crisis if something happened to him, you know. There is no heir. We need to get him married off, so he spends his time on more fruitful things than sleeping off a heavy morning in the Green Room."

"Ah, the Green Room." Bryce nodded as he sat behind his desk. "You know, that is an excellent idea. Who do you suggest we throw in his path?"

Birlerion winced as he sat down. "I told you to rest," Bryce snapped.

"I did. I slept all of yesterday. I only came up here to see you. I had no intention of doing anything else today."

Bryce sighed and leaned his elbows on his desk. Steepling his fingers, he glared at Birlerion. "I was hoping we could brief the king today and advise him of the threat to his kingdom, but it sounds like that would be a waste of time and effort."

"Yes. He was pretty out of it when I saw him. He was trying to introduce Pierien to a life of drugs."

Bryce closed his eyes. "Dear Lady," he breathed. "I dread to think what Pierien's parents will think when he gets home. This has got to stop, Birlerion."

"What are you looking at me for?" Birlerion protested. "I'm just a Sentinal; an undesirable Sentinal at that."

"He listens to you, Birlerion. You check his behaviour for some reason. I thought having Pierien here would help, but it didn't last."

"What about calling Jerrol back from Senti?" Birlerion suggested.

"I would, but the king banished him for speaking out against his policies. It's not just a case of him going off on holiday. He can't be seen in Old Vespers."

Birlerion heaved a deep sigh and scowled at Bryce. "Alright, I'll speak to him. If he instructs you to execute me, I expect you to save me."

"I promise I will do all I can," Bryce said with a grin.

"That doesn't make me feel much better," Birlerion

replied, his face grim. "So," he began ticking items off on his fingers. "One, we need to save the king from himself; two, we need to track down who owns that warehouse; three, we need to see what Lord Gillian has to do with anything; four, we need to discover who is abducting and killing young men; five, we need to block the supply of euphoria. Is that enough to be going on with?"

Bryce scowled. "There is no need to be flippant, we're doing our best." He sat back in his chair. "First, you'll sort the king out tomorrow, and then we can brief him." He ignored Birlerion's grunt. "Second, the warehouse belongs to a trading company. They just rent out space to whomever pays them. Third, there was nothing to link the suspected smuggling to Gillian except that you saw him there, and that is not enough proof of anything because it's your word against his, and we know who the king will believe. We don't even have enough evidence to go and search his estates, of which it seems he has more than one. The lad, Charlie, didn't recognise anyone. He never saw Gillian, so he's no good as a witness. As to the rest, we're no further forward," Bryce finished leaning forward. "We had a report of another lad gone missing, but no one saw anything."

"When was that?"

"Report came in this morning. Lad's not been seen for two days."

"Randolf was going to try and find the source of the drugs. He had a few places to search." Birlerion offered, trying to lighten Bryce's mood. "Is Taurillion still here or did he return to Retarfu?"

"I offered him the chance to go back. I saw no reason to keep him here, but he opted to stay. He's down in the Chapterhouse."

"I'll go and speak to him later. I could use the back-up. Give me the addresses of Gillian's estates, and I'll go and check them out. At least I'll try to see if there is anything unusual going on. If you could get anything out of Gillian's men, something we could use against him, then we could do something about it."

"We've had no success so far, but we'll keep trying."

Birlerion stood and paced to the door. "This is all connected somehow, I just know it. Gillian is the only lead we've got. Let me see what I can find on him."

"Be careful, Birlerion. Gillian is protected by his office. The king won't treat any accusations against his administrators lightly."

"He'll just have to add it to the list of things he wants to execute me for then, won't he?" Birlerion said, his irritation leaking out.

"I didn't say don't go. I just said be careful," Bryce said calmly.

Birlerion grinned at him in apology as he ran his hands through his hair. "Sorry, we are in an impossible situation."

"I know, but without proof, my hands are tied. Find me proof, Birlerion, and I'll gladly take over and set the inquisitors on them."

25

KING'S PALACE, OLD VESPERS

That evening, Birlerion returned to the palace, hoping to speak to the king. Anders should have had time to recover from his excesses of the morning. He should have known better. Wrinkling his nose at the heavy scent of alcohol and other unsavoury aromas, Birlerion watched the king with disgust. How could he have come to such a pass, to be publicly humiliating himself? Anders was jeering at his courtiers for not keeping up with him. The courtiers had more sense than the king. Those that were still conscious were only pretending to take a slug from the bottle.

Birlerion carefully approached the throne. "Your Majesty, are you alright? You don't look well."

"I'm fine," Anders snarled. "Was it you watching me? Spoiling my night?"

"You're the king, Your Majesty, everyone is watching you," Birlerion replied, keeping his voice calm. "May I assist you back to your chambers? You look pale, Your Majesty. Maybe you would prefer to recover in your rooms in privacy."

Anders considered him. "You'd like that, wouldn't you?"

"Your Majesty?"

"You don't approve, do you? You're so strait-laced you don't know how to relax. Give this Sentinal a drink. I command you to join me in a toast."

"As you wish, Your Majesty." Birlerion took the glass eagerly proffered to him by a courtier rather the worse for wear. Birlerion glared at the man until the courtier's befuddled brain understood the hint and slunk away. Birlerion carefully sniffed the drink. He had no idea what it was. He caught the eye of a footman who came over with a tray. He placed the glass on the tray and took a flute of champagne instead. He raised it to the king and knocked back the flute before placing the empty glass on the tray.

"It looks like you have out-stayed your courtiers, Your Majesty. They are looking rather the worse for wear."

Anders snorted. "Light weights. Have another drink."

"No thank you, Your Majesty."

"You refuse a command from your king?"

"Certainly, Your Majesty, when you abuse your position. It is not your place to order me to get drunk."

Anders eyed him doubtfully, and Birlerion hoped the king realised that it wasn't such a good idea to push him. Not today. "Very well, you may escort me to my chambers. This night is over," he announced grandly. His words fell flat as he realised the few people left standing were his staff and not his guests.

Birlerion guided his king's faltering steps out of the room and through the palace. His icy expression kept the guards' faces blank, their eyes averted. He manoeuvred Anders into his personal chambers and opened the inner door. He halted on the threshold, his eyes narrowing as he saw Ellie seated in a chair. Her face froze as she saw who accompanied the king, but she recovered and tottered over to them.

"Anders, darling, at last. Here I am as you commanded."

"I think it's time you went home, Ellie, this is no place for you. The king is retiring."

"That's the king's decision, not yours, Birlerion," she replied tartly as she fluttered her lashes at Anders.

Anders frowned. "Ellie?" His voice was slurred.

"That's right, my dear, I have what you asked me to bring you."

"Not tonight, Ellie. The king's had enough," Birlerion said, appalled at her behaviour. Did she have no self-respect? They had made excuses for the twin's behaviour for years, explained Ellie's excesses as a reaction to being trapped in the Veil all those years, when maybe they shouldn't have. "Leyandrii would not want you to behave like this."

"Leyandrii deserted us!" Ellie snapped. "For centuries, she left us trapped and alone."

"No one knew …"

"She should have!" Ellie hissed, her face pale with anger. "She has no right to say anything and nor do you!"

Anders' head swung back and forth before the two Sentinals trying to follow the conversation.

Ellie took a deep breath and smoothed her expression. A cloyingly sweet smile curved her lips as she said, "Anders, darling, tell Birlerion that you want me here. You do want me, don't you?"

"Yes, m'dear, of course."

Ellie glared at Birlerion in triumph and took Anders' arm and led him into the room. "Your services are no longer required, Birlerion. Why don't you go off to bed like a good little boy? You are not welcome here."

Birlerion gritted his teeth. "Your Majesty, it's late. Maybe you should provide Sentinal Elliarille with an audience tomorrow."

Ellie laughed, though her eyes glittered dangerously. "You overstep, Birlerion."

"No." Birlerion's voice was cold with anger. "I think you do."

Birlerion's sharp voice penetrated the fog of alcohol Anders was floating in, and he frowned. "Leave us," he whispered. He cleared his voice and tried again. "Leave us," he commanded. After a brief hesitation, Birlerion bowed and obeyed his order.

"Come, Your Majesty, it's time to relax," Ellie purred as she pulled him over to his bed. She helped him out of his jacket, tutting as she realised how drunk he was. "Poor, poor Anders. Were you ignoring your guard dog?" she murmured. "Never mind, you're safe with me."

"Water," the king muttered, "thirsty."

"Here, drink this." She held a vial against his lips and encouraged him to drink it.

"So tense," she whispered, massaging his shoulders. "You have to relax to get the best experience. Let's take your shirt off, shall we?"

"No, get Birlerion for me."

"It's too late, Your Majesty. Relax now, open yourself to it. Do you hear its call?" She watched as the drug began to take effect, his eyes glazed over, and his breathing slowed. Her hands began to move over his body as she helped him undress, soothing him into the thrall. Her breath quickened as she anticipated his body's response.

Anders began to shudder as her touch and the drugs took over. "That's right," she crooned as she straddled him and gasped as he thrust upwards as his body spasmed, over and over. "Yes, yes," she squealed as she reached for the stars and lost herself in the ecstasy of belonging.

Ellie stretched, her body satiated with desire. The longing was satisfied for the moment. She climbed off the king and leisurely straightened her robes. Swaying with a feeling of tired contentment, she slipped on her shoes and left the king's chambers. She had no interest in him now. He had given her what she needed, just as she had given him what he wanted. A fair trade after all.

Birlerion watched from the shadows, waiting for her to leave. He entered the king's chambers, and his concern deepened as he saw the state of the king. Anders' body was still faintly shuddering with the after-effects of whatever she had given him, his body still aroused even though he was not aware. There were glass vials lying on the bedside table, and Birlerion cautiously smelt them. They were potent and made his eyes water, and they matched the bottles he had found on the wagon. Lord Gillian was supplying Ellie?

Birlerion tried to make the king more comfortable, propping the pillow under him and pulling his bedclothes over him. He didn't attempt to dress him; Anders was far too heavy to manage alone. Filling a glass with water, he placed it by the bed and, sighing deeply, pulled up a chair and spent the night anxiously watching the unconscious man.

A few chimes later, the king stirred, groaning. Birlerion bent over him. "Drink, Anders," he said softly. Anders gulped down the water, and Birlerion filled the glass again. His pupils were still enlarged and the few words he muttered were confused and slurred.

"Sleep, Anders," Birlerion spoke clearly. "I am watching; you are quite safe."

The king slept.

Anders awoke late the next morning, his head thumping. He regretted drinking so much last night. Birlerion had been right. He ached. He felt like he had spent the night in the sparring ring. Shivering, he realised he was naked under the bed sheets. He never went to bed naked. It was too cold.

Raising his hand to head, he frowned in confusion. What had he had done the previous day? He froze as he sensed another person in the room. Opening his eyes, he met the silver eyes of a Sentinal and flinched away before he recognised Birlerion.

"Birlerion? What are you doing here?"

"Protecting you from yourself, Your Majesty."

"What do you mean?" Anders couldn't help the quaver in his voice.

Birlerion took a deep breath. "Anders, this has to stop. You are destroying yourself and allowing others to put your life at risk."

"Don't be so melodramatic, it's too early," Anders replied.

"Do you remember what you did last night?"

Anders paused, confused. He felt a sense of disquiet, and his stomach fluttered as he realised he didn't remember the previous day at all. He flicked a glance at the grave face of the Sentinal, and his concern deepened. Gripping his sheets, he closed his eyes. "I have a headache."

"Then you shouldn't drink so much." Birlerion was unsympathetic.

"I ache," he whimpered. "Maybe I'm getting sick."

"Inviting sensuous young women to your rooms with a pocketful of drugs will have that effect. At least you know you're still alive, because Elliarille could have just as easily slit your throat." Birlerion was unrelenting.

Anders flinched. He was feeling at a distinct disadvantage. The Sentinal seemed to have an answer for everything. A slow flush of embarrassment spread through him as he realised Birlerion must have found him after Elliarille had left. Licking dry lips, he felt very thirsty and hungover.

He was surprised when Birlerion handed him a glass of water, and he gulped it down greedily, accepting a refill when he had finished. He handed Birlerion the empty glass and lay back on his pillows.

They stared at each other.

Anders sighed. He knew Birlerion was waiting for him to explain himself. It reminded him of when his father had made him analyse what he had done wrong. He closed his eyes. When did this start? How had he gone so far astray? He felt a sense of yearning, an emptiness pulling at him, and his eyes flew open.

"Sire? Is something wrong?" Birlerion was leaning over him with concern.

"Yes, no. I don't know." Anders was confused, but the feeling faded as the Sentinal gripped his arm. He looked at Birlerion's hand.

Birlerion removed it. "My apologies, Your Majesty."

They were interrupted as the king's chamber door opened and a thin man entered with the king's clothes over his arm. The man hesitated before entering, then he quietly went about his duties, ignoring the tall Sentinal in the king's chambers.

Anders waved a hand. "The day begins. Meet me in the throne room in a chime." He passed a hand over his eyes. "I think we need to talk."

"Certainly, Your Majesty." Birlerion bowed and left the room. He shut the outer door and leaned on it as he exhaled. He raised a trembling hand and rubbed his face. Exhaustion pulled at him, his eyes gritty with lack of sleep. Tension hummed through him at what Anders could do to him. He needed a shave and a good night's sleep. He had one chime.

Kin'arol crooned in the back of his mind, and some of his tension eased.

Heading for the barracks, Birlerion ordered the first

guard he came across in the palace corridors to take up sentry duty outside the king's chambers. The guard blanched, but after a look at the Sentinal's face, he did as he was ordered.

Birlerion was waiting in the throne room when the king arrived. The room had been cleared of all the debauchery from the evening before. The mosaic of the sentinal tree and the crescent moon glowed brightly on the floor, and Anders gulped. A few courtiers loitered, interested to see what the king would do to entertain them today. They were to be disappointed.

Anders glanced around the room. "Leave us," he commanded. Waiting for the room to empty, he inspected the Sentinal before him. Birlerion had managed to shave and find a change of clothes. He didn't look like he had spent the night looking after him. Anders conscience twinged. He waited. He didn't have to wait long.

Birlerion dived straight in. "Sire, for the good of your people and your kingdom, this has to stop. You are destroying yourself, and you place your rule at risk, not to mention your life. The people around you take from you what they can. Your guards pay you lip service. Without a figurehead they respect, all you have will crumble to dust."

"How dare you," Anders flared, Birlerion's words hitting too close to home.

"I dare because someone has too. You make decisions when you are too inebriated or too drug-befogged to know what you are doing. You allow others to make decisions you should be making. You are losing control."

"I am not losing control. I am the king!"

"For how much longer, sire? Look at yourself, hard. What

have you done lately that's not just been for your own gratification?"

Anders stiffened. "Be very careful, Birlerion. I may be indebted to you for last night, but that doesn't mean you have the right to speak so. I am still the king. Mind your words."

"Yes, you are the king, so behave like one."

"You go too far, Birlerion."

"I shouldn't *have* to go this far," Birlerion bit back angrily.

"It's none of your business what I do."

"Yes, it is. I am a citizen of Remargaren. Maybe I came from the old world, but I gave my life to the protection of this world, and I will not stand by and let you break your oath. The oath you swore before your people, this land, and the Lady. You can hide it behind as many curtains as you want, but that oath exists, it resonates through your bones, and you cannot deny it." Birlerion looked at the king steadily. "That oath engraved in the wall behind you has guarded our world for centuries. Your rule is bound by that oath to the Land and the Lady. Yet you ignore it and encourage others to do so as well." Anders glared at him, but Birlerion met his angry eyes as if daring him to stop him. Anders could have him executed for his words if he so desired. Birlerion continued anyway. "You mock the Watches. Why? They are your source of income, they enable you to live as you do. In return, you should be protecting them."

"I don't mock the Watches," Anders said, lifting his head, annoyance flashing through him.

"Yes, you do. You forced Jerrol to hand over Stoneford to Mikkeal, and then you publicly humiliated the boy before your court when he came to swear allegiance."

"The boy was impertinent," Anders replied.

"Because you made his position untenable. You should have been proud of the way he stood up for himself, that he had the character to show his strength. Instead, you had him laughed out of Vespers. What do you think the Watches think of you now?"

Anders was silent. Inwardly writhing under Birlerion's disdain, his righteous anger, Anders realised he may have gone too far. Then he whispered. "I didn't force Jerrol out."

"Yes, you did. You disbanded the Sentinals. Where's the King's sentinal now?" Birlerion's voice hardened, and Anders flinched. "It's certainly not here. Would Jerrol have given up Stoneford for anything less than your word? You know what he's given Vespiri and the throne. Stoneford was his refuge, his home."

"Where is he now?" Anders voice was subdued. He dropped his eyes to hands no longer able to face Birlerion's anger.

"They went to Senti."

Anders closed his eyes as his stomach churned. What had he done? He abruptly realised how vulnerable he was. No Sentinal stood at his shoulder, and he felt the loss keenly. His guards no longer stood proudly to attention as he passed. No one barred entry into his chamber, except for the nervous guard he found outside his rooms this morning.

He swallowed as his conscience pricked him. Birlerion was right. He had allowed others to lead him down this path, to tempt him with forbidden desires. He was weak. He had treated Jerrol and his son abominably, and, come to think of it, his daughter as well.

Suddenly, he realised what he could do and straightened on his throne. He peeked under his lashes at Birlerion, still standing angrily before him, his silver eyes glinting with the strength of his passion. Remind him of his Oath and responsibilities, would he? Lady willing, he was doing the right thing. He began speaking the Kings Oath, the words imprinted in his memory since the day his father had explained what they meant. They burned before his eyes:

"Do your Duty, Never Falter, Never Fail,
"Lady, Land, and Liege obey."

Birlerion stared at the king in shock. "You know what this will mean if you continue," he interrupted breathlessly. "If you make me your Oath Keeper, we'll be bound together, forever. It can't be broken unless one of us dies. I'll be reminding you of your Oath every day."

The king continued, his blue eyes challenging Birlerion,

"All are one, Entwined ascending,
Keeper's Oath Never Ending."

Anders waited, his fingers nervously tapping the arm of his throne as Birlerion stared at him in silence. He had no idea what Birlerion would do. "Help me, Birlerion," he pleaded. "Please."

He let his breath out as Birlerion slowly knelt before him, meeting his gaze as he accepted the Oath.

"Lady, Land, and Liege obey. Keeper's Oath Never Ending." Birlerion repeated, his voice firm and clear. There was a brilliant golden flash from behind the velvet curtains, and the Land trembled in acknowledgement as the Oath was accepted. Those few, the Guardians who had kept faith, heard the Oath reverberate around Remargaren. The king had invoked the Oath. They didn't know who had accepted it, but there was hope.

Anders exhaled. "Rise, my Oath Keeper." He looked at Birlerion. "I'm sorry," he said simply.

Birlerion nodded. "It's forgotten, sire," he said as he rose, relief making his knees weak.

Anders watched Birlerion sway and was glad he was not the only one feeling lightheaded. Grimacing, he said, "I doubt everyone else will forgive me so easily. Could you ask

Parsillion to come and see me in my chambers? And then Bryce. I think I have some grovelling to do. After that, we need to clear the palace out and put it back to rights." He frowned at the curtains behind him, the golden glow of the Oath leaked around the edges, and he shook his head. "What was I thinking? Get these curtains removed for me, will you?"

Birlerion exhaled, visibly letting his anger go. "With pleasure, sire." He turned away, Anders was sure he was glad of the respite. The tension thrumming in the air was emotionally draining, even more for Birlerion who had stepped so far over the line of acceptable behaviour, it was a distant memory, but he was still prepared to follow his king's commands. Anders called him back and stared at him. "Thank you for protecting me," he said softly. "You didn't have to."

Birlerion smile was weak. "Someone had to."

"Well, I'm glad it was you."

Birlerion nodded. They had reached an understanding on some level, and it would strengthen over time.

26

EAST WATCH, VESPIRI

Birlerion checked his notes. Of the three locations Bryce had given him for Gillian's estates, this was the most likely. It was before East Ford. Not too deep in East Watch but far enough south to give easy access through the marshes to the coast. He had checked the other two locations, one in Marchwood, the other outside Old Vespers, just in case, but no one had reacted to his presence, and all had been open and welcoming. He hadn't sensed anything out of the ordinary. He had left Bryce at the palace trying to bring Anders up to speed with what was happening in his kingdom.

He rode up to the small manor house situated off the East Road. It was surrounded by well-kept gardens and bordered by a wooden fence, which seemed to encircle the whole plot. Out houses and barns curved around the side of the building and led down to what Birlerion assumed were more gardens. Although modest, the manor house was well built and was decorated with spires and mock crenellation, which reminded him of the family estates of old. An old family lived here.

Birlerion eased out of the saddle onto the loose gravel that covered the ground in front of the house and looked around. Kin'arol shifted as the gravel gave way under his feet. Birlerion soothed him and led him towards the grass verge. His eyes narrowed as he searched the barn. He thought he saw a movement in the shadowy interior, but he turned away as a voice spoke behind him.

"May I help you, sir?" A liveried steward stood on the steps.

"Yes, could you tell me who lives here? I have a client interested in buying a property such as this," Birlerion lied smoothly, shielding his eyes against the sun.

The steward smiled in superiority. "This land is not for sale, sir, and Lord Gillian would never sell it."

"Oh? Why not?"

"Why, it has been in his family for years."

Birlerion spun as a man erupted out of the barn and ran down the path beside the house, his bright blond hair visible as he stormed through the bushes at the bottom of the slope and climbed over the fence. "Who is that?" he demanded as he remounted Kin'arol, his muscles bunched beneath him ready.

"He works in the gardens. That's Roberts." The steward frowned after the fleeing man.

"Where does he live?" Kin'arol pirouetted under his hand.

"Woodbridge, the last house on East Street. But, wait ..." the steward gasped as the honey gold stallion leapt down the road, after him. He called after him, "Wait, what do you want with him?"

Birlerion cut south through stunted vegetation and sparse copse of trees and paused as the land levelled before him. A large lake blocked his way. Smoke rose from across the water. Labourers were working the ground, stacks of dark blocks rising in mounds around them. A rich peaty aroma drifted across the flat marshes, eddies of smoke swirled in the briny breeze off the sea, and Birlerion inhaled the sour scent of burning peat.

He turned away from the labourers and followed the road south towards what he hoped was the small village of Woodbridge and paused on the outskirts. The Mortelin marshes led down to the shelving coastline, a narrow spit of sand separating the mainland from the open seas. The largest island of the Birtolian archipelago shimmered on the horizon, a dark shadow rising out of the sparkling sea.

Birlerion's gaze swept the marshes. They were a mass of vegetation and deep channels. Grassy hummocks rose above a network of wooden boards that criss-crossed the channels down to the beach, flattened by the breeze. The sandbar, which protected the estuary from the open seas, explained the demise of the village. Trade would have moved to a more easily accessible port further down the coast.

The channels eventually joined together and widened into a broad outlet that was currently a river of dark sludgy mud that slashed through the green vegetation like a scar. It would be covered later as the tide came in and refreshed the marshes with a supply of salt-water. A rickety jetty extended out into the mud, an array of skiffs planted in the thick sludge awaiting release by the tide.

It was eerily silent, just the rustling of the grasses in the warm salty breeze and the lonely call of a solitary seagull. The place felt deserted. There was no one trying to cross the marshes, so he turned back to the village and dismounted. Leading Kin'arol, he returned to the empty central square and squinted at the sun's position. He rotated to get his bearings and faced east. He looked down the street, where a row of dilapidated buildings petered out at the edge of the marsh. In fact, all but North Street petered out into the

Marshes. He idly wondered why the village was called Woodbridge when there wasn't a bridge in sight.

He wrapped his reins around the pommel and out of the way and patted Kin'arol's neck. "Let's see what we have here," he murmured and walked around the back of the last dilapidated house in the row. He knocked on the door and waited. There was a movement in the house, and a very old woman opened the door and scowled up at him, her blue eyes surprisingly bright in her wrinkled face.

"There's no one here. They're all down at the Pollock," she said abruptly, intending to close the door again.

"I'm looking for your son. Roberts?"

"He's at work, up at the house."

Birlerion held the door. "The house?"

"The one up by the road. Takes most of the young lads around here," she scowled. "Making them soft, taking 'em away from the land."

"Takes? Do they not come back?"

"Nah, he takes them to work his estates."

"Does he not allow them to visit their families?"

The old woman snorted. "Look around you, then ask again young man."

"Roberts hasn't come home this morning? He left his work in a hurry and came this way."

"He may be after the extra work. They always need the hands when it's harvesting time. They were stacking them down by the Pollack, other side of the lake." She turned away uninterested and this time he let her shut the door.

Birlerion hesitated, frowning out to sea. He was sure Roberts had come this way. If Roberts hadn't gone home, then where would he have gone and why? The slam of a door behind him startled him, and he turned, expecting to see the old woman again. Instead, Roberts swung a shovel at his head.

Birlerion managed to get his arm up to block it, and pain exploded up his arm as the impact vibrated through him. He stumbled back, his foot snagging on the uneven ground. He fell awkwardly, his arm still numb as Roberts swung again. The shovel passed harmlessly over Birlerion's head, and Roberts cursed before turning away. By the time Birlerion had recovered, Roberts was off across the marshes, nimbly jumping from one board to the next, heading for the jetty.

Birlerion followed more slowly, gingerly flexing his arm as the feeling returned; he hadn't broken it, Lady be praised, though it had certainly felt like it. The boards flexed under his weight as he cautiously navigated the marshes. The tide must have turned. Water was seeping in, beginning to cover the mud beneath him. The tang of salt and rotten eggs grew stronger as he crossed the spongy ground.

He quickened his pace as his balance steadied, and he began to close on Roberts, who continued to head for the creek. Roberts kept checking over his shoulder in fear. Birlerion seriously began to wonder what this man knew that would make him so scared of being caught.

He was beginning to overhaul him, and Roberts started to make foolish decisions. His arms flailed as he tried to keep his balance after a wild leap, and he missed the connecting board that led on to the jetty. Roberts slipped and fell into the channel with a cry of fear, and Birlerion hurried up to see where he had gone.

Roberts was caught in the gloopy mud that the incoming tide was liquifying. He raised horrified eyes to Birlerion. "Help me," he called, "it's like quicksand."

Birlerion balanced on the boards and reached down to grab his arm.

Roberts twisted in Birlerion's grip, his eyes wides with fear. "Help me, I'm sinking! Don't let it take me, help me."

Roberts was beginning to panic as his legs were sucked into thick mud.

"Stop struggling, man, you're making it worse," Birlerion hissed as he tried to gain some purchase with his feet, hooking his toes over the edge of the board as he stretched, but the weight of Roberts combined with his injured arm giving way, he lost his grip of the board and the gloop quivered beneath him and sucked him too, pulling him after Roberts into the mire.

Birlerion tried to release Roberts, but the man had a death grip on his arm and the gloopy mud was relentless, sucking and bubbling around them as the tide continued to rise. The cold mud quivered around him, and he strained to lift his head. Birlerion tried to spread his weight but Roberts continued to struggle as the mud closed over his chest and slowly crept up to his face. As much as Birlerion twisted and turned to try to gain some purchase with his feet, there was nothing strong enough to hold him. He tried to push against Roberts, to lever himself up, but Roberts continued to pull him down, and the mud crept up his arms to his neck, and he started to pray as he was dragged down into the suffocating mud.

27

WOODBRIDGE, MARCHWOOD WATCH, VESPIRI

Birlerion jerked as someone grabbed his arm. He inhaled a mouthful of mud and coughed it out. A hard, wooden board was shoved under his chest and raised him out of the mud. A horrendous sucking noise rose around him as he was pulled out and over the side of a boat. The boat tipped dangerously as Birlerion's arm trailed in the grip of the other man. He twisted and reached for Roberts, helping to drag the man out of the mud. They all fell onto the bottom of the boat in a slimy mess, Birlerion gasping for air. His rescuer cleared the unconscious man's airways, scooping the mud out of his mouth and rinsing off his face. He thumped his chest, and Roberts choked, retching as he tried to eject the mud in his throat.

Birlerion stared at his rescuer blankly, his chest heaving. He watched the man set his boat to rights. "I heard you hated water," Birlerion said, bemused, as the man stowed the oar he had been using to lever Birlerion out of the mud and grabbed a line before sitting back down by the tiller. A bright red sail unfurled as he tugged the line, and the little boat started to move.

"I do hate the water," Jerrol admitted, keeping his eyes averted from the depths and on the rather muddy Sentinal sprawled in his boat.

"Ah, it must have been that you couldn't sail a boat."

"You must have heard wrong," Jerrol grinned, his silver eyes flashing in the sunlight.

"Thank the Lady," Birlerion said with a heartfelt sigh. He sat up and looked around him. "What are you doing here?"

"Marguerite said you needed some help."

Birlerion started laughing.

Jerrol watched him, cocking an eyebrow. "What's so funny?"

"The likes of Gillian have no idea what they are dealing with," he finally gasped, before bending over the mud-covered man lying beside him. He found a steady pulse and leaned back against the side of the hull watching Jerrol's efficient handling of the boat.

"You never forgot how to sail, then?"

"You never forget," Jerrol said softly, his eyes distant as the little boat swept out into the open waters between the Vespirian mainland and the island of Molinti.

Birlerion took the opportunity to reassure Kin'arol, who was pounding him with concern.

"Kin'arol? I'm fine. Can you make your way back to Marchwood? I'll ask Laerille to take you through the waystone to Vespers, and I'll meet you there."

"I couldn't reach you. I couldn't help you. I'm so sorry, Birlerion."

"It was not your fault."

"Where are you going?"

"I have no idea." He glanced around him. *"But seeing as Jerrol rescued us, probably Senti."*

"Make sure you return to Vespers as soon as possible. I'll wait."

Birlerion shed his jacket and shirt, washing them and himself in the sea as best he could before he rolled up the sleeves and put his shirt back on. His grimy shirt flapped in the breeze, his chest bared to the sun still smeared in places with mud. The bandages around his ribs were somewhat grubby, and his side ached. Birlerion was aware of Jerrol watching him, and he tensed.

"So, it was you," Jerrol said softly as Birlerion turned back to him.

Birlerion twisted his lips. Of course Jerrol would see it, whatever effect the Oath had on him.

"You've got a golden glow around you, and you seem ..." Jerrol hesitated. "… as if you have an added weight about you, it's difficult to describe, it's like you are even more present."

"That's what I get for lecturing the king about his oath. I guess we should be pleased he listened before it was too late."

"I'm sorry it came to this, Birlerion."

Birlerion shrugged. "The Oath and the Land are entwined. Marguerite said she would have her turn. She always said I had an affinity with the land. And now, I am bound to her just as I am bound to Leyandrii. I knew I was in for the long haul. I'd rather be involved than not." He grinned at Jerrol "Not like some sunning themselves by the sea," he said, admiring Jerrol's tan.

"Not by choice," Jerrol sighed, "though it is nice. What were you doing down in the marshes?"

Birlerion checked Roberts. He was still unconscious, so he made himself more comfortable and started telling Jerrol all that he had found out. "I mapped the locations of the missing boys, and they were all aged between fifteen and eighteen, predominantly dark-haired, and all from the south-east quadrant of the city. They were all dumped or found in the vicinity of the harbour. I was fortunate to be able to speak to the lad who had the most recent experience. He kept referring to a glowing spirit. She offered to show him the stars, and he was rambling about going back. He keeps finding his way back to where he was found, hoping the woman would come back, I guess."

"The stars?" Jerrol repeated thoughtfully.

Birlerion sighed. "He wasn't really coherent. I managed to get Healer Francis to look at him, and he said he was in a drug-induced thrall. Typically, once the drugs run through your system, you return to normal, but the healer thought he had suffered a mental trauma whilst under the influence and probably won't fully recover.

"He did say that the symptoms were similar to a drug called Euphoria, which has recently begun appearing in the city. It originates from Elothia. So I went to Randolf and asked him to see if he could find where it was coming from and hopefully stop it. Leyarille came with me, by the way. I returned driving a wagon train. Randolf sent Taurillion back with Leyarille to help, us being short on Sentinals in Vespers."

Jerrol grinned. "A good choice. Have you managed to dig Taurillon out of the Chapterhouse yet?"

"Barely. Bryce offered to let him return to Randolf after we had a bit of an altercation at the warehouses where we offloaded the wagons, but fortunately he stayed."

"Where you picked that up, I suppose?" Jerrol asked nodded at his side.

"Yes. When I returned from Elothia, the king was in full state mode, entertaining Pierien; how you managed that I have no idea."

Jerrol grinned. "You'd be surprise., Geraine was quite enthusiastic; good experience for the boy."

"With Anders occupied, Ellie set her sight on young Mikke, whom Anders had called back to court for the State dinner."

Jerrol stilled, his face tightening. "And?"

"I detached her from Mikke, and she moved back to Anders."

Jerrol exhaled. "Mikke should know better."

"Ellie can be persuasive. You can't blame the lad."

"Still. He has responsibilities now, as does Anders."

"Anders was …" Words failed Birlerion and he closed his eyes. "Well, let's say worse for wear and leave it at that. Ellie had her claws in him, and he was enamoured." Birlerion blushed. "I did give him short shrift the next day, I must admit. I've never been so angry in all my life, that our king could denigrate himself so, put all at risk."

"Ah, I think I see now. He retaliated by invoking the Oath. Well done!"

"I left Bryce and Parsillion setting the palace back to rights and followed up on reports that there was a link to the influx of drugs at the palace and a place in East Watch. It seems it's the home of one Lord Gillian."

"Gillian?"

Birlerion paused at Jerrol's exclamation. "Yes, one of the administrators. Anders is not pleased."

"I'm not surprised."

"That is one of Gillian's gardeners, apparently."

Jerrol dubiously observed the man in the bottom of the boat. "He doesn't look much like a gardener."

Birlerion chuckled. "I suppose it all depends on what he was growing. We'll have to see what he has to say."

"True." Jerrol concentrated on his sailing.

Birlerion's shirt was dry by the time Jerrol's tall sentinal tree came into view on the headland above Senti harbour. Birlerion smiled as he felt the sentinal's warm greeting. He had spent quite some time being healed by the tree in the past.

As the little boat entered the gap between the tall, curving walls of the harbour, Birlerion watched the walls pass by with a thoughtful expression in his eyes before turning towards the jetty. Birlerion jumped out and ran up the steps, and, running the rope around a bollard, he tied it off. Jerrol threw up the stern rope and bent to shake the shoulder of the man slumped in the bottom of his boat.

"Wakey, wakey, sunshine," Jerrol said, squatting beside the inert man. "We've arrived. It's time to wake up."

The man stirred, and Jerrol helped him upright. His clothes were stiff with dried mud, and as he moved, clods of it cracked and dropped to the deck.

They climbed up the steps hewn into the side of the dock and steered Roberts up to the house with the white veranda looking out over the harbour.

"Birlerion," Taelia enthusiastically hugged him and then stood back, concern on her face. "Birlerion, what have you done to yourself?"

"The king invoked the Oath," Jerrol explained, shoving Roberts down in a chair on the veranda.

"Oh," Taelia said enlightened. She looked at Birlerion keenly, and then her gaze moved to her other guest, her nose wrinkled in distaste at the state of him. "And who's this? Where have you been, Jerrol?"

"I took a boat out and came across Birlerion and his friend here trying to drown in some mud, so I bought him back for tea."

Taelia choked. "Now, Jerrol, seriously."

"It's true," Birlerion cut in quick. "Jerrol saved us. This is Roberts. He is a gardener on the Gillian estate in Marchwood. We got caught in the marshes with the tide coming in."

Taelia's eyes glinted at Jerrol. "And what were you doing off the coast of Marchwood, may I ask?"

"Looking for Birlerion. Marguerite called."

Taelia sighed in disbelief. "I thought you were retired?"

Jerrol shrugged. "Obviously not," he said, giving her a disarming grin.

She grinned back at him and kissed him. "Good," she said. "Birlerion, you must need a drink. Sit, and you can tell me what Roberts is growing in this garden in Marchwood."

"I think we'll let him tell us," Birlerion said, staring at the bewildered Roberts, who was watching them in confusion.

"Yes," Jerrol agreed, standing over him, "or we'll just toss him in the sea for the fish to eat."

Roberts slid down his seat and stared at them in horror.

"So what's it to be?" Birlerion asked, accepting a frosted glass from Taelia. He drank deeply, the cold water clearing his throat. "How long have you worked for Gillian?"

Roberts looked from Birlerion to Jerrol to Taelia and swallowed.

Taelia smiled. "Don't worry about me, I've never seen an interrogation before. I'm eager to see how it works."

Roberts turned pleading eyes on Birlerion, who shrugged. "We'll have to make sure she gets to see the whole works. I mean, this is probably her only chance, isn't it?" He looked at Jerrol.

"Sure to be," Jerrol agreed, smiling coldly at Roberts.

"About three years," Roberts babbled.

"And what is it you do for him exactly?" Birlerion asked.

"I was his gardener, honest, and then he said we had some new plants coming and we would have to nurture them very carefully."

"What plants were they?"

Roberts shrugged. "Don't know, but they came right enough. We had to build special glass houses for them. They needed the heat."

"And?" Birlerion prompted as he paused.

"They all died, as it wasn't hot enough. We had to build extra fires to warm them. We got new plants, harvested them a few months ago, had our first batch, dried the leaves out, extracted the oil, and Lord Gillian had a buyer."

"A buyer for what?"

"A drug. They called it Euphoria. Gives you a weird experience, takes you out of your body apparently."

"Who bought it?"

Roberts wavered.

Taelia gasped. "Are you going to torture him?" she asked her eyes bright with mock excitement.

Jerrol's lips twitched.

"It was a woman, like you, with the silver eyes. I don't know more, honest."

"What colour hair?"

"Blonde, very light, almost white. She had a bloke with her, looked the same as her."

Birlerion met Jerrol's eyes. "Elliarille. How did Gillian know this woman?"

Roberts shrugged. "I don't know. I just looked after the plants."

"And you never went to Vespers to meet this woman or help her with anything?"

Roberts shook his head.

"Why did you run?" Birlerion asked suddenly, "at Gillian's manor. I had no idea who you were. Why did you run?"

"Orders, not to speak to anyone with silver eyes."

"Why?"

"I dunno, Gillian was adamant."

Jerrol nodded. "But will you swear it before the King's Justice?" he asked intently, watching Roberts.

Roberts blanched. "They'll kill me if they know."

"And we'll kill you if you don't, so you're in a bit of a pickle."

"Best you write a statement," Taelia said, trying to help, "then they won't know. I'll get some paper and a pen."

The men watched Taelia in amazement as she came back with pen and paper. "You tell me what you know and I'll write it down, then they won't know it was you, and then you sign it." She smiled encouragingly, and Roberts slowly began speaking. Taelia grinned at her husband and began writing.

Jerrol's eyes ran down the statement once Roberts had finished. "That should do it." He handed it to Birlerion.

"This tells us where the drug came from but not why Elliarille and Gillian are working together, or why so many young men are going missing."

Jerrol frowned as Roberts flinched. "What do you know?" he asked, resting his hands either side of him and leaning over him.

Roberts cowered away from his silver glare. "N-nothing."

"You're lying."

"I don't know nothing."

"Which means you know something," Birlerion said.

Roberts looked at him, confused.

"What do you know about all the young men who have gone missing in Vespers?" Birlerion repeated Jerrol's question.

"N-Nothing, just that I overheard Gillian once saying be glad you're a blonde."

"What does hair colour have to do with it?" Jerrol asked perplexed.

"All the missing boys were dark haired. Not a single one was blond," Birlerion replied.

"But what does he need them for?"

Roberts shrugged. "That was all I heard."

"What about the lads from Woodbridge? You must know them all. Where are they?"

Roberts clamped his mouth shut, his face paling.

"Where are Gillian's other estates?"

"I don't know."

"Then where are the missing boys?"

Taelia drifted passed. "All those mothers and fathers worried about their children. What if it was your son? Wouldn't you want him to be found?" she asked as she sat on the steps.

Roberts swallowed. "I don't know nothing. I don't know where they went."

"But they are not at the house?" Birlerion persisted.

Roberts shook his head.

"When did you last see them?"

"I don't know, honest. I didn't notice to begin with, I was just doing my work, and one day, a new bloke would start, a week later they'd be gone. No one said where or why. I just thought they didn't like it an' upped and left. And then a couple of months later, the same thing happened."

"How many times has someone left so abruptly?"

"At least four that I remember in the last year or so."

"In the last year?" Birlerion was horrified. The supply of drugs and boys had been going on for much longer than he had realised.

"That's all I know, honest, I'm just a gardener."

"And lucky to be alive, by the sounds of it," Taelia commented from the steps.

Roberts shuddered and held his head in his hands. "What am I gonna do? I can't go back. He'll know by now."

Jerrol watched him thoughtfully. "Stay there," he said to Roberts. Birlerion followed him down the steps and out of earshot. "What do you think?" he asked, keeping his voice low.

Birlerion stared at the walls in thought. They sparkled in the sunlight, and he felt a strong compulsion to stay flood through him. Jerrol thumped his shoulder. "Birlerion, pay attention."

Birlerion dragged his eyes away from the walls and met Jerrol's sympathetic eyes. "I shouldn't have brought you back here," Jerrol said. Before Birlerion could ask why, he continued. "So what do you think? Is he telling the truth?"

"As far as he knows it, yes. But that's not much. I think I'll take him to Bryce and set the Justice on it. With his testimony, they will pay attention. They can investigate the missing lads from Woodbridge and dig into Gillian's business far more easily than I can. Maybe they'll find a link between all this that we're missing. This is beyond just me."

Jerrol nodded. "Very well, you can use the waystone on the headland."

Birlerion nodded, his eyes drawn back to the tall harbour walls. "I'll be right with you," he murmured as he strolled around the harbour to the steps that led onto the walls. Aware of Jerrol watching him, he mounted the steps and rested his hands against the wall.

A flash of excitement rushed through Birlerion's body, and a warm hum vibrated through his hands and into his bones. He had found the Oath. He heard a familiar girlish voice welcome him, and he collapsed on the steps. *"Marguerite?"*

"Birlerion, my Oath Keeper, you came. Welcome home."

"Home?"

"Yes, you'll always find us here in Senti. You shouldn't be surprised. You helped Jerrol place the Oath in the wall's foundations, after all."

"Does Taurillion know?"

"No, this is the home of the Oath, but he doesn't need to come here to find me. He knows where I am."

"Anders needs our help."

Marguerite sighed. *"Yes, he's made a mess of it, hasn't he? Do you know why? What caused it?"*

"Only that recently …" Birlerion paused wondering what 'recent' meant to a centuries old deity.

"Now, now, don't be thinking I'm old, because I'm not."

Birlerion flushed. *"Forgive me, my Lady."*

Marguerite laughed, her voice shimmering through him. *"I'll forgive you this once. Anders gave up his power, allowed others to step in. He needs to reassure the Watches of his vigilance and his protection. He has some fences to mend, but that is his job."*

"I thought my job was to protect the king? To ensure he keeps his oath to protect his people."

"Oh yes, but the Oath is the Land. I am what sustains it, and you will protect us. We are one my Oath Keeper, it's so good to have you back! We've missed you."

"But what does that mean?" Birlerion was confused.

"It means you're all mine. I know you thought you were Leyandrii's, and it is true, you were hers, but it's my turn now. I've waited for you long enough. I've never had one all to myself."

"You have Taurillion."

"Mmm, I do. But he is my companion, as Guerlaire is Leyandrii's. You are my Oath Keeper."

"What about Jerrol?"

"He is Leyandrii's Captain. I only got to borrow him. But you," she sighed with pleasure, and it rippled through his body, *"you are all mine. I've been watching over you long enough. I couldn't claim you until you accepted the Oath, but now … I'm so glad he brought you here. Let me show you what we are."* She spun around him in glee, her auburn hair flying out around her, her blues eyes sparkling, and Birlerion was lost in a burst of sensation and delight.

Jerrol sighed and turned away. He walked up the steps to the veranda of the white house, which looked over the bay. The house he had first built over three thousand years ago. "Well," he grinned at Taelia and Roberts, "you're not going home tonight, so you might as well make yourself comfortable."

Taelia stared across the harbour in concern. "Will he be alright?"

"Of course. Marguerite is so thrilled to have him, she won't let anything happen to him." Jerrol laughed as he settled in a chair next to Roberts. Taelia grinned and settled herself in his lap.

"I suppose I ought to dish up dinner," she said, reluctant to leave his embrace.

"It can wait. Let's watch the moon rise," Jerrol said, hugging her close. He ignored Roberts squirming in his chair and gazed across the still waters of the harbour as the moon slowly climbed into the sky; its silvery light shimmered across the water and caressed Birlerion's body still frozen in place on the subtly glistening wall.

The next morning, Jerrol found Birlerion sitting on the veranda steps staring at the wall. "So, she let you go then?"

Birlerion raised his face, and Jerrol suppressed a gasp at the sight of his eyes; they glowed with an inner fire. Jerrol suddenly wondered what he had looked like all those years ago when Benedict had made him his Oath Keeper.

"I doubt she'll ever let me go," Birlerion said with a gentle smile. "But then I wouldn't want her too. It's nice to belong somewhere."

Jerrol grinned. "You know you belong to us, too, don't you? You've always been part of our family. You are like my brother."

"I know, and I miss you all the more because of it." Birlerion looked around him. "How do you leave this place? The Oath is so strong here. I didn't expect to see Marguerite. I didn't realise how much I missed her."

Jerrol smiled. "It'll ease over time. She's a little excited to have you." A soft pfft drifted on the air, and Jerrol laughed. "Although I can feel the Oath, it's not the same. I no longer hear Marguerite unless she chooses to speak to me directly. One Lady is enough to keep me busy."

Birlerion frowned. "But I am Leyandrii's, too. I am a Sentinal. I've always been Leyandrii's."

"That's for you to work out between them. I wish you the best of luck with that one."

Birlerion looked at him in horror. His eyes flared as Marguerite wrapped herself around him and soothed his agitation. *"Hush, no one is making you choose. We are one. It is done, and Leyandrii approves. She watches over us, as always. We are entwined as one. Lady, Land, and Liege."*

Jerrol watched him relax. "Well, you'd better get yourself together because you need to take Roberts back with you this morning."

The light in Birlerion's eyes faded and Jerrol was relieved to see Birlerion looked more himself as he rose from the steps. "Has he behaved himself?"

"Exemplary behaviour. I think we scared him silly between us."

"Oh, I'm sure that was Taelia," Birlerion said with a grin as she joined them outside.

"I didn't realise interrogations were such fun!" she laughed.

"Where is he?"

"Making the most of the bath house. I don't think he's ever seen one before. We were hard pushed to get him out of it last night."

Birlerion chuckled. "I probably could have spent better time in it myself," he admitted looking ruefully at his creased and stained clothes. They were rimed with salt and stiffly uncomfortable.

"Never mind." Jerrol slapped his shoulder. "Consider what fun you'll have explaining it all."

"Help like yours is not required," Birlerion said before stepping into the house. "Roberts, we're leaving," he shouted. He turned back and hugged Taelia. "It was great seeing you. Leyarille is loving the rangers, as is Jared. They were both kicking up a storm last I heard, but I'll let them tell you what they've been up to. I did hear they were both placed on an accelerated path along with Kayen, so watch out."

Jerrol laughed. "So we'll have to watch out for three new rangers quicker than expected. That's good news."

"I'll keep you informed," Birlerion said as Roberts emerged from the house. He hugged Taelia again and then clasped Jerrol's arm.

"Don't forget to ask the Lady Marguerite for assistance," Jerrol said, his voice low. "She is there to help you as much as you are there to help her."

Birlerion nodded, his eyes flashing. Jerrol smiled and led the way to the waystone. Roberts baulked at the thought of entering a waystone, but Birlerion bundled him through, and they stepped out behind the Chapterhouse in Vespers. Roberts paled and began to retch. Birlerion steered him to the bushes and left him to be violently sick.

Kin'arol bombarded him with concern. *"You went so far away. Don't do that again, Birlerion. Don't leave me behind."*

"I can't promise that, Kin'arol. Though I will promise to try not to."

"Is that supposed to reassure me?"

Birlerion chuckled. *"I'm sorry. You know it wasn't intentional, and anyway, you wouldn't have fit on Jerrol's boat."*

"Tell him to get a bigger one."

"I will. Where are you?

"I'm at the garrison. I assumed you'd return here."

"I'm on my way."

Taurillion appeared out of the Chapterhouse gates, his silver eyes widening in surprise as he took in Birlerion's unusually dishevelled state. "Birlerion, what happened? Where have you been?"

"I went for an unexpected trip around the islands of Birtoli."

Peering behind Birlerion, Taurillion raised an eyebrow, his copper eyes gleaming.

"Sorry, this is Roberts; he is here to help with our investigation. We have much news to share, and I think we need to share it with Commander Bryce."

Taurillion nodded doubtfully as he watched Roberts lurch to his feet. "Let me get my notes and I'll walk up with you."

"Meet us at the garrison. I need to collect Kino."

Birlerion steadied Roberts, offering a grimy handkerchief. Roberts grabbed the hanky and turned back into the bushes, shakily reappearing a few minutes later. Birlerion grimaced at his pasty face and shaking hands. "Sorry, should have warned you. Waystones can be a difficult experience for some."

"D-difficult!" The man was shaking uncontrollably. "Why would anyone want to use them?" He began to swallow and, paling, he turned back to the bushes. He was still retching uncontrollably when Taurillion returned and silently offered a canteen of water. They waited while Roberts cleaned himself up, and then, with a Sentinal holding him up either side, they made their way to the garrison. There, Birlerion reassured Kin'arol whilst Taurillion wheedled two horses out of the horse master and then they rode up to the office of the Commander of the King's Justice at the palace.

28

KING'S PALACE, OLD VESPERS

Birlerion paused on the threshold of Bryce's office and tried to restrain his grin as he observed the dejected man seated outside. Roberts was at least a bit cleaner than he was, though his clothes were still stained with mud. He slouched in the chair outside the commander's office, pale and trembling. Birlerion wasn't sure if it was due to the after-effects of traveling through the waystone or the fact that he was sitting in a garrison behind the king's palace about to be interrogated by none other than the Commander of the King's Justice.

"Roberts," Birlerion said quietly, and the man rose.

Dragging his feet, he entered the office, and Bryce observed him as he approached. "Have a seat, Mr Roberts." Roberts sat, flicking a glance over his shoulder at tall Sentinals behind him. "You've had a couple of eventful days, I understand. Why don't you tell me what's going on?"

"Apart from being chased into the marshes and forced here against my will through that stone thing … I have rights, you know," Roberts protested.

Bryce smiled sympathetically. "Yes, they can be uncomfortable, but then if you hadn't run, Mr Roberts, you wouldn't have suffered all these indignities. Why did you run?"

"Because I was being chased by one of them." He jerked his head behind him.

"No, try again, Mr Roberts. You ran even before Sentinal Birlerion saw you."

"He did. He saw me in the barn. He's got those silver eyes."

Bryce frowned at him. "What has that got to do with anything?"

"They can see through things. He saw me, and I didn't wanna be next."

"Next for what?"

"I dunno what they do with them, but they turn up dead. We heard the rumours."

"Why don't you explain what you fear, Mr Roberts. What is going on at the Gillian Estate? Start at the beginning. How long have you worked there?"

Bryce skilfully questioned the man, drawing out his guesses and suppositions entwined with the few facts he knew. Most of it was hearsay or rumour, but it didn't paint a pretty picture. Finally, he leaned back. "Very well, Sentinal Taurillion, please escort Mr Roberts to the cells whilst we verify his story."

Roberts started protesting. "I done nothing wrong. Its them, they chased me! It's them you should be locking up, not me."

"I'm not punishing you, Mr Roberts. I am merely detaining you whilst we find out more information. You should be pleased. At least you will be safe here from whatever is going on."

Roberts fell silent as he digested the thought, and Taurillion bundled him out.

Bryce stared at Birlerion. "You look a mess," he said absently, his mind obviously busy turning over everything Roberts had shared.

Birlerion smiled as he sat in the chair. "It's Gillian. He's supplying the boys. The question is to who and for what purpose, other than filling them with drugs and dumping them in Vespers dead or alive."

"Maybe they are testing the drugs on the boys? If they are trying out different strengths, maybe they got it wrong," Bryce suggested.

"Maybe, but why dump them in Vespers and not hide them in the marshes of Marchwood? You would have thought Marchwood would be less conspicuous, unless there is another reason."

Bryce sighed. "Well, there's no point guessing. I'll get Stafford to send some cadets to Woodbridge and the surrounding villages, see if they can find out how many lads are missing. That will be a good exercise for them." He screwed his face up. "And see if they match any of the unexplained bodies."

"What about Gillian?"

"I think maybe the king ought to have that conversation, don't you? Once we have Lord Gillian, we can descend on his estate and clear this situation up." He looked at Birlerion with a wry smile. "You need to get cleaned up before the king sees you. You can't meet him looking like that."

Birlerion looked down at his creased and muddy clothes. "I'm going to start charging you for my laundry bills."

"Fine, just go get cleaned up. We need to brief the king."

Birlerion nodded and left the office.

He returned a while later, dressed in a clean uniform, his hair still damp.

"How's your injury?" Bryce asked.

"Fine. I dropped in on Hollin, and he said it was healing fine; don't need a bandage if I'm careful."

"Do you know what that word means?" Bryce inquired as they walked into the palace.

The king was waiting for them in his chambers; he too looked much improved. He was perfectly groomed, his eyes sharp and alert. He looked like a different man and Parsillion stood behind his shoulder, back where he belonged.

"Sire," Birlerion knelt.

"Rise, Birlerion. Please sit. What's up?" He indicated the chairs in front of his desk.

"We have evidence that Lord Gillian is involved in the murders in Vespers," Bryce said, cutting straight to the point. "Birlerion tracked down a witness at one of Gillian's estates. He can vouch for the fact that Gillian has been passing the boys to Vespers, though we are still unclear why or what is causing their deaths. Gillian is also growing the drugs that are being used to create this more lethal form of Euphoria. We need to bring Gillian in and question him."

"He's a prominent member of the administration. We would have to be very careful," Anders said.

"I suggest we hand all the evidence and the witness over to the Inquisitors and let them handle it," Bryce said calmly. "We can be available to support them as needed. It seems Sentinal Elliarille is also involved, but I suppose you know that since she is bringing the drugs into the palace."

Anders grimaced. "I can't exactly fault her when I instructed her to bring them, now can I? I've told her not to bring any more drugs in. If she does, we can deal with her then."

"We'll leave the Inquisitors to call in Lord Gillian. If possible, Your Majesty, sooner rather than later, we have another young lad who has been missing for nearly five days. He may not have much more time," Bryce said.

The king nodded. "Very well, I will meet with them later today and get them to send out the summons. Do we know where Lord Gillian is?"

"He has multiple residences, sire, but I would expect him to be in his house here in Vespers. He has no reason to be suspicious. He wasn't at any of his estates when I checked them a couple of days ago. If he isn't in Old Vespers, we will track him down," Birlerion said.

"Send what you have to the Inquisitors then, and we'll see how it develops. Include details on the missing boy. We can see what he knows about that as well." The king paused. "How likely is it that more of the administrators are involved?" he asked.

"There is no evidence to suggest anyone else is involved, Your Majesty, but until we know what Gillian is actually involved in, we can't be sure," Bryce replied.

The king nodded. "If that is all?" He paused, and they rose. "Birlerion, stay a moment if you would." Bryce bowed and left. Birlerion waited, watching the king.

"I hear I have more to thank you for," Anders said with difficulty. "I am ashamed that I could embarrass Vespiri so badly. I appreciate all your efforts to alleviate the damage I was doing, both with your brethren and my people."

"Sire …"

"Let me finish. Do you think Jerrol would come home if I asked him too?"

Birlerion sighed. "Where would he go? He cannot return to Stoneford; he would not oust Mikkeal now he is lord."

"I was thinking of making him my chancellor here in Vespers, with you at his right hand if you would."

Birlerion stared at him, wide-eyed in shock.

"You both know my people a lot better than I do; I need you to teach me," Anders said humbly.

"Sire, it would be my honour to serve you in any way you wish."

"If I gave you a letter, would you take it to Jerrol for me?"

"Of course, sire."

"Thank you. I'll let you know when it is ready to go; it needs some work."

Birlerion stood and bowed and then left, leaving the King of Vespiri frowning at his desk. Birlerion hurried through the palace and back to Bryce's office, where Deron grinned at him as he poked his head through the door. "I'll be at Niallarion's house if you need me."

"Birlerion, wait," Bryce called him back. "It looks like Gillian is not at home. Any thoughts where he'll be?"

Birlerion frowned. "Damn him. We'll have to go back through his estates. He may have properties we don't even know of."

"If you brief the cadets on what they need to look for, we can get a squad sent to Woodbridge. Then we can get another squad trawling through the records, see if they can find any other properties."

"You want *me* to brief the cadets? I don't have any authority."

"Stop making excuses, Birlerion. Of course you have authority, you're a Sentinal. You know the most about all this. We need to make sure the cadets know how serious it is."

Birlerion gave a resigned sigh. "When?"

"Today if you can. Commander Reece said he could have two squads ready for briefing this afternoon."

"Where?"

"Down at the garrison. You can use the main briefing room."

"You've been busy, haven't you?" Birlerion said, glaring at his friend.

Bryce grinned. "Blame Deron, he's the organised one."

Birlerion scowled at Deron. "Do you have the maps and descriptions all written out as well?"

Deron silently pointed at a pile of paper on the end of his desk. Birlerion grimaced. "Thank you," he said as he picked the pile up and left.

Bryce laughed. "Not often we catch that Sentinal out, now is it?"

"No, sir," Deron replied with a grin.

Birlerion stacked his papers in the briefing room and unfolded the large map of Vespers and a map of Marchwood. He tacked them up on the wall and stood back, frowning at the marks on the map. Sighing, he turned to the stack of papers and split it out into the missing persons and the property lists.

He marshalled his thoughts as he waited for the cadets to arrive, staring at the map. No matter how much he stared at it, he could not see a pattern. On a sudden thought, he marked Gillian's known properties. It didn't help much.

He moved to the front of the room as the cadets filed in.

He shook hands with Commander Reece as the cadets settled. "We appreciate your help."

Reece laughed. "This is an ideal project. Something that has real meaning, real consequences. We need them to be engaged in a project like this for them to get experience. Keep us in mind in future as well, please. They are all bright kids. They will all be bright rangers."

Birlerion nodded and observed the cadets as Reece introduced him. He stepped forward and began speaking. The cadets listened, riveted.

"This is not a drill. This is not some situation we created for you to practice on. People are dying right now, and we don't know why. We are asking for your help to stop this from happening again. There are at least two boys we know of who are missing as we speak. One has been missing nigh on six weeks, the other nearly a week. We don't know if they are alive or dead, but the work you do here could help save their lives and the lives of future victims."

Birlerion paused as he looked around the solemn faces. "This is what we know." He outlined the situation, the unexplained deaths, the two confused boys, obviously drug-related, and the influx of drugs into Old Vespers. He began to explain the maps.

"There's something we're missing." Birlerion stared off into distance. "It's there, I just can't see it. There's a link we're missing between the boys being drugged and their subsequent murders … and why are there two that were released still alive? It doesn't match. So what's the pattern?" He grimaced. "If anyone has any ideas, don't hesitate to speak up."

Birlerion looked at his list. "Unit One under Lieutenant Scott will travel to Woodbridge in Marchwood. Your task is to question the villagers and record every person who has left and not returned in the last two years. We need to confirm where they are or list them as missing. You need to follow the trail until you find them, match them to our missing persons list or add them to the missing list. Lieutenant Scott will hand out your assignments. Stay in your pairs. This is the real world, and you need to work together and back each other up. If there is any hint of danger, you do not engage, you track and report. A dead cadet is no use to anyone, understood?" He waited until the unit nodded. He handed

Scott the missing person descriptions. "Good hunting," he said in dismissal, and he waited until the unit had left, Jared amongst them.

Birlerion looked back at the unit left behind. "Right." He rubbed a hand over his face. "Right," he said again, re-ordering his thoughts. "The other piece of the puzzle is the drugs. We need to track down where they are coming in and how they are being distributed. We have one name. Your job is to find every property, every cross reference or partnership that is listed in the records in the Chapterhouse or the palace archives. You will be given access to both. You are not to remove anything, but anything you find must be annotated and listed, including the record or book, chapter and page. That is so the Inquisitors can follow up on it if needed. There must be a paper trail for every fact you present as evidence, understood?" He stared around the room. "This is very sensitive. You are not allowed to speak of this outside this room, not even to your parents. Even in the Chapter-house or archives, if anyone asks, you lie. You say you are researching an essay or something. You'll understand why when I tell you the names." Birlerion paused as if still deciding whether to trust them or not. "The person you will be tracing is Lord Gillian of the King's Administration and the owners of the warehouses in the harbour district." He paused as the cadets gasped. "As I said, this is very sensitive. We are trusting you to be responsible and careful. No false information, keep it clean, keep it tight."

"Yes, sir," the cadets chanted. Leyarille and Kayen exchanged concerned glances.

"Lieutenant Kopka will assign you to a location. You have two days to find what you can and report back to me here. Any questions?"

"What if they are not directly linked?" Leyarille asked, wrinkling her brow.

"Keep going," Birlerion prompted.

"You are assuming that the deaths of the boys are directly related to the supply of drugs. What if it is just a coincidence? In Elothia, Euphoria was commonplace, no threat to life, recreational, they said. We have no proof that Euphoria is causing the deaths of the boys, only circumstantial evidence that drugs have begun to appear in Vespers. What if their paths just happened to cross?"

"Interesting thought. Keep thinking it through to its natural conclusion. If they are not related, what does that mean?"

"We have two criminals, one killing boys for the fun of it and someone peddling drugs for the money or for influence," a petite red-headed girl said.

"Your name?" Birlerion asked.

"Cadet Petra, sir."

"Petra, that is an excellent supposition. Now all you have to do is help me prove it," Birlerion grinned. "Lord Gillian may be innocent of the murders, but don't assume anything. We believe he is connected to the drugs because we have a witness saying he is growing the plants on his estate near Woodbridge and I observed him receiving a drugs delivery from Elothia. We know boys have gone missing from Woodbridge. Is that coincidence or can we prove a link? Don't assume anything. Make sure you have a proof to back up every record." He looked at Kopka. "I'll be here for the next two days. Any questions, any concerns, any ideas, don't hesitate to bring them to me. We are on a clock, and there are lives depending on it."

Birlerion stepped back and let the lieutenant hand out the assignments.

Reece came up to him. "You don't hold back, do you?" he murmured.

Birlerion sighed. "We can't afford to."

29

WOODBRIDGE, MARCHWOOD WATCH

Jared cursed his luck as he escorted his partner back to the Marchwood manor house. They were being billeted in one of the barracks as they continued their house-to-house questioning of Woodbridge and the surrounding villages.

As the cadets compared notes in the barracks each evening, it became clear Woodbridge was not the only village suffering the loss of young men, and Lord William was distraught that he hadn't been aware. Jared wasn't sure how the Lord was supposed to have known. The odd disappearance over the years wasn't noticeable, easily explained as a man choosing to move elsewhere. It was when it was all collated on one piece of paper that it became obvious something more perfidious was happening.

Jared and Darius had been checking a small hamlet called Redmarsh, so called because of the local reeds lining the marshes being a brilliant red. There were maybe thirty houses in all, enough to keep two pairs of cadets busy for the day. Darius had been bemused by the reeds, and the colourful baskets the women were making out of them.

Trying to impress, he tried to cut some of the reeds for them and sliced his hands up badly. The edges were razor sharp. The women tutted and slathered his hands in a gooey paste, which stung so badly it brought tears to his eyes, and Lieutenant Scott ordered Jared to take him back to the healerie in Marchwood.

Darius bent over in his saddle, cradling his hands in his lap, his face pale and strained as Jared led his horse down the road. Who would have thought reeds could cause so much damage? Once they reached Marchwood, the healer hustled Darius away and Jared began the trek back to Redmarsh.

He hesitated as he passed a narrow dirt track that led to a small farm. Not sure why, he turned down the track, which ended in a deserted farmyard. He slowly dismounted, not sure what he was expecting. A low groan disturbed the peace, and he led his horse towards the barn. Releasing the reins, he dashed to the side of a man lying curled up on the ground. He rolled him over and clamped his hand against the bloody wound in his stomach. The man groaned again and open his eyes. They were a deep brown and filled with pain. He stared at Jared hazily. "They have my wife, my children. Help them."

"Who has them?"

"That man, Benarte's bully, he turned up unexpectedly. We didn't have his money ready. We haven't had time. It's just not possible to meet their demands." The man shifted awkwardly, and Jared removed his hand from the man's stomach.

"Let me see," he said. Jared drew his breath in at the sight of the wound, and the man hissed his breath out.

"He said he would take payment in kind instead," the man wheezed. "He ran me through, and then he went into the house. Help them please. My girls are too young to understand."

"How many men were they?" Jared asked as he folded a sack over and used it press against the deep wound in the man's side. "Hold it," Jared instructed as he left to search the barn. He found some grubby rags and a ball of string. He wrapped them around the man's torso and tied them in place. Leyarille was right, they should always have bandages on them. This was the second time today he had needed them. He left the man to peer out of the barn. It was open ground all the way to the farmhouse.

The man coughed weakly and Jared hurried across to him. "Can you hold on? Help will be here soon," he murmured. A high scream made them both freeze.

"Help my family, please," the man whispered. Tears ran down his face as he gripped Jerrol's arm.

Jared stared at him and then nodded. "Pray to the Lady for help then, because we're going to need it."

"I did. And you came," the man laughed, his face bleak.

"Lady help us, then," Jared replied. He muttered a quick heartfelt prayer of his own as he crept up to the house. "Please, Lady hear us. I offer you my sword to do with as you will, only help your people, please." He skirted the farmyard, knowing his lieutenant was going to cream him when he found out.

He almost dropped his sword when a soft voice breathed in his ear. *"Do you mean it? You will protect those who cannot protect themselves? To protect us until your last breath?"*

"I swear so," he replied, peering into a window, trying to see where the men were.

He sensed someone behind him and spun, expecting an attack, but a slender young woman with long blond hair that curled around her exquisite face, stood before him. Her brilliant green eyes bored into his, and Jared gaped at her. She raised her hand and caressed his face. *"I accept your word and your oath, Jaredion. I have looked forward to this day for a long time.*

Your heart is true, and I will treasure it forever. Never forget, if you ask for my help, you shall always receive it." She smiled at his surprised face and gestured. "That looks better," she laughed as his clothes shimmered into the silvery green high-necked uniform that Birlerion usually wore. He gasped as he realised who she was. *"I believe you offered to help. They are around the back, and there are four of them,"* she said, her face grave and then she faded out of sight, leaving him standing in full view of the window.

Jared stood stunned for a moment before instinctively dropping to the ground, his stomach fluttering. Rubbing his eyes, he suddenly froze. He was a Sentinal? With silver eyes and the cast iron stomach? He rushed to look in a bucket of water. Silver eyes gleamed back at him and he swallowed nervously.

"Get a grip, Jared," he muttered to himself. Clutching his sword in one hand and a dagger in the other, he carefully made his way around the side of the farmhouse. He suddenly paused, a thought blooming in his mind. If he was a Sentinal, he could call Ari, the little Arifel. He concentrated briefly, sending out a call for help, more in hope than belief.

When he reached the back of the house, he paused, listening. A woman screamed, and the terror in her voice made him shiver. Children whimpered in fear nearby. A sharp voice almost above him told them to shut up or they'd be next. He silently sheathed his sword and took a deep breath as he rose behind the man and calmly slit his throat, pulling the body back around the side of the house, out of sight. He rolled the body over and returned to the terrified girls. "Run to the barn, your father is waiting for you," he whispered as he wiped his dagger on the grass. They ran.

A slight disturbance in the air preceded a soft chirrup as a small kitten-like creature hovered beside him. Jaw dropping, Jared gaped at the little mackerel striped Arifel. It truly did have scaly wings that sprouted from its back. "Ari?" he whispered.

The Arifel chirruped again.

"I need some help. Can you ask Lord William to send Anterion? Whoever you can get!"

Ari disappeared and Jared peered around the corner of the building. Inhaling, he flipped his dagger in his hand and threw it at the back of the man who was holding the terrified woman down. This was not the time for principles, outnumbered as he was. He drew his sword as he rushed the men who released the woman and rose in anger as one of their number collapsed in front of them, a dagger protruding from his back. The woman scuttled back on her bottom, her dress in tatters, a smear of bright red blood across her pale face.

"Who do we have here then? A Sentinal to the rescue, is it?" The man scowled at Jaredion as he buttoned his trousers and buckled his belt. His face was smooth, his eyes hard, his body lean. He unsheathed his sword and gestured to his companion to wait. "Let's see what you're made of then, shall we," the man purred. From the way the man held his sword, Jared knew this was no ruffian, he was a trained fighter.

"I can already see what *you're* made of," Jared replied as the woman rolled into the bushes and disappeared. Jared focussed on the men in front of him.

The man hissed at the implied insult and struck. Jared parried and struck back, the ring of steel a comforting reminder that he did know how to fight. Maybe not as dirty as his opponent, but he could learn fast. He swirled away from the dust the man deliberately kicked up. He kept both men in his view, trying to rotate so they were always before him, but the other man was gradually working his way around behind him.

"So you work for Benarte, then?" Jared said, breathless at the speed of the man's strikes. He forced the man back so he could pivot.

"Lord Benarte to you, scum," the man growled, flicking his sword at Jared's arm. It sliced the material, and Jared felt the bite on his skin.

"Is that all you got?" Jared thrust, and the man skittered out of reach.

"It's more than enough for you, boy." The man's eyes flickered, and Jared ducked, and the blow glanced off his shoulder. He had forgotten the other man. Scuttling back out of reach, he regrouped, his dagger in one hand, his sword in the other. He faced the two men, breathed in deeply, and hoped his mother would forgive him if he didn't survive.

Lady bless them, he thought as he lunged. His sword screeched the length of his opponent's sword, and he flung his hand up and blocked the other sword with his dagger caught in the hilt. He jinked the sword away and stepped aside, thrusting his knife at one man as he smoothly parrying the follow up strike. He glared into the eyes of Benarte's man as he forced him back, and then the farmyard was suddenly full of men and horses.

The men were pulled off Jared, and he swayed, breathing deeply as he watched bemused as Lord William dismounted from his horse, closely followed by Sentinals Laerille and Anterion of Marchwood.

Lord William approached him carefully, watching him as if he was some wild animal about to attack, and Jared realised he still had his weapons ready. Lord William frowned at him. "Jared?" he said hesitantly as though he wasn't sure it was him.

Laerille came and stood beside him. She grasped Jared's shoulders as he didn't respond. "Jaredion?" she said softly, and he looked at her as exaltation and relief rushed through his veins. "Are you alright?" she asked, watching him in concern. He wasn't sure if he was alright or not. He felt … weird, as if he was elsewhere, observing from a distance. Was that how you felt when you accepted that you were about to die, but you fought on regardless? He looked down at his new uniform and frowned at the many slashes, some rimmed with red, but he didn't feel them; he was passed simple pain. His only thought was that the Lady would be upset as she had only just given his uniform to him.

Jaredion stared at Laerille in relief. She had her sword at the ready and alertly scanned the yard for further threats. She tucked her blonde hair behind her ear and revealed the fine scars that marred her face. Anterion loomed beside her, his solid bulk reassuring. Glancing around him, Jared tried to remember where he was and what he was supposed to be doing. "Where did you come from?"

"Ari came for us, but never mind that, are you hurt?" Laerille patted his arm.

"I'm fine. The farmer was injured. Benarte's man ran him through; he is in the barn."

"We found them. His wife sent us back here to help you."

Jaredion nodded. "I meant to watch and report only, sir, honest." Jaredion looked at Lord William, and then the Sentinals. "But they needed help, and the Lady said …" he faltered as he remembered his meeting with the Lady.

"It's alright, Jaredion. You did well. Come, let's return to the keep. Lord William's men will deal with this now." Laerille coaxed him away. "Sheath your sword for now, Jaredion," she murmured. "You can clean it later."

Jaredion looked down at his sword, surprised to see the blood staining it. He sheathed it in one fluid movement. "My daggers." He had thrown one, the other had been in his hand.

"Lord William's men will retrieve them for you," Laerille

replied, guiding him around the farmhouse. He allowed her to lead him away.

Lord William looked at Anterion and exhaled deeply. "Is he truly a Sentinal now?"

Anterion smiled. "Oh yes. I bet when we get back, we'll find one of our saplings is missing."

Lord William looked around him. "He did well. Four against one and he is still standing."

"And the people he was protecting are alive, thanks to him," Anterion said with a grin. "The Lady picks well, even if I say so myself." He knelt beside the body lying in the dust, a dagger protruding from the man's side. "He punched it through the lung. Killing blow."

"While holding off another, quite amazing," Lord William murmured, walking over to the other body. He put a foot on the man's back and pulled the dagger out with a grunt before rolling the man over. "Benarte's men. It will be interesting to see what he has to say about all this."

Birlerion cursed all the way to Marchwood, a long string of invectives that didn't make him feel any better. Jennery was going to kill him, and Tagerill probably. It should have been a simple door to door interview. How had Jared managed to get himself into such a scrape? Ari had brought Lord William's report of what had happened and a desperate request for him to come to Marchwood. Birlerion had left immediately.

Laerille was waiting for him as he arrived through the waystone. "Is Jared alright?" Birlerion asked immediately, halting in front of her.

"*Jaredion* is fine," Laerille said, emphasising the name, and Birlerion stared.

"Truly?" he said finally.

"Truly. A few cuts and bruises, but Birlerion, you need to speak to him."

"Of course," Birlerion said, taking a step towards the house.

"No, I mean *speak* to him. He thought he was going to die. He accepted that and continued anyway. I don't think he's realised yet that he didn't."

Birlerion closed his eyes. "Where is he?"

"Lord William is with him in his study."

Birlerion nodded and slowly walked up to the house. He paused on the bottom step and took a deep breath before climbing the steps and entering the manor house of Marchwood Watch. The steward bowed him into the study.

"William." Birlerion held his hand out as the Lord of the Watch stood.

"Birlerion, it's good to see you," Lord William said with relief. "I'll leave you to speak to him. These are his," he said, handing Birlerion a bundle. "We'll be near if you need us." Birlerion nodded and waited for William to leave.

He sat opposite Jaredion. The boy was diligently cleaning his sword, focused on polishing the length of the blade, over and over.

"Jaredion," Birlerion said, keeping his voice gentle, and Jaredion paused before beginning to wipe it down again.

Birlerion lent forward and placed his hand on Jaredion's stopping the motion. "Jared, look at me."

Jaredion slowly looked up and met Birlerion's eyes. Birlerion swallowed at the sight of eyes with such luminous depth. "You can put your sword aside. It won't get any cleaner no matter how much you polish it."

Jaredion stared at him.

"You did very well, Jared. You saved that family. They will all recover well and return to their home, thanks to you."

"They were going to kill them," he said, his voice lacking any emotion.

"Yes."

"I offered the Lady my sword if she would help me protect them."

"Yes," Birlerion said. "Please forgive me, Jared. I am so sorry I put you in such a position."

Jaredion's brows contracted. "You didn't. I was on my way back from Marchwood when the Lady called me off the road."

"You wouldn't have been in Marchwood if I hadn't sent you there."

Jaredion shrugged. "It could have been any of us."

"True, but the Lady chose you. Congratulations, Jaredion."

"For what?"

"For seeing what the Lady needed of you and fulfilling it. That is all we Sentinals are, you know, the Lady's protection in action. We protect what needs to be protected against whatever threatens it." Birlerion smiled wryly. "And we try to stay alive so we can continue doing so. She only has so many Sentinals, after all."

"I didn't think I could do it. Help those people I mean."

"But you did."

Jaredion's voice shook. "I don't remember killing those men, but I know my hand did it."

"I know. Sometimes, when the odds are stacked so high against you, you enter a different mindset. You expect to die, so your brain seems to calculate things even faster. It is a survival instinct, I think, your body's way of trying to survive even though your common sense says it's hopeless."

"I didn't die," Jaredion stated, though he didn't sound too sure.

"No, you are still very much alive, and I am so very glad

to welcome you as a brother. The Sentinals are a family, you know. We support each other, even if we are a bit more dispersed now than we used to be." He slowly unwrapped the bundle and hefted one of the daggers in his hand.

Jaredion's eye was drawn to it.

"It was impressive," Birlerion said inspecting the dagger. "You slit the first man's throat from behind and dragged him out of sight, thereby saving the children. You then threw your dagger at the man with his back to you, reducing your opponents by half.

"You engaged a skilled fighter and managed to hold him at bay so the woman could escape. You held your own against a man stronger and more skilled than you whilst thrusting your second dagger into the chest of the fourth man, who was trying to attack you from behind. These are honourable blades," he said firmly. "Maybe you should clean them." He held the daggers out to Jaredion.

Jaredion stared at him, mute. There was a long silence. "It wasn't honourable," he finally said. "I struck them from behind. It was cowardly."

"And why should you treat dishonourable men with honour?" Birlerion asked. "Were they acting honourably to that family in their own home? They would have raped and killed the farmer's wife," Birlerion said brutally, "and done the same to those innocent young girls as well, no doubt. Could you have stood by and allowed that to happen?"

"Of course not. I didn't," Jaredion rose out of his chair in protest.

"Exactly, you acted honourably. You prevented those without honour from breaking the law of the land and our Lady. You *protected* those people. Did they treat you with honour? I don't think so. That you had to kill is distressing. It is *always* distressing. It is against our very nature. But if you hadn't acted, they would have killed you and that family and possibly many others. Killing in defence is a necessary evil that we learn to live with so others do not have to. Clean your daggers, Jaredion."

Jaredion's face wavered as his eyes filled with tears. "Birlerion?" His face crumpled. Birlerion was beside him and had him in his arms as he finally broke down. Birlerion held him as he cried out his terror and anguish.

Birlerion rocked him as his grief abated, and he nearly missed the boy's words. "I thought I'd die," Jaredion whispered brokenly.

Birlerion tightened his grip. "But you did it anyway," he replied. "It takes a special kind of man to face that and continue. A soldier, a Sentinal, someone like you, Jaredion."

"Someone like me," he whispered, closing his eyes as he relaxed in Birlerion's arms.

Birlerion gently laid him down on the sofa, and Jaredion stiffened as Birlerion stood. "Sleep, Jaredion, I'm not going anywhere. I will be here with you." As Birlerion covered Jaredion with a rug a small black Arifel appeared. It was a tiny ball of fluff with wings and reminded Birlerion of when Ari first hatched. The Arifel cheeped and descended onto Jaredion's chest. Her vivid green eyes observed him as she settled, flipping her wings back and curling her tail around her.

Jaredion extended a cautious finger and stroked down her nose. The Arifel coyly butted his finger until he scratched her fluffy ears. She sighed and laid her chin flat on his chest.

"She says her name is Pel," Jaredion said, awe tingeing his voice.

Smiling, Birlerion drew a chair up beside him and sat down. "Then I suggest you remember it, as she is more likely to respond than any other Arifel. The Lady blesses you."

Jaredion smiled as the Arifel crept up his body and snuggled under his chin. He relaxed with a soft sigh, his eyelids drooped and he fell asleep.

Birlerion leaned back in the chair and closed his eyes. He was just as exhausted, trying to say the right things to reassure the boy, no he was a young man, to ensure no permanent damage from his abrupt baptism as a Sentinal.

"Lady watch over him," he prayed. *"Bless his healing sleep and guide him well."*

"Always Birlerion, as I do you," she breathed in his ear. *"Thank you for your care. I apologise for the need. It will not be forgotten."*

Birlerion opened his eyes and watched Jaredion sleep. His face had lost some of its unnatural rigidity, and the little Arifel, Pel, rose and fell with his chest. She raised her head and watched Birlerion stand and check over Jaredion's jacket. There were numerous nicks and tears in the material, some rimmed in blood. *"My Lady? Your Sentinal needs a new jacket!"* The cloth shimmered in his hand, and he laid it over the chair. He wished it was as simple to repair all wounds.

Sitting back down, he rested his head in his hands. Lord Benarte was involved. It got worse. He dreaded where this was going, and he suddenly felt concerned for the rest of the cadets diligently following his orders. Maybe he ought to call them all back? But if he did that, they would not find out what they needed to know. He would have to warn them and see if Lord William would assign a Sentinal to watch over them.

He stirred as Pel landed on his shoulder, and he scooped her into his hand and cuddled her against his chest. The soft vibration rumbling through her as he stroked her made him smile. "I'm fine. Just tired. You need to look after Jaredion."

He would take Jaredion home to Deepwater, let Jennery and Alyssa help him find his balance, and then he would have to hope he could find a clear trail out of all the information that would be waiting for him in Vespers.

Lord William opened the door and the Arifel disappeared. "It's getting late. Do you want anything to eat?"

"I'd love a kafinee," Birlerion replied with a tired grin.

"How is he?"

"The Lady watches him; he will be fine. He is a good lad."

"He is a Sentinal," Lord William said. "Where do you think his tree went? It's not in the nursery."

"I should think it went to Deepwater; that is his home after all."

"I'll bet that was a shock," Lord William chuckled.

"I'll go with him to Deepwater tomorrow. It will do him good to be with his tree; it may help make it all a little more real for him."

"Should we move him?"

Birlerion shook his head. "If we can leave him be, he'll wake in his own time. I'm sorry we ousted you out of your study, William."

"Don't be daft, that doesn't matter. Laerille was worried."

"Well, tell her he's fine, and he understands. He just needs some time to adjust, and he'll get that in Deepwater."

"How are you doing?" William looked at Birlerion keenly, and Birlerion was too tired to try and hide his exhaustion. "You need to look after yourself as well. You're not an army of one, remember. You need to delegate."

"To whom, William? You called me here."

"You know what I mean, Birlerion. Now that the king is reassessing some of his decisions, if you need to pull some Sentinals back into Old Vesper's, then do so. You need the support."

Birlerion nodded. "You're right, but I think you are going to need some support here. You need to keep your Sentinals. We need to keep an eye on both Gillian and Benarte's estates. I think the Inquisitors will have some questions for them once they've questioned his henchman."

30

DEEPWATER WATCH, VESPIRI

"We've been expecting you," Jennery said dryly, indicating the new sentinal tree gracing his lawn.

Birlerion grimaced. "I guessed you would be."

Jennery looked at his son and smiled. "What have you gotten yourself into now?" he asked in a tone of resignation as he pulled Jared into a heartfelt hug. "Are you alright, son?" he asked, looking into his silver eyes in concern.

Jaredion smiled. "I'm fine, Pa." His eyes strayed to his sentinal.

"Jaredion why don't you go say hello to your sentinal before your mother finds out you're home?" Birlerion suggested.

Jaredion gave him a smile of pure delight and rushed off down the slope and shimmered into the tree.

Jennery looked at Birlerion. "I'm all ears," he said politely.

Birlerion tried to look innocent. "What makes you think it's anything to do with me?" he protested. "The Lady chooses her Sentinals, not me."

"Try again," Jennery said.

Birlerion heaved a deep sigh and rubbed his face. "It's complicated." He glanced towards Jaredion's tree. "I need to visit Stoneford," he said, the longing in his voice plain to Jennery.

"Then visit Stoneford, Birlerion," Jennery said, shaking his arm. "It will take you moments by waystone. Make time for you in all this mess. Your sentinal needs you as much as you need him."

Birlerion sighed again. "I know, but it's easier said than done."

"Even Jerrol had help. He didn't do everything by himself. He had you, me, Tagerill, Bryce, even Taelia. Who do you have, Birlerion?"

"Don't." Birlerion ran an agitated hand through his hair. "I have Bryce, Parsillion, Frenerion. Taurillion is over from Elothia. And anyway, I thought you wanted to know about Jaredion? How much do you want to tell Alyssa?"

"Everything," Alyssa's voice came from behind them. "I expect you to tell me everything, especially how my son has become a Sentinal. Where is he, Birlerion?" Her voice was dangerously calm.

Jennery cursed under his breath and gave Birlerion a warning glance before he turned to his wife. "He went down to his tree, love."

"Then we had better go and welcome him home," she said, outstaring her husband. Jennery surrendered and, taking his wife's arm, led the way down to the sentinal.

Jaredion shimmered out of his tree as they approached. Birlerion hung back, leaving his parents to greet him. Jaredion hugged his mother, allowing her to search his face intently. "Jared, are you alright? What happened?"

"Never better," Jaredion replied, starry-eyed. "It's like nothing you could ever imagine; he is perfect."

Birlerion's lips twitched as Alyssa frowned at her son. There was no way Jaredion would be able to explain the absolute oneness you had with your sentinal. Though he was sure Alyssa would make him try.

"How did this happen? You haven't even graduated from the academy yet. How is this possible?"

Jaredion shrugged and smiled at his mother. "I offered the Lady my sword when she needed it; she accepted it."

"But why?" Alyssa wailed.

Jaredion looked at his father. "I'm sorry, the Lady needed help, and I was there. I couldn't stand by and let innocent people be killed; it's not in me to walk on by. You never raised me to be such a person."

"I know son. I never expected you to," Jennery said softly. "I am very proud of you. As is your mother."

"Of course I'm proud of you, it's just … it's just you could have warned me," Alyssa complained, and Jennery tried to hide a smile. "Introduce us," Alyssa said, looking up at the elegant tree now permanently connected to her son.

Jaredion smiled and hugged his mother. He took her hand and led her up to his sentinal. "Please, be welcome," he said as they shimmered into the tree.

Jennery let his breath out explosively. "Well, that went better than I expected. Whatever you do Birlerion, please don't tell her all the details."

"I wouldn't dream of it. I need to return to Vespers anyway. No doubt Jaredion will tell you what happened in his own time. He needs time to rebalance." Birlerion held Jennery's eyes. "Accepting one's death is always a traumatic experience," he said, his face grave.

Jennery stiffened, his eyes widening. He slowly nodded. "I see," was all he said. He turned smoothly towards the sentinal as Alyssa and Jaredion shimmered back out of his tree, a smile on his face, though he scanned his son's face, his concern obvious.

Jaredion protested when Birlerion said he was returning to Vespers that evening, some of his calm maturity wavering without Birlerion's silent support. Birlerion hugged him farewell, murmuring in his ear, and Jaredion nodded acceptance, though his gaze followed Birlerion when he walked off down to the waystone.

They were all distracted when Tagerill and his wife, Miranda, Alyssa's mother, joined them, Tagerill boisterously asking who allowed a sentinal to park in their back garden, and Jaredion relaxed into the familiar banter of home and the gentle teasing of his sister, Saranne, who was thrilled to have a brother who was a Sentinal; the first of a new generation.

Alyssa looked thoughtful at that, and later, as she lay with Jennery, she voiced her concerns. "Why would the Lady need new Sentinals now, Lea? What does she expect of them?"

"I don't know, love, but there aren't very many Sentinals in total, you know; a few more won't hurt. Did you notice how worn Birlerion looked? He is being pulled in all directions with Jerrol out of the picture, and he doesn't have Jerrol's support structure to lean on. He needs the likes of Jared to help him."

"Did you realise he is Anders' Oath Keeper?"

Jennery looked at her in surprise. "No, he never said."

"I felt it."

"Is that why you didn't press him about Jared?" Jennery asked.

Alyssa sighed. "I know there is nothing good to know about it, and there was no point distressing Jared. He'll tell you what he wants you to know and you will tell me." She glared at him.

"Yes, dear," Jennery said with a smile.

"Jared obviously admires Birlerion, as do we all. Birlerion is under a lot of pressure. The poor man wouldn't even stop for dinner. Maybe now he has the king back on track … and Lea, it is because of Birlerion that he is back on track," she said firmly. "Maybe we ought to go to Vespers, then you'll be on hand if Birlerion needs you."

Jennery looked at his wife in awe. Her astuteness amazed him. She had seen so much in such a short time. "I'll speak to Tagerill. Maybe he ought to go. He is closer to Birlerion than I am."

"Make sure you speak to him tomorrow," Alyssa said, snuggling down in his arms.

"Yes, dear," Jennery said as he kissed her.

Birlerion arrived in Stoneford as it was getting dark. There wasn't much that he could do overnight, so he would take Jennery's advice and stop for a moment. His sentinal called him as he walked up the road to the keep, his expectant hum increasing with every step, and Birlerion relaxed into his comforting embrace.

Niallerion rushed out of the keep. "Birlerion, is everything alright? What happened?"

Birlerion grinned, rubbing a tired hand over his face. He had forgotten they would all know about Jaredion. "Yes, fine. Jaredion is fine. He is at home in Deepwater with his sentinal."

"Jaredion," Niallerion repeated with a smile. "A new brother. The family grows."

"Indeed. Can you give me moment? I just need to stop by my sentinal. That's why I came, really. I'll stay for dinner if you'll have me. I can't remember the last time I ate."

Niallerion looked at him keenly. "Of course. Come on, I'll walk with you. Take as long as you need." Birlerion's shoulders visibly relaxed as he approached his sentinal. His hand shook as he rested it on the silvery trunk before he shimmered inside. The sentinal's thrum intensified as Birlerion collapsed on the bunk, and his sentinal wrapped him in a cocoon of love and reassurance. Golden threads spun out of the air, and Birlerion closed his eyes as he became one with his sentinal. He set aside all his worries for a moment as he sank into his blissful embrace.

It was much later when Birlerion emerged, feeling relaxed and refreshed. Niallerion was hovering outside, and Birlerion laughed. "You haven't been waiting all this time for me, have you?"

Niallerion's face eased. "You looked so strained. I was worried for you," he owned, embracing him. His relief was obvious, and Birlerion wondered how bad he had looked when he'd arrived. "And anyway, I thought you might like some company eating."

Birlerion smiled. "That would be nice," he said, remembering many nights where he had eaten alone.

They entered the keep, and Birlerion paused on the threshold at the mass of people already seated in the hall. He had forgotten that he had sent Prince Pierien off to Stoneford with Mikke. Was it really only a week ago? They both looked young and disgustingly healthy.

Mikke rose and came to greet him. "Birlerion, come sit, eat. You can tell us the news later." Birlerion smiled at the young lord's knowing look.

"Of course, my lord," he murmured, bowing towards Pierien with a grin as Niallerion pushed him into a chair. Niallerion filled his plate and he began eating. He was starving. He was fending off more food when the room fell silent as Jerrol walked in.

Jerrol grinned at the room in general. "What? Can't I come home and visit on occasion?" he asked as the room descended into chaos.

Birlerion leaned back in his chair, watching in amusement as Mikke and the Sentinals vied for his attention.

Jerrol laughed. "If I'd known I'd cause such a stir, I would have waited until later."

Mikke hugged him. "Where's ma?"

"I left her at the Towers. She wanted to see Margareth."

"We didn't hear the waystone; how did you get here?" Serenion demanded.

Jerrol shrugged. "Zin'talia needed the exercise, so we rode here from Velmouth." He looked at the silent Birlerion. "I need to speak with Birlerion, if you will excuse us for a moment? We won't be long."

"Use the study, Pa," Mikke offered.

Jerrol spotted Pierien and smiled. "Pierien, how do you like Stoneford?"

"Very much, Lord Jerrol. Your son is fortunate in such a Watch."

"Indeed," Jerrol smiled. "If you would excuse us a moment?" He waited for Birlerion to rise before leading the way to his old study, now Mikke's.

"You received the king's request then?" Birlerion asked as they sat at the table.

"Ari delivered it yesterday," Jerrol said.

"And?"

"Why didn't he offer it to you?"

"I'm not you. You've run a Watch; I haven't."

Jerrol scowled at him. "You're almost running Vespers, and you're doing it much better than the king."

"You're the Lady's Captain. Maybe he thinks you'll get him a pass from the Lady."

"You're the Oath Keeper, you could do the same."

Birlerion chuckled. "You're the statesman; I'm your right hand."

Jerrol stilled. "And you don't mind?" he asked as he absently flexed his maimed right hand.

Birlerion laughed. "Don't be daft, Jerrol. You're my Captain. I've been following your orders for twenty years. Why would I mind now."

Jerrol smiled. "You've had a taste of giving out the orders for a change."

Birlerion shook his head. "I've always been handing out orders, Jerrol. I just never had to manage the upper echelon, as it were, which I will gladly leave to you. After all, you do it so well."

Jerrol nodded, reassured. "I'll only take it on if you will truly be my right hand. I can't do it without you."

"Deal," Birlerion said, holding out his hand.

Jerrol grinned in relief as he shook it. "And I hear we have a new Sentinal, young Jaredion."

"Yes," Birlerion said pensively. "The Lady didn't hold her punches with him. He had a rough introduction, but he proved his worth. I believe he will return to Vespers by the time we get there tomorrow."

"Not tonight?" Jerrol asked with interest.

"No. I promised my sentinal I would stay here tonight."

Jerrol nodded. "Good idea. Let's go speak to the family, then. They are sure to want to know more about Jaredion, as do I." He suddenly laughed. "How did Jennery take it?"

"Better than Alyssa did," Birlerion said with a wry grin.

Jerrol was still laughing as they joined the others.

Birlerion and Jerrol arrived in Old Vespers early the next morning. Jerrol went to the Chapterhouse, intending to visit the Deane, whilst Birlerion peeled off to the garrison to check on the cadets. He arrived to find Leyarille in charge of the briefing room. Kopka was overseeing, but he was letting the cadets run with their findings. More maps were tacked to the wall, with pieces of string linking what Birlerion realised were warehouses and estates.

"Report," Birlerion said as he scanned the information the cadets had collected.

"We began with Lord Gillian, as you requested," Leyarille said immediately. "Gillian owns all these buildings in Vespers and these estates in Marchwood. We found multiple holding companies that owned a range of properties. Those have yellow pins." She looked at Birlerion. "When we cross-checked those holding companies a second name kept appearing."

"Benarte," Birlerion breathed.

Leyarille nodded. "Yes, Lord Benarte. How did you know?"

"Preliminary reports from Marchwood indicate he is involved. The Inquisitors have been informed."

"Birlerion, it just keeps evolving. Every time we find one property, another crops up, and they are across all Vespiri; it is a veritable network, even if the concentration is in Old Vespers and Marchwood."

"A distribution network," Birlerion said thoughtfully. "Or not. The question is, if it isn't for distributing drugs, what is it for?" He looked around the room. "Excellent work, all of you," he said, raising his voice. "This is exemplary work, and your commanders will be informed. Keep searching. We must root out this disease before it can affect more people than it already has. We need to know what this network is for. Keep digging." He looked back at Leyarille. "Do you have a summary I can give to the king and the Inquisitors?"

Kayen handed him a report. "It's all in there. We'll begin cross-referencing the information from Woodbridge shortly. The latest reports have just begun arriving."

"Excellent," Birlerion murmured, busy scanning the report. He stared into the distance for a moment. Leyarille watched him. Her father often did that whilst he digested a lot of new information. "Leyarille, Kayen a moment." He drew them aside and gave them a lopsided grin. "Jared managed to get himself into trouble down in Marchwood. He's fine," Birlerion reassured them, "but he made Sentinal. He offered the Lady his sword and she accepted it; he is now Jaredion. He is currently in Deepwater with his tree, but he'll return here shortly. Be there for him, would you? He needs your friendship and support now more than ever."

"Of course we will," Leyarille exclaimed, "as if you'd have to ask us that."

Birlerion nodded. "Enough said, then. He did well. You all are doing well." He turned to address the room in general. "Keep up the good work. You're making the inquisitors earn their money," he said with a grin as he left the room. He paused to speak to Lieutenant Kopka. "Anything new, send to Bryce at the palace. He will be coordinating the King's Guards to go check out these locations. He can adjust as necessary. Scott's unit will report to the Sentinals at Marchwood, and the Sentinals will relay the messages here. Advise them if there are any other locations they need to check."

Kopka nodded. "Of course sir." He returned to the room as Birlerion left. There was an excited buzz in the room as the cadets discussed his visit, buoyed by his praise. Kopka clapped his hands, "Back to work, folks, let's get the missing boys list updated as quick as possible. We need to give the King's Guards as much information as possible before they are dispatched." Anterion appeared in the doorway as he finished speaking and handed Kopka a sheaf of paper, then vanished just as quick.

Kopka rifled through them. "Listen up," he barked. "Here are the preliminary interviews. Landis, start a new list on the wall, track all the missing persons, cross them off as we find them. Haven, cross-reference their location on the map. Sid, Petra, start on these." He handed out the reports.

Jerrol was waiting for Birlerion outside the gates of the garrison. As they began to walk up the road, Birlerion laughed. "I keep meaning to ask you, why don't you create a waystone at the palace? Save us climbing this damn hill every time."

Jerrol stopped dead. "I never thought," he said blankly. He concentrated, and Birlerion felt a soft chime resonate through him, and they retraced their steps to the Chapterhouse and stepped through to the new waystone. They appeared outside Bryce's office.

Birlerion began to chuckle. "That is going to annoy him so much."

Deron spoke up from his desk. "If that is what I think it is, it's going to annoy me a lot more."

"What will?" Bryce poked his head out the door. His eyes widened as he saw Jerrol. "Well, about time, too. Look at you, tanned, relaxed. What is the world coming to?"

"It's good to see you too," Jerrol replied.

"Come in, both of you. What news?"

Birlerion handed him the reports. He summarised the findings, and Bryce cursed under his breath.

"You're sure? Benarte is involved as well?"

"We have independent corroboration. The cadets found evidence here in Vespers and in Marchwood. The Inquisitors will have to investigate him as well."

"What's this I'm hearing about young, Jared?"

"It's true, he made Sentinal. You'll see him later. He found the connection in Marchwood. Has there been any word from the Inquisitors? Jaredion captured one of Benarte's henchmen running a protection racket outside of Woodbridge."

"He did what? Why haven't I heard about this?"

"Lord William's guards brought him here at least a day ago."

Bryce called in his aide. "Deron, do you have any reports from the Inquisitors on a ..." he paused "What was his name?"

"Grant," Birlerion supplied.

"...on a man called Grant, arrested in Marchwood day before yesterday, one of Lord Benarte's lackeys."

"Nothing's come in yet, sir. I'll find out," Deron replied.

Bryce nodded. "Let me know as soon as you do." He turned back to Jerrol. "When do you see the king?"

"When I tell him I'm here, I suppose," Jerrol said, and he grinned as Bryce choked.

"You mean he doesn't know? What are you doing here? Get in there, Jerrol. For Lady's sake, put us all out of our misery so we can get on and solve this mess."

"I thought Birlerion and you were doing quite well as it is."

"It will be much easier when you control the Chancellery and those prickly Inquisitors."

"Are they not helping then?" Jerrol asked.

"Not quick enough. I had to threaten them to get someone to go out in the field, and not hearing about this Grant, there's another example of them dragging their feet. Lord Pelori is too old; it's time he retired. The whole place needs shaking up."

Jerrol grinned. "I can do that."

"Well, go and make it official, then we can get the king behind us as well."

"Alright." Jerrol levered himself to his feet and looked at Birlerion. "You're coming too. You're in this as well you know."

Birlerion grimaced and followed him out of the door.

31

KING'S PALACE, OLD VESPERS

King Anders was standing beside his desk, looking out the window, his view unfettered over the formal gardens to the solitary sentinal standing on the lawns beyond. There used to be so many more. He felt the lack keenly, very aware it was his fault. No matter what excuses he made, he had still disbanded the Sentinals and banished the King's Sentinal from Vespers. He wasn't sure he would be able to convince Jerrol to return. He didn't expect him to be so forgiving as Birlerion, not after the way he had treated him the last time he had been in Vespers, not to mention how he had treated his children. Jerrol would be even less likely to forgive that.

Anders gripped the curtain, his knuckles whitening at the strength of his grip. How could he have forgotten everything his father had taught him? He was a disgrace. Weak. That ended today, hopefully.

He had managed to placate both Parsillion and Bryce, not that he'd deserved it. They had accepted his apologies and reverted back to normal immediately, much like Birlerion. Though he was well aware his relationship with

Birlerion would never be quite the same again, and not just because he was his Oath Keeper, but more because Birlerion had risked his life and acted as if he was the Oath Keeper before he had even uttered the words of the oath. He shuddered at the thought of what he could have done to Birlerion had he not listened to him.

He even forgave Birlerion for setting the healer on him. The amount of drugs and alcohol he had consumed, it was a valid concern that he had been affected somehow. He was relieved that he hadn't succumbed to some addiction, though the healer had been clear it was a close call and recommended he forgo any of it for the near future. He did have an odd yearning for something on occasion, though he wasn't sure what it was, but if that was his price to pay, then he would pay it.

Jerrol was of the same mold as Birlerion, both committed to the Lady and Remargaren. He was so lucky to have men of such calibre around him, he hoped. He took a deep breath and turned as the door opened.

Parsillion gently shut the door behind them and stood guard outside the king's chambers. He had instructions not to interrupt, no matter what. Not that he was worried.

Birlerion and Jerrol knelt before Anders, and he closed his eyes, humbled that they would still show him respect. He would make sure that he earned it.

"Rise," he said, his voice firm.

They stood, and he stared at Jerrol. The man looked really healthy. His sojourn in Senti had suited him; the fact that it had been enforced was beside the point. Jerrol held his eyes, a slight challenge in them. He wasn't going to make this easy.

Anders cleared his throat. "I owe you an apology, Jerrol. I am so sorry for the way I treated you. It was unforgivable, but I am asking you to forgive me. For the sake of Vespiri and Terolia, for Remargaren, please forgive me and allow me to show you that I have mended my ways. I regret the pain I have caused, and if I could undo it, I would, but I can't. I can only promise you that it won't happen again and that I have the very best interests for Vespiri, Terolia, and Remargaren at heart."

Jerrol stared at Anders. "That's some apology," he said with a slight smile.

"And I mean every word," Anders said seriously.

"Very well, Your Majesty, I accept your apology," Jerrol said formally, not letting him off the hook.

Anders nodded. "Thank you," he said carefully. He indicated the chairs. "Please sit. Would you care for a drink?"

Jerrol cast a glance at him. "Water, if I may," he replied politely.

Anders nodded at his steward and he served water for all. Anders' hand trembled as he took a gulp of water and then smiled at Jerrol as he placed his glass on his desk. "Don't worry, I'm currently abstaining."

Jerrol laughed. "I remember your father saying that once. I had to use his favourite brandy to combat the effects of trealt. It made him so violently ill, he could never drink the stuff again. He was most put out."

Anders laughed with him. "I remember. It was the most expensive brandy as well," he said, and suddenly it was all alright. The stilted awkwardness melted away. He looked at Jerrol and sighed. "Will you replace Pelori as chancellor for me? He wants to retire. He knows managing the Chancellery is beyond him, and quite frankly, I only kept him on because my father appointed him. But there is a disease in my administration, and I need you to cut it out." He watched Jerrol anxiously.

"On two conditions," Jerrol said.

"Name them," Anders said.

Jerrol smiled. "Birlerion is appointed First Administrator, accountable only to me and to you."

"Done," Anders said promptly. "And?"

"My word within the administration is law. You won't overturn my or Birlerion's decisions on the whims of any lord who thinks they have the authority or influence over you to change them just because he doesn't like them."

Anders considered him. "I will agree on the basis that none of these decisions negatively affect the future viability of the Kingdom of Vespiri, Terolia, or Remargaren as a whole."

Jerrol smiled. "I wouldn't expect it any other way, sire."

Anders leaned back in his chair. "Welcome to the Administration of Vespiri and Terolia, Lord Haven, Chancellor of Vespiri. "He looked at Birlerion. "Well, my Oath Keeper? You have been very quiet."

Birlerion chuckled. "I'm just trying to figure out if my new position means I'm going to be running all over the kingdom putting out fires for both of you."

"Sure to be," Jerrol laughed. "But then, Lord Birlerion, First Administrator of Vespiri and Terolia, I'm sure you wouldn't want it any other way."

Birlerion winced. "That is quite a mouthful."

Jerrol shrugged. "It's your title, you figure it out." He looked at Anders. "Sire, we have quite a situation brewing."

"So I understand. Bryce is asking for Inquisitors to accompany his guards to the estates of Lord Gillian. There is a warrant for his arrest, but he hasn't been found yet."

"And for Lord Benarte," Birlerion said.

"What?" Anders stared at him. "They are the two most senior members of my administration."

"With the most to gain from your demise, sire. After all, you have no heir, do you? Who would step in to rule but your chancellor and his administrators?"

"It's a good job I have two new loyal administrators then, isn't it?" Anders said, devoutly thanking the Lady for protecting him and his kingdom.

"You're welcome, Anders," she whispered into his ear, and he shivered.

Birlerion grimaced. "We have much to do. The cadets have identified many of the lords' properties. We have the most likely locations. We need to assign an Inquisitor to each unit. Sire, you need to formally announce our appointments so we have the authority to brow beat these people into obeying your instructions."

"I feel I ought to mention, sire, that my wife wants to petition you for a new Chapterhouse at the Watch Towers. She believes the exploration and understanding of that heritage site has been much underestimated," Jerrol said.

Anders grinned at Jerrol. "But my Chancellor will be located in Vespers. Surely you would want your wife with you?"

"Preferably, of course, sire, but we would figure it out; she is very determined. And I of course can travel via waystone."

"Why don't you suggest to your lovely wife that she relocate to Old Vespers with you and become the new Scholar Deane of the Chapterhouse of Remargaren?" Anders suggested with a gleam in his eyes. "She could then, of course, decide to open a new Chapterhouse wherever she deemed appropriate."

Jerrol stared at him. "Sire? But Liliian …"

"Liliian told me months ago that she intends to retire. I can't think of anyone more suitable to replace her than Taelia," Anders said firmly.

Jerrol stared at him in shock. "Umm, are you sure you want that many Havens in a position of power, sire?"

Anders snorted. "I think there is a higher power you all

need to concerned with before you worry about me. The Ladies will gut you if you stray from the path long before you ever get to me."

Jerrol smiled wryly and looked at Birlerion, who laughed. "I am not touching that one; that's all yours."

"What's the use of subordinates if you can't tell them what to do?"

Anders laughed. "When you figure that one out, you can tell me. Now, I will formally announce the retirement of Pelori with immediate effect and your new appointments at the Administrators Sitting tomorrow. You will both need to be in attendance, and one of you will need to lead the meeting thereafter. Pelori will give you the details. I suggest you suck him dry before he leaves, then you can consider what needs changing."

"Yes, sire," Jerrol said.

Anders cast him a suspicious glance. "Then you can instruct the King's Inquisitors to support Bryce however he needs supporting."

Birlerion frowned. "Isn't there anything we can do before then? We don't want Benarte getting wind and disappearing like Gillian."

Anders shook his head. "We have to follow protocol. We can't circumvent the law of the land; not if you want to be able to uphold it later. And anyway, both Benarte and Gillian should be at the meeting tomorrow."

Jerrol raised an eyebrow. "Well, if they turn up, we'll make sure Bryce is on hand with one of your Inquisitors to serve notice."

King Anders looked around the Administration chamber, the dark wood of the furniture, the rich golden curtains, and the flags in his colours emphasising the formality of the occasion. He nodded at his Commanders, Bryce and Stafford, and Lord Cramer from the Inquisitors office. Lord Simeon of Greenwatch represented the Watches, Ambassador Lis'arine for Terolia and Scholar Dean Liliian was present for the scholars. Three of the lords responsible for the various departments of his administration were seated opposite him. He frowned as he noted both Benarte, who was responsible for trade, and Gillian for transport, were missing. Those present included Lord Relian who oversaw taxes and finances, a relatively new position held by Mace for education, and Lord Pelori, who led the Chancellory and the King's Justice. There were two glaringly obvious absentees. He frowned at Lord Pelori. "Did the Lord Administrators Gillian and Benarte provide an acceptable reason for placing their own business above that of the Kingdom of Vespiri and Terolia?"

"No, Your Majesty."

"And they were informed of the import of this meeting?"

"Yes, Your Majesty."

"Very well, let them be marked present for the purposes of this meeting."

"Yes, Your Majesty."

"Gentlemen and lady," he called the room to order, nodding at the elderly grey-haired woman who was responsible for the scholars at the Chapterhouse. "I have but three matters to lay before the administration. The first is the very distressing report that was laid before me by the King's Justice that Lord Gillian has been guilty of growing a banned substance in Vespiri; that he was growing this substance to sell for monetary gain and to influence decisions made by the Crown of Vespiri and Teroila. He is subsequently accused of treason and served with notice to appear before the King's Inquisitors to explain his actions. His position in my Administration is rescinded, and all assets, properties and chattels are confiscated by the crown until such time he proves his innocence. Does anyone challenge this action?"

Anders paused and looked around the room of shocked lords, inwardly smiling at the dropped mouths. "Good. Action passed. Secondly," he said without pause, "that Lord Benarte is accused of protection racketeering, banditry, and associated crimes and is subsequently remanded before the King's Inquisitors to explain his actions and the actions of his people before the crown. Until such time as Lord Benarte responds and satisfactorily explains these accusations, his position in the administration is rescinded and his assets, properties and chattels confiscated by the crown. Does anyone challenge this action?"

Anders looked around the room. "No? I'm surprised. Action passed," he said remotely.

"Remind me to never piss Anders off," Jerrol whispered, watching the king in awe.

Birlerion choked.

"And finally, it is my sad duty to announce that Lord Pelori, the Lord Chancellor, has tendered his resignation. He has asked the Crown to consider allowing him to retire as he has been suffering from ill health recently and feels that he can no longer provide an adequate service to the Crown or the office he holds. I have decided to honour his request, and as such Lord Pelori will retire with immediate effect, on condition that he agrees to provide support during a to-be-agreed handover period to his successor, Lord Jerrol Haven.

"I hearby advise and confirm that Lord Jerrol Haven will succeed Lord Pelori with immediate effect as Lord Chancellor of Vespiri and Terolia and that he will be supported by the First Administrator, Lord Birlerion Descelles. They will both accede to their positions with immediate effect. The King's Justice, the King's Rangers, and the King's Administration will forthwith report to and abide by the ruling of the Lord Chancellor's office and his First Administrator. Any questions should be directed to his office." Anders looked around the chamber. "That is all I have to lay before the Administrators today; are there any other matters to be discussed?"

The chamber was silent, the Administrators gaping at him in stunned shock. Anders smiled. "In that case, Lord Pelori, I thank you for your dedicated service. We will formally acknowledge our debt to you at the confirmation of the new Lord Chancellor. I wish you a very pleasant retirement. Lord Haven, Lord Descelles, have at 'em," he said with a grin as he stepped down and left the chamber.

After a short silence, the room exploded into chaos as the lords began protesting. Jerrol watched bemused before moving to stand before the chair that the king had just vacated. He slammed his hand down on the table. "That is enough," he said loudly, his silver eyes gleaming. He waited until silence fell. "You heard the king. I am Lord Jerrol Haven, Lord Chancellor of Vespiri and Terolia, and you will listen to what I have to say if you wish to retain your seats."

"Pelori, speak up, man, you can't allow this to happen," Lord Relian protested.

Lord Cramer of the King's Inquisitors smiled grimly. "I think you will find, Lord Relian, that it already has happened."

"But the king can't just remove Benarte and Gillian. They have rights; they have a right to reply."

"They have been offered a right to reply; they should have been here today to respond to these allegations," Lord Cramer snapped. "The king followed procedure to the letter. One would almost think someone told him what to say." Cramer glared at Birlerion.

Birlerion smiled blandly.

"Why don't you all sit, and Lord Descelles will explain the current situation," Jerrol said, his gaze slowly inspecting the lords. Birlerion took the seat at his right hand and began speaking. The lords gaped at him in horror as he outlined the deaths occurring in Vespers and Marchwood, and the links to Gillian and Benarte.

"Our first action should be to find Gillian and Benarte so they can respond to these charges and either prove their innocence or accept their punishment," Jerrol said firmly. "Lord Cramer, please have your department assist Commander Bryce with his enquires. Lord Relian, your department will need to help unravel the finances of these two men. As their assets are identified, you need to record them for the Crown until decided otherwise." He looked at the head of the King's Rangers. "Commander Stafford, with Lords Benarte and Gillian's department currently leaderless, could you assist Bryce in those enquiries? I understand your cadets have already been a great help. I will appoint interim management for those departments without. Does anyone have an issue with these actions?"

Jerrol was relieved when there wasn't. Scholar Deane Liliian spoke up. "If the scholars can assist at all, Lord Chancellor. I am aware there are cadets researching in our libraries; if we can assist them to search faster, then please let me know."

"Liliian, that would be a great help." Jerrol looked at Birlerion. "Could you bring Lillian up to speed on the research so far?"

Birlerion nodded. "Of course, Lord Chancellor."

Jerrol formally closed the meeting and thanked the attendees for their time. Lord Simeon paused beside him as the others filtered out, Birlerion and Liliian in deep conversation as they left. Simeon smiled. "Congratulations, Jerrol. All Vespiri and Terolia will be much relieved."

Jerrol grimaced. "Unfortunately not all. We still have some bad apples to root out."

"There will always be bad apples of one sort or another," Simeon grinned. "That's what keeps you in office."

Jerrol laughed and made his way to the king's chambers. The king's steward bowed him in, and Jerrol stepped over the threshold and stared at Anders.

Anders looked up. "Well? My Lord Chancellor."

"Well indeed, sire" Jerrol replied. "How did you know how to deal with them?"

Anders laughed. "I asked the Justices for the correct procedure to remove administrators who were under suspicion of treason," Anders said with a wicked smile. "They were most happy to supply the information and also the fact that, once the notices were formally served in the Sitting, I could confiscate all their assets for the crown. *All* their assets, until such time as they were proven innocent," he said happily.

"It will be interesting to see how they respond. Bryce has all his unit leaders down in the briefing room getting the latest intelligence, then they will be spreading out across Vespers and Marchwood, seizing your new assets, sire."

Anders nodded. "Let's hope they find out where they are holed up. I want this finished and finished quickly."

The next afternoon, after a tour of the Administration building, Birlerion settled in his new office. A stack of reports sat on his desk, and he wondered who had left them there. Flipping through the stack, he pulled out the cadet's reports, and he was was deep in the file when a deep voice hailed him from the doorway. He looked up and was surprised to see Tagerill lounging against the frame of his open door, and peering over his shoulder, Jaredion. "Tagerill! What are you doing here? Jaredion. Come in." Birlerion shifted a pile of reports off the only other chair in his office and dumped them on the floor. "How did you find me?"

"We asked. At the Garrison, then the Justice building and then the Administrators office and now we've found you."

Birlerion embraced his brother and then Jaredion. "Well, I'm glad you have. What are you doing here?"

"Well, Jaredion is reporting back for duty, and I came to offer you some help but it doesn't look like you need it seeing as Jerrol is back … nice of him to tell us by the way, and Lord Chancellor to boot. I can't wait till I tell Jennery and Alyssa!"

"If you'd come last week, I would've fallen on your offer gladly, but as you say, things are very different this week," Birlerion agreed.

"Still, you need someone guarding you now, Birlerion," Jaredion stated firmly. "And that will be me."

"First Lord of the Administrators," Tagerill teased. "You've done well, Lord Descelles!"

"Don't," Birlerion rolled his eyes.

"See, Serillion always said you'd be the highest achiever out of all of us. I'm glad to see you've not disappointed him," Tagerill said with a laugh. He clapped Jaredion on the shoulder. "You'll have your hands full with this one."

Birlerion twisted his lips as Jaredion laughed. "Who'd have known, huh? But Jaredion, you ought to return to the cadets and graduate."

Tagerill laughed. "He's already graduated with flying colours, and Jerrol has already assigned Jaredion to you. So no arguments."

"Don't I get a say in this?"

"No!" Tagerill and Jaredion replied together.

"Not much point being the First Administrator, if I don't have a voice."

Jaredion's face fell. "Do you really object to having me guard you?"

"Of course he doesn't. He's just teasing you," Tagerill said before Birlerion could speak.

Birlerion rose and rushed around his desk to Jaredion. "No, Jaredion, honest, I couldn't be happier with anyone else, even Tagerill. I never meant I didn't want you. I only thought you would want to finish out at the academy."

Jaredion relaxed. "You need protection, and I would be honoured to protect you."

Birlerion gripped his arms. "And I'm honoured to have you." He glanced at Tagerill. "You can at least stay and celebrate Jaredion's new assignment. I need to see someone in the city. Join us for a drink."

"I'm surprised you have time to go out drinking."

"You can't work all the time," Birlerion replied with a grin. "Come, Jaredion, escort us into the city."

"Who is this we are talking to? Where's the real Birlerion? Jared, what have you done to him?"

Jaredion laughed as he followed them out of the building and down into the city.

"I'm glad to see that you are finally acting sensibly at last. It's about time you had a guard at your shoulder."

"You haven't given me a choice," Birlerion replied, casting a smile over his shoulder at Jaredion. "But I'm sure Jaredion will do fine."

Tagerill ruffled Jaredion's hair and Jaredion pushed him away. "Your new position suits you, lad. At least you've started your new job under no illusions. I can't imagine Birlerion will be able to stay out of trouble for long."

Birlerion's protests were half-hearted, and Tagerill slapped him on the shoulder as they entered the warren of back streets. Tagerill inspected the Docker's Tavern with a suspicious eye. "Are you sure this is where you go drinking,

Birlerion? This looks worse than some of the places I used to take you to back in the day."

Birlerion laughed and pushed open the door. "Evening, Jim," he nodded at the bar man.

Jim nodded back. "He's out back." He eyed the two Sentinals. "Not sure he'll be pleased to see more of 'em, though," he said dubiously.

Birlerion laid some coins on the bar. "They are friends of mine, don't worry," and he headed out to the back room. He ducked into the dim room and smiled at the lone occupant. "Tom, it's good to see you. I'd like to introduce you to Sentinal Jaredion, and this is my brother, Tagerillion."

Tom quirked an eyebrow. "Pleased t' meet yer."

Tagerill grinned. "Likewise, I'm sure."

Tom inspected him. "I know yer name. You're from Deepwater, aren't you?"

Tagerill smiled. "Greens originally, now Deepwater, yes."

"That's right, yer held the line for Jennery, didn't yer?"

Tagerill stilled. "Yes," he said more seriously. "I did."

"Fine bit o' defending, I heard." He looked at Birlerion, "Yer brother, yer say?"

Birlerion nodded. "Yes," he said softly as he accepted a mug from Jim. Jaredion moved to stand by the door.

"It's good to have family," Tom said agreeably. "Yer never know when you need them."

"True," Birlerion agreed, sipping his ale.

"A toast," Tagerill smiled, a mischievous glint in his eye. "Too old friends, family, and new responsibilities. I give you Lord Birlerion Descelles, First Administrator of Vespiri and Terolia."

Tom's eyes almost popped out of his head. "No kiddin'," he breathed. "Lord Birlerion." He saluted Birlerion with his mug and took a deep gulp.

"I hope this doesn't change anything and we can still meet, Tom," Birlerion said.

"Don't see why not. I should've thought you'd need it more now."

Birlerion relaxed. "Good. You know I value all that you do for me."

Tom shrugged. "It's for our benefit, too, and you listen, which is more than others do. I'd say it's good for both of us."

"Well, you'll be pleased to hear that both Gillian and Benarte have received a summons and that all their assets have been seized by the Crown."

Tom's grin was pure evil. "That's good news. That Gillian, he's a greedy man. Benarte … he is just plain nasty. But Birlerion, think on. Remember a lot of folks earn their livin' from 'em. Be careful what you do with them assets; it could be bad for some."

Birlerion nodded. "Good point, I'll make sure it's done carefully. Won't be of much benefit to the king if they all fold, now, would it?"

Tom laughed and took another gulp of his ale. He sobered up. "Any news on them boys?"

Birlerion sighed. "I'm afraid not. We haven't managed to trace them back to where they've been held. They disappear and they reappear, there is nothing in between. If we can apprehend Gillian, he may be able to give us more. If you hear anything about his whereabouts or Benarte, let me know."

"Will do," Tom agreed. "Keep in touch," he said, his eyes straying to the door.

"I will," Birlerion promised as he rose. He led the Sentinals back out into the bright daylight.

"Well," Tagerill said with a huff of breath, "you know how to show a man a good time."

Birlerion chuckled. "Come on, we'd better get back."

Tagerill grinned. "I'll head back to the Waystone. No point going all the way uptown just to come back again." He hugged Birlerion. "Take care of yourself. Those men are not going to go down quietly."

Birlerion nodded. "That's what the King's Guard are for," he replied.

"And you," Tagerill thumped Jaredion's shoulder, "make sure you look after him; he's turning out to be worse than Jerrol was, and speaking of Jerrol, who's protecting him these days?" Tagerill asked.

Birlerion wasn't fooled by his casual question, he knew Tagerill wouldn't like his answer. "Fonorion." Fonorion was one of the oldest Sentinals still serving, it was time he retired.

Tagerill frowned. "We are too few," he said bluntly. "Can't you call some of the Terolian Sentinals here?"

"We are growing, with the likes of Jaredion here; the Lady will provide us with what we need."

"Well, call me if you need me." Tagerill held his brother's gaze.

"I will," Birlerion promised.

"Good." Tagerill suddenly laughed. "I'll see you later." And with a cheery wave, he strolled off towards the waystone. Birlerion smiled after him and then, shaking his head, he turned back towards the Justice buildings, Jaredion following close behind.

32

KING'S PALACE, OLD VESPERS

Elliarille watched the king with icy concentration as he circulated amongst his courtiers on his way to his throne. The receiving chamber and throne room were resplendent in candlelight, the oath engraved in the wall behind his throne flushed with a golden glow.

Anders had rebuffed her repeatedly and banned her from bringing any drugs into the palace. Her position was precarious and it was all Birlerion's fault. She knew it was him. The king no longer listened to her, had even threatened to ban her too if she didn't stop making a scene. She had toned down her histrionics, but that didn't mean she wasn't angry.

It had been five days since Anders had made Jerrol his Chancellor, and she didn't like the changes occurring in the palace.

She watched Birlerion cross the room to the throne and tensed. He paused to speak to the king, and the king laughed. He *laughed* with Birlerion, of all people. She watched him as she chewed her finger. It was all Birlerion's fault. He was always in the way, diverting the king's attention, staring down at people. If he wasn't here, then it would all go back to the way it had been. Anders had loved her before Birlerion had turned up and spoiled it.

She considered the idea carefully. If there was no Birlerion, the king would pay her attention again and she would be back in favour. She smiled at the thought, and a shudder of desire ran through her and sparked a sense of longing. She watched Birlerion intently. He was a good-looking man to be sure; he had a lean body, and she knew he trained often. She had seen him sparring in the ring. She imagined his strong arms around her; he would be ideal. The thought of running her fingers through his thick black hair was intoxicating. Her gaze moved on to the dark-haired man at his shoulder. Ah, the new Sentinal, young Jaredion. He would taste good too, and young. She could teach him to love her, both of them. She watched them with a calculating gaze.

Her brother was worrying as usual, complaining about her behaviour, annoyed about one thing or another. He never relaxed and enjoyed life. As if anyone could harm them. They were the Lady's Sentinals. Leyandrii had chosen them. She wrinkled her brow as she thought about Birlerion again. Leyandrii had chosen him first, right in front of her, and then they had stared at her as if she was stupid because she hadn't heard Leyandrii's invitation straight away. Birlerion wouldn't take Anders from her like he had Leyandrii. At least Gillian would help them. Such a boorish lord, but Ellaerion seemed to think he was perfect for their needs. Her needs. As long as he kept his mouth shut and did as he was told, all would be well.

Elliarille approached Birlerion in time to overhear him murmur an aside to Jaredion.

"What time were we supposed to meet Tom?"

The young Sentinal leaned forward and replied. "A

chime ago. Should I go and let him know you're detained here?"

"I suppose you'll have to." Birlerion frowned at her as she placed her hand on his arm. Yes, he would do just fine. Jaredion blushed as he averted his eyes from her low-cut gown, so sweet and innocent. Birlerion scanned the room as if looking for someone, and his gaze paused on her brother; he was leaning against the wall, watching the room.

Ellie drew his attention back to her. "Birlerion, where have you been?"

Birlerion smiled at her, but it didn't reach his eyes. She would make them sparkle with love for her.

"Around," he said.

"We missed you. After all, you are the life of the party these days, aren't you?" she asked coyly.

Birlerion watched her. "I would suggest that is you, Elliarille. You do so love parties, don't you? Aren't you fortunate the king is so lavish in his entertainment; where would you go otherwise?"

"Now, now, Birlerion," she laughed, though anger flashed through her. Who was he to chide her behaviour? "Be nice. We're all friends, after all."

"Are we?" he asked bluntly. The king observed them, aware of the change in atmosphere, and Jaredion shifted behind Birlerion.

Elliarille moved her gaze to him. "A new Sentinal, the first in over three thousand years. Let me look at you. Welcome, brother," she said with a smile.

Jaredion bowed. "Thank you, my lady."

"The young today are so well mannered. Young Mikkeal was just as nice," she said with an edged smile. "The Watches are turning out such nice young stock. Maybe I ought to go and visit?"

Birlerion smiled gently. "Yes, but I thought you wanted

more mature company?"

"But you can teach the young so much more than a mature man. After all, they are a new book waiting to absorb what you tell them," she said, holding his eyes.

Jaredion muttered in his ear, and Birlerion nodded. The boy turned away and left the room. "Or not so polite. Maybe I need to teach him better."

"There is nothing you could teach that Jaredion needs to know," Birlerion said, stiffening as Elliarille spun around him. She laughed as she trailed her hand across his back. She glanced towards her brother, and he levered himself off the wall. "But Birlerion, you once said I could help you feel much better," she teased as a young woman approached. Lithe and slender, she had her brown hair tied back, silver eyes gleaming in the lamplight. She wore a cadet ranger's uniform.

Elliarille watched them closely, noting the way the girl extended her hand and then stopped as she reached him. Birlerion leaned towards her as she began to speak in his ear.

"Another example of the lack of manners in the young," Elliarille interrupted them. "And here I was just saying that the young were so polite. I was obviously mistaken."

Leyarille flushed and bowed slightly. "I am sorry for the interruption, my lady."

"Ah, and you must be Jerrol's daughter, the not Sentinal," she said, drawing herself up so she could look down on Leyarille.

"Now you are showing your claws, Ellie, and I thought you were trying to show how nice you could be," Birlerion said with a slow smile.

"But Birlerion," she fluttered her lashes at him, "you love me. I don't need to show you how nice I am, you told me so." She watched Leyarille closely; the girl listened with polite interest. She smiled at Leyarille. "I've known Birlerion ever since he was made Sentinal, from a rough, uncut boy to the man we see before us today. He turned out quite well, didn't he?"

"It's a shame time hasn't been so kind to you, isn't it, Ellie? You seem to have found a preference for speaking ill of others," Birlerion said, his voice hardening.

"Be careful, Birlerion, the king will only put up with so much. You may plant your garden with a flush of new blooms, but once they are cut, what do you have left then? You can enjoy them while they have water, but even then, they will fade and die."

"But flowers that are nurtured and cared for can last a life-time," Birlerion replied, watching her.

Ellie smiled, her face stiff. "But who will look after them when you are not there to tend them?" she asked as she twirled away.

Leyarille frowned as she watched Ellie flirt and laugh her way across the room. "What did she mean?"

Birlerion stared after Ellie in concern. "I believe," he said softly, "that was a thinly veiled threat."

"Why would she threaten you?"

"She wasn't, she was threatening you, my dear. Please make sure you take care. Who did you come up with?"

"I came on my own. It's young boys that are going missing, not girls. That's what I came to tell you. There's been another body found, down near the warehouses, a new location. Taurillion reported it."

Birlerion suddenly stiffened and then cursed. "I let Jared, go off alone" he said, striding across the room, his glance swept the room. Ellaerion was nowhere to be seen.

With a smile, Ellie watched him leave, the girl at his shoulder.

Jaredion hurried through the quiet streets down towards the harbour. The stale, fishy aroma was strong on the night air, the silence unnerving. He glanced over his shoulder as his neck prickled. Someone was watching him. He picked up the pace, but the feeling intensified. He unsheathed one of his daggers as he passed a dim building, and he felt the rush of air and turned as his neck stung. "Help!" he yelled at the top of his lungs as he threw his dagger. Unsheathing his sword, he staggered. Fumbling for his second dagger, he thrust it into the wooden boards of the building as he collapsed to the ground, his hand at his neck.

He dimly heard a man cursing, and a boot connected with his ribs as he passed out. The men dragged his body around the back of the warehouse as people came out of their homes, lanterns raised. A small crowd gathered, peering up and down the empty street.

A murmur of concern rose as the sound of pounding feet grew louder. Taurillion came to a skidding halt. "Did anyone see what happened?"

"No, we just heard a shout. There were noone 'ere when we came out."

"May I borrow a lamp? Please, stay in your homes. I need to see if there are any tracks." He took the lamp that a man handed to him and cast it over the ground. *"Marguerite, my love?"* he murmured, *"do you see anything?"* Her vision overlaid his, and he saw the drag marks. His face pinched. As they inspected the building as a glint caught his eye, and he crouched by the wall. He picked up the dart on the floor, he tasted the point, and spat it out, "Chlorem," he said softly. He rose and saw the dagger, and he carefully levered it out of the wall. Hefting the dagger, he followed the drag marks back around the building, where they ended. He was about to turn off towards the Chapterhouse when Birlerion and Leyarille came running towards him.

"What is it?" Birlerion gasped as he reached him.

Taurillion held up the dart and the dagger. "I was down in the harbour with Inquisitors, we found another body. I heard a yell. The sound carries on the night air. I rushed up here and found these."

Birlerion took the dagger. "It's Jaredion's," he said numbly, as if the boy hadn't been through enough already.

Taurillion sighed with regret. "I heard him shout, but I was too far away. They got him with a dart. It's tipped with Chlorem; he didn't have a chance. I'm surprised he even had time to get his dagger out. The tracks lead up towards the Chapterhouse, but I'm assuming you didn't see anything when you came here?"

"Nothing, the roads were quiet; we saw your lantern and came to you."

"I'll see if I can track him any further, but the trail was already petering out. I think they must have picked him up."

"We'll head back to the garrison and rouse the guards. We'll get them doing a house-to-house search in this area. Keep looking and be careful. I'd leave Leyarille with you, but I'm running out of people I trust at my own back!"

"You shouldn't be travelling on your own anyway, so I wouldn't accept. You're an important man now, Birlerion. You need a Sentinal at your shoulder."

"And I will have a Sentinal at my shoulder," Birlerion replied, "when we find Jaredion; that's his job. You reported a body earlier?"

"Yes, another young lad, dumped behind the warehouse. No marks except slight burns on his wrist and ankles where he'd been restrained. Otherwise, there was no obvious cause of death. The healers have him."

"We'll stop by there later. Thanks for sticking around, Taurillion," Birlerion said, gripping his arm.

"You need us, Birlerion. It's what we are here for; to help protect the Lady's people."

"I know, but I am beginning to worry that we need to protect our people against one of our own," Birlerion said, running a hand through his hair.

Leyarille stiffened and considered who he might suspect. From the way she had acted today, her guess would be Elliarille, but she had been at court, so it couldn't be her. She followed Birlerion, silently shadowing him, watching the streets. She may not be a Sentinal, but she'd do her damnedest to protect him. She didn't know how he had the stamina, or the memory for all the things he was expected to do every day. He suddenly stopped and cursed. "What time is it? Do you know?" he asked.

"It's got to be past midnight."

"Damn."

"Why?" Leyarille asked as he turned back toward the barracks.

"I was supposed to meet Tom tonight; he said he had some news. It's too late now. I'll have to try and find him tomorrow."

They arrived at the barracks and Birlerion left Leyarille in the briefing room, plotting the area to be searched as he went to rouse the rangers. He returned with Commander Stafford and began summarising the situation. Leyarille's respect for him ratcheted up another notch as he clearly laid out the plan of attack. She listened and learned.

Commander Stafford nodded in agreement. "I've got eight units of four men I can send out now. I can assign a cadet with each as a runner to carry messages. Who do you want to go with?"

"I'll take the low end of the East Road, Leyarille will come with me seeing as she is here, send out the others either side. All report back here."

"Very well. Good luck," Stafford said before turning away.

"Stafford, send word up to the chancellor for me. He ought to know."

Stafford nodded, this time leaving the room.

"Grab a field kit." Birlerion's grin was strained. "Let's be prepared for once."

Leyarille nodded and pulled a pack out of a cupboard and slung it over her shoulder. She left the door open, pulling a couple of packs out, hoping others would take the hint, before following Birlerion out to the parade ground, where squads of rangers were waiting. Lieutenant Calver was handing out assignments. "Tosca with Scott, Statten with Landis, Nimes with Fenton ..." Birlerion left him to it and left, Leyarille close behind him.

Birlerion and Leyarille returned to the barracks with the rangers as the sun rose. The houses had been swept clean; all they had done was upset a lot of important people.

"Get some sleep," Birlerion said gruffly, rubbing his eyes. "No point missing something because we're too tired to see it. Back at midday. We start again then." He watched her drop her field kit in the control room and leave. Her eyes were red-rimmed with tiredness, much like his own he expected. He desperately prayed to the Lady that Jaredion would be alright.

Staring at the map, he tried to think where they could have taken him without anyone seeing. He had been sure they would find him in the housing that was nearest to the Chapterhouse. He considered a new angle and began jotting notes, only stopping when Kopka entered the room.

"No luck?" Birlerion asked. Kopka looked exhausted too.

"Nothing, sir."

"I want to start a new search for properties in the name of Tousette. See what you can find. Housing, warehousing, businesses, anything."

"Tousette? Who are they?"

"A very old family, who may or may not be involved. Can you make it urgent? We need to start checking as soon as possible."

"Of course, I'll rouse the cadets. Birlerion, if I may say, get some sleep. You're no good keeling over in the middle of a fight."

Birlerion grimaced and stood. "I'll go home for a couple of chimes. If I'm not back by midday, send someone to wake me up. Make sure the chancellor gets a report."

Kopka nodded. "I'll go up myself once I've started the search off."

"Thanks," Birlerion said as he left.

Kopka finished his report and stood at attention. He hadn't expected the king to be present; he felt grubby and unkempt and very tired.

"And Birlerion went home to get some sleep, you said?" Jerrol asked.

"Yes, he asked to be woken up at midday if he hadn't returned by then. I tasked a cadet to go wake him if he doesn't arrive at the briefing room by then."

"Who was the target of the new search?"

"Tousette, sir."

"And who are they?"

"I don't know, Your Majesty. Lord Birlerion just said it was a very old family who may be involved."

"A family he knew from before then," Jerrol murmured.

"Possibly sir."

"Thank you, lieutenant, you look exhausted. Go get some sleep."

"Yes sir," Kopka saluted and left.

The king spoke pensively. "Jerrol, have you considered that these people are escalating? They are targeting Sentinals now. I wonder if Birlerion's inquiries have hit close to home."

Jerrol frowned at the king. "What do you mean?"

"The other night. Elliarille and Birlerion had quite a chat. Your daughter heard some of it, maybe ask her what it was about. It didn't look very friendly to me."

Jerrol nodded. "I'll check with Leyarille and speak to Birlerion later once he wakes up. Maybe Fonorion should stand at his back; he is exposed without Jaredion. I never thought I'd ever say that about Birlerion, he is usually protecting me, and now I'm worrying about him. I don't know how he did it all these years."

"You need Fonorion at your back, Jerrol; we can't afford for anything to happen to you either."

Jerrol smiled sadly. "We don't have enough Sentinals in Vespers to go around. I'll send a message to Tagerill. Birlerion said he offered to come and help."

"Do that, and any other Sentinals who can come," the king suggested. "We need all the help we can get."

Jaredion slowly regained consciousness. His head ached; it thumped in time with his ribs. Dry-mouthed, he went to rub his lips and realised his hands were tied to two bed posts; he wriggled and realised his ankles were tied too. He was tied spread-eagled on a bed in a room he didn't recognise.

He rolled his head, but his vision was blurry and he couldn't see much. He shouted for help, and the room echoed with his shouts, and his headache worsened. No one came. He struggled against the ropes, gaining nothing but sore wrists; the ropes were sturdy and unyielding. He tried to jack knife his legs, but there wasn't enough give in the rope.

Resting a moment, he tried to think, his mind slow and sluggish. Don't panic, he thought. What would Birlerion do? Try and talk his way out, he thought, with a panicky laugh. But without anyone to con, that wouldn't get him far. He had lost both his daggers, so he had nothing sharp in reach, not that he could have reached them even if he did still have them.

He tried shouting again, but his voice was getting husky and his throat sore. After a while, exhaustion dragged him down and he dozed. When he woke again, bright sunlight flooded through the tattered curtains and he could see the room was bare and dilapidated. The silence was oppressive.

Twisting his wrists, he hissed as the ropes burned his skin. They were unyielding. Heart pounding, Jaredion tried not to panic.

"Lady, please help me," he murmured, and the image of the little black Arifel who had shown up in Marchwood filled his mind.

"Pel? Pel can you hear me?" Jaredion shouted. He had forgotten he could call on the Arifels. Continuing to struggle, he repeated the call silently, over and over in his mind.

Burning pain in his wrists made him stop struggling, his wrists were raw and he gasped in breath, calming his racing heart. A soft meep preceded a gentle thump as Pel landed on his chest and peered at him.

"You came," he breathed. "You need to find out where I am and go and tell Birlerion. He needs to come and release me."

Pel peered up at him, and tilted her head, inquisitively.

"Can you look outside, is there a house name, or a street

sign? Can you tell where in Old Vespers I am?" At least, he hoped he was still in Old Vespers; he supposed he could be anywhere. Shelving that worrying thought, he concentrated on convincing Pel to go and search outside. "Show me what the building looks like."

Pel chirruped and disappeared.

It seemed to take forever for the little Arifel to return, but when she did, she projected images into his mind of a dilapidated looking building surrounded by similar buildings, some in better repair, some not. There were no street names that he could see.

"Is there a number on the door?"

Pel showed him an image of the front of the house; number 2.

"Go and show Birlerion. Tell him I need help, urgently. You need to show him where to come."

Pel settled on his chest and chirruped.

"Birlerion! Pel, go and tell Birlerion to come here." An even deeper worry stirred in Jaredion's gut. Had something happened to Birlerion? "Pel, you remember Birlerion, he was with me in Marchwood." Jaredion shared an image of Birlerion.

Pel fluttered her wings and stirred uneasily before settling on his chest again. Jaredion glanced out the window where the sunlight no longer filled the room. The sun had moved, and time was passing. It was taking too long; someone could return at any time. His stomach fluttered at the thought.

"Alright. How about Parsillion or Taurillion? Can you find them and bring them here?" Jaredion imagined Taurillion and then Parsillion and the little Arifel rose and disappeared.

Exhaling a deep breath, Jaredion started shouting again, struggling against the ropes.

33

RANGERS ACADEMY, OLD VESPERS

Leyarille woke and blearily stared around the barracks. Someone had just collapsed exhausted into their bunk. She jerked upright. What time was it? She sluiced her face in cold water and ran her fingers through her hair, scrabbling to find a comb. She tied her hair up out of her face and rushed back to the briefing room.

Scott was running the room. A new search was underway, and there were a handful more locations to check. Returning units were reassigned or sent to get some rest. She wondered if she would get to go out again. Fenton arrived and reported that the houses on Long Street were clear, and it was crossed off the list. He grinned at her nastily, his eyes glittering. He seemed like he was going to say something, but then he changed his mind and walked away, quite jauntily for him. She ignored him.

"Where is Lord Birlerion?" she asked Scott as she looked at the maps. "He said to be back at midday."

"He went home to get some sleep," Scott replied, concentrating on the papers before him.

She took another report and began marking it on the map. "Who are we investigating now?" she asked abruptly.

"Name of Tousette. Lord Birlerion started it off early this morning before he left."

"And he hasn't been back for the results?" she asked, worried. The day was progressing and there was still no Birlerion. *Lord* Birlerion, she corrected herself. He was even further from her grasp now than he was before. Every time she thought she was catching up with him, he took another step away.

She had missed seeing him today. She would make time to find him tomorrow. Sighing deeply, she closed her eyes and rubbed her temples. An image of his face appeared before her, his hand reaching for her, and she smiled and extended her hand in response. As the image wavered, she opened her eyes and blinked away sudden tears. Returning to work, she asked, "Did he say anything? He would want a report."

"We sent the reports to the chancellor, as he requested."

"What else did he say?" Leyarille persisted.

"I don't know as I wasn't there; that was what Kopka told me when I took over. Now will you let me concentrate?"

A messenger came in the door and handed a note to Scott, and he looked across at Leyarille. "Haven, the chancellor wants to see you, now." Leyarille rose and began the long walk up to the palace. When she arrived, she found her father was frowning over more paperwork on his desk. Everyone seemed to be frowning over reports.

"Ah, Leyarille. Come in, sit." Leyarille sat. "I understand you were with Birlerion at the palace the night Jaredion was taken."

"Yes, sir," she said hesitantly, not sure what her father wanted, and whether she should call him Pa or not. She erred on the side of caution.

"The king said Birlerion and Elliarille had quite an intense conversation. Do you know what it referred to?"

"Birlerion said it was a thinly veiled threat against me, but I wasn't so sure. I thought she was threatening him."

"What makes you say that?"

Leyarille frowned. "I'm not sure, it's just there was a definite undercurrent to the conversation. She was talking about cutting flowers and he was saying they would live if nurtured."

Jerrol stared at her. "Do you remember exactly what they said?"

Leyarille concentrated for a moment. "Something about planting a garden with new blooms, but once they are cut, they die. And Birlerion replied that flowers that are nurtured and cared for can last a lifetime, and then she said something like, who will look after them when you are not there?"

She was shocked as her father cursed fluently. Her eyes widened, and she stored a few away for future use.

"When he arrives, tell him I want to see him right away."

"Yes, sir."

"And I mean right away!" her father said peremptorily. "Take the waystone back."

"Thank you, sir," she said and hurried to the new waystone her father had created outside Bryce's office, hoping Birlerion would be at the garrison when she arrived.

Ari erupted into the air in front of Jerrol and flapped his wings in his face. Jerrol grabbed the little Arifel and brought him to his chest, trying to sooth him. "Alright, alright, give me a chance," Jerrol exclaimed sitting down in his chair with a huff.

Ari calmed down enough for Jerrol to place him on his desk and remove the message tube. The little Arifel was bombarding him with images of Margareth and the Watch Towers. "You came from Margareth?" he asked as he skimmed the message. "Tell her I'm on my way," he said as he stood and called Fonorion to him.

He hurried to the palace waystone and stepped to the Watch Towers. He was glad he had taken the time to create a waystone at the towers when Venterion and Tianerille had first taken over. They stepped out into the soft evening air and hurried to the courtyard. Margareth was waiting for them, her eyes luminous, her face anxious.

"It's the Veil, Pa, it's being ripped apart, repeatedly. I've been fixing it, but I found traces of Birlerion in the weave."

Jerrol frowned. "What? He's asleep at home, isn't he?" He looked at Fonorion. "Have we had word yet?"

"Nothing yet."

Jerrol nodded. "He's obviously not woken up yet." He turned back to Margareth. "Is there anything else you can tell me?"

She shook her head. "I thought it might be better if you had a look? You know the Veil better." She had been leading them into her tower as she spoke, and as she arrived in her room, she indicated the chair in mute appeal.

Jerrol looked at her worried face and lay back in the chair, staring up at the stone ceiling. Fonorion positioned himself by the door, watching carefully, not sure what was happening.

Jerrol broke through straight away and reached for the Veil, instinctively soothing its petulant complaints. He saw the repairs immediately; Margareth had done a good job. He searched the weave and stiffened as he recognised Elliarille. He cast about, sensing Birlerion, but it was very faint.

He returned and hesitated a moment as the solid stone walls of the tower around him clicked into place, and he sat up. He looked at Margareth. "You're right. Elliarille is very present in the weave."

"Elliarille?"

"She was a Sentinal we rescued from the Veil at Oprimere. It seems she has been able to return. I think if we find her, we'll find out what is really going on." He looked at Margareth, "I think it's time I had a chat with Elliarille and Ellaerion."

Jerrol returned to Old Vespers and sent out a request for Elliarille and Ellaerion to report to him and waited impatiently. He seriously began to worry for Jaredion's safety and sent Fonorion to Deepwater, asking Jennery and Tagerill to come to Vespers.

Finally, news came that Taurillion had received a visit from a new Arifel, with news of Jaredion's whereabouts. The directions where vague, but they narrowed down the search area, and the rangers had been redeployed.

Then as darkness fell, the relief; they had found Jaredion. That knowledge drove all thought of anything else out of Jerrol's head. He hurried to the palace infirmary, thanking the Lady. He had been dreading informing Jennery and Alyssa that their son was missing.

Jerrol waited outside the infirmary, nervously pacing. He stilled as Healer Francis opened the door. "He was lucky, a bit dehydrated, rope burns, nothing that won't heal," he said, before letting Jerrol in.

Jerrol sighed out his breath and grinned as Jaredion stopped eating long enough to grin back at him. He was a bit pale, but as Francis said, he looked fine.

"You gave us a scare," Jerrol said as he stopped by the bed.

"I'm sorry, Uncle Jerrol, it was all so fast. I felt a sting, and the next thing I knew, I was collapsing on the ground."

Jerrol hugged him. "You did well to leave the signs you did. Very well."

"But I couldn't escape, the ropes were too strong." He frowned at his uncle. "But Uncle Jerrol, there was no one there, at no time. And the guards who found me said the place was abandoned and derelict. I don't understand why."

Jerrol sighed. "None of this makes any sense, but we'll figure it out."

Jaredion swallowed. "The guard said the ropes were triple cored when they cut them; there was no way I would have been able to split them."

Jerrol gripped his shoulder. "Don't worry about it, Jaredion. Eat, rest. Stay here until your father gets here. You can report back to duty after he's seen you."

Birlerion struggled up from the darkness. His head thumped painfully as he tried to form a coherent thought. He didn't remember getting drunk last night. Trying to raise his hand to face, he realised he was restrained and abruptly opened his eyes. Heart racing, he scanned the empty room. A fine sweat covered his skin as he discovered he was propped up against a wooden headboard, his arms tied to either bed post, his legs splayed out and tied to two more posts. Twisting, he tried to loosen his bonds, but the rope chafed his skin and held tight.

He searched the room, but it didn't tell him anything. It was nondescript; a single curtained window, sparsely furnished, giving no indication of its owner, but deep down, he knew. Ellie, he thought bitterly. She had finally got him on her territory. He tugged the ropes, but the bed was sturdy and ungiving. The ropes looked new and in good condition and scored his skin. If the bitter taste in his mouth was any indication, she had drugged him. He remembered the dart's sting in his neck as he had passed the Lady's temple, just like Jaredion, and he prayed the boy was alright. She had taken his jacket and boots, and his shirt was loose, unfastened down the front. Breathing slightly easier, he was relieved he was still wearing his trousers.

He tensed as the door opened and Ellie flounced into the room; her frilly shift floated around her, making her seem to skim across the floor. She placed the items she was carrying on the table next to the bed. Her face broke out into huge smile as she saw he was awake. She hopped onto the bed and ran a finger down his face. "Dearest Birlerion, do you love me?" She frowned as he flinched away from her touch. "Birlerion! You love me as I love you," she said petulantly.

"If you loved me, I wouldn't be tied to a bed," he growled, his anger showing.

"But darling, you kept saying no. You need to love me the way you are supposed to. Dear, dear Birlerion, saving himself for me all these years." She smoothed his shirt open and ran her fingers down his chest. "So firm," she breathed as she kissed his skin. She inhaled deeply, and Birlerion tried to twist away.

"My love, there is nowhere to go." She slid her hands down his body, and as she brushed the stitches in his side, he winced. Her hands paused over the wound. "So this was what you were hiding. Such a shame for such beauty to be marred," she said softly, bending to kiss his chest. She sat up and looked at him. "But that won't affect you, will it? So strong, so brave. Poor, poor Birlerion, working so hard and yet carrying such an injury." She sat up and slid her hand under the waist band of his trousers.

"Ellie, stop," Birlerion warned, helpless to stop her.

Her hand slid down and grasped him. Birlerion gasped.

"Are you ready for me?" she asked, her eyes glittering bright. "That's right. You're mine," she crooned.

Fine tremors rippled through Birlerion as he tensed. He had to escape; he had to convince her to release him. This couldn't be happening. She was high on something, and she wasn't going to stop. He twisted desperately, the ropes burning his skin, the pain steadying his panic. He had to think. "Ellie, this isn't how it should be. You can't expect me to love you like this. Untie me; it will be much better," he said, lowering his voice.

"Tell me you love me."

"I love you, Ellie."

"Say it like you mean it, as if you were saying it to *her*," she said as her hands worked harder. He struggled beneath her, trying to twist away, and she scowled. Birlerion froze at the expression on her face.

"Ellie, please," Birlerion whispered.

"You had better be ready for me," she warned. "I'll show you the way, and you will never feel the same again afterwards." Her voice was getting deeper, and her expression smoothed out. "You will be the special one, Birlerion, I know you will." Her voice softened, and Birlerion watched her with concern as she flitted between anger and happiness from one breath to the next.

"I know! This will make you feel better, and then you will do as I say." She picked up a dagger and drew the cold steel down his chest. She flicked it under one of the stitches, and Birlerion flinched. "Ah, ah behave now, Birlerion, or you will pay for it, and we don't want that, do we? Why spoil something so beautiful?" she murmured under her breath as she flicked another stitch. "So ugly," she breathed, flicking another, and Birlerion hissed at the sting as his skin split, and he shuddered as the warmth of his blood trickled down his side.

She frowned at him as he stilled, drawing in his breath, her attention caught by the rapidly beating pulse at his throat. She rested a finger on his neck, concentrating on the beat; her lips parted as she watched him. His neck stung as she held the knife at his throat. "Open your mouth," she said, twisting the knife, and he hissed through his teeth as the knife bit and blood trickled down his neck, the heat of his blood stark against his chill skin.

"Ellie, please, you don't have to do this," he beseeched, but she jammed a vial between his teeth, and he choked as the bitter liquid slid down his throat. He gagged and swallowed as Ellie crooned above him.

"See? Love me, Birlerion, like you mean it. Love. Me." She leaned over him and kissed his neck, sucking the wound she had made. She moved down his neck and bit him hard, and he jerked underneath her, and she drew her breath in. She kissed him, massaging gently, swirling her fingers lightly over his skin as she watched his eyes glaze as the drug took effect.

"Love me, Birlerion," she whispered, sliding against his body. Kissing his chest, she sat up. She undid the ties at his waist and tugged his trousers down. Smiling at the sight, she straddled him and caressed his skin. His body responded beneath her, and she quickened. "Ah yes, Birlerion come with me and I'll show you the stars." Birlerion's breathing grew ragged beneath her as he fought the drug but his body was hers and it responded to her touch and he spasmed. She pulled up and away, reaching for the Veil, and she took Birlerion with her.

Birlerion's mind exploded as he took in the vast expanse before him; his befogged mind stared at the twinkling stars and the glistening shroud that sparkled and wreathed across the horizon as far as the eye could see. Ellie frolicked in the Veil, damaging the weave as she tumbled about in ecstasy.

The threads reached for her, caressing her skin as they trailed over her, questing for more. The Veil reached for him, yearned for him, and the threads extended towards him, and he drifted closer.

He had never understood what Jerrol had meant about the voracity of the Veil, but now he could see it. It was sucking the life out Ellie, her vitality fading as she cavorted blissfully until her sexual arousal was over, and she dove back down into her body, dragging an overwhelmed Birlerion with her.

Birlerion regained his senses with Ellie draped over his body, her fingers splayed possessively over his chest. His mind spun in confusion, teased by a subtle yearning, coaxing him to return. His neck stung from the wounds she had inflicted on him, and his side burned as if it was on fire; she hadn't been gentle. His wrists and ankles were burnt raw, but it was nothing to the horror his mind shied away from. He was mortified to be so helpless. He had underestimated her and had walked straight into her trap.

She was using him to reach the veil, subverting his will to hers, controlling him and his body. He shuddered in disgust and latent arousal, his body still relaxing from its traitorous act. He gritted his teeth as she moved.

Her eyes were dark with fulfilment as she raised her head, her body replete as she moved sensuously against him. "See?" she whispered. "It would be so much better, last so much longer, if you loved me properly."

Birlerion gagged, trying to push words out through his distress, but his mouth was dry and thick, his mind sluggish and confused.

"Hush, not now, tomorrow will be even better." She reached for a glass and gently raised his head. "Drink." He clamped his lips tight. "Drink," she snapped, her anger rising. "It is just water. You will do as I say, Birlerion. I will not tolerate your behaviour. Refuse me again and you will pay for it, I promise." Her expression smoothed, and she smiled as she brushed his dark hair off his face. "You have no choice," she breathed as she straightened his clothes. "Can't you feel it calling?"

Birlerion closed his eyes in relief as she left the room, his mind spinning. She was completely mad, driven by an addiction to the Veil, just as the Veil seemed to be gorging on her. What was this twisted relationship and how long had it been going on for? He wondered how many other men had been used to feed her desire, and he shivered; he was sure it was far more than he had managed to track down.

The pull of the Veil was seductive. It was a constant call, filling his mind, urging him to return soon. The drugs running through his system heightened his senses and disrupted his thoughts. His body was no longer his, and his mind was struggling with the enormity of what was happening. He shifted and his wrists screamed a warning, the burns raw. Easing his shoulders carefully on the pillow, he closed his eyes and drifted off to sleep, exhausted and confused.

The sensation of his body being tugged about woke him. His burning wrists reminded him not to move; his head was befogged and his eyes blurry.

"Go back to sleep, Birlerion. Stop fighting it."

Birlerion thought he recognised the voice, and he tried to speak, but his voice wouldn't work, and he sank back down into the darkness.

34

RANGERS ACADEMY, OLD VESPERS

The next morning the cadets were up and back on duty in the control room, Lord Cramer poked his head around the door. "Is Lord Birlerion here?" he asked, scowling at the cadets. The man didn't seem to know how to smile, Leyarille thought.

Lieutenant Kopka bowed slightly as he replied. "No, sir, we haven't seen him here since yesterday morning." Cramer nodded and withdrew.

Finally, good news percolated into the briefing room. Jaredion had been recovered yesterday evening. He was unharmed, though he had been taken to the infirmary up at the palace just in case. There had been no one at the house where he was found; it was deserted. Still no clues as to who was abducting people. Leyarille heaved a sigh of relief, Birlerion would be so relieved. She wondered when he would drop by. He was always so busy, she missed him.

More reports were filtering in, and the cadets began updating charts and cross-checking the findings. Bryce appeared to thank the cadets for their efforts. He nodded to the room in general and moved over to the maps. It still made no sense. The locations were scattered randomly, no pattern to them at all. "Has Birlerion figured out what all this means yet?" he asked.

"No sir, he says maybe there isn't a pattern to be found, that we're looking for something that isn't there," Leyarille answered.

"Possible," Bryce mused, "Where is he?"

"I don't know, sir. We haven't seen him this morning."

Bryce stilled. "When was he last seen?" he asked quietly, and Leyarille looked up in sudden concern.

"We last saw him yesterday morning, sir; he went out with a unit to the houses on East Street. He came back, started a new search off, and went home to get some sleep. He hasn't been back. Lord Cramer was here looking for him just now," Kopka reported.

"Sir, I can go check his house and his contacts in the city. I know who they are," Leyarille offered.

Bryce stared at her and nodded. "Take another cadet with you. Report to me as soon as you can. I'll be in his office in the Justice building."

Leyarille grabbed Kayen, and they hurried out of the room.

Bryce looked at Kopka. "If he turns up, tell him I'm looking for him, and I'll either be in his office or mine. Carry on."

Kopka saluted and turned back to the silent room. "Back to work, cadets, we have lots still to do."

Birlerion reluctantly opened his eyes to the early morning light. Another day had dawned. He wasn't sure how many it had been; he was losing track between Ellie's visits and the mix of drugs she was forcing down his throat. His body ached, cramping in the unnatural position he was held in. The fog clogging his mind lifted briefly as he tried to ease the position of the ropes, his breath hissing as the blood-encrusted rope ripped his skin further as it unstuck. He was now dressed in light linen trousers, his uniform long gone, along with his pride. The sheets had been changed; his blood no longer stained them. His wounds would be crusted over until her next visit.

He had dreamt of the Lady Marguerite; she had held him in her arms, keeping him safe from harm for a few precious moments, promising him he would survive and all would be well. He just had to hold out a little longer; help was coming. Clinging to the hope, the only spark of light in all this insanity, he hoped he hadn't imagined it.

Mind churning sluggishly, he tried to grasp the end of his thoughts but they kept slipping away before he could form them. He understood now how those poor lads had suffered and continued to suffer. The cocktail of drugs combined with the impossibility of the veil would unhinge the strongest of minds. He prayed Jaredion was alright.

He clung to one fact. The missing boys had nothing to do with the king or his power, they were just a horrific side effect of Elliarille's addiction, her insanity. No wonder there was no pattern to be found. Gillian must have started supplying young men to keep her addiction going, using her to disable the king.

He lost the thought and drifted in a haze of confusion. It was something to do with Ellie. Grappling with the memory of her last visit, he wondered how they missed her paranoia? It was obvious now he knew what was happening. They had made excuses for the twins for years, and all the time they had been manipulating everyone for their own purposes, hiding the fact that the Veil had done more damage that anyone could possibly have imagined. Ellaerion had to be involved; there was no way he couldn't know what his sister was doing.

Desperately, he clung to the thought as if it was a thread that would lead him out of a mist shrouded maze. He didn't think Ellie had any idea of the damage she was doing, nor had Ellaerion. She was driven by her need, and all else was subordinate to that need. He cringed at the thought that she wanted more of him, that she would continue to suck him dry until he had nothing left. Only then would she have no further use of him, and she would move on to the next unsuspecting soul. His mind drifted on to Gillian and the fact that he had taken advantage of the king's weakness, exaggerating the impact by bolstering the market and insinuating himself into a position where he could take advantage. He had been in the right place at the right time and had enough savvy to recognise it. He would have gotten away with it too.

Birlerion faltered. Gillian could still get away with it if no one found out about Ellie. Who would come and help him? Parsillion and Fonorion were absorbed back into the king's sphere, Jerrol was grappling with the Chancellery; there was no one left to worry about him. His mind drifted, confused and alone. The Veil felt his despair, and it teased and coaxed as Birlerion struggled to ignore it. In desperation, he concentrated on Leyarille, he imagined her beautiful smile, the feel of her arms around him when he had awoken that time they had shared the bed the inn in Elothia. Her courage, her soft voice in his ear, and the Veil retreated, snarling.

He tried to call Marguerite, but he couldn't focus long enough; his concentration slipped and writhed as he tried to hold it together. He prayed for help, calling Leyandrii, calling an Arifel, but his mind drifted befogged and confused, unable to focus.

A sluggish sense of urgency stirred within him. He needed to escape before Ellie returned, but Ellie, like any

Sentinal, knew how to tie a good knot. The ropes had dried to his skin overnight, and any movement caused searing pain, like ripping open a new wound. He licked dry lips, trying to ignore a sudden desperation for a drink; his mouth tasted horrible, the metallic aftertaste unnerving him. He closed his eyes, trying to control his breathing as his panic began to rise. His mind furiously turned over endless ways to escape, a blur of thoughts, none of which he could hold onto long enough to figure out if he could use it.

Leyarille was worried.

Birlerion's home was silent and empty; it didn't look like he had been home at all. She and Kayen hadn't been able to find Birlerion anywhere; even Tom hadn't seen him, which was not right. "Didn't he see you the day after Jaredion was abducted? He said he would visit the next day because you had news for him." Birlerion normally checked in with him every day, keeping a pulse on the city. Birlerion was the Chancellor's right-hand man; it was unlikely he would be derelict in his duty.

Tom shook his head. "Must admit, I was surprised. He normally does what he says he will do."

"What news did you have?"

"There's a rumour going around that Gillian is hiring men to guard him; 'e's not going to go down without a fight that one," Tom said knowingly. "Oh, and Birlerion also asked to be informed of any sightings of a blond-haired man with silver eyes. Well 'e was seen around the warehouses the night your young friend was abducted, on his own 'e was, and by the Lady's temple night before last."

Leyarille and Kayen hurried back to the city and entered the majestic justice building without noticing the mouldings and embellishments that she usually went into raptures about. They were directed to Birlerion's office on the third floor and tapped on the door. Her heart jumped when a deep voice bid her enter, but it was only Bryce.

"He's not been home. The place was dark. I don't think he's been home at all," she said immediately, her worry evident. "And none of his contacts have seen him since the day before last."

Bryce frowned. "So the last sighting we have of him was yesterday morning after the raids on East Street?" Bryce cursed. "Pull the names of the unit he was with, and everyone who spoke to him that morning before he left. I want to speak with each of them. Bring the list to my office. Use the waystone."

"Yes, sir." Leyarille exchanged glances with Kayen. Bryce was worried too. "And the information Tom had for Birlerion was regarding Gillian. Apparently, he is hiring an army. Tom believes he is preparing to fight it out."

Bryce cursed even more viciously, and Leyarille grimaced at Kayen. "Tom also said Birlerion asked for any sightings of a blond-haired Sentinal. One was seen at the warehouse the night Jaredion was abducted and near the Lady's temple yesterday morning."

Bryce stared at her. "Go get those lists, now. I'll be with the chancellor at the palace." Bryce went to find Jerrol. "Birlerion's missing," he said abruptly as he entered the chancellor's office. "He's not been seen since the morning of the raids."

"What?" Jerrol paled. "Are you sure?"

"Pretty much. He didn't meet with his contact in the city like he promised; he's not been seen since yesterday morning when he left the Garrison to go home. It doesn't look like he made it home."

"I should have looked for him yesterday when he didn't turn up."

"You had other things on your mind, like young Jaredion, for example," Bryce said gruffly.

"Still, he's been missing for nearly two days, and we didn't *know.*" Jerrol was appalled. He should have known sooner.

"He's always flitting from one place to another; we all assumed he was busy elsewhere."

"I should have called Tagerill here earlier. I knew he needed someone at his back; he shouldn't have been alone. This is my fault."

"No, it's not, Jerrol, you can't anticipate everything."

"What can't you anticipate?" Tagerill asked as he entered the office.

Bryce looked at him and then Jerrol. "Birlerion is missing."

Tagerill froze for a heartbeat. "When?" he asked.

"Two days," Jerrol said passing a hand over his face.

Tagerill looked at him. "Two days?" His voice rose, and Jerrol flinched. "*Two days?* Why wasn't I told sooner?"

"Because we've only just confirmed he's missing. It's been a bit manic here, you know, what with Jaredion going missing and all," Bryce interjected.

"We found Jaredion last night. He's here in the infirmary; he's fine," Jerrol said before Tagerill could explode again.

"I'll see him for myself first. I'll be right back," Tagerill said as he stormed out of Jerrol's office.

Jerrol blew his breath out. "I can see this day is not going to get any better."

Leyarille returned to the palace with a gnawing sense that she had lost something. It was calling her, just out of reach; if only she could figure out what it was. She stepped out of the waystone outside Bryce's office and smiled at Deron, who cursed as he spilt his coffee. He looked at her in resignation. "Can't you make a bell ring or something before you arrive? Give a man a bit of warning?"

"Sorry," Leyarille said, shrugging her shoulders.

"He went to the chancellor's office. You can wait here or go and find him."

"I'll go find him," she said and headed to her father's office.

She found her father with Commander Bryce and Tagerill, trying to trace Birlerion's last known movements. "Our last confirmed sighting was the morning of the raids when he returned from East Street. There are no reports of anyone seeing him after that." He looked up as Leyarille entered his office. "Leyarille, you have the list of people who saw him last? Bryce start interviewing them all," Jerrol instructed.

"I'm on the list," Leyarille said. "I came back with him from East Street at about third chime. He told me to go get some sleep and be back for midday. Lieutenant Scott said he went home to get some sleep too; that's what Lieutenant Kopka told him."

"That's right." Jerrol snapped his fingers. "Get Kopka. He said he instructed a cadet to go wake Birlerion if he didn't return to the briefing room by midday. We need to know what that cadet found when he went to his house."

"Tagerill," Leyarille said thoughtfully turning at the door. "Do you know who the Tousettes are? Birlerion said they were an old family."

"The Tousettes? That was the twin's family name. Elliarille and Ellaerion. Why?"

"Birlerion started a new search for any assets belonging to them the morning he disappeared."

Jerrol exhaled. "Once you've spoken to Kopka, collate the results that have come up so far. He obviously already had his suspicions. Those are the locations we should search first." Jerrol looked at Tagerill. "Elliarille and Ellaerion have got him," he said with conviction.

"Why would the twins have him?" Tagerill asked, perplexed.

"Birlerion suspects Elliarille is involved in the supply of drugs into the city. He also got between her and the king. She blames him for her loss of standing in the palace." Jerrol frowned. "Ellie and Ellaerion are also ignoring my summons. I expected them to report here before now."

"We'll find him," Tagerill tried to reassure him. "There is no reason for the twins to harm him. They are Sentinals for Lady's sake; they follow the Lady."

Jerrol looked at him bleakly. "Not well enough it seems." He rose and went to stare out to the window. "He could be anywhere. We've already searched the city once."

"Then we search it again," Tagerill said grimly.

"They've had more than enough time to move him out of the city."

"Don't borrow trouble, Jerrol, focus on what we *do* know. We'll find him; the Lady will protect him." Tagerill stopped speaking as Lieutenant Kopka hovered in the doorway. "I'll help Bryce," he said shortly and left the office.

Jerrol frowned over the report that Birlerion had been seen at home by the cadet, intending to go to his office at the justice building. Jerrol thought briefly and stepped out into the corridor outside Birlerion's office, and the soft chime of a new waystone vibrated around him. He should have done this yesterday. Grimacing, he began a door-to-door interrogation to see if anyone had seen Birlerion the previous day. No one had.

The search continued all night. Rangers were dispatched

to outlying properties, the king's guards gradually trawling through the streets and warehouses. They found no sign of Birlerion.

Birlerion's eyes flew open as his body jerked violently, and he cried out as pain bloomed in his shoulder. Fire flared through his body, and his cry died in his throat as his breath caught. His neck screamed in agony as he tried to alleviate the pain, but he was pinned against the headboard and movement was excruciating.

"See," Ellie's light voice carried across the room; she held a cross bow in her hands.

He gasped in breath as sweat beaded on his skin. "What?" His voice wouldn't work.

"It will heighten your senses, increase your stamina. The bolt was treated, and the drug will be in your bloodstream so much quicker. It will mean you have to stay here with me, not be thinking about anyone else. It's time for us to be together. I've watched you. I know you've been thinking about *her*; I told you I would punish you if you didn't obey me."

Birlerion struggled to breathe, to think. "Ellie," he gasped in shock, his breath wheezing painfully. He sucked his breath in as the bed dipped under her weight. The bolt kept him pinned. Warmth scored a path down his icy skin and soaked into the bed. It ran down the wooden headboard and meandered slowly around the carved legs of the bed before hanging suspended, gravity pulling and distending the precious droplet into a tear until it dripped onto the floor, followed by another, collecting in a ruby red pool, seeping through the floorboards, travelling onwards.

"Hush, my love," she wrapped a cloth around the end of

the bolt which barely protruded from the junction between his right shoulder and his neck. "You will feel it all and you will love me for it. Pain is good. It enhances the spirit, stimulates the senses." She smoothed the sweat from his greying face, smiling into his dazed eyes. Her hands moved down and were busy at his waist.

"Ellie, wait," he gasped breathlessly, trying to gather his scattered wits. Her hands slid over him, and he shivered. "Let me hold you too, please," he whispered as darkness threatened to engulf him. The flash of pain in his neck brought him back; Ellie had loosened one of the ropes, and the weight of his body pulled on the bolt.

A low groan escaped his lips, and Ellie smiled in anticipation. "Yes, that's right, my love, here I am." She snuggled into his side, drawing his arm around her as she delved back into his trousers. Her hands were hot on his skin. He felt so cold, and he shivered as her hands touched him.

"Ellie." His words sighed out raggedly with his breath. "This is not how you love."

"Yes, it is." She reached up to kiss him, and his hand convulsed around her waist as she pulled him against the bolt. He drew his breath in sharply as his vision wavered. His mind was numb; he was oblivious to what she was doing as pain engulfed him. His body shook uncontrollably, a combination of shock, drugs, and stimulation.

"No," he moaned as she slid down on him. Waves of pain blocked all thought; the drugs racing through his bloodstream took possession as his body responded. His blood dripped to the floor and raced after its companions, flowing down the cracks in the floorboards, and Ellie reached for the stars taking Birlerion's shattered soul with her.

35

BRIEFING ROOM, RANGERS ACADEMY

Leyarille stepped outside the briefing room for a moment and breathed in deeply; she felt odd. She frowned as the feeling of uncertainty and loss grew within her. Her stomach churned, and a sense of despair welled up inside her. Her breath caught as pain flooded her body, and she braced herself against the wall as she shuddered. An urgent compulsion made her stand upright and start running for the waystone, her breath coming in ragged gasps as she stepped out in Bryce's outer office. Deron lurched upright, gaping at her as she rushed out of the door and around to the palace. She ran down the corridors and leaned on the throne room doors, pushing in desperation against the heavy wood.

She stopped on the threshold, her chest heaving. The Oath was flushed a bright crimson, as if infused with blood. She gasped in horror and spun away, rushing to find her father.

"Pa!" Jerrol looked up in surprise as his distraught daughter crashed through his office door. He was about to remind her of protocol, when he saw her face. "Pa, why does the Oath glow red?"

Bryce hissed his breath out, and Leyarille realised she had interrupted the Commander of the King's Justice.

"What?" Jerrol was out of his chair and running through the corridors, Leyarille close behind him. The palace guards watched them in concern as Leyarille called after him. "What does it mean?" Jerrol skidded into the throne room as Bryce hurried in behind them and gaped at the Oath.

"Birlerion is hurt," her father said, his voice anguished.

"Birlerion?" Leyarille looked at him confused, and then her eyes widened as the realisation hit her. Birlerion must be the Oath Keeper, and the Oath was flushed blood red. Her face paled. "What do we do?"

"Keep looking; they have him here in Vespers. I don't why, but I'm sure of it. Ellie prefers it here in the city; she would have stayed here." He gave his daughter a reassuring hug. "Go back to the garrison and keep looking. We will find him," he promised.

Once she had left, he went up and placed his hand on the Oath. *"Marguerite? Where is he? Can't you help him?"* There was only silence. He was no longer the Oath Keeper; that was Birlerion. Anders found him staring at the Oath, his face bathed in the red glow.

"Jerrol, any news?" He baulked as he saw the oath. "I could call him," he offered. "The oath works both ways, so m'father said."

Jerrol shook his head. "Don't. If he is restrained like Jared was, it would only make it worse. The compulsion to come to you would drive him mad, if she hasn't succeeded already," he said softly, looking back at the Oath. He rested his hand against the wall, and at the sight of his face, Anders backed out of the room and shut the doors.

Leyarille stared in horror at the number of properties, holdings and businesses that the scholars had already discovered. "And they said this was just the start," Kopka said with a scowl. "Start a new map." He looked around the room. "Listen up, people, stop what you are doing. We have a new parameter. Start working through this data, see if anything crosschecks with what we've already found." And he began dishing out papers.

"The chancellor asked for regular reports," Leyarille said numbly as she unfolded a new map and tacked it on the wall. Kopka nodded. "That would be you then. At least you can use the waystones. List those and I'll have a report ready for you to take up." She diligently began marking off the list of properties; her heart fluttered as she thought of Birlerion injured and alone, no one caring for him. *We're looking for you. We won't leave you. We're looking for you*, she repeated silently as she worked.

Later that evening, Leyarille stood outside Birlerion's home and stared at the dark windows. She had spent the day shuttling back and forth between the chancellor and the garrison. *We'll find you*, she vowed silently; whatever it takes, we'll find you. She turned, intending to return to the garrison, but her feet made their way into the Lady's temple, and she knelt before the altar and prayed for him. *"Dear Lady, hold him close. Protect him until we can protect him, please. I promise I will love and cherish him for ever if you only help him now. Even if he doesn't love me, I will protect him, I swear. Let us find him, just let us find him. We will look after him, I promise. Help me to find him, please."* It was a litany in her head, over and over. She rocked on the step as the tears fell.

"He is under great duress. His mind is fractured, and I cannot reach him. I keep losing him before I can connect. You must find him.

You have what you need. Speak to those who saw him last," the Lady whispered. Leyarille looked up and swallowed nervously as the Lady appeared before her, her exquisite face anguished. *"Not everyone speaks true. Retrace his steps and see what is. Find him for me."* The Lady smiled at her, and a feather light touch caressed her face. *"Dearest Leyarille, you have no time to waste,"* she said as she faded from view.

Leyarille spun and rushed out of the temple, aware of the Lady at her shoulder. The Lady was worried. She ran faster and rushed into the briefing room, breathing heavily. The room was empty, everyone was out searching. She began rifling through the reports until she found the ones Birlerion had requested. She laid them out and studied them, her mind racing ahead. Who had seen Birlerion last? Kopka and the cadet sent to wake him. She rifled through some papers and found the name of the cadet. Fenton! She stiffened as she read his report.

On a sudden thought she checked the housing register. She found his family's name and the address. It was in Sear Street, to the north of the Chapterhouse. She checked the map of Tousettes properties and found one in the same road. Birlerion had been on the right track, just the wrong street.

She stilled as she remembered Fenton's cocky expression. He was never happy unless someone else was suffering. The Lady's words resonated in her head. What if he'd lied? She read his report again. It said Birlerion was awake and intending to go to his office in the Justice building. She shivered with anger. Birlerion had never even made it home, so he couldn't have been there.

Fenton, she thought angrily. How could he? Leyarille stormed out of the briefing room and through the garrison. It was fortunate no one tried to stop her. She crashed into the barracks of the second unit, cadets protesting around her.

She came to a halt at the foot of Fenton's bed. He looked up at her lazily, tossing his book aside.

"And to what do we owe the pleasure?"

"You parasite," Leyarille hissed, her silver eyes flashing. "What did you do?"

Fenton laughed. "What could you possibly mean? Relis look, she's pretending to be a Sentinal. Where did you steal the uniform from? Did you cosy up to Birlerion after all? We all know you like him."

Leyarille didn't hesitate. She grabbed him by the throat and pulled him of the bed. "Where is he?"

Fenton's eyes bulged as he scrabbled at her hands. Leyarille's glare scorched the horrified cadets as one of them approached her. "Leyarille," Relis whispered. "What are you doing? Are you mad?"

"He falsified a report. Didn't you?" Leyarille spat, easing her grip and shoving Fenton against the wall. "Sentinal Birlerion is missing, and you know where he is. Don't you, Fenton?"

Relis glared at Fenton as he stood by Leyarille's shoulder. "Is that true? Do you?"

"No, I don't. How should I?"

"You were sent to wake Birlerion later that morning, but you didn't, did you? You couldn't because he wasn't there. Yet you said he was. You reported that he had just awoken, and duty done, you returned. What did you do? Tell them when he got back from East Street? You were out too, that morning. I remember you returning to report that it was all clear. Did you distract Birlerion long enough for them to get him? Was that it? Are you helping them?"

"Just because you're pretending to be a Sentinal, Leyarille, doesn't mean you get to go around questioning anyone you want."

"She isn't pretending," Jaredion's voice came from the

doorway. "You can't wear this uniform without actually being a Sentinal. And I suggest you answer the question or we'll hand you over to the inquisitors and let them torture it out of you."

Kayen peered over his shoulder. "Let's just take him now. We don't have time to waste. If he knows what has happened to Birlerion, then we need to know now."

"I think we need to visit Ellaerion's house on Sear Street," Leyarille said slowly, watching Fenton. His eyes flickered. "Or maybe the houses next door, or maybe the whole street. What about your home, Fenton? Your parents live on Sear Street, don't they. Are they hiding Elliarille and her dirty work? Are your parents involved too?" Fenton flinched back from her silver glare. She stood up, satisfied.

She looked at Jared and Kayen, her eyes widening at the matching silver eyes. Kayen had also turned Sentinal. "Kayenion, can you take Fenton to Commander Reece? We need to go and visit Fenton's parents. Tell Tagerill and the chancellor," she said, meeting Kayenion's eyes. "Ask them to meet us there. Tell them why."

Kayenion nodded and advanced into the room. Leyarille smiled grimly as she saw his uniform. The Lady was busy tonight. For good reason, she thought, as she glared at Fenton. Fenton exploded up out of his bed, but Kayenion punched him in the face, and he fell back, howling and holding his nose.

"I'll help you," Relis said as he grabbed Fenton's arm. Kayenion took the other, and they dragged the still protesting Fenton out of the barracks.

Stoneford Watch

Mikke and Serenion looked at each other as the ground trembled. "The sentinals," Serenion gasped as he dashed off to the private garden, where his and Birlerion's sentinals stood behind the main buildings.

A third tall tree was glowing gently as it settled next to Birlerion's tree. Mikke and Serenion watched it settle in awe. The deep green leaves unfurled, questing in the air. The other sentinals were rustling their leaves in welcome. Serenion carefully placed his hand on the trunk and grinned as Leyarille's name echoed through him. He looked at Mikke. "Leyarille," he said with pleasure. "She's made Sentinal!"

"But why is it here and not with her?" Marianille and Niallerion arrived to hear Mikke's question.

"This is her home?" Serenion suggested, stepping back.

Marianille laughed. "I think maybe Birlerion is her home, and until he finds his home, Stoneford will do."

Mikke glanced at her in surprise. "Do you think he knows?" He paused thoughtfully. "Does she know?" he said, slowly thinking it through.

"I'm quite sure deep down he's always known. He just won't admit it. Look at the way his sentinal is behaving," Marianille smiled.

Serenion frowned. "Something's not right," he said as he leaned forward and laid a hand on Birlerion's tree. Pain exploded in his head, and he jerked back. "Birlerion's hurt," he gasped, spinning away.

Niallerion placed his hand on the tree, and a flash of red agony slashed through him. He gritted his teeth on a hiss. "I'll go," he said softly to the sentinal. The sentinal shuddered under his hand, and Niallerion met Serenion's gaze. "I'll go," he said more loudly and left on his word, hugging his wife before he ran for the waystone.

. . .

Leyarille and Jaredion scouted Sear Street. It was deserted. Three storied grey stone buildings lined the street at regular intervals, all in darkness. The bright silver moon gleamed off clear glass windows and metal railings. Only those with money would be able to afford to live here. The house in Ellaerion's family name was two doors down. Fenton's parents lived in the house opposite.

Leyarille shivered. "I'll take Ellaerion's house. You check the Fenton's. We need to be quick before the rangers arrive and wake everyone up."

"They wouldn't dare," Niallerion breathed over her shoulder and she nearly fainted in shock. "Sorry, I met Kayenion on the way," he said as Kayenion loomed up beside him. "Where's Birlerion?"

"We think he's in one of the houses down this street. Most likely in Ellaerion's which is number 2, or number 3, which is the Fenton's."

"His sentinal believes he is badly hurt. I called the healers, so let's find him quick. I'll go with Leyarille. Kayenion, you go with Jaredion to the Fentons. We'll check the most likely first," Niallerion said as he ghosted up to the house Leyarille had pointed out and peered in the window. Light glowed from under the closed door. "Well, someone is home," he breathed as Jaredion and Kayenion forced the door and entered the house across the street.

Leyarille followed him up the steps, and after a brief pause as Niallerion knelt by the lock, he opened the front door and they crept in. A dimly lit staircase covered in a plush red carpet led up immediately in front of them. Niallerion ascended as Leyarille checked the lower floors.

Ellaerion was asleep in a chair in his study. The golden glow of the lamp sparked golden glints in his hair. He looked young and vulnerable, yet old and drawn at the same time. A heavy oak desk separated them like some immovable barricade.

Leyarille slid across it, scattering papers in her wake, and had her knife at his throat and her knee in his gut as she yanked his head back. "Where is Birlerion?" Ellaerion jerked, and her knife bit. "Don't move if you want to live. Where is Birlerion?"

Ellaerion paled as he stiffened beneath her.

"I won't ask a third time," she growled. "You know where he is, so tell me."

Ellaerion shoved his chair back violently and knocked Leyarille's arms up and away as he rolled out of his chair and to his feet. Leyarille's knife went spinning, and she launched herself at him, not giving him time to regain his balance. He folded with a gasp as he crashed into the bookcase, books falling around him and thumping to the floor. Leyarille's elbow took his head back with a snap, and she slammed him to the floor. "Now," she said, coldly calm, her silver eyes glowing with anger. "Shall we try this again? Where is he?" She pressed her thumbs into the base of his throat, and he shuddered as he gasped for breath. "I will kill you, slowly. You think you know what pain is? I haven't even started yet," she said as she increased the pressure.

Niallerion skidded into the study and halted. Moving carefully, he approached Leyarille. She was bent over Ellaerion with death in her eyes. "That you could betray a brother Sentinal … You think the Lady is pleased with you?" Ellaerion's face was turning purple and Leyarille replaced her death grip on his neck with her belt dagger. "Wait till she gets her hands on you. Wouldn't you like to offer her some sign of redemption? Show her there is some good in you? Tell me where Birlerion is," she said slowly, emphasising each word with a twist of the blade.

"First house. Top floor, back room. The door is concealed in the closet," Ellaerion stuttered.

Niallerion ran.

Taurillion rushed into the street, his copper eyes wide with fear. "This way," he shouted, rushing up the steps of the first house. "Marguerite says he is here." Taurillion burst through the door, the wood shattering around him. He dashed up the stairs, kicking in doors, Marguerite's fear pushing him on.

"The entrance is concealed in the hall cupboard at the back. Ignore the bedrooms," Niallerion shouted as he pounded up the stairs behind him. Taurillion reached the top floor and wrenched opened the doors until he found the cupboard, and, tossing baskets out of the way he felt for the door and pushed it open. He halted on the threshold in horror.

Niallerion ran into him and pushed him out of the way. He immediately turned and yelled out the door. "Jaredion, we've found him! Get the healers, now!"

Birlerion lay awkwardly on a blood-soaked bed. His only free limb gripped the throat of the blonde-haired woman sprawled over him. The woman was held in place by his grip. Her blood shot eyes bulged, and her face was contorted and purple. She was quite dead, though Birlerion didn't loosen his grip. Taurillion struggled to release Birlerion's death hold around her throat, cursing under his breath the whole time. He finally managed it, and he dragged the unrecognisable body off him, dumping her on the floor.

Niallerion flipped a sheet over Birlerion, covering the visible signs of his suffering, and began sawing through the rope with his dagger. He knelt over him and sighed out in relief when he found the thready pulse beating in Birlerion's throat. There were multiple ragged knife wounds on his neck and the bed was blood drenched in multiple places. No wonder he was so pale. His silver eyes gleamed dully through his half open eyelids, fixed and unseeing.

"Birlerion? Can you hear me?" Niallerion removed the blood-soaked cloth from around his neck. His mouth tightened as he saw the end of the bolt, and he carefully peered behind Birlerion. He was pinned to the headboard, and his blood soaked the wood and the bed behind him. This was beyond his skill to remove. Niallerion wrapped another cloth around the wound as best he could. He looked up as Leyarille skidded through the door, dragging a terrified Ellaerion with her, Jaredion on her heels. At the sight of her livid face, he would have been terrified too, Niallerion thought bleakly.

Ellaerion cried out in distress and fell to the floor beside his sister's body.

"He said we're too late, that Birlerion was with Ellie," Leyarille said furiously. "That she had taken him out of our reach." She looked at the body at her feet and smiled grimly, and then she saw Birlerion. She took in the blood-soaked bed, the awkward position of his body, his unseeing eyes, and she shook, her face paling.

"He's alive," Taurillion said as she swayed. "Marguerite is with him."

"Where did she take him, Ellaerion?" Leyarille shook the distraught Sentinal violently.

Ellaerion rocked his sister's body in his arms. "The Veil," he whispered, all fight gone. His unspoken but much longed-for desire met at last, he no longer had any purpose.

"What? Show me."

Ellaerion shuddered. "I'm not going back there."

"You have to," Jaredion replied harshly. "Birlerion's hanging by a thread. If you don't go back, he will die. She's nearly killed him."

"Show me. I'll go," Leyarille said, her fingers digging into his shoulder, and Ellaerion's silver eyes flared as he showed her where to go.

"Quickly," Taurillion snarled.

Kayenion moved to stand over Ellaerion as Leyarille stepped towards the bed. Her eyes feverishly traced Birlerion's much-loved face, now grey and lined with pain and so very still. Her heart clenched as she realised how foolish she had been in not telling him how she felt. She reached for his face, and Niallerion hastily moved out of the way. He tucked the sheets tighter around Birlerion's body and threw his cloak on top. Birlerion was ice cold to the touch.

"Birlerion?" Leyarille whispered as she rested her hand against his cold cheek and reached to find him. She gasped as she traced his path, the wide expanse overwhelmed her; the Veil shimmering seductively around her until she found him. She focused on Birlerion, ignoring all else. She was here for him and only him. Leyarille carefully teased the Veil away from him. She frowned as she sensed her sister in the bindings. What had Margareth been doing here?

Birlerion was drifting, lost and alone. She faltered as she realised that he had suffered the same trauma the damaged boys had. Would he still be the Birlerion she loved after all this? He didn't react to her presence. The Lady had said his mind was fractured, and she could see why. She worked methodically, cocooning him in her love, gently whispering that he was safe, asking for him to come back to her. She was waiting for him. But she couldn't keep the threads from reattaching. As soon as she pulled one away, another latched on.

"Marguerite?" She thought she heard his voice, though she wasn't sure. He was translucent, fading before her eyes. Losing hope. How long had he been up here?

She convulsed as a hand touched her shoulder and she was spun away. Her heart jumped into her throat. In the unending silence, she hadn't expected anyone else to be there. Ellaerion blundered into her, angry and uncoordinated. Distress emanated from him as he searched the Veil, looking for Ellie. Unable to accept she had gone. He reached for Leyarille again, desperately searching, and pushed her into the Veil. She easily shoved him away, but he knocked the unresisting Birlerion deeper into the strands. She cursed viciously as she pushed herself towards Birlerion, and then Ellaerion screamed silently as he disintegrated, his essence a fine sparkling spray that was sucked into the Veil.

Leyarille slashed at the threads. "He's mine," she growled as she tried to pull Birlerion to her. She sheltered his tattered essence, unstintingly offering hers as she worked, but she couldn't free him.

She suddenly felt her sister's presence. Margareth pushed her away. *"You can't stay here. Go. I'll help him."*

Leyarille gasped as she rocked back on her heels, the room coalesced around her as the vast expanse filled her mind. Her sister's strong and commanding voice echoing in her ears. Beside her, Birlerion took a deep grinding breath, and his eyes darkened with pain. He let out a ragged moan, and she heard her name.

"I'm here," she smoothed his face and leaned over him. "You're safe now," she whispered, cradling his head carefully in her arms. She kissed his face. "You will always be safe with me." He relaxed in her embrace as his eyes lost focus and became fixed.

Leyarille stiffened. "Birlerion?"

She was unceremoniously shoved out of the way by an elderly man in healer garb. Jaredion hurried another healer into the room, who reached for Birlerion's neck, not even trying to find a pulse in his rope-encrusted wrists.

"He lives," he said and began issuing instructions to his assistants.

Jaredion drew Leyarille away. "Let Healer Francis do his work; there is no one better," he said as she stared at the bodies of the twins. They had been laid out side by side; he fair and unmarked except for the bloody wound from Jaredion's sword; she distorted and unrecognisable as the young woman who had floated so precariously through all their lives.

Leyarille let out her breath. "It's over," she said thankfully.

Niallerion hissed his breath out, watching the healer transfer Birlerion onto a stretcher, an assistant clamping his shoulder back and front, holding the bolt in place and staunching the bloody wound. Taurillion hovered over them, his eyes never leaving Birlerion's deathly pale face.

"Not for everyone," Niallerion said.

36

INFIRMARY, KING'S PALACE, OLD VESPERS

Alyssa rushed into the infirmary and up to her son and hugged him close. "Jared! I've been so worried."

Jaredion gave her a ragged smile. "I'm fine, Ma, just a few rope burns, nothing serious."

"I know, but still, what they could have done to you. Look at poor Birlerion. It doesn't bear thinking about."

Jaredion's eyes darkened. "It was my fault; I should have been at his back."

"Son, it is not your fault," Jennery tried to reassure him. "They were prepared. They knew what they were doing. You wouldn't have been able to prevent it." *And you could have been killed*, he thought to himself.

"I should have escaped. Everyone was so busy looking for me, they didn't watch Birlerion."

Jennery recognised the guilt in his son's eyes.

"Son, you tried. You have the burns to prove it." He gently grasped Jaredion's bandaged wrists to prove his point.

"I should have tried harder." Jaredion shuddered, and Jennery grasped his arms as he saw horror in his son's eyes.

"The rope was embedded in his skin," Jaredion said, his voice haunted. "He had struggled so much it was buried, bloodied over, torn, and dried many times."

"I'm sorry, Jaredion," Jennery said carefully, pulling his son into his arms.

"If I'd only been able to escape." Jaredion's voice was muffled against his father's shoulder, and Alyssa rubbed his back, trying to offer comfort.

Jennery left Alyssa trying to console Jaredion and headed into the dim room he had been guarding. He found Taelia seated beside Birlerion's bed, her eyes fixed on his face. She looked up and smiled wanly as Jennery entered the room. "Francis will force one of us to leave," she warned. "Only one visitor at a time."

"I won't stay long. I just wanted to see him." And now he had, Jennery was appalled at the sight of him. His neck and shoulder were heavily bandaged as were his wrists. A tube ran from a bag of blood into his arm and the tube was full of a deep red blood. Even with the blood being pumped back into him, Birlerion was almost translucent, his face drawn and strained even though he was deeply sedated.

Jennery sighed out a horrified breath. "What are they saying?"

"Too early to say. They want him stabilised. He lost too much blood. Tagerill's been here all night. I only got him to go to bed because I promised I wouldn't leave him alone." Taelia tightened her grip on Birlerion's hand. "As if I would," she said softly as tears rose in her eyes.

Jennery cleared his throat. "I'll come back later," he said gruffly as Francis loomed up behind him. Jennery found Jerrol in his office staring into space. He wasn't getting much work done by the looks of it. Jennery collapsed in one of the plush chairs before the chancellor's desk.

"I met the king. He is determined to deal with Gillian

and Benarte. He's ordered me to contain Benarte in Deepwater."

Jerrol observed him for a moment before speaking, "Gillian is building his forces in Marchwood. It makes sense to separate the two. If Benarte is cut off, we weaken Gillian's hand. Bryce is readying his men to march. We leave in the morning. Anders is determined to personally bring him down."

"It would help repair his reputation if he is seen to be the restoring peace."

"Indeed."

"I've just seen Birlerion."

Jerrol looked at him and nodded. "Any change?" he asked, though Jennery knew he would have been informed already if there was.

"Taelia was with him."

"Someone is with him at all times. He needs to know he's safe, with family."

"Does he even know you're there? Jerrol, he looks so … so diminished."

Jerrol winced. "I know. We should have protected him better. I took him for granted all these years. He was always so strong, always there."

"We all did," Jennery said softly.

Jerrol continued as if he hadn't spoken. "He was always standing at my shoulder. Even now he agreed to join the Administration to help me. He was in Vespers because of me."

"He wouldn't have wanted to be anywhere else, Jerrol, you know that."

"When you think how many scrapes he got me out of … I never thought of him as vulnerable. He was always so solid and reliable. So indestructible." Jerrol leaned forward on his desk. "I forgot that he's not invincible. He is only human. How could we have ignored that? If he dies ..." Jerrol faltered.

"He won't," Jennery said firmly, trying to alleviate the fear he could see in Jerrol's eyes.

"He should have bled out. Most other people would have. He didn't."

"Marguerite was watching over him."

"*We* should have been watching over him. He should have had a Sentinal at his back at all times. We should have known he was missing. *Two days*, Lea. It took us two days to realise he was missing. It's unforgivable," he said angrily, the tears glistening in his eyes.

"Jerrol, it was not your fault." Jennery was horrified to see the same guilt in Jerrol's eyes as he had seen in his son's. "You do Elliarille's work for her if you allow this misplaced guilt to eat away at you. It doesn't help Birlerion. You have to be strong for him. Be able to help him when he needs it. Jerrol ..." He looked up as a shadow hovered in the doorway. It was Leyarille. Jennery gaped as he saw her uniform. "Jerrol, you never told me Leyarille made Sentinal." He rose to embrace her. "Congratulations, my dear."

Leyarille twisted her lips. "Thank you. It was all a bit of a rush. The Lady needed me."

Jerrol relaxed back in his chair. "We will celebrate her and Kayenion at a date yet to be determined."

"Kayenion?"

"Yes, Kayerille and Oscar must be so proud; a Sentinal for a son." Jerrol laughed bleakly. "Though I saw his tree appeared next to Parsillion's, so it looks like he has chosen to stay here."

Leyarille tried to smile. "He said Terolia had enough Sentinals already; Vespers was in more need."

Jennery saw the shadow that passed over Jerrol's face. "That is good news then. Where is your tree, Leyarille?"

"In Stoneford for now, with Birlerion's."

Jennery nodded, watching her, seeing her anguish, though she didn't say anything further.

Jerrol interrupted them. "Did you need me for something or were you just visiting?"

Leyarille straightened. "I just wanted you to know I spoke with Tom. He's agreed to meet with me until Birlerion returns. He said to tell you that support for King Anders and his administration is high. Although people have been upset by the intrusions into their homes, they understand why. And people are pleased with the way you are handling the restructuring of Gillian's and Benarte's businesses."

"What's this?" Jennery asked with interest.

"Birlerion set up a contact in the city. Keeping a pulse on the people, he said," Leyarille explained.

Jennery looked at Jerrol. "Did he now? It seems our Birlerion has more than one trick up his sleeve."

"That he does, and we need him back, sooner rather than later," Jerrol said with a sigh. "I miss him."

"We all do," Leyarille said just as gently, her eyes misting.

Jerrol cleared his throat. "Right, keep me informed." Leyarille nodded, smiled at Jennery, and left his office. "She is a blessing from the Lady, even if she is my daughter. She and Kayenion have taken over Birlerion's office. They are doing what they can to keep things running, and they are doing very well. I think Birlerion will gain a very dedicated team when he returns." His lips quirked. "Does it seem funny to you that all the new Sentinals have gravitated to him? Jaredion is determined to be at his shoulder no matter what, and Leyarille and Kayenion are guarding his work. He will be well protected when he returns, make no mistake of that. He won't lack for protection ever again."

"It will be interesting to see how he reacts to that," Jennery said with a laugh. "He was always the protector. I imagine he will find it difficult to allow others to protect him."

Jerrol nodded, his face determined. "Well, he'll just have to learn, won't he?"

Leyarille paced the throne room, casting worried glances at the red-tinged oath. As long as it glowed, at least she knew Birlerion was still alive, though whilst it was flushed red, there was much cause for concern. She had heard, he had roared back to consciousness in agony when Francis removed the bolt from his neck, the sedatives ineffective, desperately calling Lady Marguerite for help, lost and confused. Tagerill sat with him still, soothing him as best he could, his low voice rumbling late into the night, reassuring Birlerion that he wasn't alone. The healer wouldn't allow other visitors no matter how much Leyarille longed to be with him.

She had pieced together what had happened from the bits Taurillion had let fall, as well as those he hadn't. Her brief conversation with Ellaerion in the study had been frightening and now made sense. He had been as trapped by Elliarille as he had been by the Veil. Poor man.

Looking up, she sank to the floor as King Anders strode into the throne room, Parsillion in position behind his shoulder. The king settled himself on the throne and looked across the room at Leyarille. "Rise," he said.

Leyarille inspected him as intently as he watched her. The king looked clear eyed and alert and reminded her more of his father than he had at any other time.

"Your Majesty," she said softly, staring over his shoulder at the Oath.

"How is he?" Anders asked as if he hadn't had a report that morning from the infirmary.

Leyarille's lips quirked. "You probably know better than I do, sire."

Anders grimaced. "I highly doubt it," he said. "Why are you still here?"

"I am waiting for Healer Francis to say Birlerion is fit to travel and then we will take him home to Stoneford."

"We?"

"Niallerion and I."

"So you made Sentinal?"

"Yes, as did Kayenion in all the chaos at the end. The Lady used the tools she had, as they say."

Anders nodded. "Why do *you* think Sentinal Elliarille tried to shred the Veil?"

Leyarille stepped forward. "From what Ellaerion said, I think she was addicted to it, sire. And the Veil was so attuned to her body from all those years of entrapment, it couldn't let go. She provided something the Veil wanted. Between them, they found a way to fulfil it."

"How come Ellaerion wasn't addicted in the same way?"

Leyarille shrugged. "Luck? Or maybe his emotions were not so connected. He resented his sister's power over him; he resented her control and his inability to refuse her. I think that resentment filled his mind instead of the Veil's compulsion. There was no room left for it take root. She fed off people's emotions and pain. That's what gave her the power to reach the Veil and return."

"She was strong, I'll give her that," Anders said with feeling. "If it hadn't been for Birlerion stepping in between us, I doubt I would be sitting here." His eyes darkened at his foolishness.

"I think when Birlerion saved you from her clutches,"

Anders winced at her phrasing, "he became her next target. She broke her own rule not to involve Sentinals. She had been so careful for so long. She convinced herself Birlerion had been waiting for her and that he was hers to do with as she wished. She used Jaredion to get to him. I believe she lost her very humanity, trying to find it in others."

"Thank the Lady I had the sense to invoke the Oath," Anders said.

Leyarille nodded. "I'm glad for Birlerion's sake too. I believe his connection to Marguerite and the Land sustained him. I'm not sure he would have survived without it."

Anders nodded sadly. "Keep me informed of his progress; he is important to me." He looked across at Parsillion standing beside his throne. "And many others. I thank the Lady every day for her protection and her faith in us."

"As do we all, sire."

"How is Sentinal Jaredion?"

"He is fine. He insists he will be at Birlerion's shoulder as he recovers. I think Jaredion probably understands what Birlerion is going through more than most. He went home to Deepwater. He said he would return when Birlerion is ready to travel."

Anders nodded. "Probably for the best. Do you think she knew she was damaging the Veil?" he asked suddenly. "I mean, that was the only thing that really gave her away."

"I don't think so. Each time she visited the Veil, it reinforced her need for it. Her behaviour was getting wilder; that was what was causing the damage. To be honest, sire, I think her loss of control would have given her away in the end, but not before many others had suffered."

"Yes, I expect we will find many unexplained deaths laid at her door."

"Poor Ellaerion. He was hard pushed to keep protecting

her, trying to cover up for her. He literally couldn't refuse her anything, and his inability to stand up for himself caused his death in the end too. My father always said the Veil had a voracious appetite. He said it should never be trifled with. Maybe it's time we listened to him."

37

MARCHWOOD BORDERS

Jerrol strapped his sword around his waist and grimaced at Bryce as he paused in his doorway. He grasped the hilt, settling the weight on his hip and relaxed into the hum of the sword's greeting. Guerlaire, the previous Lady's Captain, had handed him this sword over twenty years ago and no matter how many times he lost it, the Lady had always managed to return it to him. The hum of greeting morphed into a familiar buzz of expectation, and he grinned as a sense of anticipation flushed through him. As chancellor he had avoided wearing a weapon, but there was no way he was going into battle without it. "I thought we had finished with all this nonsense," he said as he inspected a similarly attired Bryce.

"We will, today. To think that Gillian believes he can stand against the king. I think he must be partaking of some of his own delusions. The temerity of the man."

"It's the people he has deluded into joining him that is more concerning." Jerrol joined Bryce and they strode through the palace to the king's chambers.

"Once they find out Gillian has misled them, I think he

might find his support disappears," Bryce said.

"Let's hope so. I would hate for innocent people to pay for Gillian's folly."

"Anders is insisting he comes with us. You need to persuade him he should stay at the palace."

Jerrol shook his head. "I disagree. I think the king needs to be seen. He has to demonstrate he is in control."

Bryce came to a halt. "We can't afford to have you both on the battlefield. Especially with Birlerion out of commission as well."

"Birlerion will be back soon enough. He's better off in Stoneford where his sentinal can heal him. He just needs time."

"That's good to hear. Last I heard, Francis wouldn't release him."

"Niallerion came for him. Birlerion is strong. He holds the King's Oath and has Marguerite watching over him. He'll be fine." Jerrol wasn't prepared to believe anything else, no matter how frail Birlerion had looked.

They arrived at the king's chambers and Bryce paused, resting his hand on Jerrol's arm. "You do realise that Benarte is going to make a stand as well?"

"It is to be expected. At least we can deal with both of them." They fell silent as the chamber door opened and they stepped inside.

Anders stood staring out the window with his back to them. He wore a formal, dark green uniform, as commander-in-chief of the army. As he turned towards them, Jerrol was shocked at the sudden similarity to Benedict, his father. This was the first time Jerrol had seen Benedict's steel and determination in his son.

Gesturing at the table, Anders led the way to the map spread out across it. "Reports indicate that Gillian has amassed a force of over five hundred. I'm not sure what he really thinks he is going to achieve, but we are not waiting for him to advance on Old Vespers.

"I want him stopped at the river. Jennery can contain Benarte in his estate in Deepwater. He has already assured me he has it in hand." Anders unrolled a piece of parchment. "Ari brought the message confirming Jennery had him surrounded. If we can defeat Gillian, Benarte will fold."

Bryce leaned over the map. "We already have units positioned to the north and west of the river at Two Bridges. We can advance those. Gillian will not reach Old Vespers."

Anders' blue eyes gleamed. "I think we should show Lord Gillian what happens to traitors of the crown. His estate should take the brunt of the action. I don't see why anyone else should pay the price."

"We'll let the advance units test his defences. Give Gillian's men a taste of a real fight. I doubt they are prepared," Jerrol said with a grin. "Stafford's scouts have already penetrated his grounds. Sentinal Taurillion is with them, so we should receive his report soon."

"And then," Anders said, rubbing his hands together. "I will put that man in his place."

Arriving at the army's encampment at Two Bridges as the sun set, Jerrol inspected the preparations, pausing to speak to the healer and his assistants, Fonorion following silently behind him. Jerrol was relieved they seemed well prepared. Any fight, no matter how easily won incurred casualties. The healer had two tents set up, holding over thirty truckle beds. If he didn't need them all to the good. Jerrol approved of his thoroughness.

Joining Bryce and the king in the commander's tent, Jerrol was surprised to see Taurillion lounging in one of the chairs across the table. Commander Stafford, a grey-haired portly soldier, the commander of the King's Rangers sat beside him.

Fonorion grinned at the Sentinal and, after a quick glance around the interior, took up position outside the tent flap with Parsillion.

Anders waved a hand at the empty chair. "Take a seat, Jerrol. We were just discussing Gillian's defences."

Jerrol sat opposite Taurillion and raised an eyebrow.

"They are disorganised, unruly, and belligerent," Taurillion began. "Even if Gillian told them to stand down, I don't think they would. He has them so riled up at the injustices they live under," Taurillion's laugh was more like a snarl, "which he imposed on them, ironically enough, that they want blood and lots of it."

Anders scowled. "What a waste," he muttered.

Taurillion straightened, tugged out a wad of paper from his jacket and unfolded it, revealing a crude map of western Vespiri. Jerrol and Bryce leaned forward to hold down a corner as Taurillion began speaking. "I believe you can minimise your losses, Your Majesty, if you send a unit to infiltrate the southern defences. They are the lightest. Gillian has focused the majority of his men on his northern defences, here and here. If we can catch them unawares in a pincer movement from behind, we should wrap this up quite quickly."

Anders stared at the map. "So, if I pontificate for a bit out front, draw their attention to my visible forces, Stafford can take his men south and meet us at the gate."

"It would be my pleasure, Your Majesty." Stafford's deep voice rumbled through the tent.

Jerrol frowned at the map. "Make sure you leave some for the rest of us."

"Absolutely not," Bryce said. "You and the king will fall back to Two Bridges. You can make your speeches, but you are not getting entangled in this brawl. Because that is what it will be. I cannot guarantee your safety when we don't know what some idiot will try and do."

"I need to be seen," Anders objected.

"And you will be, but I am not wasting men's lives protecting you when they should be focused on fighting Gillian's men."

Jerrol's lips quirked. "Wasting?"

"You know what I mean," Bryce snapped, his glare unwavering.

Jerrol raised his hands in surrender. "Fine," he sighed. He hadn't expected Bryce to let him near the fight, but it had been worth a try. With Jerrol's capitulation, Bryce transferred his glare to the king who quickly agreed. They returned to planning numbers, positions and timing until, at last, Stafford and Taurillion rose. They shook hands and departed to prepare their men.

"We'll see you in the morning," Jerrol said with a bright grin, relaxing in his chair as Bryce followed them out the tent to brief his captains. A flurry of activity, directed by Parsillion, brought the evening meal, and Jerrol and Anders conversed quietly as they ate.

"It doesn't seem right allowing others to do all the fighting."

Anders laughed. "Did you never delegate in Stoneford?"

"I didn't need to, Birlerion was always there." He fell silent, staring at his glass as he twisted the stem, and Anders eyed him.

"As he will be again," he said softly. "Jerrol, please forgive me for taking Stoneford away from you."

"Sire. It is forgiven."

"It was your home. I should never have interfered."

"It is still my home, and Mikkeal will do a wonderful job protecting it."

"I am sure he will." Anders cleared his throat and changed the subject. "Three new Sentinals. The Lady blesses us."

"That she does." Jerrol smiled and sipped his wine.

Early the next morning, as wispy strands of mist clung to the river's surface, Anders' army marched out of Two Bridges, leaving the rear guard and healers waiting anxiously. Zin'talia whisked her tail as she pranced down the road. *"To think that man has the nerve to challenge the Lady's choice."* Zin'talia shook her head, causing her mane to ripple and gleam in the sunlight.

"Stop showing off," Jerrol replied as he patted her glossy neck. Her chuckle vibrated through his mind and he grinned. The sun was a brilliant glare in the palest of blue skies, so pale it was almost white, and Jerrol shielded his eyes as he squinted down the road. Tall, broad-leafed trees lined the track which veered off to the right. The branches met in the middle creating a glowing, green tunnel as the sunlight filtered through the leaves. It was a shame death and destruction waited at the end of it. "We should be approaching the borders of Gillian's estate momentarily, sire."

"I look forward to hearing what he has to say."

Jerrol winced at the bite in the king's voice. Somehow, he was sure that whatever Gillian said, it wouldn't appease the king. The king's armour shone in the golden sunlight, polished to a mirror finish, no doubt by his valet who had valiantly packed up the king's wardrobe and travelled with them.

Bryce pulled up next to the king and dipped his head. "The men are in position, Your Majesty. I have sent a herald to request a parley under your flag, but please keep out range of the archers. The scouts have marked their outer limit."

He gave a ferocious smile. "They've already wasted plenty of arrows which our scouts have collected." He shrugged. "They'll soon get them back!"

"The rules of parley will prevail. Even Gillian would not cross that line."

"I would not be so sure, Your Majesty. He is desperate, and desperate men make errors of judgement."

"We'll see." Anders was non-committal. Patiently waiting for Gillian's response.

"How far is his main estate from the road?" Jerrol asked as a runner rushed up to one of Bryce's captains.

"About another half-league, but I think we have his response." Bryce took the missive from his captain and glanced down it before handing it the king. "It seems Gillian does not wish to talk."

"More fool him," Jerrol muttered, though he wasn't surprised.

"Well, I intend to have my say." Anders kneed his horse forward. "I didn't come all this way to be ignored." His standard bearer scurried before him, the dark green flag with the silver crescent moon and sentinal tree emblazoned upon it, fluttered in the breeze.

As they passed under the trees, the land levelled out into arable fields, which led up a rise to where a grey stone mansion sat, surrounded by a hastily built barricade of woven branches and wagons.

"Do you think that is to keep them in, rather than us out?" the king enquired as he drew to a halt behind an upended bucket with a sword stuck in it and a piece of yellow cloth tied to the hilt. He observed the sword. "Bryce, you need to tell your people to treat their weapons with more respect."

Bryce laughed. "I will, Your Majesty. But it got the point across."

"True, but still, I can't shout from here. Let's give them a show of force and keep their attention firmly on the front door." The king encouraged his horse forward, ignoring Bryce's protests. Jerrol exchanged grimaces with Parsillion and followed.

"Gillian! Show yourself," the king shouted, turning his horse sideways to make his body a smaller target. Jerrol nodded in approval, and Parsillion stopped a few strides in front of him blocking the clean shot.

"You're a disgrace, Anders. You shouldn't be on the throne," Gillian yelled as he climbed on the back of a wagon. "There is nothing to negotiate. We will not stop until you're gone."

"Stop what, Gillian? Treason? Disappointing the Lady? Screwing the last coin out of your people before you stand back and let them all die?"

"You can talk. What did you do? Bring every man in your army?"

Anders smile was feral. "Yes. And I will stamp out every treasonous bone in your body. Your people have one chance to surrender."

"Why would they listen to you? A drug addict for a king?"

"And where did those drugs come from Gillian? I am sure there is more than one person behind your flimsy barricade who has been involved in your underhand schemes. I wonder if they received any additional reward for breaking the law?"

"Good business is not breaking the law."

"It is when you are murdering innocent people to support your schemes. We know all about Elliarille and your deal with her. Provide her boys to satisfy her cravings, and she would feed your drugs into the palace. You had no care for those boys nor the people who died as a result of your mis-handling of the drugs you imported. Those deaths are on your hands, and those of the people who stand with you. You will be punished for it.

"If your people walk away now, and go home peacefully, they will not be penalised for listening to your rhetoric. Because that is all it is." Anders raised his voice. "Your lord is no longer a lord. He's been found guilty of murder, smuggling, exploitation. His estates are forfeit. His position in my administration rescinded. He has no power; he can no longer protect you.

"Make your choice now! Stay and die for *his* cause, or return to your families and live a full life. You will not get a second chance."

Gillian hissed his breath out, raised his arm and clenched his fist. Parsillion lunged, his sword flashing in the sunlight as he deflected the arrow that sped towards the king. An audible groan came from behind the barrier as the people's choice was taken from them as Jerrol and Parsillion forced the king back to safety.

Bryce ordered his men to advance as the king's archers rained arrows on the barricade. Voices raised in anger and fear were interspersed with Gillian's voice ordering them to stand firm.

A return volley of arrows forced the soldiers to raise their shields, but they didn't stop their advance. The interlocking leaves of their armour flashed as they moved in unison; an indomitable force advancing relentlessly, their tall pikes marking their advance.

Bryce yelled a command and their pikes dropped and they charged the last few feet and the barricade collapsed before them. The clash of swords and cries of 'for the king' were interspersed with shrieks of terror which filled the air. A wagon exploded into flames and rushing figures were gilded by the golden blaze, armour glinting and swords flashing.

Bryce parried a blade and charged onwards, clambering over bodies and discarded weapons. Behind the barricades, chaos reigned. Men ran in all directions. It was difficult to tell what they were trying to achieve, except maybe, surrender.

Pockets of determined men tried to defend the mansion, but they were caught in the pincer movement and trapped against the walls. The momentum of the king's men overwhelmed them, but Gillian was nowhere to be seen.

Tugging his sword free of another body, Bryce wiped the sweat from his face. The heat emanating from the carcass of a burnt-out wagon was surprising.

"What are you doing here, Bryce? Shouldn't you be directing things, not in the centre of it?" Taurillion asked as he loomed out of the drifting smoke.

"And leave all the fun to you? I'm just making sure no one slips around us."

"They haven't the heart for it. The rangers have at least a hundred men detained in the barn."

"Have you seen Gillian?"

"That coward tried to run. Unfortunately for him, he ran straight into Stafford; he didn't get very far." Taurillion glanced around him. "Nothing much left to do but mop up the stragglers."

The King's Rangers carved through the defences to the south and pinned Gillian's people between them and the King's Army. Gillian's forces had nowhere to go, and they knew it. They began throwing down their weapons. Their will to fight had never been strong, and many would have fled when the opportunity was offered had they had the chance.

Anders paced as he waited for the outcome of the battle. Concern for his men uppermost more than doubt about the final outcome.

"Sire! We have Gillian, alive!" Bryce strode into the king's tent, his armour blackened and dented.

Anders stopped pacing. "Bryce! Is it done? Are you hurt?"

Bryce waved him off. "I'm fine. It is unfortunate, but you will have to deal with him."

"What are our casualties?"

"Light. Nothing serious. According to the rangers, Gillian's men surrendered in droves. It was only his personal guards that continued to fight. The healers are dealing with more of Gillian's wounded than our own. What do you want us to do with Gillian?"

"Would that he had died in the fight," Anders murmured and ran his hand through his hair.

Bryce grimaced. "He may yet."

"Unfortunately, if we have the means, we cannot leave him to suffer."

"He tried to kill you," Jerrol pointed out. "Maybe you should let the Lady decide if he survives his wounds."

Anders grinned. "What an excellent notion. Detain him for now, along with those known to be his personal guard. If they survive the trip back to Old Vespers, they can all be tried for treason. All other prisoners, let Lord William deal with them. He can decide whether he will accept their fealty or not; after all, they are from his Watch. Make sure he has all the reports and any confessions. That should help him sort the hapless from the zealous."

"It shall be done, sire." Bryce bowed and left the tent.

"Well, now that bit of fun is over, let's get the inquisitors in and see what Gillian has left to incriminate himself," Anders said, accepting a glass a wine from an attendant. He saluted Jerrol with it. "Let's hope Gillian is worth enough to cover all this expense or you'll be juggling budgets!"

38

STONEFORD KEEP, VESPIRI

The sentinal didn't release Birlerion for two weeks, and only then when Healer Tyrone demanded he be allowed to check on him. The healer now had him in the infirmary under close observation.

Leyarille sat beside Birlerion's bed and watched him with concern.

Birlerion shifted awkwardly and she started forward to help him, but she stopped when he flinched away from her. She curled her fingers into a fist and sat back in her chair and waited for him speak. He stared past her, at what she didn't know. The silence grew awkward and Leyarille struggled to find something to say that didn't sound trite.

It was something she thought she would never say, but he seemed smaller, and her heart ached for him. He moved again, a slight hiss of pain escaping his lips as he cradled his right arm. The bolt had damaged several tendons and he moved his arm with difficulty. Lines creased his face, and she wished she could kiss them away, but he had made it clear, he didn't want to be touched.

"Shall I get the healer? Do you need something for the pain?"

"No, I'm fine."

"But you're suffering needlessly."

"The draughts make me too sleepy. When I start training, that will help my mobility."

Leyarille pinched her lips tight against the obvious retort that he was in no fit state to start training. She worried that he would never heal from everything that he was suffering. Desperately, she searched for a different topic. "Tom sent his best wishes."

"Thank him for me."

Silence descended again, and Leyarille fidgeted, unsure what else to say.

"You don't have to sit with me. I am sure you have better things to do," Birlerion said, still staring at the wall.

Leyarille gritted her teeth. She couldn't get passed his formidable defences. Giving up, she rose. "I'll drop by tomorrow to see how you're getting on."

Birlerion didn't reply.

The next day was no better and Leyarille left almost in tears with sheer frustration.

Mikke finally suggested she return to Vespers. Birlerion seemed uncomfortable in her company; he wasn't ready to socialise. She nodded slowly in agreement. Maybe if she gave Birlerion a couple of weeks before she returned home, he wouldn't be so distant.

Birlerion relaxed as she left. Although he knew they all meant well, their tentative concern just set his teeth on edge, as if they thought he would break if they said the wrong word. A tear leaked down his cheek as he admitted to himself it was very possible. He swung from feeling absolutely nothing to drowning in utter despair, and he didn't know how to manage it. It was as if Elliarille had smashed all his control and he had nothing left. He shuddered as the memories intruded and destroyed his peace.

Tyrone glared at Jerrol as he accosted him outside Stoneford infirmary. "You have to give him time. He's confused, grappling with major trauma. You saw what happened to the boys that survived. He suffered the same, if not worse. It's not something you get over quickly."

"I know, but he will recover, won't he?"

"He is improving. Physically, he should make a full recovery, but his control is fragile. Just be there for him, Jerrol. He needs to know he is safe, with family. You are his family."

Jerrol sighed in acknowledgement and went to sit with Birlerion and watched him sleep. Concern rippled through him as he realised Birlerion wasn't fully relaxed, even in sleep. It was as if some internal battle that no one could see was going on inside him. Tension ran through his body, along with his pale face and the creases between his eyes, it was clear he was suffering. Jerrol was at a loss. He didn't know how to help his friend. Leaning back in his chair, he closed his eyes. He was exhausted. The meetings were never ending, sorting out the mess Gillian and Benarte had left was consuming his every waking moment, and he needed his right hand back.

Suddenly aware of being watched, Jerrol opened his eyes. Birlerion's silver eyes gleamed in the dim light, and Jerrol slowly leaned forward. He reached for Birlerion's hand wrapping his remaining fingers around it, and tightened his grip, giving Birlerion's hand a little shake. "Hey, how are you feeling?"

Birlerion tried to speak, but it came out as a croak. Jerrol offered him some water, and after taking a sip, Birlerion cleared his throat. "Like I've had way more sleep than you have."

Jerrol gave a bark of laughter. "True. I underestimated the demands of the chancellor's office," he admitted.

Birlerion smiled. "You need to learn to delegate."

"I need someone I trust to delegate to," Jerrol replied softly.

Birlerion's smile slipped, and he closed his eyes and Jerrol watched him in concern. "Maybe later," Birlerion finally murmured as he tightened his grip on Jerrol's hand, and Jerrol watched over him as he dozed off.

When Birlerion woke again, Jerrol still held his hand. His head was resting on his arms on Birlerion's bed, and he was asleep. Birlerion looked up as Tyrone entered his room and frowned at them. "I was debating about waking him up," Birlerion said quietly, "but he needs the sleep."

Tyrone grunted. "How's the pain?" he asked.

"I'm fine," Birlerion replied.

Tyrone squinted at him. "You don't look it. Take this."

"I can't sleep my life away," Birlerion protested softly, not wanting to wake the sleeping man beside him.

"And you won't, but there is no point suffering unnecessarily. You have a long way to go, Birlerion. Don't make it more difficult than it has to be."

Birlerion sighed and took the glass. Tyrone hovered until Birlerion's tension eased and his eyelids drooped, and he dozed off again.

When he woke, Tagerill was sitting beside him, trying to read a book by the light of a dim lamp.

"I didn't know you could read," Birlerion said with a slight smile.

Tagerill looked up and grinned. "I thought it was time I

should learn, you know. I might be missing out on something."

"Not if that book is anything to go by." Birlerion chuckled.

"Well, if I'm wasting my time ..." Tagerill tossed it aside. "And I thought I was bettering myself."

Birlerion's eyes glinted at him. "I don't think that's possible." Tagerill laughed, extremely relieved to see a glimpse of the old Birlerion.

Birlerion progressed. He did what the healer told him, dutifully did his exercises, began light fitness training, and finally left the infirmary. Tyrone let him go with reluctance, but what Birlerion needed now couldn't be provided by healers. He needed to start living again.

When Jaredion arrived in Stoneford, over a month later, he found Birlerion sitting outside his sentinal, a rug over his lap. They stared at each other. Birlerion had been relieved to hear the boy had been found. He hadn't expected him to start profusely apologising for letting him down.

"Jaredion, stop, you don't owe me anything. If anything, I owe you an apology for sending you off on your own that night."

"But if I'd managed to escape ..." Jaredion paced restlessly in front him. "Everyone was looking for me."

"Classic distraction strategy," Birlerion said with a nod. "You couldn't say Ellaerion didn't have his wits about him."

"If I'd been at your shoulder as I should have been—" Jared continued.

"You'd probably have been taken then as well," Birlerion said morosely.

Jared stopped pacing and stared at him. "Will you let me?"

Birlerion stared back at him, perplexed. "Let you what?"

"Return to your shoulder? Let me prove I can protect you."

Birlerion looked at him in surprise and gently rotated his shoulders. "It might get a bit boring guarding a convalescent," he said sadly. "You should take the time to finish at the academy."

"I belong here, behind you," Jaredion said, staring at him stubbornly.

"I'd prefer it if you stood *beside* me. Bit difficult to talk to you if I can't see you."

Jaredion grinned in relief. "You won't always be convalescent."

Birlerion nodded. "True. I need a sparring partner anyway, once they let me hold a sword," he said with a scowl.

The keep watched in concern as Birlerion began to move among them. He was like a like a ghost, remote and withdrawn, but never alone. Jaredion always stood at his shoulder. They began sparring, but Jaredion and others could see Birlerion's heart wasn't in it, he was going through the motions, but he had no spirit.

Niallerion voiced his concerns to Tyrone. "It's like he's not here. He spends chimes in the bath house or pretending to spar in the ring. He doesn't initiate conversation; he only responds to direct questions, and even then, he doesn't really answer."

"It takes time, Niallerion. He has made amazing progress. I was worried he wouldn't even come out of his sentinal. At least he is making the effort to interact with you all. He may not be the Birlerion you knew, but put yourself in his position.

"For one moment, just imagine what he has been through. How would you react? If someone restrained you against your will, drugged you, took away your power, your control, violated you, how would you feel?"

Niallerion stared at him and gulped.

"Exactly," Tyrone said. "Add to that, the torture, his injuries, the Veil. It's amazing the poor man is even functioning at all. Just be there for him, Niallerion. Be patient. Listen when he needs to talk, be a shoulder for him to cry on, because he will need it. Let him rage at you if he needs to. He is full of anger, anguish, shame. Be ready for it. Because when he breaks out of this numbing shell he's in, you'll wish he was back in it."

Niallerion retreated and went to find Mikke. As he passed the stables, he found the stable master berating one of the stable lads.

"What's happened?" Niallerion asked.

"Kino let himself out of his stall again. They didn't close it properly."

"I did, sir. I swear. He just finds a new way to open it."

"Third time this week," the stable master complained.

"Where does Kino go?" Niallerion asked.

"We find him by Birlerion's sentinal every time," the stable master replied. "We don't have time for this. Go and get him," he said to the stable lad.

No," Niallerion said. "Leave him. I'll go get him."

Hurrying through the courtyard towards the private gardens at the rear, Niallerion slowed as the honey-gold stallion came into view. He was tossing his head as the sentinal's leaves above him rustled and swayed. Niallerion bit his lip, hope blooming in his heart that Birlerion wouldn't be able to resist the blandishments of both his sentinal and his Darian.

After what seemed far too long, Birlerion shimmered out of his sentinal and extended trembling fingers towards his Darian. The stallion pushed closer, nudging Birlerion until his arms embraced the horse's neck, and Birlerion buried his face in Kin'arol's mane, and his shoulders began to shake.

Niallerion swallowed back tears as he watched. Finally, a crack in Birlerion's defences.

Later that week, Niallerion cornered Jaredion whilst Birlerion was back in the bath house. "Jared, can't you help him. You know what he's been through."

Jaredion was aghast at the thought. "What I went through was nothing like what he experienced. They just tied me down. She tortured him for days. What he suffered …" Jaredion paused, horrified, "would break most of us," he admitted.

"How do we help him?"

Jaredion sighed, staring at the bath house wall. "However he will let us. When he's ready, he'll let us know."

Birlerion soaped his body again; he couldn't get clean. He flushed with mortification as he tried to rid his body of her scent, her touch. He felt dirty, ashamed, even embarrassed to have been discovered in such a vulnerable position. He had let everyone down and continued to do so. He knew Jerrol needed him, but he couldn't face returning with everyone knowing what had happened. The way they would look at him in disgust. He thumped the side of the bathtub as his anger finally stirred.

"No-one will look at you in disgust," Kin'arol murmured. *"They love you, as do I, and there is nothing disgusting about you."*

Birlerion ignored his Darian as embarrassment flushed through him, tightening his gut. "How dare she? How dare she?" The litany ran through his head as he dressed and went to find his sword. Jaredion found him pounding the sparring target with ferocious anger and went to find Niallerion. They watched as Birlerion swung over and over again in an uncontrollable rage. The target finally disintegrated, and Birlerion collapsed to his knees. Niallerion rushed over and gathered him in his arms as Birlerion shuddered into tears.

After that, Birlerion began working properly in the ring, the sparring master slowly helping him build his strength up, replacing the destroyed targets overnight without comment. Birlerion's strength returned, as did his skill. He was lethal in the ring, and the sparring master often had to step in as Birlerion's control slipped.

Birlerion began to spend more time with Niallerion and Marianille, just sitting watching her baby grow, soothed by the growth of innocent life. His face would soften as she placed his hand on her distended stomach as the baby kicked, and he would look up at her in wonder.

Around him the keep began to prepare for Mikke's Joining. Mikke had finally asked Saranne to join with him, and the Watch was thrilled to find out she had said yes. Jerrol and Taelia paid fleeting visits from Vespers to check on the preparations and on Birlerion. As did various other Sentinals, who dropped in unannounced.

39

STONEFORD KEEP

A week before the joining, Leyarille found Birlerion sitting in her father's favourite spot under the King's Sentinal. He was staring out across the moonlit keep.

"I'm so sorry I failed you," she said, her voice breaking. "I should never have let you go home on your own."

"You never failed me," Birlerion replied, staring at the moon.

"If I had paid attention, understood her threat, she would never have…" she faltered, "hurt you."

"It's not your fault; I didn't understand it, either. It's the Veil. It is rapacious. She was trapped a long time; it had to have had an effect."

"She's taken you away from me, and now I can't find you," Leyarille said, tears colouring her voice. She reached for Birlerion's arm and stopped as he stiffened.

Birlerion remained silent.

"Will you leave me a trail when you're ready, so I can find my way home?" she asked, her heart breaking as she watched his rigid face. She turned away, tears filling her silver eyes as she stumbled back down to the keep.

Birlerion watched her go.

The next morning, Birlerion took his anger out on the training targets, yet again. He was filled with a burning rage that threatened to overwhelm him. Anger at himself, anger at Elliarille, and yes, anger at Marguerite. She had left him to suffer. They all had. And then he felt angry for thinking such terrible things about his friends who had done everything they could to help him. He was being unreasonable, he knew it, but he was just … so … angry. The target disintegrated under his ire.

"So this is where you ..." Birlerion spun, his sword swinging at Tagerill before he had a chance to finish his sentence. Tagerill's sword was up and blocking, instinctively. Birlerion pounded him in fury, forcing him across the training ground, their swords clashing violently and loudly. Tagerill defended himself, blocking the blows raining down on him. He had no chance to retaliate; the unrelenting pressure was astonishing. Tagerill was beginning to realise he was in trouble as Birlerion wedged him up against the railings. He blocked the ferocious blows, his arms vibrating with the power of the strikes until the sparring master rushed up and hauled Birlerion off him.

Tagerill was relieved when he saw the blind rage finally fade from Birlerion's face as he stilled in the sparring master's arms and stared at him, chest heaving. Birlerion's fury was replaced by a haunting look of despair as he saw his brother for the first time.

"Tage?" he whispered, releasing his sword in horror.

Tagerill grinned weakly. "My apologies, brother. I should have given you warning." He slowly eased upright and took a shaky breath. He pulled Birlerion into his arms and held him tight as he saw the distraught expression on his brother's face. "Birler, it was not your fault. I'm sorry. I shouldn't have surprised you." Birlerion shuddered, his body rigid, and Tagerill tightened his grip, rocking him gently as he murmured reassurances until Birlerion slowly relaxed in his embrace.

Tagerill finally released him. "Come, let's get something to eat. Enough practice. I don't think that target's getting back up any time soon," he said with a grin as he stooped to pick up Birlerion's sword. He tugged Birlerion's arm and then gently led him out of the ring.

Onlookers drawn by the sound of fighting scattered at the ferocious expression on Tagerill's face as he led Birlerion back to the keep and into Mikke's study. He pushed the unresisting Birlerion into a chair.

"I could have killed you," Birlerion said, and Tagerill shivered at the lack of emotion in his voice.

"Nah, you couldn't. Not on your best day," he replied, trying to ease the fraught look on brother's face.

"I didn't see you."

"But you do now, and as you can see, you didn't kill me."

Birlerion covered his face with his hands, and his shoulders began to shake. Tagerill crouched in front of him, watching him in concern. "Birler, I'm here now. You're safe. You're home."

Birlerion raised haunted eyes. "Home? Where is that, Tage?"

"Home is where you make it, Birlerion. Stoneford, Vespers, Greens. You choose where you want your home to be. No one else. The Lady will be with you, no matter where you go."

"I-I feel lost, empty inside. I'm not sure I know where home is anymore," Birlerion admitted, his voice low.

Tagerill gripped his arms in sympathy. "You'll find your way," he promised. "It takes time, the Lady will guide you."

"Will she?" Birlerion asked, and the desolation in his voice cut through Tagerill.

"You are the most pig-headed, stubborn, obstinate Sentinal I've ever had the good fortune to know, Birlerion," Marguerite said from the doorway. Her hands were on her hips, and Taurillion hovered behind her with a huge grin on his face.

Tagerill leapt to his feet. "Marguerite?" He stared in shock at the petite, brunette deity standing before him.

Marguerite smiled at Tagerill, her sky-blue eyes sparkling as she patted his face. "Give us a moment would you, Tagerillion?"

"Of course, my Lady." Tagerill backed out of the study and glared at Taurillion as Marguerite shut the door on him. "What are you doing here? What is *She* doing here?"

"Marguerite was worried about Birlerion, and seeing as he wouldn't respond to her, she took matters into her own hands, as you can see. Isn't it amazing to see Her back?" Taurillion laughed, his happiness overflowing.

Marguerite stood over him, but Birlerion couldn't look up. His eyes were fixed on the floor. He heard her sigh, and tears gathered in his eyes.

"Oh Birlerion, my dearest one. What are you doing to yourself?"

At that, Birlerion did look up, startled, and met her vibrant blue eyes. She was right in front of him. She cupped her hands around his face and his tears fell. "That's right, let it go," she soothed. "You can't hide behind it anymore."

Birlerion's shoulders shook as Marguerite broke down his barriers one by one. She soothed his distress, embracing him close as she wrapped him in her love. The humming sensation of the Oath entwined them both, and it filled him with a sense of belonging.

"You've never been alone. You're mine. How could you ever forget that? My dearest Birlerion, you are as beloved now as you ever were. And now it's time for you to bestow your love where it is needed. She needs to be loved as well, you know." She kissed his brow, light as a feather, and faded away. The Oath hummed happily through his veins, letting him know he would never be alone again.

Jerrol watched his daughter carefully. Her face was pale and there were dark circles under her eyes. She had done what she could. It was up to Birlerion now.

Jerrol hugged her. "Why don't you go and soak in the baths and relax some of those muscles? You'll have the place to yourself. We are all going down to see Jason before all the excitement tomorrow. Won't be back till late."

Leyarille nodded, brightening slightly at the thought of some peace and quiet. She dutifully headed off to the baths, pleasantly surprised that the coals were already lit and the water was steaming.

She was relaxing in the tub, laying supine in the water when the latched clicked and the door opened. She sat up in surprise as Birlerion hesitated on the threshold, a towel over his shoulder.

"Birlerion!"

"I'm sorry, I thought it was free. I'll go."

"No, no wait. If you give me a minute, I'll go. I know you need the baths."

Birlerion shuddered. "I don't *need* it exactly. I just like them." He smiled shyly, hesitating in the doorway. "We could share it if you want?"

Leyarille's eyes widened as she stared at him in shock.

"Only if you want to," he said, backing out the door.

"Don't you dare go," she replied, casting around for her towel, but it had fallen to the floor.

Birlerion slid back into the bath house and closed the door, settling on the bench opposite her. "I'm sorry," he said, watching her try to lean over the side and revealing a lot of bare flesh.

Leyarille stopped her flailing and turned back to him. The water covered her up to her chest, though she felt quite vulnerable under his clear gaze. She crossed her arms under the water. "For what?" she asked, her voice equally soft.

"For pushing you away. I couldn't believe you would want to be with me knowing …" he faltered, "knowing everything. That I was unable to protect myself."

"We protect each other. That's who we are."

"I felt ashamed."

Leyarille's eyes filled with tears as he struggled to explain.

"And angry. She took away my power, my control." His eyes dropped. "Control over my own body," he said with difficulty.

Leyarille stood. Towel be damned. Water sheeted off her body as she climbed out of the tub. She wrapped her arms around Birlerion, and he buried his face in her neck. She silently cursed Elliarille as he shuddered in her arms.

"I am so sorry, my love. You should never have been placed in such a position. We all failed each other," Leyarille murmured into his hair.

"I can't get rid of her. I can't sleep. She invades my dreams when I least expect it, and then there's the Veil. It keeps calling me."

"Hush, my love. We'll fix it, one piece at a time. We'll deal with it together." She raised his head and kissed his tear-stained face, gently wiping the tears from his cheeks. "If you'll let me," she finished softly.

Some of the tension in his body eased as he held her eyes

as if searching for the truth of her words. She observed him, watching her, and then he kissed her. Leyarille stiffened in surprise as his hands slid around her waist, his touch on her skin sending thrills through her body, and then she leaned into him in case he misconstrued her reaction and thought she didn't want him.

He suddenly pulled back, his eyes crinkling as he realised she was naked. "You'll catch your death like that," he said as he swooped her up in his arms and dumped her back in the tub, the water sloshing over the sides.

"Birlerion, be careful, you'll hurt yourself. You shouldn't be lifting …" Birlerion stopped her protests with another kiss.

"Hush, my love," he said when he pulled away. Shedding his clothes, he prepared to climb into the tub. He faltered as she took in the damage to his body. So many new scars; his skin was patched with angry red marks, which would fade to silver in time. Tears filled her eyes. He had taken so many injuries, protecting everyone else, and they had failed to protect him the one time he had needed it. Birlerion climbed in the tub and, after hesitating a moment, sat opposite her. "It will be alright," he promised. "I … I just need a little time."

"Of course," Leyarille whispered. She stretched her legs across the tub, her toes searching for his. "Take all the time you need. I've spent years trying to catch up with you." She smiled sadly. "I can wait as long as you need me to." Leyarille held his silver gaze as he slid his foot under hers, tentatively seeking the solace and comfort she offered. She tangled her toes with his, silently wishing she could smooth the strain off his face. Warm water lapped her body, and she realised he had moved, slowly sliding around the edge towards her, and she moved to meet him.

They sat side by side, shoulders touching, thighs touching, and as the heat from his body suffused her, Leyarille waited. It had never been so hard as at that moment, when she was desperate to touch him. This would be up to Birlerion. She would never force him to do anything. Ever.

Birlerion raised a hesitant hand and smoothed his fingers over her cheek. "I am so sorry for pushing you away," he whispered. His fingers left a trail of scorching desire across her skin, and her lips parted as she gasped.

Birlerion captured her lips, his tongue venturing into her mouth, and she accepted it gladly. As she hesitantly explored his mouth, luxuriating in the intimacy, her fingers trailed over his damaged skin, and Birlerion shivered. She froze. "Don't stop," he murmured against her lips. "Please, don't ever stop loving me." He pulled back and met her gaze. "Your love is the only thing that is keeping me sane."

"I've loved you all my life, and I'm not stopping now," she whispered as she wrapped her arms around his neck and tugged him closer. "I would never do anything to hurt you, but you'll have to lead the way. You'll have to let me know what you can cope with."

Birlerion placed his hands either side of her face. "You could never do anything that I couldn't cope with. You are not *her*, and I will not allow her to ruin what we have." He hesitated, his eyes dropping as he released her. "If you still want me, of course. I'm not much of a prize."

Leyarille didn't think she had heard any words that could hurt her more. He still didn't believe he could be loved for who he was. She mirrored his action, capturing his face between her palms. "I will never stop saying this," she said, striving to keep the pain out of her voice. "I love you, Birlerion. You, and only you. I will stay by your side for as long as you will have me. I will love, protect, and worship all of you, if you'll let me. You are the most beautiful person, both inside and out, and you deserve to be loved, by me, if you'll have me."

Birlerion's answering smile made her heart clench, and she kissed him. Peppering his mouth, his cheeks, his eyes with fluttering kisses, she leaned into his body, her skin on fire wherever it met his.

"I love you, too," Birlerion whispered as he kissed his way round her ear and down her neck.

Leyarille couldn't stop the smile spreading over face as she tilted her head so he could reach more of her skin. His soft caresses left a trail of burning heat, and her skin tingled long after he had moved on as she writhed under his touch.

Some while later, Birlerion leaned back against the side of the tub and relaxed as he pulled her back against his chest, he wrapped his legs around hers to keep her in place. Leyarille kissed his wrists, leaving the softest kisses on his poor scarred skin. He had rubbed off so many layers of skin with his struggling that he would have scars forever. He shivered beneath her touch, and Leyarille knew it was in response to her touch, not in fear of some terrible memory.

She leaned back against him and relaxed. Her head fit just right under his chin. She kissed his arms as he wrapped them around her. She wanted to kiss every part of him. She sighed.

"Why the sigh?"

"My father is going to tease us about this for years, you do know that? Do you think he planned this?"

Birlerion's laugh rumbled below her. "Him or Marguerite, though there are worse things to be teased about, you know."

"True," she agreed. She turned in his arms and straddled his lap. He stiffened before relaxing beneath her, and she kissed him lightly on the mouth. "You never have to do anything you don't want to," she said, snuggling against his chest. She smoothed her fingers over the jagged scar on his neck, and as the warm water lapped against them, she reached up to kiss it. She couldn't stop touching him.

"I'm sorry. I can't help it. Sometimes I flash back." Birlerion was apologising again.

"Hush, no more apologies. We'll overcome it, together," she promised, her silver eyes glinting up at him.

He smiled, his gaze heating. "Together," he agreed, his head dipping to meet her halfway, and they lost themselves in each other.

Stirring, Leyarille said, "We're getting wrinkly; we ought to get out."

Birlerion chuckled. "As long as we get old and wrinkly together, I don't care."

Leyarille rose and pulled him up out of the water. "Come on, I have someone you need to meet." They helped each other dry off before shrugging damply into half-buttoned shirts and trousers.

Leyarille smiled as Birlerion's eyes went distant and he twisted his lips. "Does Kino have an opinion?" she asked as she took his hand.

"Everyone has an opinion. Though he approves, if you weren't sure. He says you'll make me happy, if I have the good sense to let you," he replied. Lacing his fingers with Leyarille's, he smiled as she tightened her grip and he followed her through the keep towards their sentinal trees. She tugged him inside her tree and wrapped her arms around him. He hardly had time to greet her sentinal before she pulled him down on top of her.

"I've wanted to make you happy all my life, and I'll spend the rest of it ensuring you are," she whispered as the happy thrum from her sentinal filled her head and Birlerion's from the expression on his face. He melted into Leyarille's arms and she concentrated on helping him release the last of his pain and replaced it with her love.

Leyarille cupped his face and deepened the kiss, heat flushing through her veins and sparking behind her eye lids. She opened her eyes and drowned in Birlerion's luminous silver gaze, which devoured her. Unbuttoning her shirt, Birlerion slid her sleeve down her arm, kissing her exposed skin with the lightest of touches. His lips curved as she shivered under his touch, and Leyarille couldn't resist kissing his dimples as she raised his chin. "I've always wanted you," she whispered, "all of you."

"You have all of me," Birlerion replied as he sank into her embrace. "I love you, Leyarille."

"I knew you were mine." Leyarille chuckled. "I'll never let you go, you do know that, don't you?"

"I never want you to."

Leyarille traced the new lines on his face, and her vision went blurry as her throat tightened and tears welled.

"Shhh," Birlerion whispered as he shed his clothes and helped remove the last of hers. "We have our own memories to make."

Leyarille grinned up at him through her tears and wholeheartedly threw herself into helping him make the first of many.

Much later, Leyarille watched Birlerion as he slept in her arms, sheltered by her sentinal. His precious face was relaxed; he was at peace at last. Gently, she smoothed the new lines of pain and loss. She kissed the silver scar that bisected his left eyebrow. He had suffered so much, she wanted to protect him from everyone and everything. "You're home, Birlerion, where you belong," she whispered, and he smiled in his sleep. His arms tightened around her, and she kissed him again, relaxing into his embrace. Her breathing slowed, and she fell asleep too.

40

STONEFORD KEEP

Mikke and Saranne were joined under the towering sentinals in front of the Lady's altar, watched by their family and friends and King Anders of Vespiri and Terolia. The keep heaved with people; some even had to overflow into the village. There just weren't enough rooms for so many important guests.

The Lord Chancellor and his First Administrator stood with the king and watched the party flow around them. Commander Bryce was in a constant flap with so many visiting dignitaries and important members of the government out of the city at once.

Birlerion watched Leyarille twirl around the dance floor in her brother's arms, and his grave expression softened as he watched. The Lord Chancellor flicked him a calculating glance and distracted the king.

Prince Pierien paused beside Birlerion's elbow and grinned. "Hey, Birlerion, you ought to know that Tagerill is betting that you won't dance tonight. I thought that maybe you could help him lose that bet."

Birlerion raised an eyebrow. "Are you sure that's what he

was betting against, Your Highness? I would have thought Tagerill was more astute."

Pierien chuckled, watching Leyarille search for Birlerion each time she faced him. "That's what I thought, so I took the bet. I can't wait to see his face."

Birlerion smiled as his gaze followed Leyarille. "I will do my best to assist you in winning your bet, Your Highness." Pierien laughed and melted into the crush.

Jaredion paused beside him, and Birlerion's smile faded. "Stop fretting, Jaredion. I'll still be here tomorrow. Your sister only gets joined once. Enjoy it."

Jaredion smiled sheepishly. "It doesn't feel right. I should be with you."

Birlerion sighed. He had two of them keeping a close eye on him. "I expect that is because the Lady asked you to stand at my shoulder; let's not strain her request too much. Why don't we agree that just for tonight, you can check on me once a chime. Will that make you feel better?"

Jaredion grinned. "Much," he said and dived back into the crowd. Birlerion shook his head and sought out Leyarille again. Birlerion suddenly realised the king was speaking his name, and from his expression it wasn't the first time.

Birlerion tipped his head. "Sire?"

The king's lips twitched. "I was just saying to the Lord Chancellor here that we have a surfeit of estates. I suggested you choose one. He thought you might be difficult and I should just bestow one on you. Would you be difficult?" he enquired.

Birlerion's gaze strayed back to the dance floor, and he smiled. "Not at all, Your Majesty."

"See," Anders said, turning to Jerrol. "I said you were wrong." He turned back to Birlerion and found him gone. He frowned. "Where did he go?"

Jerrol laughed. "He's making sure Pierien wins his bet."

He watched Birlerion cut in on Leyarille's current partner and observed her delighted surprise as he took her in her arms. They seemed to melt into each other for a moment. Birlerion murmured in her ear, and she laughed up at him before he twirled her away.

Many eyes followed them, though the Sentinals only had eyes for each other and didn't notice, nor would they have cared if they had.

There was a stir, and the music stopped. Niallerion stood forward, a huge smile on his face. "Apologies, folks, for the interruption, but I have some news. Marianille and I have a beautiful daughter. They are both well. She is blessed by the Lady, and we've named her Melisarille." He was lost in the crowd of well-wishers who surrounded him, and Birlerion and Leyarille took the opportunity to slip away.

Jaredion skidded to a halt in surprise as he saw Birlerion wrap Leyarille in his arms and brace her against the wall.

"Leave them be," Jerrol said from behind him.

"But that's Birlerion and …"

"It's part of his healing," Jerrol said with a grin, steering his nephew away from the oblivious Sentinals.

"But …"

"He's got a Sentinal at his back, well his front, I suppose." Jerrol laughed. "They are all around him, and there are enough to keep eyes on him today. Enjoy the day, Jaredion, there will be plenty of time for you to protect him."

Jerrol continued to chuckle as he went to find Taelia. She would be so pleased.

The End

If you have a moment and you enjoyed reading Sentinals Banished, then please do leave a review and tell other fantasy readers what you enjoyed. Reviews are so important to independent authors to drive visibility and to help us to continue publishing our books.

Sign up to my newsletter via the link on https://linktr.ee/helengarraway to find out more about my books and download a free novella set in the world of Remargaren, the setting for my epic fantasy Sentinal series.

Novella: Book 0.5: Sentinals Stirring

Thank you for your support.

Helen Garraway

www.helengarraway.com

GLOSSARY

Deities

Leyandrii (Lay-ann-dree): Guardian of Vespiri
Marguerite: (Mar-guh-reet): Leyandrii's sister, Guardian of the Land
Guerlaire (Guh-LAIR): Original Lady's Captain

Stoneford

Jerrol Haven: Lord of Stoneford Watch
Birlerion (Bur-lair-rion): Sentinal
Leyarille (LAY-er-rill): Jerrol's daughter
Mikkeal (Mick-i-all): Jerrol's son
Margareth (Mar-gar-eth) Jerrol's youngest daughter
Taelia (Tay-lee-ah) Scholar, Jerrol's wife
Fonorion (Fuh-nor-i-on): Sentinal
Serenion (Sir-REN-ion): Sentinal
Tianerille (Tee-ann-er-rill): Sentinal (Watch Towers)
Venterion (Vent-air-i-on): Sentinal (Watch Towers)
Zin'talia (Zin-Tar-lee-ah): Jerrol's Darian Mare
Pil'Penia (Pill-pen-ya): Mikkeal's Darian
Kin'arol (Kin-ah-roll): Birlerion's Darian

Jason: Former Lord of the Watch

Old Vespers

King Anders: Ruling monarch of Vespiri and Terolia
King Benedict: Former monarch of Vespiri (dead)
Chancellor Pelori: Leader of the Government
Lord Gillian, Benarte, Cramer, Relian : Administrators of the Government
Commander Bryce: Commander of the King's Justice
Commander Stafford: Commander of the King's Rangers
Parsillion (Par-sill-i-on): Sentinal
Frenerion (Fren-nair-i-on): Sentinal
Marianille (M-a-ri-an-ill): Sentinal
Niallerion (N-i-al-air-i-on): Sentinal

Rangers Academy

Commander Reece: Commander of the Cadet Academy
Captain Calver: Adjutant to the Commander
Lieutenant Scott, Kopka, Parnent – Unit leaders
Cadets: Kayen, Fenton, Sid, Petra, Relis, Lucas

George: Birlerion's contact at Docker's Tavern
Porter: Docker
Timmin: Wagon driver
Jim: Owner of Docker's Tavern

Chapterhouse

Liliian: Scholar Deane of the Chapterhouse

Deepwater Watch

Lady Alyssa (A-liss-ah): Guardian of Deepwater
Leander Jennery: Lord of Deepwater
Hugh, Jared and Saranne: Alyssa and Jennery's children
Tagerillion (Tagerill) (Taj-er-rill-i-on): Sentinal

Miranda: Tagerill's wife
Denirion (Duh-near-ion): Sentinal

Marchwood Watch

Lord William: Lord of Marchwood
Anterion (Ant-air-i-on): Sentinal
Laerille (Lay-er-rill): Sentinal
Roberts: Lord Gillian's Gardner

Elothia

Grand Duke Randolf XIV
Duchess Guin'yyfer
Gerhard, Wilhelm and Rosie – Duke and Duchesses Children
Owen – Commander of the Elothian Army
Taurillion (Tor-rill-ion) : Sentinal
Allarion (Al-LAIR-ion) Sentinal

Birtoli

Emperor Geraine : Ruler of the Birtoli Empire
Crown Prince Pierien : Geraine's son
Roberion (Roe-bear-ion): Sentinal

ACKNOWLEDGMENTS

Thank you so much for staying with me throughout the adventures of Jerrol and his Sentinals in the magical world of Remargaren.

You may think this is the end, but I have one more book in the series to share, and then the prequel where we take a closer look at Leyandrii and Guerlaire and how the Sentinals first came to be.

The title for Sentinals Banished was voted on by my newsletter subscribers, and I would like to acknowledge (with their permission) each person who voted. Thank you so much for taking the time to give me feedback, and I hope you all love Sentinals Banished.

Susan Manbridge, John Gilligan, Patty Biggs, Arthur Hollak, Kathleen Ebling, Tonly Blyton, Barbara Harrison, Geoffrey Gudgion, Davin Palin, Neil, Rachel, Nancy Portz, Bill Sturdevant, Kaye Adams, Laurie Robertson, Leah Rosson, John Howser, Eleanor Joy Dixon, Daisy Wood, Shawna Gregg.

Thank you to my wonderful editor Maddy Glenn who continues to push me to delve that little bit deeper and Jeff Brown of @jeffbrowngraphics who designs my wonderful cover. Maps were designed by Tom of Fictive Designs.

And finally, thank you to Michael Strick my alpha reader, who is one of my greatest supporters, and fortunately, loves my books. His early feedback helped drive the book you now hold in your hands. Thank you Michael, for your continued support.

ABOUT THE AUTHOR

Award winning author, Helen Garraway, has been writing about the world of Remargaren, a fantasy world of her creation since 2016.

Sentinals Awaken was Helen's debut fantasy novel published in 2020 followed by four further books and three novellas in the Sentinal series.

An avid reader of many different fiction genres, a love she inherited from her mother, Helen writes fantasy novels and also enjoys paper crafting and scrapbooking as an escape from the pressure of the day job.

Her very own Arifel keeps her company as she continues to create and explore more fantasy words, coming in a book near you soon!

You can find out more about Helen's work on Patreon, and/or sign up to her newsletter via helengarraway.com or on Social media.

Patreon

Join Team Arifel, Team Darian or Team Sentinal and get access to the first chapters of my new books first, free bookish downloads, polls, early sneak peeks and for Team Darian: a Sentinal mug and free ebooks, and for Team Sentinal: a signed paperback of new releases and a patreon exclusive Sentinal hoodie.

CPSIA information can be obtained
at www.ICGtesting.com
Printed in the USA
BVHW050216030223
657743BV00002B/4

9 781915 854018